TRUTH
BE
TOLD

30131 05802124 4

LONDON BOROUGH OF BARNET

Praise for *Guard Your Heart*

'Profoundly powerful, subtle and effective.' *Guardian*

'Outstanding. A comprehensive, and emotionally charged foray into the North's complexities.' *Irish Examiner*

'Divin, whose day job is in community peace building, succeeds in blending a call for empathy with a compelling, engaging narrative.' *Irish Times*

'A deeply affecting, powerful book.' *Irish Independent*

'Divin skilfully maintains two attractively distinct voices [and] . . . sets her story with an insider's knowledge of the dynamics of Derry . . . absorbing.' Geoff Fox, *Books for Keeps*

TRUTH BE TOLD

SUE DIVIN

MACMILLAN

For Grace

Published 2022 by Macmillan Children's Books
an imprint of Pan Macmillan
The Smithson, 6 Briset Street, London EC1M 5NR
EU representative: Macmillan Publishers Ireland Ltd, 1st Floor,
The Liffey Trust Centre, 117–126 Sheriff Street Upper
Dublin 1, D01 YC43
Associated companies throughout the world
www.panmacmillan.com

ISBN 978-1-5290-4098-2

Copyright © Sue Divin 2022
Extract from 'If I was Us, I Wouldn't Start From Here', by Damian Gorman,
commissioned by the Poetry Jukebox, used with permission of the author.

The right of Sue Divin to be identified as the author of this work has been asserted by her
in accordance with the Copyright, Designs and Patents Act 1988.

All rights reserved. No part of this publication may be reproduced,
stored in a retrieval system, or transmitted, in any form or by any means
(electronic, mechanical, photocopying, recording or otherwise),
without the prior written permission of the publisher.

Pan Macmillan does not have any control over, or any responsibility for,
any author or third-party websites referred to in or on this book.

1 3 5 7 9 8 6 4 2

A CIP catalogue record for this book is available from the British Library.

Printed and bound by CPI Group (UK) Ltd, Croydon CR0 4YY

This book is sold subject to the condition that it shall not, by way of trade or otherwise, be
lent, resold, hired out, or otherwise circulated without the publisher's prior consent
in any form of binding or cover other than that in which it is published and without a
similar condition including this condition being imposed on the subsequent purchaser.

Supported by the National Lottery through the Arts Council of Northern Ireland

Especially in a broken home like ours
Where broken doors and windows feed the cold,
Each generation has a sacred task:
To tell a better story than it was told.

Damian Gorman
(From 'If I Was Us, I Wouldn't Start From Here',
commissioned by the Poetry Jukebox)

Chapter 1

TARA
Derry, 15 August 2019

Everything holy in our house is in the attic, under a layer of dust. Nan says it's the same for the whole country, thanks be to God. Still, she's the one who sent me into the roof space on a mission to recover the lost Child of Prague statue she wants to give to the neighbours. Their daughter is for getting married tomorrow and is dreading rain. Nan swears putting their faith in a battered ornament of the baby Jesus will bring blazing sunshine. Since my ex, Oran, got shot in the leg, I'm done believing. I flash the torch into the eaves. I can't remember the last time I was up here. Years. Nothing's changed except the dust is thicker and, as I straighten, I realize with a thud that my head now hits the roof. I rub my temple. The true miracle is that we even *own* a Child of Prague or that I can be arsed looking for it. My family only wheel out religion for special occasions. Weddings. Funerals. First Holy Communions. My first Holy Communion was my last Holy Communion which, judging by my mates, is fast becoming a new Irish tradition.

'It's in a box,' calls Nan from the landing below.

'I could be a while,' I say, looking at the boxes piled everywhere. They must breed up here. I sneeze and wrinkle my nose.

'I'll stick the kettle on,' says Nan. It's her universal solution. 'Shout if you need my help.'

As if she's going to swing herself through the ceiling with no

1

ladder when she's wheezing with the exertion of walking down the stairs. I sneeze again as my eyes adjust to the light. If I wasn't grounded, I wouldn't be in the house, never mind hunting religious icons. I glance about, wondering where to start. Where do baby Jesus statues in red robes and gold crowns hang out? Shoeboxes? Old suitcases? With pound-shop Christmas decorations?

I hunker down by a pile of leftover carpet bits and start rummaging under lids and pulling at knotted string round boxes. One corner is infested with ancient crockery, wrapped in yellowing *Derry Journal* papers from last century. Books and magazines are jammed in old sports bags. The titles are all student medical stuff. Was Mam a wannabe brainbox one time? No one needs learning for wiping bums in a care home on minimum wage. There are ring binders too, with paperwork and handwritten scrawls. Hardback notebooks. Faded file blocks with curled edges and blurred blue ink. But no Child of Prague.

Crawling across uneven planks, I stir dust. A red suitcase with copper fastenings catches my attention. A spider scuttles as I make my way over. The suitcase looks old enough to be Nan's. Certainly ain't mine. Furthest I've ever been from Derry was a wet weekend in Bundoran for slot machines and candyfloss. Budget airlines are beyond our budget. No chance of a flight to Glasgow to see Oran, even if Mam would let me, not that my fake ID would cut it anyway. Bits of rusted metal from the clasps flake away on my fingers as I twist them. *Click*. The lid is stubborn at first, like time has glued it in place, then it unsticks. Shining the torch in, I gasp. White lace. A wedding dress. Last thing I expected to find in our attic. Neither Nan nor Mam ever married. Nan has hardly left the house this millennium, except for her blue rinse community club, and, when it comes to men's bits,

2

Mam's too busy cleaning them in nursing homes to have time for their higher purpose. We're women's lib central. Three generations of Connollys. No posh double-barrelled surnames. No wedding rings. All Ms no Mrs. I drop the lid and lean back against an old deckchair. So why have we a wedding dress?

I juggle the torch from hand to hand, thinking. In primary school, Father's Day was torture. Teachers would think they were all politically correct saying, 'Sure make a card for your granda or your uncle.' But I didn't have them neither. The last time I bothered to ask Mam about Da was after the Love for Life talk in first year secondary. 'You're the love of my life,' she'd said. 'End of. As for the birds and the bees? Bees come with a sting. Work on being an independent woman first, right? Us Connollys and men – it never works out. It's a family curse.'

As I stare at the white lace, I mind the mortification of turning sixteen in April. Mam produced a banana and a pack of condoms in the kitchen. Nan laughing in the rocker. They made sure even if my face was ketchup, I knew which way was up. The thought stirs warmth low in my stomach. Oran hasn't messaged as much recently. I bury my face in his hoodie. Ma's raging I still wear it and that I hide it from the wash. It smells of his deodorant. I haven't had call to apply the banana lesson yet but maybe, maybe if he's allowed back from Scotland . . . Not that I'm supposed to be in contact with him at all. He was kicked out of the city by the New IRA. Mam says he's trouble. Says I deserve better. What Mam doesn't know doesn't harm her.

I chew my lip and twirl the torch. The beam hits the rafters in the far corner and shines on a heap of scrapbooks and junk. On top is a grey cowboy hat. Mam used to love country music. Laced with a few gins, she goes all soprano. Ducking under the lowest beams and worming round cardboard mountains, I grab the hat.

My fingers leave marks on the felt. Banging it with my palm induces a sneezing fit. The hat turns from grey to black. Perfect. It'll match my entire wardrobe. The fit of it's a bit on the large side, but it works at an angle. Finders keepers. I focus back on my mission. The light beam swings behind the red suitcase and there, peering out from newspaper, tucked inside a shoebox, is the Child of Prague statue. I grin, recognizing my ticket to freedom. The grounding this time was for smoking. Mam didn't buy the rationale that technically, due to Nan's emphysema, nicking her fags was an act of charity.

Removing baby Jesus from his blanket of newspaper, I kiss his porcelain cheeks. With this statue, Nan will go soft and, since Mam is on night shift, my prayers will be answered. Tonight is the August bonfire. I don't even know why we do bonfires – something political or religious. Either way, it's an *Us and Them* thing. I. Am. Going. I'll even live feed it from my phone for Oran cos he'll be mad at missing it. Unless he's wasted. Again. Glasgow is parties 24/7 he says. The guns did him a favour. I wonder.

'Nan?' At my holler from the attic, she sticks her head round the kitchen door. 'You sure this statue needs to be broke to bring sunshine?'

'Aye,' she shouts. Then dissolves into coughing from the effort.

I take a last look at the immaculate Child of Prague with his wee gold crown and red cape, then drop him down onto our landing below. As he hits the wooden floor, his head snaps, a clean crack. The momentum bounces the severed head down our stairs.

'Perfect,' says Nan, when she catches her breath. 'I'll get the glue.'

*

Me and my mate Lena drape ourselves over the city walls. Below us, the weans from the good families are messing with community workers, slipping down the banking on plastic and Fairy-liquid slides and kicking about at cage football. Other kids in white runners and shorts are sorting through piles of planks and junk under the green, white and yellow bunting across the street at the back of the Meenan shops, helping older lads with the finishing touches. The bonfire is three storeys high – jammed with British Army Para flags, Union Jacks and a massive 'F**k Soldier F' sign. I'm not up on alphabet soldiers. Something to do with the Troubles. In a few hours, they'll light it with petrol bombs and hopefully someone will have a few cans to share. Once the cans are empty and we're full, we'll join the alcohol-free community gig in the Gasyard. We're wise to them. They can make you empty your pockets but not your stomach. Unless you puke.

A banner wraps the low railings where a couple of men stand smoking: 'Free Derry says no to state terrorism'. Watching them watching us, I find my nails digging into my palms. They're the kinda ones that pull more than punches. Self-appointed vigilantes. Think they rule the place. I might not understand much but, trial by jury? Innocent until proven guilty? No torture? When we first did about rights in primary school, our teacher sounded out 'U-ni-ver-sal'. Meaning, like, for everywhere. Guess we're off the map. Out of this world. Somehow, here it's OK to shoot teenagers in the knees. That stuff, everyone understands. So much for peace.

'Least they're only burning wood this year. They took the tyres out of the bonfire,' says Lena. 'Two hundred and thirty of them. Was in the *Journal* and all.'

'Where'd they even get two hundred tyres?'

5

She shrugs. 'Businesses fly-tipping on the sly to avoid recycling.'

Oran had different ways of burning tyres. Scorching black circles with cars on the roads round the city at 3 a.m. Sometimes it was a bit mad being with him. I'll never admit it, but Mam is probably right. He's bad news but he swears he's gonna change. I'm like the only person left in the world who still believes him and maybe that's why we're still meant for each other, because hardly anyone believes in me any more either, except him. All the rest are like 'You got *potential*, Tara, but you gotta start using it'. My phone pings an alert and my heart flips. It's him.

Luv ya. Don't be missing me too much.

I read his text five times. Not like him to be going all cheese. Another alert springs up. Oran's on live feed from Glasgow, driving, one hand on the steering wheel, the phone in the other. I hug my phone. So maybe it's not a call just for me, but at least he texted and now I'm seeing him. I clasp the mobile to my chest and lean against a tree on Grand Parade to watch in private.

'You going to record it to watch again under your duvet tonight?' Lena laughs.

I grin and give her the finger, but when I look back at the screen my smile fades as the scenario sinks in. Something's wrong. Oran's a definite headcase – but this is crazy. He doesn't own a car so it must be stolen, and he sure as hell shouldn't be driving and streaming. On both counts, he's framing himself with clear evidence. The footage is bumpy as he drives round some industrial estate, taking corners with drift and handbrake turns, the speedometer gradually picking up and engine noise rising above the music blaring from the radio. I can't make out everything he's saying, but as he flicks the camera view back to himself, clearly identifiable, he's mid-spiel going on about the

6

New IRA. Lambasting the ones who kneecapped him for joy-riding and anti-social behaviour. Just cos not everyone trusts the police shouldn't mean self-appointed men in balaclavas should dole out street justice. He spits his words. 'What gives them the right to say I can never see my mam again in Derry? I'd have better rights if I was in prison doing time.' One by one he names them. Gives their home addresses. 'Carry this on your conscience every time you see my ma walking your streets.'

I pale. Like WTF? Everyone knows who pulled the trigger but naming them? On social media? Either he's deliberately burning his bridges, or drugs and forced exile have melted every last viable brain cell. He'll never set foot in Derry again.

I straighten up, livid, and start shouting at the phone, as if he'll hear me across the airwaves. As he careers round side roads and alleys, Oran's eyes are rolling in his head. He's spaced. This footage is seriously incriminating. And dangerous. He's not even wearing a seatbelt. Either he doesn't realize, doesn't care or he's doing this on purpose. I flick out of the live stream and pull up his number on speed dial. Twice it rings out as I pace about. Minutes later, screaming in frustration, I flick back to the video.

The camera is now flipped to street view, the engine screeching and the car racing past grey industrial walls in a blur. For an instant, he switches the view back to himself. The tears are tripping him; his I'm-alright mask replaced with a vacant hopelessness. Then it's back to street view. Dead ahead, at the end of a long straight, is a low concrete wall. Beyond it, a yard of rubble and junk. I'm thinking that Oran's playing chicken. At the last second, he'll pull the handbrake and spin. Then I hear him say one last word: 'Bye.' And as the car speeds on, the penny drops.

I can't not watch. What I see sears my brain. Glass smashing,

7

metal grating, buckling, the mobile tossed from his hand and ricocheting, bashed from ceiling to floor, still live-streaming the chaos, from blue sky to black tarmac, windshield and wipers, white clouds to grey brick, as the car hits the wall, flips, somersaults, slides and crumples. A strangled cry sticks in my throat. I can't let it out because if I do, this will be real.

Lena runs to me as I collapse onto the cobbles. Silence. Stillness. The final screen view is of blue sky beyond a broken windscreen. I paw at the phone as if I can reach Oran. Save him. But all I can hear is silence. No radio or commentary. Stillness. Nothing. Not even breathing. And all I can think of is the snapped head of the Child of Prague.

Nothing will fix this. Not glue. Not even miracles.

Chapter 2

TARA
Derry, 24 August 2019

Oran is dead. My Oran. And this last week or so, something inside me is wired bad. Broke. Like inside broke. Not money broke. Like the scream's still strangled and can't escape.

It never even made the news but because he's dead, the suits, some do-gooders from Belfast, are paying for our youth club to go on holiday. Cos we knew him. And so we don't riot. Or joy-ride. Or lose it completely. That's the bones of it once you filter through the jargon of 'diversionary cross-community peace-building residential'. It's August and pissing like October. I draw RIP in the condensation on the bus window and watch it drip away into nothing. I don't want to be here. I don't want to be *anywhere*. Maybe they're right, and getting away from it all will help.

'Why do we have to link up with Protestants?'

Lena asks the question we've all been swallowing in case it sounds screwed. She gets away with it on a technicality – her being Polish, even though she's pure Derry.

'Funding requirement,' says our youth leader, Emer, as we pull out of the estate.

Aka we're not worth the money if it's just us. But since we couldn't afford it otherwise, we'll all sing 'Kumbaya' till it goes viral and fake smile for the group photo. Ma says I've got to move on from moping round the house, like I'm supposed to be over this already. If it wasn't for Lena, and the fact there's nothing much else to do in the last week before back to school, I wouldn't even be on this trip. I've already bought art pencils. Ma's scoured the free uniform shop for second-hand blue shirts. Last year's skirt's shorter. Oran would've liked that.

I jam my runners flat against the seat in front and stuff in my earphones.

As the bus weaves through the Glen streets, I see all our old hang-outs. Alleys. Lamp-posts. Street corners. It's been the longest ten days of my life. Oran was seventeen, one year older than me, but he looked fifteen in his coffin. Innocent. Angelic. Like he should've topped the Christmas tree instead of himself. My arse. He never denied being off the rails, but he was *my* boyfriend even if we were supposed to be split since April. Even before the hormone fest, since primary school, he was a friend. A kick-about mucker for street football, a share-your-last-Rolo, lemme-copy-your-homework kind of friend. A mad chancer who chanced his arm once too often. I wasn't for saying that at his wake. I wasn't for saying anything at his wake. Not now. Not ever. It's pointless. Nothing changes.

People shouted crap loud enough on Facebook. Like folk get their kicks from joining a hate fest over his dead body. *He didn't get shot in the first place for saying his prayers. Had it coming to him. No smoke without fire. Should've wised up sooner if he couldn't handle getting sent away.* So what if he wasn't a saint? Weren't the bigger sinners the ones who dragged him away from half-ate Easter eggs to shoot him in the leg and kick him out of the city?

Lying awake each night this week I could still hear the whispers from the wake. Decades of the rosary mixed with adults nodding intelligent and pronouncing it serious like 'Anti-Community behaviour'. Acting like it makes sense Oran got shot in the first place. 'Went lenient. Spared him the lucky six' – two in the thighs and two in the ankles for bonus. 'Not the proper kneecapping. Only a flesh wound to wise him up.' As if blowing a hole through a teenager's leg and evicting him to Glasgow solves everything. I crank up the volume in my earphones, like beats will silence voices.

Our bus passes the bookies. White paint on the roof still says, 'Death-drivers will be shot.' They're PC enough to replace 'joy-riding' with 'death-driving' yet they'll pull a trigger instead of giving someone a fair trial? The guns are Troubles zombies – refusing to work with the cops cos they represent the 'state' yet still thinking shooting solves shite. No one puts up signs saying, 'Addicts will be helped' or 'Wanna job? Come on in'. I'd paint them kinda signs if I was in charge. Instead, the guns give themselves names, the New IRA, Dissidents, and they lord about defending their community. Oran was still sixteen when they did him. They called it a punishment attack. Nan called it child abuse and she hugged my head tight into her chest until I stopped sobbing. Mam said we wouldn't talk about it again. 'Don't give it any headspace.' It was for the best to let go and forget about it.

As the bus crosses the Foyle Bridge, I twirl my hair around my finger. If Oran had kept his gob shut, if he hadn't done himself in, would our youth club still have been funded? Jammed into this bus for outdoor pursuits? Obviously meeting Protestants will blow our minds and we'll be model citizens. Aye, right. I can't help thinking the whole set-up is just so the suits will feel righteous for investing their spare change. Apparently, this is the peace process and we're living the dream. I wipe the bus window with my sleeve. Harder task wiping memories.

Out of Derry, misty fields zip past. Emer twists round in her seat, watching me and Lena with that leader look. It's wrote all

11

over her – this trip's a tin-opener move to prise me open. I blank her and take an interest in scenery. 'Sudden death,' the parish priest called it. Catholic holy-speak for the obvious. In the coffin Oran was dressed fancy in a shirt and tie, the lower half of the coffin closed to hide his injuries. Make-up to disguise the worst of the bruising. Blue lips. Cold hands. I shiver. No more vampire movies. His funeral had fifty mourners. Before they pulled it, I screenshot the 9,537 views on his Facebook Live goodbye.

I glance at Emer, already halfway up the bloody bus with her mind-reader skills.

'How're you holding up?' she says, commandeering the seat in front.

'What's it matter?'

'Matters if you want to talk,' she says.

I shrug and mess with my phone. Nope. Nan says talking's for touts – snitches grassing on their own communities. And for politicians. Where would I start talking anyway? The time he mooned me in primary school? Our first drunken snog at an alcohol-free disco? First time we shared highs off tabs? First time I rode shotgun as he drew doughnuts with car tyres on Racecourse Road? Every good memory is bad. Yet it wasn't . . .

I sigh. Talking will just earn me lectures that'll make me feel more screwed. Why am *I* the problem? I'm no more screwed than street justice. Steal a car. Get caught. Do time. Normal. Steal a car. Get summoned by the New IRA? Told to turn up at a specific time and place to be shot? Get brought there and handed over by your ma? Like WTF? Grown-ups only want to talk when they think they have answers.

Emer's still staring at me like I'll utter something prophetic. I've no words. Everything's messed. My head, brain, heart and fists are on different planets, fighting separate wars. How am I supposed to process that, a week after Oran topped himself, the suits fund our club? And some other club from Armagh, because Emer says that's how it works in the north of Ireland. If they fund one side of the fence, they've gotta fund the other. Twisted equality. Emer's still staring. She's clearly not for budging till I say something.

'Why didn't they fund us *before* he died?' I sigh.

'Good question,' she says. 'Ask the politicians.'

There's chewing gum stuck to the back of the seat. Blackened gunge. Lena elbows me as we pass the protest sign in the Sperrins. 'Say no to gold mining. No to cyanide in our water.' Greta Thunberg is Lena's middle name. Ten-years-to-save-the-planet mantra. Ten weeks and we're screwed by Brexit, my nan says. Road spray spatters the windows.

'If politicians can't give a shit, why should we?' I say. 'Nan says there's been no government here for like two years and they're still getting paid. Is that true?'

'Two and a half,' says Emer. 'Mad world. None of the rest of us earns a living staying in bed.'

'Nan does,' I say. 'She's on disability.'

'That's different. Besides, world peace and prosperity are a bit beyond my remit, but I am trying to wake you two up to your potential.'

'Who cares?' I say, folding my arms.

Lena elbows me like *don't push it*.

I used to care. Used to plague my teachers with questions like a proper swot before I wised up. Used to think you could change stuff. Then I watched Mam slogging her guts out to pay red bills. Watched Nan coughing her lungs out waiting years on hospital appointments. No one's looking out for ordinary people. No one can explain why. So why care?

Emer interrupts my thoughts as she stands to head back up the bus. 'Look, the weekend's not about having to talk,' she says, 'but if you want to, you know I'm here.'

I chew my finger.

Our bus pulls in at a filling station for a pee break and half of us disappear round to the wheelie bins at the back instead for smokes, vapes or snogs. I pick nicotine. The youth workers fake selective blindness and head for cappuccinos. I drag on a cigarette nicked from Nan.

'Weren't you for giving up?' says Lena.

'On what?' I say.

She rolls her eyes. I flick ash and stump out the butt with my runner.

'Maybe I just did,' I say. 'My head's fried.'

'Oran or more?'

'Everything. Oran . . . School . . . as if anything we do's gonna change our future. Why bother making an effort? I don't really want to do sixth-form A levels and stuff. Except art. Obviously.'

'So why go back?'

'What's there to go forward to? Can you see me on the Tesco tills? I'd be fired on day one. Ma's like, "You are so lucky school took ye back and these are your best years . . . Don't make the same mistakes I did." . . . Like HELLO. I *am* her mistake.'

'Your mam still say nothing about your da?'

'Zipped. Maybe she doesn't know who he is.'

Lena rolls her eyes. 'Can't imagine your mam like that.'

'Maybe Oran was right. Best to go mad, enjoy it and die young.'

'You need a bloody couch,' she says. 'And therapy.'

'I know.' I laugh. 'Seems like Emer reckons that too. Wanna be my shrink?'

'Aye.' She wags her finger, all melodrama. 'Stuff the back story, Tara Connolly, and get on your game face. You're a fighter. Not a quitter.'

I give her the middle finger.

She grins. 'Cheer up. Seriously. Residentials are mad craic. We've a stash of tequila and there could be talent on the other bus. Who knows?' She elbows me in the ribs as the youth leaders holler from out front that the bus is leaving.

Back in our seats, Lena digs in her bag and fires me a Twix and some salt-and-vinegar Tayto. 'Would you go with a Protestant anyways?' she asks.

I shrug and lick chocolate from my fingers. 'Not now. Dunno. Maybe if he was well fit.' I pick at my nail. My words feel like betrayal. Catholic guilt, Nan would say. If I meant so little to Oran that he'd top himself, why does the thought of fancying someone else punch so heavy?

Another hour trundling along with the head torture of the younger teens giving lilty to 57 billion green bottles, and we pull into some outdoor pursuits place with wee cabins and boats stacked outside on trailers. Middle of nowhere. Mountains and, somewhere close, the whisper of waves. I take a photo on my phone of the bus tyre treads reflecting in the puddle. Everyone's all 'I hate this place', 'There's no 4G', 'Christ, is there even WiFi?' Then there's a race for dorms but the leaders are a step ahead. The Protestant crew aren't here yet but our lads are siphoned away from the girls and they've names listed on the doors. They're force mixing us. At least Megan Carey's in a different dorm from me. It's like she gets her kicks out of being on my case. Miss ever-popular-totally-perfect. Last thing I need on holiday. It's bad enough at school.

'It's about trying to make new friends,' says Emer, 'but no

boys in the girls' dorms and no girls sneaking in with the boys. When I count you onto the bus home, I want the same number I came with. No less and *definitely no more.*'

Giggles and fake puking sounds. I get it, but the ache of missing Oran hits the same way as always, when I'm not expecting it. It wasn't that we'd even got that serious yet but he's the only boy I've dated steady. What is it with my family? Never mind Mam, Nan was a single parent before it was even a thing. She never talks about that stuff – she's just all 'us women gotta be strong, Tara'. Mam puts it simpler – 'We don't need men. We're grand as we are.'

In their feminist garb they're all 'individuality is our best card. We're our own women'. Sometimes I listen. Their mantras were a perfect back-at-ye argument for the two helix piercings at the top of my ear and the neon blue streak dyed into my hair. They go well with my new cowboy hat. When she first saw me in it, Mam paled, then muttered 'No matter,' and went back to peeling carrots. Megan has slagged me sick all week over it. I blank her. Show the real underneath story and you're dead. Teenage rules are pick your vibe and go with it. I choose individual. Arty with a mix of goth and a shedload of attitude. Black suits my mood.

I bag a top bunk and apply filters to the tyre photo as Lena reads the list off the door. The four names we don't know are *them*. Bethany, Hannah, Grace, Faith. They sound shit holy.

I'm lamenting my sleeping bag – bright orange with flowers, like Nan salvaged it from the 1960s – and Lena and the others are touching up eyeliner, when we hear the second bus trundle across the cattle grid. We jam our noses against the dorm window, our breath misting the glass. Teenagers in jeans, hoodies and trackie bottoms mill about waiting for bags.

'They look kinda like us,' says Lena.

'Expecting martians, were ye?' I say. She kicks me in the ankle and I lean down to rub it.

'O-M-G.' She spells out the letters slow and low and I squish further along to look, knowing it means serious eye-candy. Except I'm wrong. Way wrong. It takes a moment to really sink in. A weird out-of-body feeling. Like holy mother of . . . The air is sucked from my lungs and now my friends are staring at me and back to the window like ping-pong, and I can't breathe, tranced out watching a girl step off the bus and she. She. SHE. Looks just like me. The same wavy black hair. Same fair skin. Same nose. Cheek bones. Stance. *Everything*. The exact same as me, only airbrushed posh instead of goth. If individual is all I've got, now I'm nothing. The burning floods from my stomach, rising to my ears. Anger. Hot and frightened.

'Talking of looking like us . . .' says Lena.

'Shut it,' I say, slapping my hand flat on the wall. 'Like sweet Jesus. Seriously?'

'I know she's a Prod, but you have to be related. She's your clone, Tara. You sure your mam didn't have twins split at birth? Your one there does make-up way better, though.'

I shove Lena. Her eyes go wide as she lands on a bunk. Something is so wrong and my head can't get it. How? Just how? *Is* she something to me? Banter and footsteps sound down the corridor, coming towards our dorm and then she's there. Right there. Flaunting it.

'Hi. I'm Faith,' she says. Then, as she sees me, she drops her bag. Puts her hand to her mouth. Takes a step back. Three other girls jostle in through the door frame and then the whole room goes eerily still. As they freeze, I lunge. I don't even realize I'm doing it until – *thwack* – I punch her in the chest and she staggers as I barge past. Running. Fleeing. Up the corridor. I hear Emer

17

shouting 'Tara, stop!' But I don't care. Out the door. Past the buses. Through the gate. And on and on. Gravel. Puddles. Hedges. Gates. Trees. Mud. Fields. Up and on, over and through, until my muscles burn and I fall on my knees, coughing. No way am I for crying. Bitch. I don't care about anything or anyone or any of this. All I can see in my head is a girl who looks just like me, only upgraded.

Bog water is soaking through the knees of my jeans. Hit and run. The look on her face was like a sick selfie when I punched her. I shiver in the dusk. Am I victim or villain? Sure doesn't feel like I'm in the driver's seat. Feels like my life's the car crash.

Chapter 3

FAITH
County Down, 24 August 2019

I'd been hoping that this weekend maybe I could tell Jack how I'm feeling. Or even a youth leader – one who wouldn't go all religious on me. Just to get the words out of my head. Now? I can't think straight.

My head is cold against the hostel bathroom tiles. I splash icy water on my face. Live a lie long enough and it becomes the truth. I've tried that. Now it's looking like my parents have been living one too. I need answers. Maybe this girl can give me some.

That's what I was thinking, right before she punched me.

I've my foot jammed against the door but my friends are whispering outside. Course they are. They saw her too. My double. After a series of 'You alright?'s and door knocks, they go to find a leader. Only Bethany remains. I move my foot and click the door open before I get in bother. She's hugging the walls, unsure what to say.

I grab loo roll from a cubicle and wipe away black bits on my cheeks where the mascara has run. As I concentrate on the mirror, I study my eyes again. Emerald green with distinctive flecks of brown. Pretty rare, even for Ireland. The type of green is really bright, too. Mum's eyes are blue. Dad's too. A simple chart of dominant and recessive genes in GCSE science plus a closer examination of extended family photos had planted a small doubt two years ago, but I'd dismissed it. Blue-eyed parents with a green-eyed kid. Not impossible. Not likely, either. No sign of it in my wider family. My question mark from that day is still scratched by compass point into the varnish on the school lab bench. Jagged and jammed with dirt. I have a mole on my neck, just like Mum. Freckles too. And she still has the umbilical clip and wristband from when I was born. But what about Dad? Since that biology lesson, I'm obsessed with people's eyes – friends, uncles, the tenor section in the church choir, men buying the papers in the village shop. No one. Not one soul has eyes like mine. Until now. I rub my ribs and visualize the moment again. When she thumped me, I saw her eyes clearly – they are just like mine. All of her is like me. Exactly. Only she's more confident. And aggressive.

'Got a comb?' I try to act normal. Pretence comes scarily easy. I've been doing it a while.

Bethany hands me one from her bag. 'You OK?' she says. 'I saw her hit you. They'll send her home for sure.'

I stare at her. It dawns. She's right. For a second, the real me shows up. 'No!' I say, dragging my fingers through my hair. 'They can't. I want . . .'

Bethany hugs me, plastering me with reassurances, reading it all wrong. The stress is fizzing but I bite my tongue. I must talk to Tara. 'Where's Jack? Can you get Jack?'

Bethany goes quiet, avoiding my eyes. 'Jack's gone,' she says. 'He ran after her. I think he mistook her for you.'

I groan. Even Jack couldn't tell us apart? My youth leader bustles up the corridor, all facts and forms. What? When? Who? Am I bruised? Upset? Do I want to call home? I look down, gasp, then grip my fingers tight round Bethany's comb before stuffing it into my pocket. My youth leader's eyes follow the movement and then she looks at the side of my head.

'So, she pulled your hair, this other girl?'

'I . . . uh . . .'

Already she's scribbling.

Did Tara yank my hair? There's no pain there. It wasn't like a catfight – she just punched me in the chest and ran. I've zero memory of any hair-pulling. What's blatantly clear though is that there's another girl on this planet who looks so like me she could virtually be my twin. To get rid of my youth leader, I spill the facts of the incident dutifully. Compared to my questions, hers are easy answered. It's obvious she hasn't clapped eyes on my stunt double yet. Probably thinks the lookalike bit is just girlie hysteria.

'Anything else I can do?' she asks.

From the confusion, I have one clear thought. 'Yes,' I say. 'Please don't send her home. But . . . could I get a different room?'

She nods. 'I'll see what I can do.'

I smile. My everything's-fine mask is well-rehearsed. Sometimes even I can't tell the difference. Once she's gone, I lock myself in the toilet cubicle. It's a bit rank. Not the best place for taking deep breaths but the only place I feel safe. I look at the comb. It's netted with a clump of my hair. Far more than normal. Long. Black. Wavy. I pull it from the comb and chuck it in the loo, watching the fronds sink in the water. Weird. I genuinely don't think Tara pulled my hair, but if she didn't, what caused this? I've enough on my mind already without needing another problem. Instinct draws my fingertips to my head, tracing their way across my scalp until I freeze, feeling the smooth patch. Was that what my youth leader had noticed?

Willing my sense of touch to be wrong, I go for the visual and reach for my mobile. After minutes of staring, unblinking, at a contorted angle into my phone camera, I throw up.

Chapter 4

TARA
County Down, 24 August 2019

As my anger and the night temperatures cool, it dawns on me – I'm lost. My phone's on 4 per cent. No reception. Not exactly Google Maps territory. Arsehole of nowhere with sloping mountain fields and wiry plant stuff that tangles my feet. My runners squelch with bog water. The field is clattered with seaweed. Like WTF? Seaweed? I plonk myself onto a stone wall and look around.

Not a bloody street light for miles. Someone should introduce them to tarmac. The moon's already up, gawping in and out behind clouds like some two-star horror flick. On my phone camera, I take a slo-mo. Something about the tones of grey trailing across the brightness. Trancing out to it gets me thinking. I'm in the shit. Again. Emer'll give me a bollocking. Ma'll rage. I'll be grounded. Megan will slag me to hell. It's all patterns. Patterns I'm stuck in. Always repeating. Screw up. Get grounded. Act sorry. Be good. Get angry. Screw up. I don't know why I do this shit. It just happens. Especially these last two weeks. Who am I kidding? These last two years.

I kick my heels against the wall. Apart from sheep bleating some place, it's mad quiet. No cars. No drunks padding the streets after pub closing. Not that there's even streets. I try to think what way I came but it's a blur. All I know is it was uphill and that something in me just kept running. Running like when

I used to be on the team. Fast. Before I quit. Now I don't know my way back. Even if I find it, I'll have to face her and they'll make me say sorry and when I think on it, that's not even the scary bit. Scary bit would be just seeing her. Like seeing a selfie I never took of me in a pastel blue sweater. Posh. Sorted. Faith. I say her name over and over in rhythm with my kicking heels. Do I want to see her? I can't suss it. Maybe I do. Maybe I don't. If Nan and Mam won't tell me about Da, could Faith help solve my mystery? Is her da my da? Bloody hell, is my da a Prod? Is that why Ma won't spill? Lena's right – Faith and I look so similar, it can't just be fluke, can it? Are we related? Sisters? Half-sisters? Twins? My head's a blender.

I don't know how long I sit there. Soggy. Cold. Messed up. I know it's getting dark though and I couldn't fill a fart with everything I know about outdoor survival.

I pull my knees up to my chest for warmth. I can't even stick some dubstep on my phone for company cos the battery's died. Mizzling rain is soaking everything. My hat's dripping. If I was her, someone would be out scouring the hillside. If I was her, it'd matter that I was missing. Everyone would be out searching. Like even from her clothes, she's in the 'in' crowd. Centre of attention. She's going steady with the best boyfriend, aces school, even maths, and has family dinners every Sunday. With dessert. Everybody loves her. She never screws up. Never loses it, sees red or throws punches. Plus, she's going to be an astrophysicist and if she was here, she'd float to our hostel guided by starlight, never once stepping in cow shite.

I gawp about me. Feck. I really am lost. I do have a cigarette left though and no Lena to bollock me about it. I dig my lighter from my pocket and suck in deep, holding the flame to the tip until it glows orange.

A thin line of dot-to-dot light below traces bits of wiggly coast. Squares here and there of yellow windows. Some in clumps. One of them's gotta be the hostel. A smaller light is bobbing much closer. Crawling uphill in zigzags. I stare at it as I blow smoke and stub out my cigarette butt on the wall. The light stops moving. A shout. 'Faith? That you?' A male voice carries in my direction on the wind. It doesn't sound Derry. My eyes can make out a shadowy outline. He tries again. 'Faith? It's only me.'

I cough. The light bobs more quickly uphill, its line straighter. Edging towards me. As it gets closer, I can see it's a teenager. He's about my age but taller with short hair, joggers and a hoodie.

'What happened?' he says as he picks his way across muck to the wall. 'Thought you were for the Olympics the way you hoofed it up that hill. Impressive.'

'I'm not Faith,' I say.

He stops mid-stride about four metres away and swings his phone-torch beam onto me. 'Aye right,' he says. Then goes real still. There's just enough backlight catching his eyes for me to see him study me. Slow. My hat. Face. Hoodie. Jeans. Runners. Back to my face. His own eyes narrowing in concentration.

'Say something,' he says.

'Feck off.'

'Jesus,' he says, dropping to his hunkers, sitting on his boot heels. 'You're not Faith. But you look . . . ' He sucks in a whistle. 'Who are you?'

'Tara,' I say. 'How'd you know I wasn't her? Who are you?'

'I'm Jack,' he says. 'And it's obvious from the attitude on you. Plus, the accent. Hat. Piercings. The fag.' He nods at the cigarette butt. 'Wouldn't have found you, apart from that glowing.'

'Right Sherlock, aren't ye?'

He stands and walks closer, right up to me, staring like I'm a ghost.

'Regulation check on perfume?' I jump from the wall. 'Back off, alright? I'm not your bloody girlfriend.'

He rubs his eyebrow and steps back. 'Too weird. You look . . . Where's Faith? What happened?'

A sick feeling churns in my stomach. Yer man's probably my best ticket back to the hostel, but tell him the truth and I'll be lost out here all night. They'll pull me shivering from a bog of sheep piss in the morning. I can't *not* answer. He's glancing about the hillside and back at me. The model boyfriend, charging up mountains like a knight in bloody shining armour to rescue his distressed damsel. She was worth it. None of our crew found me. I drop my shoulders and nudge a globe of rabbit poo with my runner.

'I hit her,' I say.

'You what?' He steps close so quick I feel his breathing on my face, see him squaring his shoulders, eyebrows narrowed.

I clench my fists. I could hit out. Kick even. Or spit. With luck, the shock might stall him enough for me to leg it but he's tall and athletic. Strikes me, he's pretty alright for a Prod. He speaks kinda country, though. Some guys I would fight. Not him. He's the sort of lad built for Gaelic or, given that he's one of them, rugby. I tilt my chin and stare defiant into his eyes. For a moment the turquoise of them catches me and I drop my gaze to his boots, hesitating. Camping out without a tent isn't my style and the cold's drilling into my bones. 'Look, don't be mad,' I say. And for once, I spill the truth. 'It was like a bullet seeing her. I freaked.'

Jack steps back like it's him I just caught with an uppercut. He walks a slow circle round the top half of the field, clasping his hands behind his head and glancing my way every so often like he's checking me out in some kind of risk assessment. As he knocks flat some yellow weed things on stalks, I'm kicking myself over picking the wrong time for bloody honesty. I will die here. Froze and mummified in sheep shite, to be resurrected in five centuries and pinned with some mournful history saga of warring tribes.

Finally, he makes his way back to me, hands stuffed deep into his pockets. As he looks up from his boots, I'm caught again by his eyes and find myself tongue-tied between saying something streetwise feminist and coming over all Disney princess. The silence sits awkward while we study each other.

'It's bloody foundering for August,' he says eventually, arms hugged tight across his chest for warmth. 'Do you come here often?'

It takes a second, then we both bust nervous laughing because the whole thing is absurd. 'All the time,' I say. 'Never leave the place. Turns out but someone's nicked the signpost back to the youth hostel.'

'City folk, no doubt,' he says. 'Happens I was for heading back that direction.' With his head, he gestures downhill. 'Wanna walk together?'

In the fading light, we squidge and squelch our way down the mountain. Our breathing goes in fits and bursts with the exertion but, once beyond the fields, our footsteps pick up a rhythm, a steady scrunch, sliding on the mosses and wet gravel of a narrow backroad. Cars here must be size zero. Apart from an occasional inhaled comment on the madness of this, Jack says almost nothing until we turn a corner and, in the distance, see the glow of the hostel windows. I'm several metres ahead of him before I realize the crunch of his boots has stopped. When I turn, I can just about make him out in the blackness, stood with his head cocked to the side, eyeing me.

'What's the story?' I say.

'Exactly what I was wondering,' he says. 'How we gonna play this?'

I screw my face up in the dark as it dawns on me again that facing my youth leader, facing everybody, facing *her*, might be an occasion well shy of a picnic. Something inside me also lifts though about how Jack said it. There's a *we* in this. Like I'm not on my own, even though it's all my fault.

'It's just me in bother,' I say.

'You think our leaders won't be mad we both disappeared for a couple of hours? Or that Faith won't be off her rocker about me mixing you up with her?'

'Yeah, but truth is I threw a punch.'

He shuffles.

'You wanna go ahead on your own?' I say. 'I could mosey about. Follow in a bit. There's no call for you to take the fall.' I bite my lip. 'You don't have to have anything to do with me . . .'

Real slow, he walks up to me. Reaches out. Rubs the fabric of my sleeve between his fingers.

'You're soaked through,' he says.

'To my fecking knickers.'

Jack slaps his hand to his face and shakes his head. 'You are *so* not Faith. This is surreal on steroids.' He folds his arms.

Shivering, I take my hat off to comb my fingers through tangled hair. Even though it was under the hat, it's sodden. The prospect of pissing about in the rain even another ten minutes is as appealing as a brick in the face. The prospect of facing my youth leader, worse. My shoulders sag.

Jack's studying the hat. 'You ever watch old cowboy movies?'

I shrug. 'Wet Sundays. With Nan.'

'*Butch Cassidy and the Sundance Kid*. The blaze of glory bit at the end where they both know they're dead but they face it together?'

We don't even make it past the buses. I'm still steeling up my defences, readying for the shots when there's drumming on windows from the dorms. A shout. Megan-bloody-Carey. She'd grass on her granny for a Happy Meal. By the time we're sucked into the blazing lights of the corridors and main hall, my muscles are tight, my brain racing to spit obscenities and kick out about the shite of everything and how-would-you-be-if-your-whole-identity-got-stole-by-an-impostor and who-gives-a-toss and the-whole-world-can-go-jump because why-should-I-care-anyway?

The youth leaders leap from a huddle of conspiracy over steaming mugs in a corner, and three men decked out all super-hero-meets-mountaineer in high-vis wet gear with head torches and maps surround us like we're refugees. I'm about to launch into get-the-feck-off-my-case when Jack lets rip, only different. Like a pro, he's blazing guns of apology, concern for the tormented youth leaders, the hassle we've caused, *so sorry*, and 'Where's Faith? I need to see Faith'. It's like he aced GCSEs in adult manipulation and deflection.

Gawping in silence, dripping, I find myself bear-hugged by Emer, tight as a strait jacket, her sentences alternating between foghorn loud and supportive whispers and what-in-hell-Taras and thank-God-you're-OKs. Then Jack's shipped off to the boys' dorms and I'm in the kitchen towelling my hair and Emer's making me hot chocolate like I'm all prodigal at the same time as she's chewing my ear off about 'totally unacceptable behaviour' and me dousing the club with shame and oh-my-god am I really-the-feck-OK cos she'd nearly had to call my mam. And. And. And. And I'm quiet. And peeling off wet socks and wondering if Faith paints her toenails black too and how the world, or even tomorrow, could ever feel the right way up again, and thinking that if Oran were here he'd give me a tab and the world might feel saner and how Nan's 1960s psychedelic sleeping bag will feel like I've won the lottery and what-in-under-Jesus is a kayak anyway because apparently we're for them first thing.

Chapter 5

FAITH
County Down, 25 August 2019

Faded life-jackets every shade of orange. Black wetsuits. We're a troop of human slugs traipsing the kayaks off the beach into the breakers. The rig-outs give us a kind of uniformity, though everyone's sticking in their own youth group huddles. Armagh and Londonderry. We were hardly off the bus last night before our crew discovered we could rile them just by saying 'Londonderry'. They spit back 'Derry'. Stirring each other's heads seems like a game we're expected to play. Northern Irish rules. Protestants and Catholics. Catholics and Protestants. The whole 'love your enemy' thing gets glossed over. So much for all the 'get to know you' cross-community ice-breakers our youth leaders roped us into last night.

I study them as the shingle crunches under our old trainers. It's not so much about hate these days. It's just we don't know them. After the Troubles, grown-ups still hugged the good-fences-make-good-neighbours line. Stitched it so we rarely mix. Different schools. Different sports clubs. Different ends of towns or villages. As we pile into kayaks, we don't look that different. Splashing and messing. The last thing I want to look is different. Bad enough feeling it. I just never expected to look the same as someone else exactly.

I eye Tara laughing with a group of friends. Today, we look even more alike. Only the blue stripe in her hair and the brighter orange of my life jacket tells us apart. I keep my head down, conscious of the whispers. I skipped breakfast. I'd hardly slept, and it took ten minutes to clip back my hair to hide the bald patch. Dark strands laced my pillow. This is no hair-pulling thing. It's different. Scary. When I think about it, I have been de-fuzzing my hairbrush more often this summer, but it just didn't seem significant. I tried googling it in the small hours but the reception was so bad the buffering drove me demented. Jack found me skulking in my new dorm and handed me marmalade-loaded toast just before everyone got chivvied to the wet changing. He knows me well. He's been glued to me ever since, but it's like he swallowed a mute button. Apart from toast, all he's given me is shrugs and apologies. Like everyone else, including the leaders, I catch him glancing at times between her and me. Every time I look at her, my head spews questions.

In the water, the kayaks bob chaotically. Our instructor blows a whistle. 'Listen up. Paddles like this.' He demonstrates the wide handgrip, the slicing twist through the water. 'On my next whistle I want yous to paddle into a line. Not just any line. Paddle yourselves into alphabetical order by first name.'

'In our own youth group?'

'No, eejit. Yous are all one group. You've two minutes.' He blasts the whistle.

Paddles scrape off fibreglass. Boats spin. Shouts and laughter. Everyone's talking. *Bethany. Colin. Caitlin. Caoimhe.* 'Come again?' *Diarmuid* . . . 'That Irish?' 'Feck off.' 'I'm only asking.' *Joaquim.* 'Jesus. Where'd they find you?' *Me. Grace.* 'Quit drenching me!' *Harry. Hannah.* 'Thirty seconds . . .' *Jack. Lena. Megan. Niamh. Pádraig. Omar.* 'Swap. Swap.' *Reuben. Tara. William.* The shriek of the whistle carries across the water but we take a minute to settle. We shout our names in order. Then he

31

tells us to shout the name of the person to our left in order. Then our right.

'Stars the lot of ye. Another game, then we'll paddle the coast. On my whistle, shift yourselves into order by age. Youngest to my left. Oldest to my right.' The splashing and jostling drowns the whistle. I'm in the thick of it, trying to suss my position, when Tara's kayak clips mine.

'April,' she says, looking fierce, like it's my fault I'm in her way. 'When's your birthday?'

'February,' I say. For a moment it's like we're alone on an ocean. I bite my lip. 'I'm sixteen. You?'

'Same,' says Tara. She points her paddle. 'You're in the wrong place. Get up the line.'

As I steer myself up closer to Jack, it hits. Tara and I can't be twins. I'm older. Something about that feels good. In time with my paddling, I count from February to April. Three months. What are the options? Weirdly similar distant relations? Sisters? For a moment, I'm lost in processing the thought and don't realize I'm headed for the breakers. My kayak is drifting off course, pulled by the tide. The wave of emotion hits as the real waves ditch me into the white horses. The paddle slips from my grip and I'm flipped over. *Splash.* I find my feet, blinking and spitting saltwater.

'Stunt double's as bad as Tara,' a girl shouts. One of their group.

I hear laughter, the flap of paddles flat onto water like belly flops. Through the muffle of water in my ears, I hear Jack's voice returning an insult. The instructor blows the whistle and paddles in my direction.

'I'm OK,' I call, righting the boat. The words repeat in my head. *I'm OK. I'm OK.* I whisper it to myself as I flop undignified into the kayak, then realize I should have got the paddle first. *Am I OK?* Metres away, there's an almost identical human being to me. My parents are keeping secrets. I'm keeping a secret. We're all letting on things are normal. *I'm OK.* Thoughts and choppy waves rock me everywhere. Am I adopted? In our family photo album, there are pictures of Mum and Dad with me in hospital the day I was born. My little toes turn in, just like Mum's. Three months between me and Tara. *Think logically.* The evidence says we're not twins. Not full sisters. Half-sisters? I look nothing like my dad. Is he my real dad? Sea-spray and laughter. The clunk jolts me.

Jack slides my paddle across the front of my kayak. 'Don't mind them,' he says. 'Pack of wasters.'

I smile my thanks and grip the pole tight. Determined. If Tara wants to, she can hate me but, already, I'm finding answers. Already, I know my next question. *Who is Tara's dad?*

I look to my right – towards the older side of the wiggle of kayaks. Jack has paddled into place two up from me. He's glancing down the line. Four clear places between me and Tara and I know he's doing the same biology sums.

'We need to talk,' he mouths.

I nod. 'Later.'

We're getting the hang of it. Our kayaks cut at different speeds through the water, slicing each other's wakes. Having capsized once, Bethany acts like an escort as we follow the coast.

'My mum got an email one time from this woman in the States,' she says. 'Thought it was a scam at first, but it wasn't.'

'Yeah?' I say. 'What was the story?'

'Ancestry stuff. Family tree research. Turns out she was a second cousin billionth removed or something . . .'

I frown. 'Your point being?'

Bethany giggles. 'Mad thought. Think your dad ever donated sperm?'

'Euurrk! No!' My stomach churns with a crass mental image.

'Aren't you curious? Tara's still in my dorm. I could be your undercover private eye . . .'

I chew it over. 'Did she say anything last night?'

'Barely a word. Whispered two seconds with her friend . . .' Bethany angles her paddle towards a blonde girl in a kayak ahead. 'Lena. Word is that Tara got a legendary dressing down from her leader. I'm not surprised she was quiet. Or we could try Megan? She seems to have something against Tara too.' She nods in the direction of a brunette.

For a second my stomach flips. Megan's like a supermodel. Racing through the water like she was born with a paddle. For a moment I'm all caught up watching her, and the guilt of it floods me, just like every other time, until I hear her call to some of our lads and realize she's the one who dissed me when I capsized. 'What makes you think I've something against Tara?' I say.

Bethany shrugs. 'She only tried to floor you on sight.'

I mull it over as I paddle, watching her ahead of me at a distance. When I think about her, my insides have a sick-fizz feel. Scared but curious. She has a neck of brass and I'm all bottled up in glass. Mad thing is, she could be a godsend. The coast veers to our right into a new bay. On the beach a minibus and trailer are waiting.

'How come Jack's so quiet on it?' says Bethany. 'Didn't you two talk?'

I shrug. 'He's not exactly chatty this morning.'

'Well, he was gone ages last night. Get him on his own and he's bound to spill. The pair of them walked back in together off the mountain, so he must know something.'

Some of the group are already out of the kayaks and messing in the shallows. Bethany has a point. She's also in my church and, even though she's my best friend, I don't know where she really stands on some of the tangled stuff in my head. Would I lose her friendship if I shared my secret? Would she spout bible verses and distance herself or offer hugs? A familiar low whistle catches my attention. Jack's still at sea, hanging back for me. If anyone's going to help me find answers, it'll be him. Just him. I can trust Jack.

'This could get complicated,' I say. 'Do me a favour? Give me a bit of space for now.'

Bethany looks miffed. Rolls her eyes like 'are you for real?'

'I'm serious. Just drop this, OK? Let me do it my way.'

She splashes off in a huff. I paddle straight to Jack.

Chapter 6

TARA
County Down, 27 August 2019

Lena shakes the bottle of tequila in my face. 'Wake up! Coast's clear. We. Are. Go!'

I sit and rub sleep from my eyes. 1 a.m. Right on cue. I never thought I'd fall asleep fully dressed but every day here I'm drained. I'm feeling muscles grumbling like they haven't in over a year and I'm clean out of fags. Abseiling, banana-boating, paddle-boarding, bouldering and all the bloody peace stuff like threading your life story into a bracelet of beads from Morocco or some place. But not even that, all the gossip-mongering and stares about her and me, and me and her, and my head won't stop spinning and flashing questions and images of Oran and shite. Knackering. It's like I'm operating off pound-shop batteries and everyone else has swallowed Duracell. The others are already ducking out the window with their sleeping bags in tow. I glance over where the girls from the Armagh group sleep. Empty beds. 'Everyone's in on this?'

'Aye. Well, the older ones anyway. The lads already have the fire going.'

'What about—'

'Faith? Yeah. Far as I know. What do you care anyway? She's too self-obsessed to worry about. There's drink. Boys . . . Maybe it's time you moved on?' Lena winks. I grin, knowing rightly she's got her sights fixed on Joaquim. It's the last night of the residential and there's definitely more in the air than just team-building. All the shite-talking reconciliation sessions have been about *respect* and how we're all the same, even if Prods keep their ketchup in the fridge and we keep ours in the press. Through the activities, adults seemingly oblivious to the intense eyeing-up at angles across the room, persistent in blethering crap about 'we all bleed red' and 'tears are all the same'. Mam's banana lesson might have had more impact on cross-community relations.

Grabbing my cowboy hat and phone, I dive out the sash window after Lena.

The fire is a stroll up the coast, far enough so the sound won't carry to the leaders on the night air. The stars take my breath away. Billions of them. Like someone scraped them off Derry and turfed them here. I hold my phone up to take a picture but they're too far off to focus. Weirdly, the whole being outside thing makes stuff feel different. I never realized that. It's not the same in concrete. I bag a place by Lena on the far side of the circle. Close enough for the glow to warm me, far enough from Faith to avoid comments. Or maybe not.

'I see the other half has found her hat again.'

I glare at Megan. Lena digs me in the ribs. 'Don't take her on. She's winding you up.'

As if I didn't bloody know. I bite my tongue. Last thing I need is another lacing from Emer. I'm already yellow carded for punching Faith. Red will mean I'm temporarily barred from the club and, if I end up in a barney with Megan, she'll grass on us all. Lena hands me a bottle. One swig and I feel a familiar warmth in my throat. Mad, but as the bottle circles like pass-the-parcel, it strikes me everyone's muddled, and not in the hammered sense. The *them and us* thing from the first day's all blurry – like every teenager knew all along that hormones were the total solution to building peace. Lena's stargazing in Joaquim's direction and they're not the only ones. Opposite me, on the other side of the beach fire, I can make out Jack and Faith, the silhouette of them lit orange, sparks rising over their heads. Even though they're not holding hands, they're shoulder to shoulder, whispering. Probably been together like forever. That could've been me and Oran.

As the drink starts to kick in, so do the memories. Oran was fun when drunk. We used to laugh like crazy. 'Boys can burn you,' Mam said when she heard we were dating. 'Mind you choose careful. Not like me.' Ma and Nan each had their man. Then their man was gone. Least I'm not left pregnant like they were. I had been almost ready to go the distance with Oran. He should've been my first.

At the next pass of the bottle, I down more than a mouthful. Falling for bad-news ones must be inbred. Watching through the campfire sparks, I study Jack and Faith, imagining I have my sketchpad. It's real subtle, but there are some differences between her and me. Like the mole on her neck. Or her freckles. The slope of her ears. If she can pull him, Mr Gallant with the turquoise eyes, is it just pure inside me that attracts trouble? I pull the hoodie up round my face and breathe through the cotton. It's faint, but the scent of Oran's aftershave is still there. I suck it deep into my lungs and smooth the fabric on my cheek like a forever memory.

Lena whispers as she passes me an open bottle of cider. 'Keep it.' Her grin is lopsided. Joaquim's tugging her to her feet. 'Enough fire in me already. You OK? I'll be back in a bit.' She winks.

As I drink, I mess at burying my runners in the sand. I twist the blue bit of my hair round my finger and glance about. Jack is looking straight at me. I yank my hat down lower and play with a shell. Bollocks. Not that I even have the headspace for wanting to compete, but it's obvious. Out of me and Faith, he knows he's got the winner. I haven't even got a smoke.

'Hat's for hiding your face?' says Megan. There are chuckles from her gang. I lift a pebble and chuck it in the fire. *Don't get riled.* Not everyone's paired up. Our crew brought drink but half of their ones are teetotal. Faith is sipping Fanta. Leastways me and her are not the same in that. Instead of booze, their crowd's passing round marshmallows. Pink, white, and chocolate digestives. Grace, one of their ones from our dorm, hands me a stick and plonks on the sand beside me.

'Some mouth on her, that Megan,' she whispers. 'You OK? You look sad.'

I shrug. The biscuits reach me. 'What's the score with these?' It comes out a bit slurred.

'You've never done s'mores? Where've you been all your life!'

With the first marshmallow, I forget to concentrate as I knock back cider and *whooom*, the whole pink blob goes up in flames on the stick then frazzles black. For a moment I watch it burn like something tragic, then the giggles take over. Grace hands me another and this time I ace it. After that, I'm expert. Dishing advice to everyone. Glorying in biting into the melted silk with chocolate crunch. Across the fire, I catch Faith watching me and Grace. She's jealous I'm having more craic because far as I can see, she doesn't drink and Jack hasn't even snogged her. He's gone. Probably for a pee. I catch myself wondering what it would be like seeing him pee, then I keel over in the sand in a giggle fit with hiccups. I'm flat on my back caught by the stars again when Megan pipes up.

'Toul' ye,' she says, all loudmouth. 'Her ma was so desperate she used a turkey baster to get pregnant. That's why she's no da.'

'Aye,' joins in one of the lads. 'And her nan went with her brother way back and that's why she's no granda.'

'Jesus, Faith. If Tara's ma used a turkey baster, maybe your dad's a God-fearing wanker!'

Faith reddens at the crude hand signals. Jack appears back beside her. It takes a second to get that the comments are assuming me and Faith are half-sisters. A second longer to get what they're saying about Ma and Nan. Then my brain sees red. I'm on my feet. Dizzy. Fuming. Megan and the ones flanking her fire up their hands as I kick sand, pebbles, seaweed into their faces. For a moment it's glorious, but the swing throws me off balance and now Megan's on her feet shoving me over. My hat flies off as she tugs my hair and we're squirming on the ground to taunts of 'catfight, catfight . . .' Some voices join in, jeering, others panic, shushing our cursing. Hands, legs, feet. I taste salt from blood in my mouth and still I'm scrabbling, punching, kneeing and I know I'm getting the better of her cos she's tiring. Wriggling but with desperation in her eyes. I don't see how dangerously close we're getting until suddenly there's screaming and it's me and my left arm is burning. Burning. I can't think. Flames lick my sleeve and Megan's sneering as I'm twisting, turning, frantic and *BAM!*

Jack rugby tackles me to the ground. Shoves me into the sand. The flames go out, but Megan is still laughing and my arm is killing me and I find my feet and run, racing in drunk zigzags, sand filling my runners and socks, legs heavy from the exertion. Running, snot streaming. Running away from all of them until somewhere at the back of the beach I collapse in grasses, curled in a ball, hiding in blackness.

Nothing is fair. Ever. Ever. Ever. I'm rocking. Cradling my arm. In the moonlight I can see blisters are appearing where the hoodie's completely singed. Oran's hoodie. I press the fabric to my nose and collapse in a coughing fit. Smoke. It only smells of smoke. The ache is overwhelming. This is all I have of Oran's. How am I gonna mind him now? My stomach's telling me I'm gonna puke. From drink. From marshmallows. From . . . Jesus but my arm hurts. The skin stings. Hot like it's still burning. I'm left-handed. What if I can't draw for art? What if they kick me out of school? Or the club? I bite my finger, whimpering. The pain is real bad and they laughed. They all laughed. Well, maybe not all, but Megan did. But it won't matter cos I'll get the blame. I started the fight. My head spins and my throat burns from fighting back tears.

'Tara?'

There's torchlight from a phone on the beach. Two silhouettes. And suddenly I taste the salt of tears flowing down my cheeks and I'm sniffing because it's Jack and Faith and I can't take any more of this. I want home. I want my ma. I want my *da*. Jesus – did I just think that? I cower in the grass, willing invisibility. Confused by my own thoughts.

'Tara!'

The pool of light races towards me and Faith drops to her knees at my feet.

'Jack, get sea water. Something cold. Quick.'

He scans around, then runs. For the first time, I'm alone with Faith. The moon glints in her eyes. Same eyes as me and, without thinking, the inside questions spill out, slurred and jumbled. 'Do you hate me? Is your da my da? I never meant to hit you. Honest, I—'

'Sshh . . . ' she says. 'It's OK.' She smooths the hair back from my face.

Jack plonks beside us and hands something to Faith. He's

41

soaked, bare-chested and shivering. Plus, he's wearing my hat and I'm raging cos it suits him.

'Knew there'd be trouble when I saw you.' He winks. 'But I never thought you'd steal the shirt off my back.'

I find myself studying his abs. Then I realize, it's his T-shirt, soaked in cold sea water, that Faith is pressing gently onto my arm. She's quiet. Concentrating.

'You're burnt,' Jack says. 'We gotta get you back to the hostel.' Already he's on his feet, holding out his hand, but I hesitate, unsure.

'I don't need help,' I say. 'I'm grand . . . I'll only land you in bother.' My head is pounding and I'm struggling to get what's going down but that question about Da – it feels urgent. I need an answer. Now.

'Wise up,' says Jack.

Faith thumps him. 'Tara,' she says gently. 'Everyone needs help sometimes.'

I look back and forth at the pair of them, trying to summon the courage to ask again about her da.

There's no need. It's like she reads my mind. 'I don't know the answer,' says Faith.

'But I—'

'I don't think my dad is your dad. I don't think he's even my dad.'

Jack pales. 'I thought you weren't for saying till you had proof?'

'That's never what I said,' says Faith. 'I said I wasn't for asking Mum and Dad until I was sure.'

'But—' Jack sits in the sand.

'Not now,' says Faith. 'Tara's hurt. If I run ahead for help, can you walk with her?'

'No!' I say. Jack and Faith look confused. My head feels woozy

42

trying to get the sentence together. 'Why'd you shove me? Gimme my hat.'

Jack removes my hat from his head and plonks it on mine as he stands. 'I rolled you in sand to put out the fire, eejit.'

I stagger to my feet but my legs buckle. Jack catches me, hoists me into a front-way piggyback and nods to Faith. 'You run. We're good. I got this.'

I feel the steady stride of Jack underneath me. Watch the moonlight glint off water and sweat on his back as my arms lollop around his neck. The beach is spinning but it feels safe to be wrapped round him. As we pass the burning embers, the campfire fight is fuzz in my mind. Empty bottles lie strewn round the abandoned cinders and final glow. I wipe my nose on what's left of my sleeve.

'You smell of beer and smoke,' I say.

'Look who's talking.' He picks his way through seaweed onto firmer sand. 'Don't suppose you've any chewing gum on you?'

'Yeah. Why?'

'Happens I'd prefer to avoid a grilling two nights in the one week. Reckon you can stand a minute?' He slides me gently over his shoulder until my runners touch the sand, then steadies me with hands on my waist. 'There's no hiding you're hammered but the sea water sobered me up fast. If I smell like toothpaste, they might yet think I'm an angel.'

I'm dizzy with the effort of standing. As I trawl my pockets, my stomach lurches and I puke violently. He catches me under the armpits as my knees buckle; holds me steady as I survey the damage to his Nike runners.

'Oops . . .' I hiccup and spit yuck.

'Not really one for first impressions, are you?'

I offer him my last piece of gum as an apology. He bites it in half and hands me back a bit. 'You *are* an angel,' I say, struggling to string the sentence together. He raises an eyebrow. 'Like, Faith is so lucky to have you . . .' The words still slur. He rolls his eyes then loops my arms round his neck.

'Jump.'

Somehow, he laces his arms under me and swings my legs round his waist before staggering into a stride. Our ears rub. Maybe it's because I'm drunk, but something about him feels secure. My head bobs as he paces up the beach and I mind primary school wheelbarrow races with Oran. A year nine disco with my arms around his neck. Our first kiss . . . I blink, feeling fresh tears hot on my cheeks. I gulp in the cool air and try to block the flood of memories. Holding hands up the Glen. Lighting my first cigarette off his. Messaging into the wee hours. I chew my fist to stifle the whimpers.

'That arm killing you?' says Jack, as he picks his way across shingle. 'Not far now.' His breathing is heavier with the exertion, the beach steepening.

'I'm too heavy . . .'

'Much lighter than marching with a Lambeg.'

'That mad Protestant drum? You play that?'

'Aye,' he says and starts to whistle the sash, striding to the beat.

'Put me down. I can walk here.' I squirm my way out of his grip and stagger in the sand.

'Sure?' He frowns, studying me. 'I was only messing. You look like death warmed up.'

From nowhere the image invades. Oran. In the coffin. And it's my Oran I want, not Jack. The ache crushes my chest and the rage burns. Jack is not Oran. Jack shouldn't be here. It should be Oran and I don't understand but suddenly I lunge towards Jack and shove him hard. Second time this residential I've hit a Prod. He staggers, confused, then I kick sand and punch him, uncoordinated, drunk, arms flailing.

'Hey!' Jack shouts, ducking and weaving round my blows, trying to grab my arms.

'Tara! Tara!' Another voice. 'It's OK. I'm coming.' Two outlines racing across the sand to me. My vision blurs and I melt, gooey like marshmallow, into the sand. As Jack catches my fall, I recognize Emer.

'Why'd Oran have to die?' I say, then pass out.

When I come to, there are voices. Leaders' reprimands in abrupt bursts in some other room. Low collective mumbles from teenagers, like prayers in school assemblies. The whole gang of us is getting a dressing down. Orderly shuffles of footsteps to dorms. Opening my eyes, I find I'm half-sideways, belly down on a yoga mat, propped up with my own elbow and knee bent in triangles. Faith is kneeling at my head and Emer is stroking my hair, talking low. I moan. Emer whispers reassurances. There's a man, the kayak guy, hunkered by my arm with a green first-aid box and black-handled scissors. He smooths white cream onto my arm, and the cold of it makes me jolt.

'Easy,' says Emer. 'You'll be fine. Sshh.'

Again, I moan. My head is pounding and I'm parched. Real thirsty. Sell my soul for an ice cube. The man puts the white lid back on the cream and I move my arm to look at the little bumps of angry blisters.

'It'll take a week or so,' says Faith. 'But it'll heal up. It's not a deep burn.'

Looking at her still feels weird. Like déjà vu. I stretch my muscles.

'You want to sit up and have some water?'

We're staring right at each other and for a second, I come over all sci-fi, like, *can she read my thoughts.* That really would be a curl-up-and-die moment, with all the shit in my head.

'Yoga mats was never really me,' I say.

Emer grins, her face washed with relief. 'That's my girl. Glad you're back in the room.' She helps me sit and Mr Kayak is all wrapping gauze and a neat bandage round part of my forearm till I feel like I'm channelling an OCD zombie. Faith passes me a bottle of water then sits cross-legged on the floor, glancing over at scribbles on youth-work forms, while the two adults distance themselves and chat in low mumbles.

'Faith,' says Emer, glancing back, 'you've been a star. I'm sure you're wild tired. Why don't you get some kip so you're better set for orienteering tomorrow? I'll take it from here.'

Mr Kayak packs up too. The scissors glint as he plonks them back in the kit with the creams and stuff.

'Tara, I'm gonna have to chat with your mam,' says Emer when we're alone.

I groan, already hearing the bollocking. 'Gawd, please?' I'm doing my best baby-seal eyes but am mortal resigned to doom. It'll be a grounding or a marathon of house-cleaning retribution, or worse, she could put parental locks on the WiFi till I'm twenty-seven and make me eat broccoli. I stare at the bandage on my arm, hoping it'll play like a sympathy card, and for some mad reason, even though the first-aid kit's gone, my mind's still seeing the scissors glinting. My brain's whirring all computer-code-break but somehow its message is lost in the programming. I rub my forehead.

Emer's cupping her chin in her hands as she watches me. 'Your arm's gonna heal up fine,' she says. 'But it's not so much that I'm worried about.'

'I'm grand,' I say, straightening up and looking about. 'Don't be worrying my mam. She's on double shifts this week and—' And then I see it. Oran's hoodie. Slung like rubbish into the grey plastic pedal bin in the corner and shredded from how they'd cut it off me to treat the burn. I'm caught breathless, choking again on the scream that won't sound and that image drilled bright neon. Everything. Is. Not. Grand. Everything is still shit.

Chapter 7

FAITH
County Down, 27 August 2019

'What's with the bandana?' says Jack. 'You look like a fortune teller.' He slows his stride, waiting for me to catch up.

'Not like I haven't worn one before,' I snap, defensively.

Jack takes a step back and raises an eyebrow.

I clasp both hands behind my head, feeling the fabric of the bandana. Last night I found the word for it online. *Alopecia*. Losing hair is a thing. It can go slow or fast but pretty much everything says it's related to stress. I know it's because I can't talk about how I feel. How I might love. Years of clapping to Sunday-school songs about the way and the truth and the life, yet I'm banking on lies and illusions. Now my own body has turned into a ticking time bomb. I'm going to have to come clean. Come out with it and face the music. The hymn music is what's terrifying. I'm not figuring on them singing 'Gentle Jesus Meek and Mild'. Not that I dislike our village, but living in a city or having parents who aren't religious would make this so much easier. I'm also thinking, wondering about Tara asking about my dad and the suspicions I've carried. 'I think the church would have something to say if I got into fortune telling,' I say. 'You think there's people can read the past instead of the future?'

'Aye.' He grins. 'They're called historians.'

We're midway in the straggle of teenagers snaking up the mountain path. Everyone's turned out like model citizens. Coats on, shoelaces tied after the previous night's grilling. Still, the last day buzz is carrying us. Ordinarily, Jack would be out front but, despite the banter, he seems deflated. For no reason, my legs are lead. I stoop to pick wild bilberries growing in the rocky soil, relishing the burst of sour on my tongue and the chance to catch my breath. Jack is looking over my shoulder and I know he's looking for her, somewhere in the rear with her youth leader.

'What do you think?' I say. 'Like really? I feel like now I have to find answers.'

'About Tara? About your dad?' He shrugs. 'I think it's your call. I mean, if you want to find out if he's not really your dad or if Tara's related it could be good but it could go wrong. It's a risk . . .' He looks out over the pine trees and across the bay then drops his head. 'Why now? Why is this suddenly so important to you?'

'I need to know the truth!'

'Why? You've two parents who love you. And each other. I'd give my right arm for that this summer. Couldn't you wait? Like keep in touch with Tara and maybe in a few years . . . Why the rush? What's so bad about the way it is?'

'I . . .' Jack's looking at me now like 'haven't we known each other forever?' And he's right. He's like a brother, he knows me better than anyone – but he doesn't know this. No one does. Will he get it? Will he freak, thinking that sometimes I look at girls the same way he does? Will he understand that I need to know if I've a different dad in case my current one rejects me? When I tell them, Mum and Dad will be hurt. Maybe mad. Disappointed. It could come down to 'change' or leave . . . Best case, I'm guessing they'll suggest therapy and prayer. With boys, at least, that's what they do – I've seen how that goes in American movies. Not. Good. Worst case, they'll disown me. If they do, I need a place to go. Not for the first time, I wonder if Tara is the same as me in that way, in how she feels, not just how she looks. I've tried to read her, watched her closely with Grace toasting marshmallows. I don't want to be able to tell, though, because if I can tell about her, can everyone tell about me? Can Jack?

'Just tell me,' he says. 'Walk and talk.'

With his broad palm, he pushes me gently between the shoulder blades to get me moving. Our steps fall in time and for a moment there is no sound except the wind and the scrunch of gravel under our boots.

'Can't you just trust me that it's important? I love my parents but I . . . It doesn't add up. Not just the eye thing. Blood groups too.'

'Blood groups?'

'Didn't you ever listen in science?'

'Only when Miss McNally was teaching . . .'

I punch him on the shoulder. Jack's at home on a rugby pitch. I'm in my element in the science lab. 'Everyone inherits their blood group from their parents.' I say. 'I'm O negative – Mum filled it on the forms for this trip. Last time Mum and Dad gave blood, I was with them. Mum is A positive and Dad is B positive.'

'And in English that means?'

'That it's unusual I'd be O negative if they were both my actual parents.'

'Not impossible?'

'Six per cent chance. I googled it yesterday.'

'So, it's unusual you'd have green eyes and even more unusual you'd be O negative?' Jack kicks his boots into the caked mud as we walk.

'Yip. And you know what? It's probably a billion-to-one odds that I'd meet someone who looks identical to me, even down to their eye colour, with the same blood group and living on the same part of the planet . . . unless we're related.' I put my hands on my hips and stop.

'What? How come you know Tara's blood group?'

'I saw her emergency form when the leaders gave her first aid last night,' I say.

Jack kicks a stone and we watch it bounce down the slope. Below, Carlingford Lough sparkles in the sunshine. Mountains rising out either side of the bay. 'What's your plan?' says Jack. 'This time of year's tough for your mum. You going to talk to your parents or are you going to wait?'

'Neither,' I say. 'I'm going to talk to Tara. Today.'

'But she's really messed up right now.'

I stare at Jack. 'How do you think I feel? Anyway, this is about me and her. It's nothing to do with you.'

He shuffles a few steps backwards up the slope. 'But what if I want it to be?' He turns and strides off, leaving me wondering.

Jack's hands are still stuffed in his pockets as we catch up with the others at the boulder. Our two youth groups are merged. No one really cares who's who. Some of us are reading the story of *Clough Mór*, the Big Stone, off the visitor panel. The rock type doesn't match. 'It was giants fighting. Lobbing missiles.' 'No, it was a glacier.' Who cares? Everyone's scrambling, giving knee ups, shoving feet, pulling arms to clamber onto the massive boulder, phones angled precariously for group selfies. It's perched high over a valley, steep pine forests falling away to the sea. We gawp at the views. Tara is one of the last to arrive, her hand clasped onto her cowboy hat to stop it blowing away. Wind whipping at her oversized borrowed hoodie. It's like she's shrunk into herself. Head down. No eye contact.

'Hey, Tara!' says Megan. 'You lonely down there on your own?'

From within the group piled on the boulder there are mumbles of dissent. Jack swears. It might even be his boot that dislodges Megan. As she slides down the far side of the rock, Jack jumps down to Tara.

'Come on,' he says, cupping his hands to give her a step. She hesitates, then accepts his offer.

I meet Jack's eyes as he scrambles back onto the boulder. For a split second I swear he blushes. 'You wanted to talk to her?' he mouths, then jumps to his feet, leading the lads in a chorus of hollers and precarious ninja moves perched high over the forest. Tara is scratching initials into the rock with a stone.

'Hey,' I say. 'How's the arm?'

'Surviving,' she says.

'Your mum collecting you early?'

She shrugs. 'Emer phoned her, but we've no car. How come you knew what to do?' She hugs her injured arm into her chest.

'I volunteer with St John Ambulance. I know first aid.'

I watch her stare across the valley. Is it even fair to ask? The lads leap to the ground. As they distract everyone going buck mad, whooping and rolling in the heather, I'm alone with Tara. I close my eyes and feel the wind brush my cheek. When I look again, she's staring straight at me.

'Would you even want to be related to me?' she says.

'Of course.'

'Seriously?'

I nod.

She scratches at lichen on the rock. 'But you seem so . . . perfect,' she says quietly. 'What if I wreck everything?'

'You think I'm sorted?' I arch my back and tighten the knot

on the bandana. 'Two words – shit and fan.'

For the first time Tara grins. 'Welcome to my world.'

'Do you really not know who your dad is?' I say.

Tara shakes her head.

'But you want to find out?'

'Yeah.'

'Me too.' I breathe deep, deciding whether to risk the next question. 'Would you do a DNA test? You know, to get proof? See if we are related?'

'You think I'm some trash case like the morning chat shows?' Her fingers clench.

'No. Really, no.'

'Why then? That stuff's big bucks. Isn't it blindingly obvious we're related?'

She's sucking the end of her hair, and somehow I know it's not an angry thing, no matter all her in-your-face attitude, and just as I'm wondering how I know that, the answer arrives: when I'm nervous, I do the same.

'Truth?' I say. 'I think we must be related. Science, biology, it's my thing. I like facts. Clear answers.'

'How's a DNA test gonna find my da?'

We lock eyes. Green eyes with brown flecks. For the first time I notice that hers are welling up as she studies me. She glances down at the bunches of teenagers across the mountaintop, then speaks. 'Look, you might've sussed – my boyfriend died. I'm on my own. Mam's on her own. Nan's on her own. Everyone else gets to play happy families but apparently we're not good enough. If Da's out there somewhere, I wanna nail him, but I can't bankroll some private-eye genetics company. Mam's burnt out working and the bastard's never coughed up a penny of maintenance.'

I swallow. 'Haven't the foggiest notion what it costs or how it works. I'll find out though. Can't be that difficult. I'll raid my savings. For the sake of a saliva sample or something, wouldn't it be worth it? At least it'd be a first step. With a DNA test we could confront our parents.'

'Who needs spit when we're the spitting image? What I need to know is Da's *name*. An address. Like, why do you even care? Am I missing something?'

I bite my bottom lip to stop it trembling. I've never said anything. Not even hinted. In my head this was always going to be said first to Jack. But the words just kinda happen. 'Last night, I was watching you with the others. You're so able to be . . . yourself.'

'Big deal,' she says. 'Like that's working out so great.'

'I was jealous.'

Tara crinkles her nose. 'Jealous? Of me?'

'You're not afraid to stand up for yourself.' I wipe my palms on my fleece. 'You fight back.'

She shrugs. 'Like I've any choice.'

I run my fingertip over the rough of the rock. 'Did you ever have other questions? Not about your da. About . . . yourself? I mean, on the outside, we look the same, but maybe we're . . . different.'

'Plain as spuds our personalities are wired different. That what you mean?'

'No. Different like . . . you know.' I keep my gaze fixed down on the rock. 'Who we like and stuff.'

Tara hesitates. I can feel her eyes on me, but I can't meet them. 'You think I'm gay?' she asks eventually. 'After me telling you about Oran dying and shit?'

'No,' I say, feeling my lungs tighten. 'I know you're straight. I mean . . . me.' Tara stares, looking down at Jack messing with the lads, then back at me.

'Oh,' she says. 'But what about Jack? Wait, am I getting this right . . .' Without thinking, she scratches her bandaged arm, then winces. 'What's this to do with finding my da, maybe our da, anyway?'

'This,' I say and show her the silver cross on my necklace. 'It doesn't exactly work with the fact that I . . .' Every outside bit of me is playing this cool, but inside my brain is writhing. My heart pumps. I've whispered this to no one but my bedroom mirror. Now, it's like my mirror-self looking back at me. Despite everything, I can feel a connection and for the first time ever, I blurt the words to another human being. 'I like girls.'

'I don't get it,' she says.

My shoulders droop as I try to summon strength. Even whispering it is scary. Plain scary. This time, I brave the actual word. 'I'm lesbian.' I cringe, yet feel lighter. Like a boulder just rolled off my back. I suck air into my lungs and glance about to check no one else is listening. I needn't have worried, everyone's prancing about, distracted like mountain goats.

'Look, I get *that*,' she says. 'What I mean is, what's the big deal? What's it got to do with finding your real dad?'

'My family are Evangelicals.'

Tara looks blank. How can she not understand? Maybe it really is different in the cities or for Catholics or even anyone who isn't a believer. I rub my temples, then spell it out. 'Evangelical Christians. As in seriously religious Protestants who think being gay is a sin. "Adam and Eve, not Adam and Steve" stuff? Have you heard of that?'

She grins. 'Mam waggled her fork raging at the telly once when a politician said that. Dropped her fish finger. Only bible in our house is clattered with dust on the living-room shelf.'

'My parents aren't like your mam.' I crinkle my eyes to stop the tears and maybe this is where I should stop talking because I hardly know Tara, but this has been a muddle in me since, since really forever and I look away because I can feel the wet trickling down my face because there's never even been a chance of finding a way out of this mess – having a place to go if coming out goes wrong. Until now. My heart is pounding. 'I've prayed so hard,' I whisper, not even looking at her. 'It'd wreck them if I come out. You're the only person I've told. "Gay" isn't in my parents' vocabulary. Not unless it's linked with the word "abomination".'

Tara wrinkles her nose and thinks for a minute. 'That sucks.'

The youth leaders have everyone sat down a short distance away now for a picnic and the focus is all on the Tayto multipacks. It's like the world is deliberately giving us space. I lift the bandana just enough to show her my head. Three tiny bald patches barely hidden under carefully arranged hair clips – each smooth like a drawing-pin head. Tara's eyes widen. 'I'm losing hair. I think it's from stress,' I say. 'I don't think I can keep quiet much longer about being gay. I have to find my real da. Even if he's useless, soon he may be my only family.'

'That bad, huh?'

'Could be. Also, if I can prove they've kept a secret this major from me, I figure they might be less harsh on me being . . . flawed.'

Tara slides herself across the rock and sits beside me. 'It's not a flaw, eejit. That is so the wrong word.' Together we gaze across the landscape. Blankets of pine trees below us fall away to open water. 'I'll think about it,' she says. 'That DNA thing. Right now, I'm just, like, I don't even know where I'm at. Every day's a drag.'

I sigh. She looks at me again, but this time with a faint flicker of something fierce. 'If we *are* family,' she says, 'I'll do Foyle Pride with you, rainbow flags and all. No one should treat you like shit. You've got rights.'

As we slide off the rock, she glances between me and Jack. 'Maybe it's not my business,' she says. 'But shouldn't you tell Jack? Like, you're lesbian but he's your boyfriend?'

I crinkle my nose. 'Jack's not my boyfriend!' I say. 'He's my cousin.'

Chapter 8

TARA
Derry, 21 September 2019

Motorbikes thunder down Shipquay Street. The roar echoes under the archway into Guildhall Square, vibrating in my bones. Everywhere smells of fish and chip vans, onions and burgers, like the community is having one last bash at summer, even though we've been back at school these last three weeks. Not that I've made it in every day, or even on time. Already my form teacher's threatened detention if I don't get a grip, but somehow Mam has come over all hugs and chocolate in between shifts. Whatever Emer said to her must've been magic. No ditch-the-attitude lectures. No groundings. Instead, Mam's like, knocking the door to get me out to school, out to anywhere, when I can't be arsed. It's her who called Lena. This morning, I wouldn't have crawled out of bed but for my friend pestering me something suffocating until the duvet lost its appeal.

Now, up on the city walls, we're swimming our way through a sea of leather and chrome, shouldering past gangs of baldy men with neck tattoos and beards. Lethal. Lena was right to pester. Best Saturday ever and all we're drinking is cheap raspberryade from Yaya's coffee shack.

'How did we not know this was on every year?' I say. It's my first Roaring Meg Bike Show and the whole place is Harleys, Kawasakis, bikes, trikes and skeleton transfers. Goths rule. Now that I'm here, I'm glad Lena's fifty million messages dragged me out the door. Something in me feels born for this. All the bikers have helmets strung over their elbows and I fit right in with my grey vest top and black cowboy hat. Lena's in her element too. Across the planet, Extinction Rebellion is brewing and outside the plastic-free shop kids are painting *Save the World* banners. The sun is shining and protest and revolution is in the air.

'I'm not sure bikes and the environment are really a united cause,' Lena says, over the din of voices and rock music blaring from speakers.

'Like, who gives a shit?' I'm taking in the mad neon negatives taped up for an outdoor exhibition along the interface railings that used to be there to stop riots. The Guildhall. The War Memorial. Some wee church. The colours – purples, pinks, turquoise, greens and yellows – are my kind of art. Ahead of us two women, decked with leather bracelets and bandanas, are holding hands and snogging as their Alsatian pees on the cobbles. Not for the first time, I wonder about Faith and feel crap that I haven't got back to her on the DNA science stuff. I don't even know why, except that I can't even seem to make a decision on what socks to wear each morning – and they're all black anyway. It's weird that thing with her hair. My mam would've probably cheered if I'd turned out lesbian. Way less fears of teenage pregnancy. I've been thinking about Oran too. Parked on the walls, right where I watched his last video, is a massive rasta-coloured trike clattered with Bob Marley stickers. Radio blasting reggae. As we pass it, my feet drag. The image of Oran's face before the crash jolts back and my skin goes all goosebumps. I need a cigarette but I'm all out.

'Wanna check out Bishop Street car park?' Lena's mind-reading. She tugs me past charity collectors in high-vis vests rattling buckets and into a family area with twirling teacup kiddies rides and ice-cream vans. We queue for a ninety-nine cone – full works with flake, sprinkles and red syrup. The sugar rush lifts my mood. Our eyes drift past the families with pushchairs to the teenage boys, strutting street cred in the cage football. Sitting on a kerb, I lick whipped vanilla and breathe in the smells of vinegar and energy drinks from the picnic tables. Mam says you can forget any boy, even one you really liked. It just takes time. Emer's trying to convince her my head's bent and I should see a counsellor. Or some community support group. I overheard Mam fobbing her off on the phone again. Says it's pure rubbish. *What's done is done.* Strikes me, she's like that with her own skeletons too. She never talks about the past. I'm wondering about it even more these days after meeting Faith. Surely to God Emer must have mentioned Faith to Mam? If she did, why is Mam tighter than a tadpole's arse about it?

'Why's it called the Roaring Meg festival anyway?' I ask. 'Who was Meg?'

Lena's wild smart. Nothing she doesn't know. 'Didn't you ever listen in junior history?' she says.

'Me? Listen?'

'At least back then, you showed up.' She folds her arms. Gives me the WTF teacher look. 'Roaring Meg isn't a person. It's a cannon. Up in one of them corner bastions. You've probably climbed on it billions. During the Siege of Derry, it was the loudest cannon they fired up towards the Jacobites on Creggan Hill.'

'Enough of the lecture.' I'm eye-rolling. 'So basically, we're at a festival named after a big gun that shot Protestants way back whenever?'

Lena slaps her forehead into her palm. 'Eejit. Four hundred years ago it was Protestants stuck inside the city walls. Mind the bit about them being so starving they ate rats and dogs?'

A vague memory surfaces of me at the kitchen table, drawing Siege menus on tea-dyed pages with burnt edges. And a bollocking after Mam noticed the matches had scorched more than the paper. The table-top still has black melty bits. 'No way. That'd mean Catholics were attacking Protestants. Not them attacking us.' Sometimes I forget Lena is Polish and doesn't get this Northern Irish stuff.

'Yes way.' She's got that 'are you like totally thick?' look. 'You seriously think Catholics were always the angelic victims and Protestants did all the attacking?'

I shrug. 'Brits out. If they don't want to be Irish, they should just go back home.'

Lena blinks.

'What?' I say, after minutes of her watching me crunch the ice-cream cone, like she has X-ray vision.

She shakes her head, all FFS. 'Did you take in nothing on that residential last month? You honestly think Protestants should go "back home" if they don't want to be Irish? They've been in Ulster four hundred years. They live here.'

I wipe my fingers on my shorts. The only history I know is the street stuff Oran used to spout. Lena did GCSE. Politics and history fry my head. 'Dunno,' I say. 'If there's a United Ireland, do you think Protestants would go back to Britain?'

Lena stands. Hands on hips. 'In the States, there's millions of Irish-Americans. You think they should all come back to Ireland? Or what about me? You think with Brexit, I should go to Poland?'

'Course not,' I say. 'You were born here. I'm not like racist or anything.'

'So why would you say Protestants should go back to England?' She smirks. 'What if you're half Protestant, like on your da's side? Will that make *you* a Brit?'

'Feck off,' I say, jumping to my feet. A dad walking past with a toddler scowls at me and I dissolve into giggles. 'You know I'm no Einstein on history.'

'I think you'll find Einstein was a scientist . . .'

I shove her lightly in the ribs. Milling through the crowds, Lena points out Roaring Meg. I'm inhaling deep on the cigarette smoke of passing groups of bikers. Thinking about history and science and how Faith wants to put them both together to see if we've got shared DNA. Faith is like Einstein – way smart. Like really, if I were for hunting down Da, I'd know sweet FA about where to start. I take my phone out and snap some images of lads in leather. Silver-zipped jackets. Customized bikes. Later, I'll edit them with a new app on my phone. Fuzz the backgrounds. Apply filters. Sometimes they come up real good. Lena angles herself against the city walls in the sunshine and I take a few portrait shots in sepia and show them to her.

'AirDrop me that, would ye?'

'Sure,' I say. Then study her. She's gone all coy. 'Any particular reason?'

'Maybe,' she says. 'Keep a secret?'

'Course,' I say. Our heads dip, all conspiratorial.

'Know the way it's nearly Extinction Rebellion day? I'm planning my own wee rebellion. Of a different kind. Interested?'

'You even need to ask?'

Lena tells me the plan like it's a covert operation. She's sussed the bus to Armagh. Two hours away. Twenty quid for a day return. Less with fake student ID. 'Two cathedrals and a planetarium according to online stuff. Pick a Saturday your mam's working, and we'll be back before she notices you're gone.' She finishes triumphantly.

'Twenty quid? Aye, like I'll check me trust fund. Cathedrals?

What even is a planetarium?' I give her the thumbs down.

'Did I forget to mention Joaquim's been texting me non-stop? And that your maybe-big-sister lives near Armagh? And her pretty hot *cou-sin*?' She sticks her tongue out at me. I return the favour. Both of us can do the rolling tongue thing. That I do mind from science. Can Faith roll her tongue?

'C'mon,' says Lena. 'Aren't you up for it? Don't kid me you didn't like Jack even an itsy bit. I reckon he might have had a thing for you too if you'd just stopped thumping him. It's well time we did something mad.'

I go quiet and flick through the pics on my mobile. It's just over a month since I watched Oran on this same screen. But it's more than five months since he got kicked out of Derry. Almost six since I last snogged him on the back seat of a stolen car out the back roads. Right now, I don't know what I feel about boys. Or what I think about Lena calling Faith my maybe-big-sister. Or DNA stuff like late-night crime-scene-hunting for my da. Our maybe-shared-da.

'You OK?' says Lena.

'Huh?' From the shoulder tilt, hands on hips thing, it's obvious she's waiting on an answer but I can't mind the question. I rub my knuckles into my forehead, feeling suddenly exhausted. 'Think I'm gonna make tracks home,' I say, already relieved at the thought of the four walls of my room and no crowds. No such luck. As I turn, Megan Carey's poncing her way in our direction, all Queen Bee with a squad of older lads swarming. I tense. Lena loops my elbow and starts me walking, but despite her diagonal track, the crowd's still moving in currents, and I know, like warped destiny, the flow's gonna take us straight to them.

'Hey,' says Megan. 'Heard you're for dropping out. That true?' She chews gum.

My brain wants to wisecrack something about fake news but my tongue's disconnected.

'Only, like, you missed art twice and Miss was saying about commitment and all and how some people have the maturity for year thirteen and others got to *grow up*.' She's posed all catwalk with the lads laced round her and one of them elbows another, all testosterone, muttering how they'd help me and Lena grow up some night if we were up for it, and all I can do is stare. At. My. Feet.

'Pricks,' says Lena. 'As if.' She tugs me past them, towards Guildhall Square and the bus depot, but we can hear their laughter at our backs. 'How come you didn't diss her back?' she says. 'It's not true, is it? You're staying at school, right?'

I shrug. How can I explain the whole world's gone fuzzy or that Oran shows up in my head pure uninvited every time I see the lamp-posts he used to shimmy up hanging flags, or walls still scribbled with the black permanent marker he carried everywhere for no reason? Everything, everywhere in this city reminds me of him. All. The. Time. All the good memories tangle up in sequence moving faster and faster, twisting and spinning, then *bang*. The images from the phone. The sounds of metal crumpling into concrete. Maybe it's Derry. Maybe if I could just get away for a bit to where there are no memories.

Waiting at the 10a bus stop, I'm fidgety. We're scrolling TikToks to pass the time when my phone pings. Nan. Traditionally crap texting.

Betty look babysitter 2mor nite 7. £20 U up 4?

Clarity kicks through the brain fuzz as the bus pulls up. Cash – we're sorted. 'I'm in,' I say.

'For what?'

'Rebellion.' I smile. 'Armagh.'

Chapter 9

FAITH
County Armagh, 29 September 2019

Apples. The boughs in the orchard are heavy laden, like my thoughts. The air is scented with the mossy freshness of early autumn. Rubbing my fingertips on the rough bark, my eyes study the ripening Bramleys. Each one is unique. Shape. Colour. Size. Next week, our church will celebrate harvest. Unless I can come up with another excuse not to go, I'll be right up front, hatted and in the choir, singing songs of thanks and glorying in God's handiwork in Creation. That bit, I enjoy. It's feeling a fraud that's digging at me. Was I created wrong? Inside, I just can't be the person they expect me to be any more. Staring up at the branches, I imagine Newton, deducing the laws of gravity from an apple falling on his head. I imagine Adam and Eve, distraught, cast from Eden over original sin. I imagine William Tell, forced to let fly an arrow towards the apple balanced on his own son's head.

Sitting at the base of a tree, I mess with a stick, bending it, testing how far it'll curve before snapping. I try to imagine coming out to my parents. Saying the words I said to Tara. Even in my mind, they won't vocalize. Thinking of Tara, I check my phone for the nth time. Three days since I last texted to see if she's decided about doing the DNA test. Still no response. And that's before telling her what I've managed to find out about the process. Tapping Chrome, I bring up the pages I've saved and scour them again as if the constant re-reading might light up a new revelation.

GENEcheck. Half-siblings vs Unrelated. Using our simple sibling check, individuals with different biological mothers can determine the likelihood of a shared biological father.

I stall, as usual, at the word simple. If only it was as simple as me and Tara scraping cotton buds inside our mouths and posting them off. That I'd had to make out I was sick to miss church is like a self-fulfilling prophecy. My stomach churns as my brain again tries to fathom any possible way forward.

Our recommendation is that to enhance accuracy of the test, samples from the two individuals and samples from both mothers are submitted. A DNA sibling test will not always be definitive. The more genetic information submitted, the higher the chances of a conclusive result.

Originally that had seemed like the hard bit, the having to get a swab from our mothers as well as us to see if we're related. Plus a swab from Dad and an extra test to see if he fits the picture – or not. Guess I'm more naive than I realized. Finding out it's illegal to do a DNA test without parental permission until we're eighteen? Impossible. If only I'd realized before I ordered the kit, I'd have saved myself three months' pocket money. Swiping the screen off, I pocket the mobile and lift the jute bag. There are no solutions for the big stuff, but I still make a mean apple crumble with a brown sugar crust. Learning how to sweeten up my parents could become an act of self-preservation. I stand and set to gathering windfalls, bruised and fallen apples, as I mooch about in my own mind. Overhead, wisps of cloud scuttle in a westerly breeze. Goldfinches, with their red masks and black and gold markings, dart as blurs of colour through the orchard. I close my eyes and listen to the soft flurry of their wings beating the air, the breeze rustling the leaves. Then footsteps. Familiar ones, with

Jack's whistling, approaching from the farm.

'Dobbing church?' He tramps towards me in wellies, fresh up from the chicken sheds. 'Who are you and what did you do with my cousin?'

'Hey.' I smile. 'You helping out your dad?'

Jack hesitates. 'Well, I'm helping. Farm won't run itself.'

He doesn't have to say more than that. Even with the easy grin he carries, it's in his eyes that my uncle's off on a bender with the drink again. I know Jack so well, the weight of it is written all over him. With me, he doesn't hide it and something in that train of thought makes me feel pathetically two-faced. I need to come out to him. I kick a fallen apple in his direction. He kicks it back.

'What's up?' he says. 'You sick? You never miss Sunday morning service.'

I set down the half-full bag, apples tipping it over at an angle. 'I'm not exactly sick,' I say, pausing to think if there will ever be a right moment for this.

'But?'

Leaning my back against a tree, I feel the knots of the bark through my T-shirt. Over Jack's head, a blackbird trills on a branch. Why is explaining myself so hard? On the one hand, I feel like I'm only just beginning to figure myself out. On the other, I feel like I've known this for ages but wasn't ready to admit it. It still feels taboo.

'What if,' I say, 'I'm not exactly who you think I am?'

'This about you wanting to do a DNA test? Did Tara reply?'

'Yes, but not exactly. And no.'

'Come again?'

'It's just something about me I need you to know.'

'So, she hasn't contacted you at all?'

I shake my head. 'It's actually nothing to do with her. Just stuff about me.'

He angles himself against a tree trunk and there's that look about him now, like the morning ten months ago when I found him down by the shuck, firing stones, and I'm hoping, hoping, hoping this won't floor him the same way.

'You're not pregnant, are you?'

'No.' I roll my eyes.

'Thank Christ for that,' he says. 'I'd have been right mortified if my angelic cousin lost her virginity before me.'

For a moment it's just birdsong and rustling leaves, then together, we're laughing. He doubles over, cheeks reddening, and when he straightens up, he has that impish big brother look about him. 'You do know you're stuck with me as your cousin, no matter the results of any test.'

'Technically if Dad isn't my real dad, then your dad's not my uncle and we're *not* actually related.'

'You saying they'd no call to drag me to your every birthday party even when I was the only boy? That our annual jam jar tadpole-hunting escapades in primary school count for nothing? All that arsing about together on bouncy castles since we were toddlers? Suffering Sunday school together?' He tilts his head. 'Way I see it, cousins is more than just biology. Aren't I closer to you than my own two sisters?'

I nod, then bite my lip. Since we were kids, we've been in and out of each other's yards near every day. Family farms, back to back in the Armagh countryside. Jack's always been there for me just like I was for him after last Christmas when his mum and sisters walked out for good. His dad's interpretation of a 'merry' Christmas had gone way too far for a happy new year. Their wheelie bin clinked with empty beer and whiskey bottles. I look at Jack, wishing suddenly his eyes were brown-flecked green. I suck my hair. The opportunity is slipping and it's clear he has no sense this is about anything other than DNA. If I want to, I can duck the issue. Wait it out and say nothing until university. But then again. Instinctively my hands go to my head, smoothing the hair and clasping at the back. There hasn't been much change, except now I study the plughole after shampooing to assess the damage. It's coverable, but for how long? His hands are stuffed in his pockets, welly boots kicking at the moss in the grass. I swallow. My brow feels hot. I breathe in deep through my nose, filling my lungs with the honey scent of orchard air and feel my throat tighten. This is the moment. The hum of a car engine on the back road passing the orchard clicks me into action. Soon, my parents will land back from church. Dad'll carve the roast at the head of the table and afterwards Mum will be up to her arms in a sink of bubbles, I'll grab the tea towel and everything will tick over like the world is upright and proper.

Sitting down by the tree roots, I pull my legs up tight to my chest. Jack hunkers down opposite. 'I need to tell you something weird,' I say. 'And honestly, I don't know what you'll think.'

'Shoot,' he says.

'I'm . . . gay.'

Jack coughs. His eyes dart to the distance across the fields, then back to me. 'You're kidding, right?'

'No.'

'But you've had a boyfriend. I've seen you at a school disco. Two years ago.'

'Jack. Listen to me.'

He's standing now. Shuffling about. Eyes everywhere then back to me and away again.

'Jack!'

'Gary Blakeman and you. Snogging.'

'I had to figure it out. I had to try. Once. Just in case. Maybe. But . . .'

Finally, he stills. Squats down close by me and looks straight at me with his clear turquoise eyes. 'Holy shit,' he says. 'This is real. You're actually gay?'

I nod.

He's shaking his head, staring. 'But you can't be gay. You're the most Christian person I know. Your parents . . . Jesus, the church . . .'

My bottom lip trembles and I look up to the clouds, still racing across the blue as I feel the tears welling. For a moment, I think I can hold this but then the burn in my throat rises and the dam bursts. I bury my head in my knees, sobbing. Trying to gulp air into my lungs as I feel each fresh burst of shame and hurt and anger and fear flood. Without even Jack on my side, this will be impossible.

In seconds, he's beside me, his right arm across my shoulders, and as I rock back and forth, he gently pulls me in. 'Sshhh . . . I'm sorry . . . Sshhh . . . that all came out wrong . . . Sshhh . . . I'm an eejit. Forgive me. It's OK. It's OK. It's OK.'

He waits for me to speak, tugging up handfuls of grass and firing them away. A single robin hops at the base of a tree, brazen, almost curious about our conversation as it hunts grubs. Rustling up a tissue from a pocket, I rest my chin on my arms.

'I'm so messed up,' I say.

Jack's avoiding my eyes. Unusually quiet.

'Say something. Anything.'

He picks at a loose thread in his jogging trousers. 'I dunno what to say.'

I wipe my cheek with the palm of my hand. Feel where the

salt tracks of tears are drying in the sunshine. It's not like Jack's ultra-religious. I'm way more religious than him, but maybe all the years of Sodom and Gomorrah in Sunday school have left their brand. He tugs again at the thread and then stops, seeing a small hole begin to unravel in the material.

'Actually,' he says. 'If I was better at this, I do know what I'd have said straight out.'

This time he does look at me. 'I'd have said, of all the people I know, you're the least messed up. You are so . . . so honest-to-God decent and human.' He pauses, reflecting. 'Look, I don't know if there's a right way to ask this, but, are you sure?'

I suck my lip, nodding.

'Did you tell your parents?'

'So they could drag me to church for healing prayer like a mad satanic thing? No. I was going to keep it quiet a while yet. Until I don't live here any more. Like when I'm at university or maybe . . . maybe if I do have a different dad I could go there?'

'And what if you find someone before then?' He hesitates. 'What if you like . . . a *girl* and you wanna . . . God this is weird. I mean, not you weird, conversation weird. Can two girls even, you know?'

'Kiss?' I say.

'And that. Like you really don't feel anything for boys?'

'Do *you*?'

'Feck off.' Jack grins. 'OK. Fair dues. I'm just processing this. You came out to me first?'

I go to nod, then realize it'd be a lie. 'Actually, one other person knows. Tara.'

Jack stands. Ambles away. Grabs a branch over his head and does chin-ups before facing me again. 'Speaking of Tara,' he says. 'She looks like you but she's actually really different. Do you know . . . I mean . . . does she like girls too or . . .'

This time I know I'm not wrong. He's blushing. For definite. 'Jack Duggan!' I stand and kick the stretch back into my legs. Jack's hands are clasped over his head, his eyes shut. He's come over all boyish, the grin on him lopsided and shifty. I fold my arms, relishing his embarrassment. 'Any particular reason for asking?'

'Other than her being bloody magnetic and gorgeous?' He opens his eyes. 'All the lads were saying how she's so fierce and individual and . . . my head's melted. Like she's your image but yet she's so unique and she might even be bloody related. It's twisted. Is it even *legal* that . . . that I like her? Maybe she's gay too—'

'She's straight. One hundred per cent.'

Jack breathes out through his nose and I can see the smile on him even though he's staring at his welly boots in the grass. After all he's been through, he so deserves a break.

'If there's ever a way of doing one, a DNA test might prove she's *not* related to you,' I say.

Jack looks at me. Eyes wide. 'Joaquim messaged. That's what I came over to tell you. Lena and Tara are for Armagh this Saturday. Wanna come?'

Chapter 10

TARA
Armagh, 5 October 2019

I feel like a deviant and it's great. At least something's clicking back into normal. 'Gimme a second till I catch a smoke,' I say as we step off the bus at Armagh station. Lena's itching to reach the Mall, some big park in the middle of town. Joaquim's only like texted full-on *Romeo and Juliet* for the last two hours once he knew we were on our way. I dip round the corner and light up.

'You know,' says Lena, pacing, 'that if a lad who doesn't smoke snogs you, you'll taste like an ashtray?'

'Piss off.'

She laughs, then winks. 'Maybe you'll wanna think about that some day? Soon?'

I crinkle my nose. Oran smoked. We shared cigarettes. 'Keeps me skinny,' I say.

'And kills you.' She frowns. 'Cross-country running had you way better toned. We could use you back . . .'

'I'll think about it,' I say. What I don't say is right now my nerves are shot. Or that I was only letting on to have music belting in my earphones the whole road from Derry. Or that despite her eye-rolling, I *am* doing more thinking about everything than I ever did. About Oran. About Mam. About Nan. About Faith. About . . . me.

Lena's shuffling. Impatient. 'The thing about walking,' she says. 'It requires moving your feet? Ideally in this direction.' She goes all drama with large steps. I grin. It's actually hard, but class at the same time, seeing her so head over heels desperate. I miss that feeling. Stubbing out the butt with my runner, I follow her along the footpath. Looking about, Armagh is all pillars and spires and posh marble town houses with square grid windows. Proper period drama stuff off the telly. As we get closer, I find it's me in the lead and Lena's suddenly gone all foot-dragging-hair-fixing.

'You do know he's already mad for you?' I say.

She's biting her lower lip like it's gum. 'But—'

'But nothing. I mean look at the cut of me compared to you.'

She gives me the once over, taking in my ripped black skinny jeans, scuffed green Adidas, grey long-sleeved T-shirt blazoned in teal with *girl=superpower* and the black hat I've near permanently adopted since August. The biggest effort I managed was looped silver earrings. She's sporting purple jeggings that hug her figure, a mauve vest top, perfect white denim jacket and make-up to die for. 'Like at least one of us made an effort,' I say.

She smiles. 'Thing is, you don't even get that you have it natural without trying. You're so arty you'd look good in loo roll.'

We pass a college and, on the corner, a courthouse, all pillars, steps and triangles like a Roman temple, caged in by black railings. Opposite is a long park looking majestic with a necklace of trees, proper posh. As we cross the road, a grey-bearded man does a double take at me, looking me up and down like I'm out of place, then raises his hand and nods like a gesture of recognition. I glance back over my shoulder as we reach the Mall and catch him still staring from the opposite pavement.

'Pedo,' I whisper to Lena but she's all oblivious, focused on three people leaning on low green railings behind a war memorial. Joaquim, Faith and Jack. Joaquim's grinning like his numbers have landed. Faith's holding her elbows tight and Jack, his dark hair spiked up at the front and wearing a leather jacket with jeans instead of joggers, is staring. Right. At. Me.

'Hey.' 'What's up?' 'What's the craic?' There's high fives and banter and 'good to see ya's. Joaquim and Lena's straight at the holding fingers thing and obviously counting the minutes till they can split off and snog some place quiet without a flurry of wolf whistles. Faith gets kinda fast-chatting how this park used to be a racecourse way back when and how some Georgian archbishop built half the town and it's actually a city on account of two cathedrals both called St Patrick, and I'm thinking how come she's a sponge for every historical fact ever, and like WTF really was the deal with that man? When I turn, I'm weirded out cos he's still there by the courthouse looking in our direction.

'Hey,' I say low to the others, 'without, like, obvious looking, what's the story with yer man over my shoulder?'

They glance. Jack swears under his breath and Faith pales. 'Let's take a walk to the far end,' she says. 'He knows us from church.'

'Hear that?' says Jack.

I'm listening as we walk the length of the park but all I can hear is lorry brakes, traffic buzz and leaves rustling. 'Hear what?'

'Jungle drums.'

'Not the Lambeg type . . .' I say.

'Nope.' He smirks. 'Rumour mill. Guess we should've thought about it, but people we know seeing you and Faith together? Apparently, it's like being punched in the chest . . .'

I elbow him, thinking back to my first reaction to seeing Faith, and he laughs. In the top field we cop a squat in the grass by a couple of sculptures. Drawn in by a black sphere, a globe drilled with tiny circles, I hop up to investigate while the others reminisce about our residential. A plaque on the ground calls it 'Turning point'. *Look inside . . . we all live under the same stars.* There's moulds of four people cast into the metalwork. Fitting myself into the nearest one, I peer through the eye sockets and it's mesmerizing, like the starry skies over the beach the night of the fire. I'm lost in the peace of it until I see another pair of eyes, turquoise, peering in opposite. They disappear and suddenly there's a whisper so close to my ear it tickles. 'Any significance to you choosing the man's shape?'

Peeling myself from the mould, I look closer at the imprint cast into the metal. 'Like what the . . .' I snigger, then regain composure before looking at Jack grinning. 'Art is beyond gender,' I say, all authoritative, staring at the penis shape imprinted with the human outline on the sphere. 'Suppose you were leant up against a woman on the other side?'

Jack raises both hands. 'Caught red-handed. You're like seriously arty, aren't you? Not like Faith. She's for medicine at university since she was playing doctors and nurses at three.'

'And you?'

Jack shrugs. 'Dunno really. She's the sorted one. Two more years and I'm done with books. Maybe I'll work with cars and bikes. Give me a spanner over a pen any day.'

'That's cool,' I say, thinking I'd have better odds guessing a Grand National winner than my own future job. Lena, Joaquim and Faith are sat chatting on the grass and I'm staring at the building opposite, thinking something about it looks wild familiar. It's got that imposing history vibe of some former fame but the windows are all narrow-barred and dirty with disuse. My head's ticking over that I've seen them before. In a painting?

'What's that place?' I shout back to Faith, knowing she'll be all glory Wikipedia.

'The old Armagh Gaol. It's not used any more. There's an underground tunnel the whole length of the Mall which they used to march prisoners from the courthouse straight to their cells.'

I mull it over a second and then remember. The Bogside Murals in Derry. Full size on one gable end of the flats is a hunger strike one with the big Jesus-lookalike IRA man. Stood in the background is a female prisoner dressed in a blanket. Behind her, a window – dead identical to the gaol opposite. Nan says that's where women always were in the Troubles – suffering in the background, keeping the pain behind windows. It's about the most I ever heard her say about the war here. These days the only thing she's worried about remembering is her medication.

Oran was way more mouthy on history. And suddenly in my head it's just like yesterday again and we're standing at Free Derry Corner, him going on about how the blankets were a protest against wearing prison uniforms and being treated as criminals when they were pure political, and some other bitchy English politician giving out until the Ra turned it up and went all hunger strike. He was fierce proud of it. I spin on my feet and do a kind of fist pump salute. 'Up the Ra.'

Stonewall. Lena's giving me WTF eyes. Jack's gawping. Faith's gone Tipp-Ex and I'm kinda wishing I could blot out the comment cos now that I think on it, it's not real cross-community material but, like, everyone says it, don't they?

'Feck's sake,' I say. 'Chill. It's just a saying.'

'It's not *just* anything.' Faith jumps to her feet and marches right up to me. 'Terrorists. That's what the IRA were. Murderers. Still are. Aren't they the ones who shot your boyfriend?'

I feel my fists tightening, teeth gritting. Scary how fast the heat of anger's brewing from inside my ribcage. All of a sudden

I'm switched to hating her, hating her for saying that, cos our side is IRA and our side is Catholic and our side is Ireland and our side is right and tricolours and equality and good, and that's what I know. Not textbooks or GCSEs. Stuff. Everyone. Knows. Street history. And I was coasting keep-out-of-bother-Tara, mind-your-gob and honest-to-God, I was actually even enjoying the trip of being some place different and seeing Jack and now, now I'm raging cos she's messed with Oran and messed my head, and worst of all, is she like *right*? It *was* the New IRA kneecapped Oran but that's not like way back then. Then was a proper war, fighting against Brits and for freedom. Lena's all headshaking at me, but inside I'm powering up for the strike, cos if this is like a words battle Faith will floor me and my head's hot and I feel the curl in my fingers and then . . . then Jack's in the middle, channelling World Cup referee hand signals with chest out and back offs and she-didn't-mean-its that might be directed at me or maybe at Faith, and he's yanked my arm, dragging me off stage, out of the picture, off the field and onto the path.

'C'mon,' he says. 'Walk with me a minute. Breathe.'

I'm all footsteps on tarmac and sucking in air and striding fast by Jack and wondering. How. Does. He. Know. This. Stuff? How did he know to be all apologies that night off the mountain, and how did he know to be carrying me drunk after the fight at the fire, and why is he with me and not Faith, and how did he know that I'm so, so, so fecking glad he cut in because last thing I wanted to be doing was hitting Faith again, and that's where it was heading despite me cos, well, cos I don't even know why but it was. Fact.

Now we're at some other statue with a list of dead soldiers' names – they're everywhere in this place – and I pull out my cigarettes and light up by a cannon on wheels. Feck but I can't seem to get away from guns anywhere. Even the bloke topping the statue to some South African war is sporting a sash of bullets as he toots his bugle all proud immortal. Jack sits down on a bench and waits as I pace about puffing smoke like Mr I-Am-Fire dragon from *The Hobbit*.

'Why'd Faith flip her lid?' I say when I'm done burning shoe rubber.

'Can't say I was all honey either about what you said.'

'Why?'

'Happens I agree with Faith.'

'So why not diss me like she did?'

'Because, well . . . to be honest, I say "No surrender" same sort of way when I'm out with the lads. So, I get that you didn't mean it bad. Also because . . .'

'Cos what?'

Jack hesitates. 'Because I figure when you're both calmer, it'll sort out.'

'You're like Mr World Peace. Who taught you this stuff?'

Jack sighs. 'My parents.'

'What are they, mediators?'

Jack laughs kinda strange. 'Nope. Mum did want them to *get* mediation counselling stuff but Dad was staunch no way. They fought like screaming heavyweights before they split on New Year's Eve. I was the only one strong enough to drag my dad back to bed when he was ranting half-comatose with drink, so I stayed. Mum and my sisters moved out.'

'Oh,' I say, developing a sudden interest in paving slabs.

'C'mon,' he says, standing after a minute. 'While we're all serious, I may as well show you something.'

I follow him as he walks back up to the courthouse end of the Mall, watching the country swagger of him from behind. He stops where they'd met us – at the largest memorial in the park. It's topped with a woman, head bowed, and footed with poppy wreaths. Again, the lists of names, this time world wars, and an inscription from Armagh. *To her children who fought and fell. In sorrow. In thanksgiving. In hope.* I look about at the black benches with red poppies and crosses designed into the metalwork and then back at the fresh wreaths with the *Brave Thirteen*, *No Surrender Club* and *Lest We Forget* handwritten messages.

'Isn't Remembrance in November?' I say.

Jack nods. 'Thing is,' he says, 'we don't just remember the world wars here. These poppies are for remembering the thirteen apprentice boys in the Siege of Londonderry. You must know that already? That's three hundred years past, yet our band still marches for it every August. The Somme was a century ago and no one's for forgetting anytime soon. The Troubles? The IRA and that? It's not even gone twenty-five years since they were murdering innocent people.'

I'm staring at him, hands on hips cos I know this is not the whole story. I know something of it is about Brits and street protests and Loyalists and soldiers and our side fighting for votes and equality, but also I'm remembering Lena all eye-rolling when I thought it was the Catholics stuck starving inside Derry's walls in that siege, and there's all them years of me turning Bic biros into pea shooters in history class. What if the only thing I really know is that I don't know shit?

'OK,' I say. 'But we weren't even born then. Why's Faith so het up about it all?'

'Because her grandparents were blown up, murdered in an IRA bombing before she was born. Happened in 1996, but her mum still battles depression because of it.'

The air whistles between my teeth as I suck in. Holy. Shite.

I'm becoming the resident expert in cobbles and paving slabs. For a moment I stare at Jack's boots, wondering if he's gone way more Protestant-rub-your-nose-in-the-dirt-gloating. When I look at him though there's nothing of that *No surrender* bollocks happening. In the bright blue of his eyes it's more of a shit-are-you-OK-maybe-I-shouldn't-have-told-you-that look.

'Kinda deep,' he says. 'Sorry.'

I listen to the breeze rustling the trees. Watch the bees air-hopping amongst bright flowers in neat rows edging the memorial. There were wreaths and flowers on Oran's coffin in the hearse. I take a deep breath right into my belly. 'I need to talk to Faith,' I say, almost surprised at how scarily mature it sounds. 'But would you mind if we talk about something, anything, else for a bit first?'

'Sure. Wanna see my motorbike?'

Parked in a bay halfway up the side of the park is a black motorbike with flashes of orange. On the back, an L plate. Jack runs his fingers across the seat like he fancies the arse off it. Lifts the helmet from where it's hooked onto the mirror and looks at me all intent, like my reaction could slay or save. All I can think is *OMG for real, he's a biker?* And gawd, but can he see my heart pumping cos this is like lethal brilliant. And maybe it's cos Oran was wheels mad too, or maybe it's cos the Roaring Meg Show is still in my system, but I'm remembering conversations and leather and chrome and testosterone, yet for no understandable cause I find myself coming over all coy and sniff-nodding like a pro.

'LXR?' I say, sounding like it's not something I just read off the bodywork. 'They're great sports bikes. What's the engine size?'

'Only a 125cc,' says Jack, eyes wide. 'You're into bikes?'

'Just recent,' I say. 'Customs more than sports. Choppers especially.'

Jack's grinning Olympic. 'Me too,' he says. 'My dad has an old Honda Shadow in the barn. I'm working on it for when I'm nineteen. The engine is bigger so I gotta get two years under my belt with this one first.' He pats the seat. 'Wanna try it for size?'

'Sure.' I shrug, swinging my leg over all done-this-millions and praying I don't tip the whole thing crashing. Curling my fingers round the handlebars, I study the dashboard. Digits and dials. Jack pointing, explaining, leaning while I listen and nod and then, cool as, he swings his leg over the back and sits in the pillion seat on account of 'sure it's easier to explain it this angle' and he could be talking Dutch or Chinese or Zulu-Martian-Brazilian because all I'm taking in is that his chest is against my back and the heat from his thighs is pressed right into mine and *oh my gawd* I can feel his heart thumping. As he's all bike enthusing, I'm blinking, processing my insides fizz-flipping like a cola-bottle pancake, but my head is all *WTF, Tara? Remember Oran?*

When he sits back, Jack's hand touches mine and, seeming all accidental, brushes the skin on my thigh where the denim on my jeans is ripped. Again, I blink. I can feel the deep breathing in his lungs and mine. For a moment, it's beautiful. Then I'm all took over with a strangle of not-knowingness and an inside panic, of stuff going mental that I've no words for, and Jack must sense it for he slithers back higher onto the pillion seat and the bike tilts with the weight shift. I suck my bottom lip.

'Sorry,' he mumbles.

I'm shaking my head something fierce and he's probably thinking I'm busting angry and, in a way, I am, but slinking slippery through my head is a thought I'm trying to catch and when I pin it, it's this. *You.* Are. *Angry. Tara. Not just angry with everything general or even the guns or Oran or your useless, deserting, invisible feck of a da. No. Face up to it. You're angry with* you.

My senses are come over superhero-crystal, listening to birds twitter, taking in how the breeze smooths the grass like velvet by the cricket runs, smelling aftershave off Jack's skin as he sits behind me like a whisper. I twist in the seat. His brows are furrowed, Adam's apple bobbing in his throat as he looks skyward. I lift his hand. Feel the roughness of it. A proper worker's hand. Mesh my fingers in his cos . . . cos I want to. Then he looks at me.

'You don't need to be sorry . . .' I say, biting my lip. 'It's *me* who's sorry. See . . .'

His shoulders relax. 'It's just . . . I thought . . . If I've picked you up wrong . . .'

'Jack,' I say. 'I think . . . I do like you. It's just . . . I'm not ready. I'm not over Oran. Truth? I don't even know how to start dealing with that.'

For a moment, we're both quiet. 'Makes sense now,' he says. 'I never could work out if you were hitting me or hitting *on* me.' He smirks as he dismounts. Holds his hand out to help me off the bike. We glance back into the park to where Lena, Joaquim and Faith are sat chatting. 'Are we OK as friends?'

I smile and tap my runner off his boot. 'Sure, and given that we might be related . . .' I do the fake cringe face.

'I was thinking about that again in bed last night,' he says. 'I don't think it's possible. I mean, if Faith's dad isn't actually her *real* dad, then she's not my *real* cousin.' Then he blushes and I twig that he's just admitted thinking about me. In bed.

I let him squirm a minute before going to his rescue. 'See, if you wanted to be my best friend right now? You wouldn't even flinch about playing gooseberry to Lena and Joaquim and getting them offsides a bit.'

He nods. 'Think I can manage that for you. Just promise me something.'

'What?'

'No punching my cousin. She's one of the sweetest people I know and right now she's got enough going on dealing with her own crap.'

I salute him with a 'Yes, Sir,' and loiter behind as he entices Lena and Joaquim into the Bull Cafe across the road.

Faith turns as I approach. I'm all hands in pockets and churning words over in my head again because this stuff? Apology stuff? I've more aptitude for piano tuning. She's still scowling, but gentler than before, like teachers hovering in 'just this one last chance, Tara' territory.

'Hey,' I say, foot shuffling a daisy clump. 'I'm real sorry. Sometimes I'm just pure-born eejit.'

She stands, all ballerina looking in her leggings and pastel blue jumper. I watch the corner of her mouth twitch. Then it breaks out into a full smile and before I know it, she's hugging me, all girly. 'I'm sorry too,' she says. 'I shouldn't have mentioned Oran like that.'

She lets go and my head starts thinking *Is that what sisters feels like*? Now I'm wishing I'd said yes to the DNA test because probably now it's too late. Since she's already out to Jack then probably she's all happy families with her parents too, and she won't need me or some new gobshite excuse for a different da. I study her hair. It's like a meticulous arrangement of chopsticks and hairpins with a sheen of hairspray lacquer keeping it in place. I wonder.

'Jack explained about your grandparents . . .' I say. 'Must be tough for your mum. I guess I was lucky, the Troubles never impacted my family.'

Faith nods. We lean up against the railings round another statue. A wee girl, barefoot with a bucket and spade. I'm wondering why the girl looks sad and why she ended up here when all the other statues are grown-ups and then I read the inscription about a railway disaster in 1889 and see more names. And ages. Boys and girls, mammies, daddies, grandas and grannies. Then Faith starts to talk. She tells me about how her grandad was a policeman – Royal Ulster Constabulary. This time I'm like proper-concentrate bite-your-tongue serious listening and whatever-the-feck say nothing anti-cop like the graffiti round my way. She's all wistful on how her mam, Sarah, was fourteen, listening to The Fugees on the radio and waving bye to her parents through the living-room window. How her parents climbed into the blue Ford Sierra in their driveway, and how it should have been just Faith's grandad in the car but her grandma got a cancellation for a perm at the hairdressers in town if she could get there fast, and so her grandad was dropping her in on his way to work. The tabby had a new litter of kittens and he'd to shoo her off the bonnet in a hurry, so on that day, that one day, he forgot the mirror checking under the car thing.

Faith tells it in a way like a Once-Upon-A-Time that she's heard over and over. How the fireball boomed bright orange at the end of the driveway. How the bonnet landed by the porch. How the skeleton of the car lay contorted and black with the doors blown wide and how the glass of the windows shattered, not just in the car but the whole house. How, for weeks after, her mam says the place smelled like fireworks and how The Fugees were still playing on the radio – 'Killing Me Softly'.

When she's done, I'm thinking I'll have a degree in paving slabs and how on the Derry Walls for me in that mad moment it was cobbles, and how it must've been glass and living-room carpet for Faith's mam and how the woman in the prison blanket, the one on the war memorial and the wee stone girl in front of me with the bucket and spade are all the same. None of them are blaring trumpets like the men. Nor clutching rifles. No looking stalwart-valiant. No, the women have shoulders sagged with the weight of violence. They look like they've their own story to tell about the lists of names.

'Your mam was only fourteen?'

Faith nods. 'For years she was seriously messed up. Drink and . . . she doesn't talk about that bit much. But she goes on about the Troubles all the time. It's like something in her got stuck there. Then she met my dad . . .' Faith hesitates. Touches her hair. 'Well, she met Philip, and it was love at first sight. They got married. She got therapy. They got me. It all happened pretty quick.'

The leaves on the chestnut trees flap as it starts to spit rain. 'Should we go get coffee with the others?' She says it like 'enough of the heavy talk'. We start to wander.

'Faith,' I say, knowing in five minutes we'll be knee-deep in frappuccinos and chit chat. 'I never did answer you about the DNA test. I guess it's probably too late, but if you still want to, I'd do it. Jack said you did the whole rainbow coming-out thing. Did you tell your parents too? I mean if your mam got through all that trauma, I'm sure she'll be really supportive.'

Faith stops in her tracks. Shakes her head. 'I can't tell them. Not yet anyway. My dad . . . well, Philip, is an elder. It'd be seen as a disgrace.'

I look at her, confused with the way she says it. 'An elder? A disgrace?'

'Elder – like an advisor or almost leader,' she says, reading my face.

I shake my head. 'Not that bit. The other bit. You make coming out sound like you've done something *wrong*, not just how you were *born*.'

'It *is* sinful, according to how we read the bible. And that's what makes it even more crucial that I find out if Philip's my real dad. If he isn't, then there's a dent in my parents' holier-than-thou image. Maybe then it'll be easier for them to forgive me . . . or it'll change how much it matters.' She bites at her fingernail. 'They told me I was born premature. Now, I'm not so sure.'

I scratch my head trying to get with her scenario and thinking how I thought I was the screwed-up one. 'So, you want the DNA result as ammunition, like blackmail, so your parents can't go mad holy about you being gay because maybe for years they've lied to everyone about your da being your real da?'

'Exactly,' she says. 'But less blackmail and more like Girl Guides *Be Prepared*.'

'And in your religion, that lying would be a big deal?'

'Yes. It'd mean my mum had sex outside marriage which is obviously also a sin . . .' She stops when I nearly choke on her words.

'Wouldn't it be easier to just ask them?' I say. 'Compared to me you're positively holy.'

She sighs. 'It's impossible anyway. I ordered a DNA kit. When it arrived during the week, I read the small print.' She jostles in her bag, produces a small box and holds out one of those instruction manual things most people bin. 'We can't do the test. We're under eighteen. Without parental consent, it's illegal. We'd have to fake the signatures and dates on the paperwork.'

Now I'm hands on hips, looking at her like 'girl, you live on a different planet'. My heads whirring, like drinking at twelve is illegal, smoking from thirteen is illegal, fake-ID-clubbing at fifteen is illegal, drugs are illegal, skipping school is illegal, joy-riding is illegal . . . We. Are. On. My. Territory. Only mad thing is, I didn't break the law about underage sex, but I'm hoping on that one at least I'll reach her definition of sinner. After all, it runs in my family. I wouldn't exist if Nan or Mam had 'saved' themselves for a wedding night.

'I think,' I say, cocking my head to the side, 'we're both looking very *eighteen* today. How about you lead Department of Science and I handle Ministry of Forgery?' I thrust my hand out all business for a handshake and watch her face rearrange itself from some holy version of WTF through OMG to hallelujah! When we shake on it, her grip is firm. By the time we meet the others in the cafe, I've her instructions memorized and, in my pocket, two swab kits.

Chapter 11

FAITH
County Armagh, 6 October 2019

Our church is jammed with fruit and vegetables, sheaves of wheat, artistic arrangements of flowers in vases on each windowsill. Everywhere there are baskets of apples – Red Russets, Widow's Whelps, Bramleys. 'The women have truly excelled themselves this year,' says our pastor, acknowledging the harvest decorations. I join in the impromptu round of applause. The children too have helped in the display. Autumn leaves in oranges and browns have been turned into collages of animals and birds. Corn dollies, their twists and braids of wheat stalks in woven spirals are neatly arrayed or hung twirling by windows. As they spin, they catch my attention, reminding me of the DNA spirals in my biology textbook.

Bethany's mum sounds the intro on the keyboard and hymn books rustle as the congregation stands to sing. 'We plough the fields and scatter . . .' Chests swell with pride as the harmonies ring out from our choir and the traditions are kept. Today we will thank God for his provision and marvel in Creation and today I am thankful to be part of the occasion. Thankful to be stood next to Bethany with the other sopranos in the choir, thankful to be part of this family and thankful that in church we still hold to the tradition of ladies wearing hats. Right now, I'm all for every belief in head coverings.

It's a full turnout. In the back row, even Jack's father is suited and booted, stood beside Jack, who is equally scrubbed up in his shirt and tie. There is a predictability to this that wraps round me like a soft blanket. The children's story will be the parable of the sower or the feeding of the five thousand. The gospel reading, Jesus as Lord of the Harvest and the disciples as fishers of men. The Old Testament reading will be more difficult to guess. Maybe Isaiah or Jeremiah or the message of how the Israelites were to leave the gleanings at the edge of the field to help the poor, just as we should be generous with giving our own gifts to help others.

As the service progresses, I look about. In the front row, Mrs McKeever, my first Sunday-school teacher, is subtly passing Mentos at seat level. Behind her, my parents intently listen as Mr Oakes reads the first lesson from the lectern. My mother is wearing a special new Sunday outfit. The blue cardigan suits her eyes and my dad is sporting a matching tie. I can't imagine how it would feel to not be part of this. Last Sunday was just a blip on my part. Here is where I am meant to be. I vow to myself never again to skip church. If God is truly love, there will be a way through this. These are good people. My people.

Halfway through church, the children leave in whispers of restrained enthusiasm and are ushered out to the hall for crafts and bible stories. The pastor clears his throat. 'Our announcements today are somewhat serious. You will no doubt be aware,' he says, 'of the impending legislation to be imposed against the will of the people in Northern Ireland.' Nodding breaks out through the congregation. 'In just over two weeks, on October twenty-second,' he continues, 'if our politicians fail to find a way to restore our local government at Stormont, abortion will become legal.' There are low murmurs of discontent. 'For half a century since the 1967 Abortion Act, our politicians have faithfully resisted the extension of this UK law to Northern Ireland. We must support them in continuing this battle.' I join with everyone clapping. There are comments of 'Life is life,' and 'Both lives matter,' from the congregation.

As the pastor raises his hand, we fall silent. 'Not content with just imposing abortion laws, London politicians at Westminster have also seen fit to threaten us with the legalization of further immorality.' He nods as he gazes across the congregation from the pulpit. I'm racking my brains. Mum and Dad are always talking Northern Irish politics. I'd have to move to outer Mongolia to avoid it. In July it was how we smashed the unofficial world record for no government. All August it was the fiftieth anniversary of the start of the Troubles. These days, it's Brexit at breakfast and evening updates on the eternal stalling around pensions for Troubles victims. Supper is sidetracked into how Republicans brought down our whole government all because of wanting an Irish Language Act. There's been no movement on anything for two and a half years. Have I been that zoned out recently that I've missed something important?

'I'm sure you're already aware of it,' says Pastor McKenna, pausing, before continuing in a low voice, emphasizing every syllable like it's treason because, after all, we are British and the British politicians should be on our side. 'London has voted, that unless our devolved government is restored by the twenty-second of October, they will also impose the legalization of same-sex marriage.'

As the congregation respond with tutting and shuffling, I feel red heat rising in my neck and flushing across my cheeks. Please let it not show.

'It goes without saying, that we must all pray that sense and morality will prevail.' The energy in the room electrifies as he begins to raise his voice and I try to count the ceiling rafters to focus my attention on anything other than the tirade I know will follow. Words from the book of Leviticus . . . *detestable in the eyes of the Lord . . . fornicators, adulterers, homosexuals.* I study his fingers gripping the edge of the pulpit as he spiels on about marriage as a sacred union between male and female. There is a ripple of 'Amen' through the congregation. 'This truth we know,' he says. 'God is love.' For a second, I lower my guard and listen, wondering if God is inclusive in what he means by love. The pastor nods his head but then his voice booms and all I can hear are words of hate, sin, abomination and hell.

I feel frozen. More like I'm stuck in a fridge than hellfire, staring at the metal frame of the seat in front as he calls the church to action. For the next two Wednesday evenings, there will be special prayer meetings. At the back of the church there is a petition. He counts on our full support. The pens are laid ready. There are options to join protests and vigils in Belfast. Together, we will make our views heard. 'Democracy must prevail,' he says. 'English politicians have no right to impose immoral legislation against the will of the Ulster people.'

Bethany nudges me and I realize I have missed the cue to stand for the next hymn. It's a modern one. Lyrics of freedom and release from fear are projected onto the wall. With all my heart, I try to join in but my throat burns and the words stick. The congregation are all singing as normal. Hats bobbing. Some with arms raised. Others with eyes closed. Lost in worship. This is normal. What has just been announced is normal. It is just me. I am not normal. Suddenly my legs feel wobbly and I don't know how I'm going to function through the rest of this service, never mind the rest of my life. Clearly, the afterlife isn't for being an amusement arcade either. Maybe I should confess and seek prayer to change. But then again, I *have* prayed about it myself for over two years with no result. All that's happening is that I'm feeling clearer that this *is* who I am. I glance to the back wall where I see the petition set on the table, ready for signatures. Then with a slight movement, Jack catches my attention. Like everyone else, he's singing, but he's not looking at the lyrics, he's looking at me. When our eyes connect, he holds his hand in a fist across his chest on his heart in a silent gesture of solidarity. Somehow, I manage to return a weak smile.

I zone out for the sermon, fearing it'll be more of the same. It's something about Ruth and Boaz and how God provides for the faithful. That story was always one of my favourites, but all I can think of right now is what if she'd been gay? Would God have provided for her then? Would Boaz have kicked Ruth out of the cornfield instead of marrying her? Worse, would she have had to marry him anyway?

Standing for the closing hymn and grace, I'm already planning a swift exit. Waiting in the car is by far the better option than risking hanging around and dissolving into floods of tears. No. There won't be a Noah's Ark to ride out this one. I grit my teeth. Hold it together. Just hold it together. The final Amen is sung and I lift my clasp bag and make for the side aisle.

'Wait up,' says Bethany. 'What's the rush?'

'I . . . I . . .' My eyes dart to the double doors now open at the back of the church.

'Oh,' she says. 'You're for signing the petition. Good call. I'll go with you.' She loops her arm through mine and I find myself tugged into a queue gathering by the table as the hum of casual conversation rises around the church. My dad, up front in the queue, already has the biro in hand. He signs, then heads to talk to the pastor. As we shuffle forward, my heart lurches into my mouth. Where is Jack? I need him. Leaning on the wall, I scan the crowded room. There. Through a break in the people, I see him bobbing his way towards me. He'll help. I know he will. Then mid-stride, he stops. Raises his eyebrows. Tilts his head. I follow his gaze and . . . dear Jesus. Can this get any worse? It's Mr Stillen. The grey-bearded man who saw Tara and me meeting yesterday at the Mall. There is a definite man-on-a-mission sense to how he is weaving through the groups of friends chatting. His direction of travel is clearly towards my mother. I watch, helpless, knowing that within minutes my mum will hear about Tara. All our plans for stealth, the safety net of the DNA test, everything is at risk. Jack is looking around. In a fluid move, like a rugby tackle with manners, he grasps Mr Stillen by the shoulder and, engaging him in a conversation, manoeuvres him towards his father, my uncle. Ouch. My thigh bangs the corner of the table. I turn just as Bethany hands me the pen.

On the varnished oak surface is the petition. A grid where we're expected to put our name, address and signature. The issues are merged – as if they're all the same. Abortion. Same-sex marriage. A spiel about how these decisions should be made by the people of Northern Ireland for the people of Northern Ireland. For the first time in my life, I find myself wondering if we're always shouting about how British we are, how come we don't want these British laws extended here? Then again, I'm pro-life. Not that I've really thought about it too much. My head is too crammed and twisted with questions and thoughts and—

'Hurry up, will you? We've the Sunday roast on.' The lady behind chastises me.

'Do you think these make a difference?' I say, stalling.

'Of course,' she says. 'What are we if we've no voice?'

Bethany is impatient. 'Just sign,' she says. 'My mum wants to chat with you.' She holds the page flat for me, thinking that's the issue. I stare at it, gripping the pen till my fingernails turn white. On the list, there are already twenty-seven names. Twenty-seven names of people I know and love. Twenty-seven people who don't want me to ever find love. The queue behind jostles me forward. If there is any choice at all, it is this. Be brave. Like the lady says, find my voice, or sign. I imagine how they'd react if I turned, hands on hips and said, 'Guess what? I'm gay.' Hell would truly be unleashed. But not on them. On me. And in that moment, I know I can't face the truth. Not yet. Not here. Swallowing, I scribble in my details, then drop the pen and walk out the door.

'So keen she's taking the hymn book home.'

I turn on my heels. Not only have I walked out accidentally with the church hymn book, I've also walked past my mum chatting with Bethany's mum. All I can think is, at least she's not chatting to Mr Stillen. The sooner I can get her and Dad into the car and head for home, the better. 'Oh,' I say. 'Sorry. I'm in a daze. Not sure I'm feeling one hundred per cent.'

Mum reaches out and drapes her arm over my shoulder. 'That's not like you, pet. Same bug from last week?' She puts the back of her hand against my forehead. 'You do feel a little clammy. Let's get you home.'

Bethany saunters up. 'Did you ask Faith yet?' She nudges her mum.

Mrs Speers smiles. 'Ah yes,' she says. 'Before you head, maybe some good news will help you feel better. I know it's only October, but I've been thinking ahead to our church carol service. Faith, would you do us the honour of singing the opening solo this Christmas?'

'Wow,' says Mum, in a way that I know fine rightly means

Mrs Speers has already talked it through with her. The three of them smile at me, expectant, and I feel exactly the way I did when Adam Trowley asked me to the formal last year. Half-thrilled at the compliment and half-terrified at the expectation. That time, I found an excuse to say no. This is different because, well, because I'd love to sing 'Oh Holy Night'. It's my favourite and it might only be our village church, but it's a big deal. The focal point of the service. Apart from Jesus, obviously. In the space of one hour, church has taken me from hellfire to heaven. Where do I fit?

'Aw,' says Bethany. 'She's lost for words.'

'Are you sure I'm the right person?' I say, finally finding my voice. 'Only, I'm not sure I'm good enough.'

'You're perfect for it,' says Mrs Speers. 'You sing like an angel. What more's there to worry about?'

I smile.

'Of course she'll sing.' Mum clasps my hand. 'Right now, I think we should get you home to rest. There's your dad now.'

Beige. The colour of my bedroom carpet is exactly how I feel. A kind of blend in, fit in, walk over me, but don't ever notice me shade. Not the real me. Having kicked off my shoes, I lie on my back alone on the floor of my room, clutching the DNA kit to my chest and thinking. Thinking about signing that petition. Thinking about denial. Thinking about how I'm so chuffed to be asked to sing solo but also confused. Is that the voice I really want right now? Deceit seems like a game I'm destined to play, whatever angle I view it from. Right now, the choice is this:

Option One: Keep hiding the truth of who I am and say nothing.

Option Two: Come out.

Choose Option One and I'll last until my next haircut, if I'm lucky. I'll have to invent more deceit about what's stressing me out enough to lose my hair. Choose Option Two and the reaction from family and church could turn me bald overnight. That leaves:

Option Three: Add both options together. Stall the big revelation. Do the DNA test. Then come out. Maybe.

Tara phrased it like the DNA test is for blackmail. Ammunition. I don't mean it like that. It's a safety net. Problem is, how will my parents see it? I don't want to dishonour them. They do love me. I'm their only child. Dad, biologically or not, has been part of every bit of my life. Until now. When Mum was feeling low, it was always Dad who took me to swimming lessons, encouraged my wobbly handstands at kiddies gymnastics or bought the Friar Tuck's chicken boxes when Mum wasn't up to cooking. Now I'm playing turncoat, potentially.

Not for the first time, I wish I was more like Tara – all guts and go. Compared to her I'm a doormat. I'm the one who suggested the DNA test – this 'Peace of Mind' test as it calls itself in the info leaflet. When I gave her the two swab kits yesterday, she pocketed them without a blink. Point blank no issue that we're stealing our parents' DNA without consent. I circle my fingertips in the carpet fluff as I mull it over. When it comes down to the practicalities of this, why am I so hesitant? Is it just because it's illegal? Then it hits me. Tara has nothing to lose. Maybe it's harsh to think it, but she doesn't have a dad right now. Not even a stepdad. I do. And if I steal his DNA and prove he's not my real father, what does that prove about me? After everything he's done for me, it feels low. Spiteful.

In my brain, I churn the arguments, the pros and cons, over and over. The word for it finds its way into my consciousness.

Ethics. We did a bit about it in GCSE science. And religious education. And with the word, comes the realization that this level of deceit is beyond me. It's not who I am.

The house is filled with the aroma of roasting chicken. From the clanking in the kitchen downstairs, Mum is full tilt in the final stages of cooking dinner. But if I don't do the DNA test, I'm left back with only Options One and Two and truth is, they don't even feel like viable options right now. I grit my teeth, realizing my thought process has come full circle without solution. *Think logically. There has to be a way.*

I reroute my thinking and ask different questions.

Is there a way I can do this with less deceit? More honesty?

Is there a way I can do this without stealing anyone's DNA?

Closing my eyes, I let my brain whir through different permutations. Exploring things from different angles. Coming at the problem sideways until . . . *Yes. Maybe. It's worth a shot.* I sit bolt upright, suddenly focused.

As I enter the kitchen, the windows are steamed from spuds boiling on the hob. Mum is in the corner, apron on, rubbing together butter, sugar and flour for the crumble. Dad, still in his Sunday suit, is drinking filter coffee at the table.

'Feeling any better, love?' My mum smiles.

'I've to do a test,' I say, diving in before my courage leaves. 'It's a science thing. I need one of you to do a swab.' I hold up the two clear bags with cotton buds on the long sticks and the plastic tubes, playing it as cool as I can muster.

'What's it for?' says Mum, wiping her fingers on her apron.

'I'm learning about genetics.'

'In school biology?'

'It's about cells and DNA. Hereditary stuff in families. Either of you can do it – you just rub the cotton bud inside your cheek.'

The glance between my parents is subtle. The clunk of my father's mug on the table, gentle. 'Homework on a Sunday?' He raises an eyebrow. 'How about you do that one, honey? Science never was my thing.'

Before they've time to ask any further questions, I hand my mother her swab kit and she watches as I do my own swab. 'Simple.' I smile after rubbing the swab inside my cheek and placing the sample in the tube. 'Now you just do the same.'

'This is part of your A level?' she says.

'It's important I learn it,' I say. 'Genetics is vital in many medical career paths.'

She nods. Then, before my eyes, does the sample and hands me the tube. All done, without a lie. So maybe I didn't correct her assumptions that this is for school, but she's handed me her DNA in full knowledge it's for a test and watched me do my own swab without stopping me. That's consent, right? Casually, I pocket the samples.

'I think I am feeling better,' I say, checking the pots as Mum chops and sugars rhubarb. 'Want me to take some dinner to Jack and Uncle Steve later?'

'That'd be great,' says Mum.

The whole way through our Sunday meal I'm as helpful as can be. I set the table. I make the gravy. I carry dishes. I don't put my elbows on the table. I nod in the right places as they discuss politics. I act interested in hearing about the lady at church whose elderly dog has had to visit the vet three times. I chirp happiness when Mum tells Dad about me being asked to do the Christmas solo, and above all, I contradict nothing, absolutely nothing, either of them says about anything from this morning's service.

I don't even blink when Dad talks about how some ladies in the church have volunteered to sort placards for the anti-abortion and anti-gay-rights demonstrations. In my pocket, the two completed tests jostle safe in their tubes. It feels bitter-sweet, like the rhubarb crumble – a sharp tang disguised with sugar. To complete the plan, all I need is to carry dinner and a third swab up the lane. I know Jack will understand. Loading the dishwasher takes the last of my patience, then, finally, Mum hands me two microwaveable tubs, one jammed with chicken, roasties, veg and gravy, the other with crumble.

Fuchsia bobs red and purple in the hedgerows with the last of the orange-red montbretia. Brambles are heavy laden with blackberries, ripe for the picking. Soon, after the first frosts, I'll twist rosehips from branches and make syrup. The jute bag with the tubs swishes against my leg as I amble along the dirt and gravel track. Nearing my uncle's farm, I listen out for clinking tools in the shed. Hardly a Sunday afternoon passes without Jack tinkering and today is no different. There's the familiar chart stuff low on the radio in the background, and as my eyes adjust from the sunlight to the shadow, I see Jack in overalls, squatting at the rear of the motorbike. Sometimes I swear it's the Honda Shadow he stayed for, rather than his dad, when his mum and sisters left. The mud shields are pristine burnt orange and black, the chrome polished like a mirror. It's a classic from the 1990s but his dad hasn't ridden it in years. I watch Jack lost in concentration in his natural habitat of grease and engine fumes.

'She roadworthy yet?' I say.

Jack looks up. 'Almost. That dinner?'

'Comes with a cost. A request.'

'Intriguing . . .' he says, wiping his hands on a rag hanging from his pocket. 'If I comply, do I get dessert?'

'Crumble and custard.'

'Sold. What's the ransom?'

I set down the bag and produce a swab and tube in carefully sealed plastic. At first, he doesn't follow the explanation, rolls his eyes at my attempt to explain ethics, but then he leans back on the brick wall and stuffs his hands in his pockets.

'Let me get this straight,' he says. 'No science jargon. With samples from you, your mum, Tara and her mum, you can get a clear result on the maybe-sisters thing but you'll still know nothing about your dad.'

I nod.

'You refuse to nick your dad's DNA because it's against your conscience but with my DNA you can run a test to see if I'm related. If that says no . . . your suspicions are proved right.'

'Exactly. If a test says your DNA is not related to mine, then he's not my real dad.'

Jack tilts his head. 'And I'm not related to Tara.'

I raise an eyebrow. 'Correct,' I say. 'Seems that, with the right motivation, you have a pretty strong grasp of biology.'

Chapter 12

TARA
Derry, 10 October 2019

My head is still wired from today's lunchtime banter. All the talk was pills. Started innocent enough with Lena needing a headache pill and next thing everyone's giggling about pills for highs, pills for lows, pills you can nick from your nan and sell, and then, like, the actual pill and what age you can get it without your mam knowing . . . Is everyone like way ahead of me on this stuff?

All I need is an invisibility pill. Not once this week have I made it to art class on time, never mind my other subjects, and it's getting harder inventing excuses. Mam is all determined I stick school out. Health and social care is just the ticket, she reckons. According to her, art's not a serious subject. Not one that can land you money unless you're a silver-spoon-weirdo with an accent all clipped BBC. I'm hesitating now, my fingers on the classroom door handle, thinking the moment requires either a what's-your-problem-saloon-door-swing or a swallow-your-dignity-grovel-apology. Maybe take a leaf off Jack and try a straightforward sorry? After all, it's already the go-jump attitude that has me late. Not the done thing to tell my form teacher she's way last century for getting on to me about the blue streak in my hair and the double earrings. Wasn't my fault I'd had to sneak a cigarette in the toilets to recover from the bollocking. And, since I was the only one in the bogs, it was a prime chance to swipe some free period-poverty stuff. Daren't be seen dead lifting it if anyone else is there. Canteen suicide. Problem is, now I'm ten minutes late. I blow into my hands and sniff. Will Miss Tierney smell the smoke? I'm still standing there when she opens the door.

'Joining us anytime soon?'

'Aye,' I say, head down, shuffling towards my usual desk at the back, then stopping when I realize Kelly McCafferty's nicked it. Only one free now is at the front where the enthusiastic lemmings usually park themselves. Just my luck it's right beside bloody Megan Carey too.

'Hey,' she says.

I don't even answer, cos it's kind of weirding me out that she said a nice hello, even if it was just the one word. When I pull sketches out of my art folder, I can see out of the corner of my eye that she's craning over my work. When I look up, she's actually smiling. It's pure freaky. I find my charcoal pencils and set to building texture and contrast. Why we've to draw a cabbage is beyond me. In my head, I'm seeing it all psychedelic, sliced, a fusion of shapes and Andy Warhol panels. Miss Tierney wants it bog-standard still life. 'The Savoy in its natural glory.' Took me three lessons to work out Savoy was just posh for crinkly cabbage.

When Miss Tierney nips into the art store, Megan is suddenly all elbows on my desk, turning my page to see the drawing. 'You're lethal at art,' she says. My head is blown. Did Megan just say more nice stuff?

'One of my mates wants to go with you,' she whispers. 'Mind from up on the walls at the bike show? The tall one with ginger hair? He's nineteen. Pure hot. Huge feet.'

At her last comment I'm all nose-wrinkling *eh?* She does the eyebrow-raise of experience. 'You know what they say about boys with big feet . . .'

'Big shoes?' I say, switching pencils and working on a different bit of the drawing.

She laughs.

I'm guessing I know what she means and maybe if Oran had been around during summer I might be ahead with all that stuff but, for now, I'm stuck in the starting blocks. Has everyone else crossed the line? And why's Megan gone sugary on me?

'His parents are away next weekend. Mega-party in the pipeline. He even knows about Oran and says he'd be grand for helping you get over him like in *any way* you need.'

Something about the way she emphasizes *any way* makes clear they've been talking about me in one particular way. Less about me getting over Oran and way more about her friend getting a leg over me. I blink.

'What?' I say. 'You think I'm a cheap slut?'

When I hear pencils drop at other desks, I know I've said it too loud. The classroom is growing ears. Megan steps back. Pales.

'No,' she whispers. 'I just thought you might wanna get, you know . . . hooked up? I meant it as a favour. Like an apology for . . . At the beach, I was as drunk as you. It all got a bit out of hand, right?'

Now I'm on my feet, walking forward. 'Out of hand?' I say, holding up my arm even though it's all healed. 'Last I remember you burnt my hand.'

Megan's gone all jazz-palms-performing-surrender but I don't care. If my anger is usually cadmium red, this time it's titanium white. Pure seething. She thinks I'm a cheap date for her sidekicks? Or that I look desperate?

'You wanna sleep around?' I say, not caring who hears. 'Knock yourself out. Or up. Just stay out of my hair.'

For a moment, Megan's pupils dilate like she's terrified. Then she turns on her bitch face. 'Awwwh, still playing the grieving girlfriend? Don't think you've a monopoly on everything Oran,' she says. 'So happens you weren't the only one went with him.'

For a nanosecond the walls suck in. Iced silence. Then it's paper ripping, hair pulling, paint-water flying, jeering, shouting and Miss Tierney diving from the storeroom swearing like a hardcore hurley player, all arms and threats and my brain is like *Jesus wept, but she's no posh Savoy cabbage now* and *Holy Christ, I'm for the office serious this time*. Worse, when I finally calm down, Megan's sobbing in the far corner and, flung across the floor every which way like piñata party sweets, are the contents of my blazer pockets: Two cigarettes. One lighter. Sixteen stashed Tampax.

I. Am. Mortified.

Retribution in the principal's office is swift. A final warning. A week's suspension. A decree to attend a meeting with Mam next Friday. And there's the door. Close it behind you.

Slinging my schoolbag over my shoulders, I stride fake-confident across the teacher's car park, convincing myself to turn at the gate and give the whole place the two fingers in case anyone's watching. When I reach the railings, I do spin, but rather than launch into all glory-feck-yous and good-riddances, the principal's words hit me: 'Think hard, Tara. What do you want? This is your last chance.'

My throat tightens. I swallow. What *do* I want? I want to be home. Fast. Safe. In my room. Where nothing, no one, can trigger me. And, quick as I think it, I know that's a lie because even in my room memories of Oran invade. Fact is, everywhere I am, he is too. The bastard has jammed my thinking gear and there's no fecking eject button on those memories, those images. Did he really go with Megan? Did he two-time me? Or was it when we were broke up? All of a sudden, I'm running; school bag pounding on my back, shoes slapping on the pavement, sprinting guilty-as-sin-shoplifter across zebra crossings, through the estates. Each suck of air is out of sync, rhythmless, my core burning, muscles screaming. But I. Am. Not. Stopping. Not stopping because running is think-less, care-less, mind-less. Not stopping because it's the only solution I've got. Not stopping because—*BAM*.

The impact makes me stagger on my feet, two-litres-of-cider style. It drops the old lady in the pink coat to the pavement, her bouquet of flowers thrown from her hand. Sweet mother of God, I've killed a pensioner. In. My. Own. Street.

The lady groans. Phew. Maybe I'm not for death row. I'm a sudden flurry of so-so-sorries and Oh-my-gawds and 'can I help you up' and 'will I call an ambulance?'

When she's back on her feet, I scoop up the bouquet with further utterances of sorry and my feckin-eejitness and 'Could I even get you a cup of tea cos I only live across the road?' I point. 'Right there.'

And she's looking at me funny. Looking at my house. Quiet, studious. Then back at me till I'm all come over thinking OMG she's a mafia granny like in the movies and tonight there'll be a squad of tuxedo-hitmen with SS tattoos and end-of-the-world firepower sneaking infra-red-assassination-style up our stairs. I. Am. So. Dead. How will I explain this *and* school to my mam?

'I'm grand, lass,' says the lady, dusting down her coat. 'Could you help me fix these flowers to the railings?'

'The railings?' I say.

She nods. Hands me a purple ribbon. And I set to because right now I'd swim the Sahara for this here lady on account of her being neither dead nor Italian. When I've secured it with tight knots and a big loopy bow, we both step back in silence. I'm trying to mind if there was a car accident sometime and wondering if there's a politeness protocol I should know about asking or not asking, then quick as we met, she's just 'Thank you,' and off again in her Yaris.

I cross the street and fish out my door key. A padded envelope snags the door as I enter. The test has arrived. The parcel won't fit into my pocket which is jammed with hastily re-stashed Tampax but no one's in, anyway. There's a gap where Mam's bike gets parked next to the banister and the house is quiet. Thursday afternoon is Nan's big afternoon out. The community bus lifts her at midday and all the blue rinses in the estate blether over free grub at the centre. Keeps Nan going, Mam says. The parcel is addressed to me and since I get mail, like, never, except for some random dog charity junk mail thing twice a year, I know Faith has done her DNA samples. Even her handwriting is five-star classy.

My bit's already done too, hid in my left runner under the bed. I had been going to put the two tubes in my underwear drawer but a sneaky sixth sense reminded me about the time Mam raided it. Not for borrowing underwear. Euurgh. Pure just checking for tabs and cigarettes. Or maybe to see if I'd ventured on to condoms yet. Stashing the stuff in the shoe was genius cos it even reeks. No way would Mam check there. It took three mornings of swabbing saliva off her after-coffee chewing gum rescued out of the pedal bin and I'm not for bin hoking again. I've even stuffed the third day's chewing gum into the tube to make absolute sure the science geeks have enough DNA.

Being home early feels weird. Half-days are usually me and Lena up the town talent-spotting in the Richmond Centre. Being suspended and close to kicked out is more ice-cube-in-microwave territory. Thin on hope. Maybe it's the running catching up, or the weight of the principal's words, but I'm treading slow up the stairs to my room. By the time I reach it, I'm shaking. Fifteen Red Bull wouldn't have a look in. Closing the door tight, I slide down and sit in a crumple with my chin on my knees. Sweet Holy Jesus and the crib at Christmas, Mam will go Halloween fire rocket. She'll have to take leave off work and all for the meeting next Friday. Not. Good. Three hours till she's home. What in under Jesus will I say? I find my phone and try random-gif-scrolling therapy. Consider messaging Lena, but she'll still be in class. I mooch through Snapchat and Instagram but it only magnifies the crapness. Everyone's like: just woke up, perfect make-up, perfect life, win a yacht. Only I'm in the karma wheelie bin. I flick to Photos hoping for better distraction but with a slip of a finger, I'm in camera mode. Selfie direction. Staring at myself. All I'm seeing is my green-brown eyes loaded tragic with that question. *What do you want?*

Outside school, all I wanted was my room. Alone in my room, all I want is school. I want my friends. I want canteen laughter. Savoy cabbage. Take me back and I'll even eat it. Raw. I grit my teeth. I'm not doing the crying thing. Not. Doing. It. But now more wants are spewing. I want Nan to be well. Mam to get a break. I want family – not the up-the-duff kind – cousins, aunts, uncles. I want answers. Answers about me. About Dad. About Faith. I want to get unstuck about Oran. To know how to stop being angry and wise up. To stop with the hitting and running and burning and thinking. I want my one last chance. My face is adopting the look of a hayfever victim. Rapid eye-blinking, nose-running. My brain, constant info dumping, wants, wants, wants as I stare at myself in the camera. With a final stab my brain downloads its last three wants. The cross-country team.

A cigarette. Jack. But hey, Tara, why not just take the cigarette? You're a loser. Unfit. Unloved. Stinking like an ashtray. Pick the easy option. No way Jack'll be tickling his fingers across the cotton rips in your jeans again. Shape of you. You're stuck. In your head. With Oran.

I do want a cigarette. I don't want a cigarette. I *need* a cigarette. The principal has my cigarettes. Confiscated. With my lighter. Pending doom next Friday.

I need a cigarette. Nan is out. I'm stealing one of hers. Right now, before I can sprout a conscience.

Super-quick, I'm down the stairs, into Nan's once-was-the-good-room bedsit, crossing the rug, reaching for the packet by the clock on the mantelpiece and . . . wheeze.

Nan's in. Actually in. Not out blue-rinse socializing. All sudden like, I switch to just-decided-to-battery-check-your-Argos-clock . . . I'm imagining her beady eyes drilling into my back but when I turn, Nan is looking away. Staring out the window. Her wrinkly hands worrying at the velour of the armchair, the change in her breathing and the slight nod, the only acknowledgements of my existence. Finally, she looks at me. She's puffy-eyed, angled light through the blinds glinting off wet tracks on her cheeks. She looks . . . old. And OMG. My nan cries?

We're staring at each other like it's a don't-blink game, because us Connollys aren't cut out for crying. Connollys are hardcore. Except for during 2 a.m. movies when the dog dies or after a stubbed-your-toe-vertical-on-the-dresser accident. Even those are usually just put-the-kettle-on numbers. Nan's clearly been crying serious tissue mountains. I'm thinking it's down to more than a cancelling of her community lunch.

'G'on, pass me one while you're at it,' she says, attempting a weak smile. 'Looks like we're both having one of those days.'

Nan cries *and* she knows I smoke?

I don't know why, something about straws and camels, but soon as she speaks, I'm in floods of tears. Top gear. A trickle to Niagara Falls in under fifteen seconds. The lip-wobbling sets in with the nose-streaming and no matter how hard I rub my eyes with the backs of my hands, it's still torrential. Nan's chair creaks. Wheezing and stick shuffling, she's right there. Big arms in a purple cardigan wrapping themselves tight, tight, tight like a forever hug. These last years she's been shrinking as fast as I've been growing but now it's her holding me up and not caring that my tears and snot are soaking her blouse, or that her slippers will probably be in a puddle by the time I'm done.

'Ah, doll,' she says, over and over. 'It'll be grand. Whatever it is, we love you.'

And now I'm anybody's informer. Splurging for Ireland. Oran. Seeing him crash. The wake. The funeral. How it's all replaying constantly in my head. The not sleeping. Then Megan Carey. The fight at camp. Stuff she said about Mam. And Nan. The fight in school. Her maybe going with Oran too. Me being suspended and the principal piling it heavy about last-chance saloons. I'm about to even spill into the whole why's-Faith-so-perfect and I'm pure screw-up when I realize now might be a good point to stop talking. I'm not real sure how much, if anything, Emer said to Mam about Faith. All I know is Mam hasn't mentioned anything about lookalikes and the shoe-stash and parcel are still safe upstairs and I'm such a failure at everything else, I'm determined I'm acing the DNA quest. It'd take Voldemort and the Grim Reaper combined to stop me posting it all off.

'Poor love,' says Nan. 'I knew home early wasn't a good sign.

I'd no clue you were shouldering all that. There was me and your mam agreeing to say nowt about the Troubles so that you'd be free of them. Seems like they sucker-punched you anyway through Oran. How about we put on the kettle?'

I muster a smile, still in shock that I spoke out stuff from my head. Then I realize I haven't asked how she is herself. I glance out the window. Hung on the railings opposite are the flowers tied with purple ribbon. 'Did someone die in a car accident?' I say. 'Someone you knew?'

Nan hesitates. 'Well, he died in his car.' She holds the back of her armchair for balance. 'Nothing accidental about it, mind. It was a long time ago. I'm fine, lass. Just the day that's in it. I do think a cuppa tea would do the trick.' She lifts her bag. 'Would you nip to the shop for a couple of apple turnovers and twenty Benson? Either I'm losing my marbles or my cigarettes have been rightly vanishing this last while.' She hands me a tenner and coins, then steers herself to the kitchen. 'Don't take all year about it,' she says, when I still haven't moved a couple of minutes later.

Nipping up the stairs for my jacket, I can't resist opening the parcel. If Faith *is* related to me, it's clear who got the brains. The instructions are all wrote out like a science experiment. Sign the declarations. One for me. One for Mam. Easy enough forged. Add my two tubes with swabs into the prepaid envelope with Faith's three tubes. Seal. Post. Wait. Know.

'Back in two ticks,' I shout to Nan, as I bound down the stairs and out the door. Something about posting the parcel in the red postbox by the shop feels decisive. Positive. Clear. In McGinty's afterwards, the shopkeeper gives me the evil eye asking for cigarettes, even though I say they're for Nan and even though I'm sixteen. As I dawdle home reflecting, I'm reading the message on the pack. *Smoking can cause a slow and painful death*. I'm thinking about Nan and her lung wheezing. Thinking about what Lena said about ashtray kissing. Thinking about my principal's question. And somehow the answer's there. I want my head showered. On the inside. I just don't know how.

Opposite my house, I stop once again at the low railings and look at the flowers tied with purple ribbon. I notice the card for the first time and stoop to read it:

In Loving Memory of Sam Carmichael. Age 24. Murdered by the IRA. 1982.

I wonder about the lady in the pink coat and about Nan's tears. Maybe I was wrong telling Faith that my family escaped any damage from the Troubles. Maybe it's just that no one in my family ever talks about that stuff. Faith said her mam got helped through talking. Jack said his mam wanted his da to do therapy talking stuff. Crossing the road, I'm remembering that Emer tried to convince Mam I should talk to someone. But talking feelings aren't a Connolly thing. Cups of tea and stoic smiles are how us Connollys sort crises. And smokes. Problem is, I've been doing that for weeks now and I'm still wired. I did manage to say some stuff to Nan. Her hugs helped but I know she's off the pace with lifehacks for my generation.

At the doorstep, I set down the Bensons and paper bag of turnovers. Digging out my mobile, I bring up a number and think. She had said if I ever wanted to talk . . . I message.

My head's fried. Only got one week till they kick me out of school. Help?

I don't even reach Nan and the steaming mug of tea on the kitchen table before my mobile pings Emer's response.

Ever heard of Art Therapy? You'd be perfect for it.

Chapter 13

FAITH
County Armagh, 12 October 2019

Early on a Saturday we go. Almost religiously. The second Saturday of every month for as long as I can remember. My mother doesn't even have to ask any more – it's just what we do. Driving the winding back road into Armagh, we pass orchard after orchard, a pick-your-own pumpkin farm all set for Halloween and chocolate-lime-striped ploughed fields strung with black poles and looped cabling. At a crossroads, a farmer has made hay bale sculptures. A huge spider, ready for Halloween in a few weeks. Not that my family celebrate Halloween. Instead of bonfires and trick or treat, the church puts on Christian alternatives and games for the younger children. At least the toffee apples are delicious.

Reaching the outskirts of town, Mum is jittery, tapping the steering wheel with her fingers. She never sleeps well the night before we visit the grave. So long as she's sleeping well other nights, it's fine. I know my role on these days. Sponge and stick. If she needs to talk or cry, soak it up. If she needs support, be a prop. This morning I watched her take the normal two sertraline. Small blue tablets to quell the anxiety and depression. In bad spells, she'll phone the doctor for a script of diazepam. The round orange mirtazapine have worked at times when her anxiety causes insomnia, but if it's one of those days, she doesn't leave the house. Her weekly pills are sorted in a colour-coded plastic tray. Not just by the days. By morning, afternoon, evening and night. There are times I already feel like a doctor, even without the training and qualifications. Not that I can find anything to help my own issue. I've taken to a beanie hat and have been googling more, but there doesn't seem to be any treatment for alopecia. The only thing that helps is the removal of whatever's causing the stress. I stare out the car window and into the October skies. Today's fielding a four-seasons-in-one-day vibe – that mix of intermittent blue skies laced with heavy downpours and occasional hail.

When she's driving in this kind of mood, Mum stares straight ahead. No radio. No talking. I tilt my head back on the headrest and let my thoughts wander. When our route flanks the Orange Hall, the Mall and the Gaol, I think about Tara. Two nights ago, she texted. The DNA samples are posted. A week to ten days the kit said it takes for results. No going back now. By midterm break, we'll know – one way or the other.

The road skirts the town centre, passing the police station with its high protective fencing and Ulster in Bloom flowerbeds. After the City Hotel, we veer off to towards Keady. No one I know lives here. The houses are pretty, but this end of town's Catholic. Bilingual street names in English and Irish. The GAA club. Catholic schools. Chapels. I haven't been in any of them. Is Tara's school much different to mine? My head muses. Catholic schools usually have green in their uniforms. State schools often have red or blue. Only the handful of integrated ones seem to avoid flag colours. Mad that twenty-five years into peace, adults still label us with colours from the age of four. Colouring by religion.

We turn right at the supermarket and drive until the road turns back to country lane. Country folk can be precious about their land. I've heard their talk – selling quicker and cheaper to someone of the 'right' religion rather than territory falling into the 'wrong sort' of hands. Kerbs might not be as painted as in the cities, but people know where they're welcome all the same. A specific hedgerow. A side of a river. Sometime, someone Protestant must have bequeathed land here for the graveyard. It's a private one, not council run. There's a *splish* of our car wheels in muddy puddles as we pull in. Mum clicks her seatbelt undone, then closes her eyes and breathes deep to the bottom of her lungs, counting to ten. I'm not sure the way her generation keep revisiting the past does any good. For them or for us. Picking at scabs stops healing. Causes reinfection.

Pulling back the bolt, the iron gate rattles as I swing it wide. The graveyard is old. The near end has a necklace of rough stone walls with lime moss and ferns. Caws and clacks of crows ring out as we tread lightly under ancient trees, bent with wisdom and skeletons of climbing ivy. Behind my mother, I pad the spongy path of fresh-mown grass, the damp blades sticking to my shoelaces. The gravestones here are simple. Weathered. No imposing Celtic crosses or holy statues like the Catholic graveyards. Simple round-topped or flat-cut headstones in grey or black. *Donaghy. Stewart. Hamilton. Gibson. Gamble. Smith.* Apart from the distant hum of traffic the only sounds are the chatter and call of birds, the swish of our coats and the crunch of autumn leaves and twigs beneath our feet. *Fulton. Booth. McCullough. Shields. Hall. McKee.* English and Ulster-Scots names from generations of Planters. Some of the oldest stones are fallen, snapped and laid horizontal like jigsaw pieces. Others have weathered writing, their surrounds coloured white and yellow with lichen. Amongst the names, the relationships, ages, bible quotes and references, some stating the old townlands of generations in family plots. *Worthy of remembrance. Always in our thoughts. Faithful friend. In loving memory.*

Approaching the more modern end, the headstones are smaller, angled sunlight glinting off engraved gold lettering and the sheen of varnished black stone. I stop and stand quietly beside my mother at her parents' grave.

David McClay and his wife, Ruth McClay
Aged 43   Aged 41
Murdered by terrorists
6th November 1996
John 3:16

With her left hand, Mum reaches for mine. Her right hand brings the bouquet of white roses to her face. She smooths the petals across her nose and breathes in. Autumn is hard. Each month holds a string of 'last time' memories. The last time they were at her school prize-giving. The last time she had ice cream from Macari's with her mum. The day they left her brother to Aldergrove Airport for the plane to university in England. Her dad's last birthday trip to the Archway Lounge for sausage rolls and chicken vol-au-vents. The next time her brother came home was for the funeral. After graduation, he became part of the 'brain drain', staying permanently in England. I squeeze my mum's fingers. She sighs. Ruffles my beanie hat.

'Don't know why you've taken to wearing that old thing,' she says. As she replaces the old flowers with the new ones in a vase on the grave, I wonder who made the choice to immortalize the memory of violence on the headstone.

'Mum?' I ask, pointing at the inscription. 'Did you want those words? The ones about terrorists?'

She hugs me in tight. Arm around my shoulder. 'I was

fourteen, pet. The minister chose them. Along with Granda. It was what people did then with IRA murders.'

The warmth of her shoulder soaks through to my cheek. 'So why not name the IRA?'

'They never claimed the bomb.'

I blink. No one has mentioned this before. Even though I know no one ever did time for my grandparents' murder, all the family talk always blamed the IRA. Sensing my uncertainty, she turns me to face her. Hands clasped on both my shoulders. Her eyes are wet.

'Obviously, it was them,' she says. 'Who else in those days would blow up a policeman?'

I rub my knuckles, wondering if it's OK to ask more questions.

'Love, what's bothering you?' she says.

I gulp, wondering for a moment if she knows about the alopecia, or Tara, or . . . the other stuff. She glances at the grave. No, it's the now questions she has sensed. Thank God. 'Was it tougher because you never got justice?' I say.

'I'd have liked to know the truth.'

I think of the bible verse. The one about how the truth sets you free. I've been thinking about it a lot recently. I hunker down in front of the grave as I frame my next question. 'If you'd known the truth, would you have forgiven?'

'They did a lot of that in South Africa. Truth and reconciliation.' She sighs. 'I'm not sure it would work here. People need to ask for forgiveness. Confess their sins. Repent. Hard to forgive someone unless they admit they're wrong.'

I pluck blades of grass at my feet. Play with the green stain on my fingers. Isn't forgiveness the Christian thing? *Forgive us our sins as we forgive those who sin against us?* 'What if someone isn't sorry? Or if they don't think they're wrong?' I ask. 'Can you

117

forgive them then?' Two magpies hop through the grass. If only everything was so black and white. *One for sorrow. Two for joy. Three for a girl . . .* I can't look at my mother. She's gone quiet.

Leaves rustle as the wind changes, causing a flurry of red and gold and sending sycamore seeds spinning. I change the subject off the one in my head. 'What about Uncle Steve?' I say. 'Jack says he's still devastated about the split. If Auntie Bea could forgive him for drinking, wouldn't it be better for Jack?'

'That's different,' says Mum. 'It's not repentance he needs, it's help. Counselling.'

I look up at her. 'What about?'

'That, I don't really know.' Mum pulls her coat tight as rain starts to fall. 'He's a private man. Won't talk about his troubles for love nor money. That's the difference between him and me.'

'Eh?' I say.

'Well, I knew your dad since secondary school. He was my first real boyfriend in my early teens and we were really in love. And then . . .' She glances back to the gravestone and reaches for my hand as a comfort. 'After the bombing, I just wasn't me any more. I fell to bits and we drifted apart. I'm not proud of my behaviour. It was the trauma. Through my teens, I'd bottled it up. I fell in with a bad crowd and so did your Uncle Steve. We were both close to turning twenty by then – just friends mind, but there was a lot of drink. Like so many people during the Troubles it was a way of coping. Philip was like a knight in shining armour.' She squeezes my hand. 'At the time, he was trying to rescue his brother, but he kind of got two for the price of one – getting both me and Uncle Steve back on our feet. Falling for Philip gave me hope. And you. I'd something to live for. He encouraged me to get counselling and . . . well, the rest is history.' She smiles. Twists her wedding ring.

'But Uncle Steve,' I say. 'For years he was sober. Teetotal. Now he's back on the drink.'

Mum nods. 'Whatever was eating at him back then, he never talked about it. Not to my knowledge anyway. Keeping stuff inside can be the death of you.'

Both my hands reach for my hat. If I talk about my feelings, my sexuality, will I be expected to repent? If I don't ask for forgiveness, will it split me from my family? Already it's killing me. My head is frazzled. Walking back to the car, there's a sudden downpour. Huge raindrops pelt the grass. Mum and I quicken the pace, stepping over muddy puddles and tracing our way back through the lines of graves. I glance up as an elderly couple approach in the opposite direction, smiling, walking with their arms looped. When I say 'Hello,' out of politeness, they hesitate, staring. Something about them strikes me. I'm still trying to work out what, when Mum calls me to get a move on. Maybe it's their love, their lightness, despite being in a sodden graveyard. Damp soaks through my coat. By the time we reach the gate, we're running.

Back in the car, the windows steam. Mum lets the engine turn and fires on the radio. As the aircon demists the windows, I watch a rainbow appear. Solid. Bold. An arc of colour in front of grey clouds. In the mixture of rain and light, I see the elderly couple again. They're stood at a grave a few rows back from my grandparents' one. As Mum drives off, it hits me. It wasn't just their initial sweetness as an old couple, nor the way they suddenly stared. It was their eyes. The brightness of them. The colour. Hers were green. So were his – emerald green, with brown flecks.

Chapter 14

TARA
Derry, 15 October 2019

I'll grant it, the vibe is more slice-your-ear-Van-Gogh than tell-me-about-your-mam-Freud. Not a sofa in sight. Can't be proper therapy, can it? Jury's out. Poker-faced is how I'm playing this. Leastways for now. Emer's turned all you-got-this-girl positivity. Picked me up. 'You got this.' Parked the car. 'You got this.' Walked me to the archway at the Playhouse Theatre. 'You so got this.' More she said it, the more I'm downing Red Bull, praying for wings. Like is everybody in here a psycho nut job? Am I? There are five others. All teenagers. None of them coming across as total screw-ups.

The room is all wooden-plank floor with the smell of that whizz-polisher they use in school corridors. On shelves and surfaces round the edges are jam jars of brushes, pencils and chalks. Assortments of paper in different sizes and colours. And at the far end, sprawled across old newspapers, a car boot sale's worth of papier-mâché and air-dry clay creations. Some of them aren't half bad. Down the centre of the studio is one huge table. The heavy-duty plastic type with a sag in the middle and half a century of adolescent graffiti and penis drawings etched into it with blue biro and compass points. I kinda like it. Not that I'm saying that. I'm not for saying anything till I suss out the deal.

The biggest surprise so far is Ingabire. She's the facilitator. Says to call her Inga. She never used the words 'art therapist'.

She's pure not Derry. I don't mean that like racist. From the words she uses, she's a long-term blow-in, but her accent's a blend of how we say stuff local mixed with my old French teacher and a different kind of tuning to how she strings phrases together. And man, that woman's got poise. And a serious patterned headscarf. She is to multicolour what my wardrobe is to black. In round room introductions she says she's from Rwanda. One wisecrack says, 'Don't you mean Africa?' and she's like, 'Right continent, but happens there's a lot of countries in the mix there and mine's called Rwanda.' I'm loving her attitude. Real sass but not making a dick out of anyone. Generating smiles and laughs. Strikes me, if we do gotta talk therapy stuff, she could be a winning ticket. Meaning not just that she's sound but that she's neutral in the *them and us* stakes. Also meaning she's not likely caught up in the usual shite-talking about the rights and wrongs of what happened to Oran. I wonder what her own backstory is, but she doesn't say.

Part of me still wants to reverse gear out. I keep on my hat. My eyes darting at the other teenagers. Have they got as much riding on this as me?

At the weekend Emer chatted to Mam. At our house. She made a special point of coming round when Mam was off shift. Even brought a pack of Tunnock's Teacakes. Over the obligatory cuppa, Mam was all sighs and 'can't believe it's come to this'. Predictable, she remained staunch fixated on the therapy-is-middle-class-shite mantra until Emer reminded her of the importance of throwing my school principal a major we-are-sorting-this line at the big meeting this Friday. Mam buried her face in her hands and God's honest, I never felt so bad for causing hassle my whole life. Every day she gets up earlier, covering extra shifts, dark bags under her eyes. On Sunday, I came over all good-daughter. Made her a cheese toastie for brunch and took it to her in bed. It was her only day off in a fortnight. Sitting good as Buddha on her spare pillow reminded me that we did used to have Mam–daughter time. Nail polish nights. Rice Krispie buns. *X Factor* or *Strictly*. I guess my hormones caused teenage drift and working to cover bills got her tangled. Then Nan got sick and the hospital waiting lists got long.

Toastie munched and fingers licked, Mam had leant against the headrest, and angled herself with me, shoulder to shoulder.

'You really want to do this art therapy?' she'd asked.

I nodded.

She stroked my hair.

'You know you can talk to me about anything?'

Except Dad. Except Grandad. Except Faith. Except you're always working.

'Mam,' I said. 'You do remember I'm sixteen? I know stuff . . .'

She rolled her eyes, all is-this-about-boys? quizzical.

'For one,' I said, super-serious, 'Santa.'

She blinked. Raised an eyebrow.

'Like we don't even have a chimney. We did that conversation way back, so . . .'

'So?'

'So, you don't need to frazzle yourself with extra shifts saving for Christmas. We can make do. If we need the food bank again in January, I can do it . . . and I'm real sorry you have to take time out for my school meeting.' With my thumb, I traced the tartan patterns on her duvet. 'I was thinking, if I do get chucked out, my dole money could help . . .'

For a moment, she just looked at me. Then she hugged me epic. Real tight. 'I'll fight every bit of the way for you, love. No one's throwing my daughter on the scrap-heap.'

And that's what's going through my head when Ingabire starts into explaining the task. The news that Mam thinks I'm still worth the fight. In primary school, that was stuff my heart knew. Recently it felt like frayed elastic. When Oran gave up on himself, it was like part of me gave up too.

Ingabire scatters colour printouts across the table. The swish of it brings back my focus. Photos of patterns on walls, pottery, canvas. 'This is *Imigongo*. It's a tradition from my country. In Rwanda, just like Northern Ireland, people paint walls with their culture.'

I'm already studying the patterns. Black. White. Red. Grey. A beige-yellow. There's something cave-drawing-like about the colours but it's all spirals and geometric designs, not mammoths.

She hands round chalks. Lifting one, I roll it between my fingers.

'In Imigongo wall art, we paint patterns. In Derry murals, you paint history. Sometimes pretty traumatic history. The thing about Imigongo is that we make art from dung.'

'As in . . . shite?' asks the girl with pink spiked hair and a *Respect Pronouns* T-shirt.

'Precisely.'

There's a collectivized *Yeeurk* and nose holding.

'Doesn't it stink?' asks the boy with a nose piercing.

'No. Cow dung is mixed with ash. It kills the bacteria and the odour. We transform something harmful, something that stinks, into a statement.'

I lift one of the pages and study it more closely.

'Look at me,' says Ingabire.

I jolt, thinking I've done something wrong, but she's talking to us all. She holds up some blank sheets of paper.

'What's different about these pages from the usual ones you get in school?' she says.

'The paper's black,' we all say.

She nods.

'Brighten your dark feelings with colour. Every one of you in these workshops is taking part because something tough has happened. You need to know, I'm never going to force you to talk about that. As we build trust, I'm hoping you will feel that, here, you *can* express yourself. But expression is not always in words. And pain doesn't have to cripple us. Work with it, get real and honest, and you can turn pain into purpose.'

She talks more. Stuff about confidence. Respecting each other. It's not about how artistic we are but about the authenticity, the truth we bring to the task. She had me at black paper and shite. As she repeats the task, making sure everyone's grasped it, my mind is already out of the blocks, racing, imagining, whirring. I'm fidgeting, insides itching to get started. Maybe it's cos today I decided to quit smoking. Maybe it's cos it's two months since Oran died. Exact. All day I've been jittery. Not a bean of concentration. With this, however, it feels good to have my brain buzzing. Colours. Designs. No one's ever told me to draw something from my own life through pattern. To express my feelings in chalk. Or to take my personal crap and transform it into art. Clearly, Ingabire doesn't speak Savoy cabbage.

We work in relaxed silence. Some world-music chill-out track playing low in the background. At times, Ingabire circles the table. Admiring work. Hunkering down beside someone and quietly chatting. She talks to the girl with spiky pink hair that looks electric. Then to the nose-ring guy in the T-shirt with the Manhattan skyline on the front. When she stands by my shoulder, I can't look round. I just keep sketching. Filling in the patterns of tracks. Staring at the black void in the middle. I know what's going there. I just don't want to draw them. Not yet. All day it has felt wrong that everyone else has moved on from remembering Oran. Kicking around at home felt like I was more than just suspended. Glazing out with Nan to *Homes Under the Hammer* and *Bargain Hunt*, I'd felt disconnected. Lonely.

In our workshop, I don't notice the time. I don't even really notice the others at the table. The paper is soaking up everything I throw at it. The reds, greens and yellows becoming something I have to express. Have to finish. Especially because of the day that's in it. Faster and faster my hands work, adding detail. The pattern round the outside is tyre treads. From the cars he used to nick. The next loop inside is bricks. Cracked and graffitied. The third frame is made from the shapes of cobbles. Then in the centre is a kaleidoscope of every chalk colour on the table, swirling like it's pulling you into another dimension. Like the high off drugs, only a one-way trip. A vortex. In the middle, I have a choice. Thinking it's a pen, I accidentally suck on the end of a chalk stick and then swear as I try to wipe the dust-taste off my tongue.

Spiky-pink-hair smiles at me. 'You're like Picasso on fire,' she says.

I smile back. Her own drawing isn't bad.

She screws her nose up. 'I'm better at painting with words,' she says.

'Eh?'

'Performance poetry.'

I nod, clueless. Then make my decision. Ingabire said she wanted honest, so she's getting it. As I complete the last strokes of chalk, I know the moment is captured. Only when I stop drawing, does the impact hit. My chalk clatters to the floor and my hand springs to my mouth. Truth on a page looks like my inner demons. No hiding from them now. Oran's eyes are staring at me, spaced out. Tripping. Pupils wide. Just like they were two months ago to the day up on the Derry Walls. There's a strangled squeak. Everyone gawps in my direction and it dawns. I. Made. That. Sound. Even in a room of headcases, I'm the sky-rocket. I. Hate. This. My chair screeches as I shove it backwards. In one swift move, I lift my page, crush it into a ball and fling it into the corner. The art room door bangs behind me as I flee up the corridor. They can chuck me out of school. Imprison me in some zero-hours minimum wage life. I. Can't. Do. This.

I. Can't. Do. Anything.

I bounce off the walls. Kicking at skirting boards. Swearing. Eventually, I curl up in an armchair on the second floor near the lift. No one's about. If I stay put another half hour, Emer will be back. I'll say it was cramps. Girl stuff. If I come across calm, she might even believe me. I swing my feet up on a coffee table and pull my hat down low over my eyes. The theatre seems empty, but if anyone passes, they should read the huge invisible feck-off sign.

The footsteps are light. The shoes orange. Somehow I know when I look up the hair will be pink.

'Hey,' she says, plonking herself down opposite. Pure uninvited.

'Hey,' I say, not wanting to be a complete arse.

'I always used to run too,' she says.

I tilt my head up a weeny bit. Her name's Dee. I remember it now from the introductions.

'When they first put me into care, they virtually had to bolt my bedroom door. Lost count of how many foster parents gave up . . . Meant it, you know. Your art's in a different league. Bet it runs in the family?'

I shrug. Neither Mam nor Nan know a paintbrush from a Toblerone.

'You're in care?' I say.

She nods. 'Ma's got early-onset dementia. Can't look after herself, never mind me.'

'Oh,' I say.

'Dad's a vanishing act.'

'Same,' I say.

'Yeah, it's a bit shit. I visit the care home. Sometimes she still recognizes me. Mostly not. You know, Ingabire is ace. Way her face lit when she saw your drawing. You gonna come back to the room or what?'

I look at Dee proper. She's not winding me up.

'Don't think I can talk about it,' I say. 'Not in front of a whole group.'

'Don't have to,' she says. 'I never opened my mouth for the first five weeks last spring. Only went to keep the social happy. Ingabire helped me find my voice. Bet now the social wishes she could shut me up.' She stands. Offers me her hand.

I hesitate. Unsure.

She thinks for a minute. Hands on hips. 'Whose eyes were in your drawing?' she says.

I gulp. Blink. Chew my lip.

She doesn't move. Keeps her face all no-pressure-but-I'm-interested.

I wipe my palms on my jeans. 'Oran,' I say. 'My boyfriend.'

'He died?'

I nod. 'Exactly two months ago.' Then the word just says itself, without me even processing it. 'Suicide.'

'God,' she says. 'That's a right head-fry.'

I can't help it. The smiling thing. It just happens. 'Yeah,' I say.

'It is.' And then I realize, it's not jammed in my head any more. I'm actually talking about it. Dee's looking half-smug got-ya, only in a good way. Wandering together back up the corridor, I'm still feeling nervous, just not at choke-back-vomit level. No more Usain Bolt sprints. My decisions are made. In the school meeting on Friday, I'm telling the truth. Sorry, Mrs McClenaghan. My head's been fried. Note to self – practise a way of putting that better. Also, keep my cigarettes. I'm done smoking. Only running I'm doing from now on is cross-country. Plus, though I'm not for making promises about talking, I'm sticking with Dee and Ingabire. If Mam's gonna fight for me, I gotta start believing in myself too.

'One question,' I say, turning to Dee before we go back in. 'What's the deal with pronouns?'

Chapter 15

FAITH
Belfast, 21 October 2019

Bethany's family isn't into politics. Just religion. She's lucky. Or maybe the better term is blessed. In the car coming up the motorway to Belfast, I try to sum it up for her again. 'Remember that petition? The one in church? The Unionist politicians, the pro-British ones they—'

'Our side?'

'Yeah, you could put it like that. They're making one last-ditch attempt to stop the London laws coming in. Fail and, at midnight, abortion will become legal in Northern Ireland.'

'Wasn't there gay stuff too?'

'The protest is just pro-life,' I say. *Otherwise I don't think I could be here*, I don't say.

Dad's driving. Mum's in the passenger seat. We're part of a convoy heading up to join the protest. The clear indication my parents are taking this seriously came when they urged me to take the day off school. Life skills, Dad had said, while Mum nodded.

Mum peers back round the headrest. 'Bethany's right though,' she says. 'Although the protest is focused on abortion, it's the same set of laws that will legalize gay marriage. And something too against coercion in proper heterosexual marriages, but that bit's OK.'

'Oh,' I say, staring at the tailbacks at Lisburn.

We rarely come to Belfast. The only places I know are the

SSE Arena, where our youth group went to see the Belfast Giants playing ice hockey, and CastleCourt shopping centre. Usually, we catch the train from Portadown. Seeing Dad navigate the stop-start traffic through the city centre, I now understand why. Will I still think of him as 'Dad' if the DNA results say otherwise? They're due any day.

This morning, right on cue to mark my rising anxiety levels about it all, I found another bald patch. Behind my left ear. Maybe it was there before and I didn't notice. That thought made me paranoid. Delayed me getting down for Mum's special fried breakfast. The potato bread had gone cold. The egg, congealed. I'd zapped it apologetically in the microwave. None of your hash browns and beans for us. A real proper Ulster fry. Delicious.

'Way to a man's heart is through his stomach,' said Dad, winking at me.

I guess it's wisdom I won't ever need. Not how he means it anyway.

Driving across to the far side of the city, the houses get fancier. No terraces here. Houses like mansions. Big gardens. Trimmed hedges. Bet they don't even own welly boots – unless they're designer gear. Gardeners probably cultivate their organic vegetable patches and wildflower meadows at the rear. Arriving near the estate, we park on a side street and enter the grounds on foot. Parliament buildings are always on the news. 'A Protestant parliament for a Protestant people,' Sir James Craig called it a century ago when it was set up. Stormont, it's known by. It domineers the top of the hill, striking with its four storeys of white brick, row upon row of windows and a pillared entrance. Everything about it screams government, except it has been empty for nearly three years – politicians refusing to meet. Each side blaming the other. These days, to govern, they're forced to share power. That was the peace solution. Now it's a problem. They won't work together, so they're not working at all. Despite the religion some politicians spout, they don't seem to remember the parable of the plank and the speck of dust. The basics of Sunday school – take the plank out of your own eye first so that you can see clearly to help your neighbour with the dust in theirs. Today, however, the lights are back on. Crunch time. The Unionist politicians have called a special session. Whether it works or not is a different matter.

'We'll leave it in God's hands,' Dad says, as we walk up the wide avenue. 'But we'll put our own to good use.' Gripping our orange and white placards, we join the other pro-life protesters.

The protest has begun early so that politicians will see us as they arrive. We gather under the statue of Sir Edward Carson. The group is a mixture of men and women. Mainly middle-aged or retired. Bethany and I are the youngest. Looking at them, I'm reflecting on what Jack said. When Dad invited him along last week, he'd muttered something about a school test and bolted from the kitchen.

'You're seriously going?' he'd asked me the next morning on the bus to school.

'Of course,' I said. 'Life is precious. It's in the Psalms. God knits us together in our mother's womb. He knows us before we're born. Why won't you join us? Aren't you pro-life?'

'Ish,' he said, twisting a button on his school blazer. 'But what guy is going to be seen dead in a protest *against* women's rights?'

'My dad.'

'OK. What *unmarried* guy who doesn't fancy the forty-year-old virgin thing? Like how could I know what it's like to be a woman in that situation? What if it was rape or the baby was gonna be born dead? What if the mother was fourteen?

131

What right have *I* to speak on that?'

'But what about the rights of the child? They can't speak at all.'

He slouched down in the seat. 'Look, all I'm saying is there are grey areas. Shit happens. Maybe the message needs more love and less judgement. I thought . . .' He shook his head.

'Thought what?'

'Never mind.'

'Tell me.'

'I just thought you of all people would get that?'

'Meaning?'

He hesitated. 'Meaning when you come out. When you choose to tell your parents, the church. I hope they'll choose grace over bible bashing.'

I'm still thinking about this as the pro-choice campaigners begin marching up the hill. They're much louder, much younger, more diverse. Our protest is deliberately silent. The unborn have no voice. Problem is, the people in Northern Ireland all feel that way with no government. Last month over 20,000 pro-lifers staged a peaceful candlelight protest at Stormont. Pro-choice campaigners have been marching the streets too. Does any of it matter a bean if politicians won't run government?

As the two groups eyeball, it's tense. They holler and chant their demands for free, safe abortion as they stride up the avenue behind their banner. Raising their homemade placards high. I can't help smiling at the one with a drawing of scissors. *Mr Politician – if you cut my reproductive rights, can I cut yours?* They are to festive what we are to dull. It's attractive, but it also turns my stomach. Sweeping up the wide road, they regroup for publicity. Standing behind placards of huge letters, they spell out D-E-C-R-I-M-I-N-A-L-I-Z-E-D.

Face-off in place, there's nothing to do but wait. Bethany and I scroll our phones. Some of the group pray. Nearby a lady is explaining facts about abortion at such-and-such weeks and survival rates of babies born prematurely. My ears prick up, my brain conjuring questions I've never thought about before. Like the weights of babies at birth. I remember when I turned thirteen, Mum showed me the wee plastic bracelet from Craigavon hospital. *Baby Duggan. 6lb 7oz.* I'd marvelled that she'd kept it and that something so small ever fitted my wrist. Fifteen was the first time I'd questioned the dates. My birthday is barely seven months after their wedding. Too curious not to ask, I'd noticed how Mum carried on peeling spuds, gazing into the sink as she'd muttered something about prematurity and then gone to empty the bin. Today, surrounded by placards with pictures of a fetus in a womb, I'm processing the lady explaining that an average baby weighs around seven pounds at birth. At two months premature it's five pounds. Not concrete evidence, but the maths of my months and weight doesn't add up. Mum may say I was premature but if that's true, I was born unusually heavy.

Some of the adults are on a news app, following the political debates in the chamber. It's like a political stunt. Before they can do business, the rules say they have to elect a speaker. Dad explains it's like a neutral person who controls the debate. Problem is, rules from the peace deal say the speaker must have cross-community support. Unionists and Nationalists. Catholics and Protestants. Since half the political parties refused to even show up today, everything hangs on the only remaining Nationalist party. It's worse than a pantomime. The protest outside is more civilized. Everything inside is school playground cheers and jeers.

Ten minutes. Twenty minutes. Forty minutes. Bethany and I

are bored senseless. And cold. Sat on its granite base, the statue of Carson towers over us. Dad is a fan. A bronze plaque says the statue was put here by 'Loyalists of Ulster'. Bethany has earphones in. I'm playing mindless app games when a message alert pings. It's Tara.

Twenty-three emojis and *OMG THEY LET ME BACK INTO SCHOOL*

????

Near expelled last week. Back now. Sworn angelic.

Yay!

Any results back yet?

It has been such a weird day, I haven't checked emails. Before messaging no, I open my app. Seeing my inbox, I jump to my feet. Suck air in through my teeth. The email is there. Right there. Everything inside me is switched on electric. I can't open it. Not here. I need privacy. Time out. This could change everything. EVERYTHING. The grown-ups are all engrossed in the live-streaming political shenanigans but not Bethany. Looking up, she mouths, *What?* I'm all subtle headshakes. *Nothing*. She raises her shoulders, furrows her brows. Mouths: *A boy?* I roll my eyes and shake my head. Where can I go? I look about, dizzy with the expectation of knowing.

Mum turns. 'You OK, pet?'

'Is there . . . I'm a bit stressed. Is there anywhere I could go and sit away from the protest?'

Mum does big parental-concern eyes. Thinks a minute. 'Actually,' she says. 'There's a perfect place.' She points to a smaller statue at the edge of some trees, a stone's throw away. 'The statue of reflection. Our victims' group visited it once.' She smiles. 'Take Bethany with you.'

In a pool, a black metal man and woman kneel opposite each

other. Their sculptured bodies make a bridge as they embrace in grief over a divide. Boulders are inscribed with *Jerusalem. Hiroshima. Berlin. Coventry.* It doesn't say Belfast. Mum says in this country, people can't agree enough on who classifies as a victim. There are proper innocent victims, but the jury's split over ones injured after causing harm to others. Strikes me it's a bit like how they say bullies were often victims of bullying themselves. We don't have shared memorials. I turn my mobile over and over in my hand, trying to build the nerve to look at the email.

Bethany tugs my sleeve. 'What's the craic?' she says. 'Someone message you? Anyone *special*?'

'Nothing like that,' I say. *Nor likely to be for a very long time. Maybe never.*

Her head tilts. 'Spill,' she says. 'I sense gossip.'

'Could you give me a minute?' I say. 'On my own?'

'Seriously? You did this at the residential too. I'm your best friend. Something's going on with you. You're acting different. Don't think I don't know.'

My heart quickens. 'Don't know what?'

She sighs exasperated. 'You've some kind of secret. Since the residential. I reckon it's your lookalike. Tara.'

I breathe deep. 'OK,' I say. 'Give me a few minutes, then I'll talk. Promise.'

Sitting by the pond, I stare across the stately lawns and the protests. Somehow they both seem meaningless compared to this email. Bethany saunters in slow circles. I cradle my mobile in my hands. Close my eyes. Listen to the rustle of leaves. Focus. *Ready? Ready as I'll ever be.* Eyes open, I tap in. Nothing in the subject line gives any hint. The email from GENEcheck is third in my inbox. Order ID: 387ST5Y as its randomly generated reference code beside *DNA Profiling Test Results* in the subject line. My arms start to shake. I breathe in deep through my nose, filling my lungs with cool autumn air. Then tap the screen. The first bits are all preamble. *DNA Profiling Test report for your case.* Scientific waffle and confirmation of processes and certification. My eyes are darting about, failing to focus in any logical order on the text. Somewhere, it must say it plain and simple but all I'm seeing are lists of something called *Locus*. Numbers and letters. Columns marked *Alleles*. Something about *Direct Index*. Then the jargon starts to change to clearer words.

Tara's name. Her mum's name. My mum's name. My own name. Circles. Green circles. Red circles. Scrolling the screen, finally I see it.

From the samples supplied we have obtained the following result:
Relationship: Half-sister
Probability of half-siblings versus no relation: 96.76%

It's true. Tara *is* my half-sister. It's singing at me off the screen.

But there's more. I glance over to the Carson statue. See Mum and Dad chatting, holding their placards. The jargon in the email has moved on. Jack's name. Stuff about Combined Relationship Index. Then the stuff I can understand.

The genetic evidence indicates that the tested relationship is practically impossible.

The probability of relationship is 0.8%. This result means Jack Duggan is excluded as being related to Faith Duggan or Tara Connolly.

I read it once. Then again. And again. The Stormont buildings and grounds begin to swim and melt. I fall to my knees like the reconciliation statue. Maybe it's a prayer. Maybe it's just a curling into the safety of my own self. My dad is not my dad. Fact. Scientifically proven. My parents have lied. Or, another thought, is it just Mum? Does Dad . . . Philip . . . my stepdad, even know? I glance across at the slogans carried by the campaigners. Even if she wasn't pro-life, my mum wouldn't have had the option of abortion. Today might make it legal, but it definitely wasn't then. Did she just marry Philip out of shame, or did they marry for love? In my hand is the proof I've wanted. Now I have it, challenging my parents seems impossible. What if I accidentally wreck their marriage? No way am I strong enough. Not for this. Not for coming out, either.

Mumbles. Voices. Shouts. Cheers. I look up, panicked, thinking everyone is watching me. I needn't have worried. Every eye is focused on the politicians spilling out of the building. Mainly men. Suits. Ties. Some women. It doesn't take any news app to read the result. The pro-choice protesters are manic cheering. Hugs. Whoops. Jumping with their placards. It shouldn't, but something in me lifts. I can't celebrate abortion, but some of their protesters are wearing rainbow badges. It's a historic day for them. It is for me too – in more ways than one.

Bethany coughs. I've forgotten she's even here. 'Enough. What the flip is going on?' she says.

'With them?'

'No. You.'

'Can you keep a secret?'

She nods.

'Swear?'

'Honest to God and hope to die.' She goes melodramatic hands in prayer and looks up to heaven.

'Give me a second and I'll tell you. I've just got to send a text.'

Bethany does like a fake strangling-me mime. I scrunch my eyes and try to capture the thought that's spinning through my brain. Tara has faced so much. She's so brave. If I have half her gene pool, surely I can be brave too? Pulling up her last message, I tap in a response.

Hey, half-sister . . .

No way! Really?

Yes way. Definite.

OMG! And your da?

Not related to either of us. Jack isn't our cousin.

WTF! Are you OK? We gotta celebrate. Can you come to Derry? Halloween is massive.

I bite my nail. It'll take a huge dose of deception to reach Londonderry but the more I think about it, the more I'm desperate to be with Tara. In one email, I've lost a dad but gained a sister. If Philip isn't our dad, then who is? Where do we go with the mystery now? We could think things through together. Besides, going out in Londonderry could be fun. The random thoughts stop racing. I focus and think. Maybe there, away from everyone I know, going out could even be a safe place for *coming out . . .*

Bethany is virtually dancing in frustration, waiting. Before she explodes, I tap one last message.

YES. I'll come up. And OUT . . . You want me to bring Jack?

Chapter 16

TARA
Derry, 31 October 2019

I'm diving into my third pack of Wrigley's Extra and Lena can't help but remind me gum is the latest thing she's dropped to be green. Something to do with it not biodegrading. I don't care. Woke is overrated. If the oceans turn to plastic, I'll own up. My fault. Sat on the bench at the Derry bus station, my legs won't keep still, rearranging themselves in different triangles every three minutes. When. Is. This. Bus. Coming? I wanna smoke so bad, but no way. Two weeks is a milestone. I'm not exactly counting, but like two weeks, two days, three hours? I'm done tasting of ashtrays.

'Why the nerves?' says Lena.

She can talk. Biting her nails to shreds over Joaquim. 'I'm not nervous,' I say.

'My arse.' She grins. 'Question is, is it your sister or her cousin that has you all jitters?'

'Jack's not related,' I spit back, over defensive.

'Ex-act-ly.' Lena folds her arms and does the head tilt catch-yourself-on look. Checks her nail polish.

I'm allowed to be nervous. This is the first time, the first proper, genetically proven, in writing, known-in-advance meeting with my sister. I, Tara Connolly, have a sister. A. Sister. A proper breathing living relative my own age. Fact.

It's epic. No one's taking this away from me. I've boxed my

way the full twelve rounds through this last fortnight, head held high, perfect behaviour, bouncing on my toes and absorbing any hits without a whimper. On time for school. Tick. Homework. Tick. Telly watched with Nan. Tick. Pasta dinners sorted. Tick. Wheelie bins dragged out without moaning. Tick. Tuesday night art therapy. Tick. I even volunteered at Nan's blue rinse community day, doing face-painting for all the weans. Shoot me if I ever draw another butterfly or Spider-Man. Worth it though. At the end, they gave me a huge box of Celebrations and twenty quid. Vodka. Tick. Clubbing. Sorted.

Community face-painting also gave me the idea for the Halloween costumes which, until then, had bugged me like crazy. One thing's clear – Faith and Jack have zero concept of the vital nature of dressing up. Their heads were fried enough with the getting here without their parents knowing. Preparation for the Halloween business? In my hands alone. On a budget of biscuits. Lena has sorted Joaquim. She's going as a nun and he'll be rigged out in a priest's collar. It'll look class when they're snogging later. She's got a miniskirt and fishnets to go under the habit. Real sexy.

All week, I took to scouring charity shops religiously after school. Waterloo Place. Shipquay Street. Cancer Research. Kinship Care. Rainbow Pet Rescue. I was almost for giving up and going as a binbag when I struck gold in Bishop Street Barnardos. His and hers long-sleeved tops. Black, skeleton bones front, back and down the sleeves. Combined with pound-shop face paints these were perfect. I rummaged around but there wasn't a third. I did find a sombrero, chucked from someone's Costa del Something hungover market splurge. Then, squished on a hanger between a puke-coloured size twenty jumper and size six pink jeans, I spied another T-shirt. The absolute ticket. I held it against myself to check for size and inspected it closer. Fifty pence well merited. Would Faith dare to wear it? Our conversation on the big rock came to mind. Worth a shot. In the end, it would be her choice. Either way, I'd be proud of her.

This morning I took to cleaning. It was when I kicked an odd ankle sock and a pair of period pants under the dresser that it dawned. Faith would be staying in my room. And Jack. OMG. Like an actual boy. Sleeping. In. My. Bedroom. A full surgical operation was required. A *Nanny McPhee* or a *Sorcerer's Apprentice* option would've been helpful.

Two hours later I was wrecked. It was tidied, vacuumed, aired, sprayed with deodorant and resprayed for good measure. After changing the bedsheets, I'd starfished out on the duvet and set to thinking. Lena had her bit covered easy. Even told her mam about Joaquim. Agreed he'd be staying on their sofa. So long as he does his sleeping there and nowhere else, her parents are sound. Not that there'll be much sleeping tonight for anyone and not just on account of fishnet tights. It's Derry Halloween. The best night of the year. In. The. World.

One pack of chewing gum later and intensive brain scrambling for my inner guru, I'd still no solution. How could I tell my mam and nan that my half-sister they don't know exists is staying the night? Or that I'm sixteen and for the first time ever, I'm gonna have a boy who is SEVENTEEN and definitely NOT my cousin sleeping right there on top of the spare duvets dragged from the hot press not two feet from my pillow? Me in my Primark PJs and him . . . OMG, like will Jack even *bring* PJs? I smell my breath. Chewing gum is way better than cigarettes. I must not eat baked beans. Mam is on night duty from six tonight. By the usual reckoning, that'll mean she's sleeping until four. Leaving at half five. If we stay in town until five, we've time enough to dodge

Mam, get home, get ready and be out for the carnival. Tight, but possible. Nan will likely be beached in front of the telly too narked with the constant trick-or-treaters interrupting *Emmerdale* to give a monkey's about what friends I have upstairs getting glammed up for town.

Lena nudges me. The Armagh bus is swinging into bay three. My eyes scan the windows. Maybe they'll have changed their minds. Maybe their parents will have copped on and spoiled the party. I can't see them. My chest tightens. Still no sign. Beside me, Lena goes manic cheerleader. I follow her gaze. There. Queued at the back. Stuck waiting for others to move forward. Faith. Joaquim. Jack. They've spotted us now too. Waving and grinning. As they reach the steps by the driver, Lena runs forward and without a blink she's full snogging Joaquim like get-a-room. Inside, I'm wanting to race over too. Wanting to group hug Faith and Jack. My feet have other ideas, taking the tarmac for treacle and sticking right where they're at. I'm all pocket hands and lip-biting, sucking the blue bit of my hair and not real sure if I can even look up – except I can't help that bit. I'm too . . . I don't know what I am. And, all sudden, I do. I am hugged. Gripped tight by Faith and Jack. Jack's lifting us both and spinning us dizzy. I feel the smile beaming from my face and hear them laughing. When he sets us down, Faith hugs me again.

'Hey, sis,' she says. The two most wonderful words ever.

'Hey, sis,' I say back.

We wander through the Peace Garden, causing a flutter of pigeons. On our right, the Peace Bridge towers over the river. The far bank is mixed. This side is mainly Catholic, though these days it doesn't matter that much. As for tonight, no one will give a shit and no one will know anyway because everyone will be in costume. This whole place will be standing room only. The clock

142

on the Guildhall tower is already lit green, making it eerie like a vampire castle. Joaquim points as a Fyffes banana walks past towing a kid with a velvet shark on its head. They think that's impressive? An initiation is needed and Lena and I have it planned. Up the steps at the rear of the Guildhall, we steer Faith, Joaquim and Jack into City Council HQ. Usually it's all polished corridors, school trip, history and citizenship stuff. Not at Halloween. It's the one time everyone is proud of the suits. Our local ones anyway. They don't just embrace this stuff. They lead it. Faith gasps as we're plunged into an alternate universe. Scraps of old discoloured bandages and cotton wool are strung across corridors like ancient Egyptian cobwebs. Black and red bunting. Draped skeletons peer round corners, their bony fingers backdropped in black cloth and displays of autumnal oranges. Suspended above on a broomstick is a green-faced witch, her gnarled fingers reaching down to grab passers-by. The royal statues look like they've been resurrected from some vault. Tangled in webs. Queen Victoria fitting right into the horror of it for once with her stone hand blown off from the Guildhall bomb way back in the Troubles. Wee kids are bouncing off the woodwork. Harry Potters, pirates, firefighters, Cinderellas, wizards – all hyper on green candyfloss, towing parents towards the Jeepers Creepers storytelling cave and haunted-house rooms. We finish at the huge entrance. The centrepiece is a Celtic Samhain/Mexican Day of the Dead bride and groom. A wedding scene with skeletons. Orange pumpkins. Top hats. Mood music and lighting effects. Leading the Armagh crew down the front steps into Guildhall Square, we hit the markets and food stalls. It's in full swing. 'Monster Mash' and 'Thriller' blasting through skeleton faces on amps. Marquees jammed with people and decorated freakish autumnal. Jack, Faith and Joaquim go complete goggle-eyed. Food stalls. Crêpes and coffee. Face painting. A selfie booth. Helium balloons. Free glitter and henna tattoos.

'This place is lethal,' says Jack.

'Wait till you see tonight.' I grin.

'Anyone hungry?' says Lena.

We grab burgers and squish round a picnic bench. The plastic tablecloth is splattered with hand-scrawled *Help Me* writing and bloody handprints. We discuss plans for tonight like a military operation. Where we'll meet. When. Where we're stashing the booze to get through the no-alcohol barriers. What we'll be wearing.

'Wind that back a minute,' says Jack. 'No way I'm wearing make-up.'

'Yes way,' chime me and Lena. 'If you don't, you'll be the one looking like a freak.'

Jack does narrow eyes at me. Dead gorgeous.

'Trust me,' I say, not letting on he's got me melted.

When Lena and Joaquim head for the Creggan bus, Jack and Faith and I mill about. I don't want us to catch the bus to the Glen yet. I daren't be home too early. Mam's gotta be out or Halloween will turn nightmarish for real. The craft village has been transformed into a Village of the Damned. Ghouls with missing eyes. Zombies. Pumpkins on stilts teasing toddlers. Everywhere the smell of pizza and doughnuts. The sound of excited chatter from the crowds. It's the weans dressed as zombie brides that reminds me. Clatters of them all thinking they're original as hell in last year's communion dresses and fake blood.

'I was doing some thinking,' I say.

'Dangerous,' says Jack.

I elbow him. 'About my dad.'

'*Our* dad,' says Faith.

'Aye. Couple of months ago I found a wedding dress in our attic.'

Jack and Faith look at me like 'and what?'

'Mam's not married. Nan neither. Could be a lead,' I say.

'I think I might have another one,' says Faith, 'but I've no clue how to follow it. I met someone in a graveyard.'

Jack rolls his eyes. 'Say it like that and it sounds seriously dodgy.'

'An old couple. No idea who they were but it was their eyes. I noticed when they stared at me that both of them had green eyes. That's rare enough, but his were more emerald green, with brown flecks.'

She looks at me.

'He's way too old to be our father but his eyes, they were the closest I've seen to ours.'

'You've got great eyes,' says Jack. 'Both of you . . .' He's looking at me.

At the craft village exit we walk into a dark corner. It's rigged with light projections to look like neon ghosts are floating in the air. Dry ice creeps across the pavement. 'OMG. How sick is that?'

Dragging Jack and Faith over, I flick through my phone camera settings and snap a group selfie. AirDrop it so we all get a copy. Seeing me and Faith together in the photo is still a head-fry. So identical unless you study way hard. Her freckles. The more sophisticated line of her eyebrows. I think my hair is fractionally darker and thicker – like Mam's, but it's the extras that define us. My piercings. The subtlety of her make-up compared to my can't-be-arsed goth. The loose way I like my hair, compared to hers all up in clips. Today she has it under a broad Alice band. Real sophisticated. Even I can see it. She oozes class compared to my common. If I didn't like her, I'd hate her. As we trek back down Shipquay Street to the Glen bus stop, the worry hits. My house. Our wee terrace. It'll look common too. It was like nothing to Faith to pay for that DNA kit. She's the one leading all this search. What am I contributing?

At the stop, I go quiet. Phone-scrolling through images. She's the rocket scientist. I'm pure sky-rocket. Jack probably just came along so I don't mess up Faith the same way as I've messed up most other shit. Definite, I've already screwed up my one chance with him after that day at the Mall.

'Scroll back a second.'

I jump, not having realized Jack's staring over my shoulder. He reaches round and flicks at the screen. 'You're seriously good at photography,' he says. And his arm is touching mine. Well, his jacket is anyway. The backs of his fingers touch my hand on the phone. Faith seems wild interested in the library. Maybe . . . Ingabire said it last week in art therapy, too. Says it's a confidence thing being able to own up to being good at something. It occurs to me that I *am* dead good at art. Faith has science. I got art.

'Yeah,' I say. 'I'm not bad.'

I'm thinking more about it as we ride the bus back to my place. I'm remembering that when I was younger, we used to play Cluedo. Nan, Mam and me, hunkered round the board game on the living-room carpet on rainy Sundays. There was always more than one detective racing to solve the mystery. Sometimes, I won. So far, we've only used science, the DNA stuff, to hunt for Dad. Science isn't the only kind of evidence, though. In the movies, the private investigators are always clicking cameras. Why didn't I think of it before? Surely to God, stashed away somewhere in our house there must be old photos?

*

As I've instructed, at the house, we go for hiding in plain sight, hollering a hello at my nan as we clump up the stairs. She pokes her head out into the hall as I'm turning at the top banister, Jack and Faith ahead of me, out of her line of vision. 'Hey, Nan. Want me to paint your face for Halloween too?'

She does her crinkly smile. 'Have fun,' she says and hobbles back to the sofa.

Twenty minutes later and Faith is in the bathroom fixing her hair and thinking about the T-shirt. She's getting quieter. My confidence is growing. Her face is a perfect Mexican Day of the Dead lady. Cobweb and diamond pendant on her forehead, black round the eyes with red flower petals on the outer circle. Blacked-out nose, bright red lips with stitching and swirl patterns of flowers and vines in bold greens and blues across her cheeks.

Jack moseyed about my room, scanning my posters and flicking through my art pad while he watched. Half-curious, half-petrified. The skeleton T-shirt is tight across his chest, in a good way. Like the lads who wear their sports tops close-fitted to show off their muscles.

'You're not doing me as a woman, are you?' he says, sitting tense in the chair for his turn.

'Depends what you mean by that,' I say, all coy.

There's a flit of panic in his eyes, followed by intrigue.

'Man spread,' I say and nudge his knees apart so I can lean in closer to his face. I work deftly. Highlighting the stern bone structure, the cut of his jaw. For him, it'll only be three colours. Black, white and a turquoise to bring out his eyes. Close up, working at the detail, I can feel his breath on my cheek. I tilt him forward and draw a cross, centred on his forehead. Cobwebs radiating from it in intricate lines. His breath is on my neck. My

147

jeans brushing his as I lean in and concentrate. He's keeping statue still. Hands splayed on his thighs. When I step back, I swear I catch his eyes on my chest before he looks up at me. Can he hear my heart racing? For the final touch, I toss him the sombrero. OMG. He is hot as hell. Serious stern and powerful. I'm turning to goo just watching him assess his new look in my mirror. My. Bedroom. Mirror. The biggest grin breaks out across his face. He's looking at me, then back at his reflection, shaking his head and laughing.

All sudden I come over like a wee girl. Sucking my hair and toeing the carpet. Inside I'm so fizzing I don't know how I'm gonna keep my hand steady enough to do my own face paint. Jack senses it. In two strides, he's over in front of me. Gently, he pulls the blue bit of my hair aside and tilts up my chin till I'm looking direct into his turquoise eyes. For a moment, he's quiet, like he's trying to read me.

'You really don't know how class you are, do you?' he says.

I shrug.

'Can I ask you something? I hope it's OK.'

I micro-nod, about to pee my knickers.

'Last time, you were . . . struggling. Oran and that. If I've learned anything about you, it's that you always put on a brave face. Maybe you paint that disguise even better than this one.' He circles his hand round his face. Then he sets a hand on my shoulder. 'How are you really? Like . . .' He hesitates. 'You'll tell me if I need to back off, right? I'm trying to understand and . . . I could be wrong, but it feels like you're in a different place from last time we met.'

'It was Armagh . . .' I tease. Part of me is kicking myself cos the conversation Jack is trying is real and I've pure head-the-balled it into a joke but this talking stuff? I'm only learning. Only just starting with Dee and Ingabire, and last thing I want is Jack thinking I'm a head-wired loser. He's still looking at me and OMG, he's so fit my legs are turning to butter.

'I don't mean that. I mean like . . . headspace? Feels like you're flirting . . .' He pauses. 'You've no clue how hard it was to keep my hands to myself when you were this close . . .' He's leaning his face right in for effect when we hear the bathroom lock unclick. As Faith emerges, Jack steps back, angling himself against the dresser. I start combing my already combed hair and check out my black cowboy hat in the mirror. Faith coughs like she needs to announce her presence. We turn and smile. Then we smile proper. She's wearing the T-shirt. Blazoned across her chest are strips of bright colour. Lettering reading clear and proud: *I'm so over the rainbow*. Jack gives her a huge hug. I'm only slightly jealous.

'Did you say you had vodka?' she says.

'Since when did you drink?' says Jack.

I hand her the already opened bottle. She looks at it, looks at us, then takes a huge swig. 'Since tonight. Think I might need it.'

The city centre is swamped with costumes, winter bobble hats and beanies. The night air is cold but clear. Perfect for fireworks. We find Joaquim and Lena at McLaughlin's Hardware on William Street and then lock hands into a snake so we stick together, weaving our way through the crowds to reach the dual carriageway by the River Foyle. No cars tonight. The only traffic on it will be the carnival. The whole length of the quay is jammed. Kids with Poundstretcher glow toys. Cowboys and Indians. Jokers and harlequins. Monks. Pirates and presidents. Toddlers with spider dummies and green dinosaur onesies, hoisted high on their parents' shoulders. Werewolves. Fortnite characters.

Superman and Wonder Woman, arms looped. Four huge Lego men. An old couple in Charlie Chaplin matching outfits. Cookie Monsters. Killer clowns. Stripy convicts. Velvet witches. The atmosphere is pumping. Music blasting from speakers strung up on lamp-posts. Police in their fluorescent yellow jackets lining the road as we wait for the carnival.

Amongst the buzz and chatter, we huddle for warmth. Jack's knuckles touch mine. He keeps them there, looking straight ahead. For a moment, I remember last Halloween. Me. Oran. A shedload of drink. Lounging on the swings in Bull Park until the wee hours. Stupid freezing. Snogging. I think about Ingabire in art therapy. She's always on about mindfulness. Being conscious of how we feel. She calls it 'the Now'. In my Now, Jack's knuckles are still right there by mine. I do miss Oran, but Jack is warm. Present. Maybe Halloween shouldn't be all about the ghosts. I'm liking the warmth in my blood and it's not just vodka. Taking a deep breath, I slowly weave my fingers through Jack's. It doesn't feel like betrayal. It feels . . . exciting. As the blare of rhythm and bass announces the carnival, Jack squeezes my hand.

The five of us stand transfixed. Everything evil and ghoulish is out on parade. I bloody love it. So what if I never rock brainbox sophistication as good as Faith? Sisters is not about competition. Sisters is about togetherness. Sisters are a team. Right now, Faith is rocking that T-shirt. And me? I'm grinning the whole width of my face – even without the Day of the Dead stitching. My hand is warm and, stood here between Jack and Faith, I'm feeling much less . . . haunted.

Chapter 17

FAITH
Londonderry, 31 October 2019

I'm loving the carnival. It's also flipping everything I thought I knew. The Day of the Dead skull face paint? The rainbow T-shirt? Tara is so off-the-scale talented. And thoughtful. Posing different ways, looking in Tara's bathroom mirror, there wasn't one angle that didn't make me smile. Or freak. It felt so right. Yet so wrong. Like my brain, heart and body forgot to be on the same planet. How does a person function when different parts of them hang out in different headspaces?

A stripy orange, white and black serpent inflatable billows over the crowd like an escapee from snakes and ladders. Its fangs and forked tongue lick heads and bobble hats. Our church teaches that Halloween is evil and that being gay, at least being in a gay relationship, is sin. They also teach us to love our enemies, serve others generously and give to charity. An army of kids in red wigs troop past, samba drumming for twirling dancers with decorated umbrellas. They're acting out some legend: stories so old, no one knows if they're true. Is some of my church-teaching myth? Is some meaningful? What do I believe? I'm not sure I know any more what's real. Or even which bit of me I *want* to be real. Maybe it's the vodka. I didn't plan that. After gripping the sides of the washbasin in Tara's bathroom and staring at myself in the T-shirt and face paint, it just seemed . . . necessary.

A choreographed troop of ravens swoop past, pirouetting in

twirls and bows to a backdrop of honky-tonk organ and screams. I'm entranced by blue-eyed black dinosaurs like ginormous stick insects. Their sparkling reptilian limbs and inflatable heads bob under the control of spiky-haired stilt-walkers attacking the crowd, causing *oohs* of delight. I'd no clue Halloween was so creative.

Before this, the only thing I've ever done around Halloween is apples. Apple bobbing, apple pie, toffee apples. Even the whole peel an apple in one go and chuck the peel over your left shoulder to ward off the devil. Dad said it was superstition. The devil was a prowling lion. Letting us think he's just a wee red cartoon with two horns and a pitchfork was all just to make evil seem harmless. The same dad who sneaked in as the tooth fairy to swap the baby teeth under my pillow for shiny coins or who helped Mum fill my Christmas stocking with chocolate money and toys. The dad who's not my real dad but who hugged me into bed and read stories every night through primary school. What would he make of me being here?

Tonight, there's not an apple in sight. I'm not missing them. I hug my arms in round myself to keep my hands warm. Maybe no apples, but I sure as hell am feeling every bit the gooseberry. Joaquim and Lena. Tara and Jack. I smile, watching Jack lean down to speak into Tara's ear. Everything in my heart is glad for what I sense happening. Mega cute. I'm proud to be wearing this T-shirt too but I'm also the only one. Can I ever keep my religious beliefs and the T-shirt? Is there any scenario where I can go beyond just the T-shirt? Find a real relationship? Questions and more questions for which I've no answers. Circles I can't square. Can anyone? My head is so messed right now, wearing my identity on the outside is the most I can manage. Liberating but scary. Like freedom still needs a flak-jacket. But what if I did meet someone? Being out in Londonderry is way different to Armagh. That's still a no go. I tap Jack. Indicate the vodka bottle stashed inside his jacket. He frowns. Mouths, *You OK?* I smile. *Sure.* He passes the bottle. Gestures to keep the bottle low. It's a family event. While I drink, he entwines his fingers back with Tara's. The heat of the alcohol in my throat makes me cough, but it's calming. Makes me glow inside and forget the questions.

Now the carnival's really kicking. The music pumps so loud no one feels the cold. Lena cheers as a glowing earth made from plastic bottle waste orbits its way past us, emblazoned with the words *Wake Up to Climate Change.* A giant willow deer ridden by a skeleton follows, charged after by a horde of whooping Vikings with *How to Train Your Dragon* helmets. Wicker heads from Easter Island. Neptune carrying a glowing egg. Nymphs on water lilies. Finn MacCool and a pipe and drum band. Jack's feet are tapping. Our heads tilt upwards to a hot-air balloon tethered with speakers blasting out feel-good pop and rock. Fifty Highland dancers fling themselves screaming in unison at the crowd. A mechanical raven, built high as a house, scans over people with its neon-pink eyes. Happy chatter carries on the night air. Now Tara's jumping, waving at a girl with pink hair dressed as some kind of crackpot doctor. She's part of a team of performers on bikes, trikes and penny farthings. Every bike sprayed a different vivid colour and all collectively towing a float with a massive inflatable rainbow. Around it dance teenagers in black leather and gothic-themed drag. The girl waves back to Tara.

'It's Dee.' Tara turns to me excited. 'I just realized. You gotta meet Dee.'

As the carnival ends, a huge boom echoes over the water. The crowd turns one-eighty to face the wide river where a barge is anchored for the display. A DJ blasts bass rhythms and beat drops, leading everyone in a countdown to the fireworks. I jostle to see over a pirate with a three-pointed captain's hat. I needn't have worried. Once the show starts, every head in the crowd is strained upwards at the clouds of sparkle. Roars, crackles, bangs, twisters. Tens of thousands of people *oooh* and *aahhhh* for the colour combinations, blasts of glitter and floating neon smoke. We whoop for the big explosions, hush for the fountains of reds, greens and yellows raining down. The finale builds and builds, explosion after explosion radiating across the night sky. I cast my eyes over the oceans of people jamming the dual carriageway and riverbanks. In the previous generations, explosions divided us. Tonight we stand together. Through mass cheering, applause and whistles at the end, the DJ belts out 'Don't Look Back in Anger'.

It's disorientating as the crowd begins to disperse. Swathes of people in groups, hands chain-linked like us in a snake, weaving left and right, zigzagging over roundabouts, up kerbs and between buildings.

'Dee's gonna meet us,' says Tara, glancing at her phone. 'Waterloo Place.'

I'm caught up in the euphoria, but dizzy, concentrating on my feet and keeping a tight grip on Jack's hand. As we turn a corner, I can hear a familiar blast of street preaching through a megaphone. Their Sunday suits and placards are out of place amongst the surge of stormtroopers and zombies. It's not my church, but it has many of the same trappings.

'Change of plan,' says Tara. 'There's Dee.' She steers us over to where the pink-haired girl and at least half the leather-clad teenagers off the rainbow float are gathered. Their chanting is drawing a crowd eager for a spectacle. Through the megaphone, a man is preaching bible verses, the black leather-bound volume clasped upright in his hand. He's met with jeers. I cringe. He means well. His fellow churchmen, and a few women, grip their placards tightly, uncertain of their safety. I don't want my eyes to scan the words on their posters but they draw me in. Messages of being found out by your sins. Messages of hell and damnation. Turn or burn. Old school. Alongside the bible verses, even though the law is now passed, are messages against abortion rights and gay marriage.

'Am I going to hell, mister?' taunts one of the lads with Dee. As he turns and snogs the boy beside him, my head spins. I've never seen a real-life gay kiss before. It's cool, but last week I was in a church group not unlike these preachers. Which side am I on? One of the placard ladies is staring at my T-shirt. Giving me the evil eye. Jack turns. Maybe it's the confusion on my face, but he drops Tara's hand and tugs me closer. I trip over my feet as he tries to pull me on through the crowd, away from the tension. I stop. Dig in my heels. I want to see this. I *need* to see this. I'm trying to process something but my brain is dizzy. This is not his call. Letting go of Jack, I duck and weave my way back through the crowd towards the sound. I hiccup and giggle as I reach the front row. Proud of my freedom. But things are turning nasty. The crowd begins to shift as marshals in high-vis vests approach and suddenly, I'm not so sure I do want to be here. I turn a full three-sixty but everywhere is a sea of faces, scarves and beanie hats. I'm lost. Can't see Jack or Tara or Joaquim or Lena and the turning has my stomach and head all over the place and oh God. I feel sick. Shivering with cold. I scan for any familiar face but it might as well be a *Where's Wally* scene. There are hundreds of people, buildings and streets I don't know. Folk jostling me sideways, forwards, backwards. Still the megaphone blaring and the crowd taunting.

'Go read your own posters,' shouts a girl. 'God is Love.' As she turns away from the protest and preachers, I'm shoved right into her. She does a double take, then smiles. Pixie eyes and pink hair. 'You gotta be Tara's sister,' she says.

My mobile's vibrating in my pocket. Jack phoning on repeat. I don't need to answer. Dee's already spotted them. Arm around my shoulders, she steers me to the soup station in Waterloo Place. Jack is a picture of relief. Tara is all hugs and thank Gods and high fives with Dee. Some of Dee's friends are with us too. Camp as Eurovision and not a care as they queue for free soup. I look at the signage on the station. Street Pastors. This is a church too. Or maybe a group of churches. One of the ladies in a bobble hat catches my eye and smiles. 'You look foundered, pet. You want soup or coffee?' I know she's seen my T-shirt, yet she doesn't seem to care whether the rainbow is for gay rights or Noah's Ark. It's like the megaphone man was in a time warp. The soup warms my fingers and insides and slowly my world turns the right way up.

As we cradle steaming cardboard cups, we huddle, suddenly feeling Baltic now the crowds have dispersed. Some place warm is on the agenda. I'm zoning out in a world of my own as they plot a solution. Like a sheep, I follow, hands shoved into my armpits for warmth as we walk across the Guildhall Square, now empty of markets, and under an arch in the city walls.

Jack nudges me. 'Only other time I was here was for the Apprentice Boys' parade round these walls,' he whispers. He holds a finger over his mouth like it's a secret best kept between us. Flaunting being a Lambeg drummer might not be a wise move. He's not the type to deny his identity, but he'll play it low-key in some circumstances. Lads are like that if they're outnumbered or on unsure ground.

We stand by a building. It's only when we're nearing the front of a queue that it dawns on me: this is a club. I'm not eighteen. None of us are. No one else seems to have realized. I'm about to ask when the bouncer eyes us. One look at the height of Jack and he's waved through. Tara's next.

'You're hardly going to stop my girlfriend?' Jack says.

Digging in her back pocket, Tara pulls out student ID. The bouncer glances at it and waves her through. Then it's me. I'm stuck. Clueless.

'For gawd's sake,' says Tara. 'She's my identical twin.'

I stare at her, then cop on. Holding my head high, I march right on through, then, safe in the club, dissolve into giggles in Tara's arms.

'Don't you ever go out?' says Lena.

'Just bowling or to the cinema,' I say. 'Never clubbing. But more than that, tonight's my first time coming out too.'

Dee slaps me on the back. 'Seriously, girl? We gotta get you a drink.'

I am dancing. Dancing with three girls and two teenagers who look like they want to be girls or maybe they are or maybe they just don't care and I don't care either. I lose track of time, worries and drinks and I don't care about that either. My head happy spins and moves with the rest of me, in time to the music. Somewhere, Lena and Joaquim are in a pair and, standing with our drinks by a bar table, Jack and Tara are vibing ever more togetherness and I'm grand. I'm no longer feeling left out because dancing here, everyone's in a circle. The circle isn't about pairs, it's just about being. Being and smiling. Being and laughing. Being and dancing. It's a circle that doesn't need to be squared. It's fine as it is. In it, I'm fine as I am. The beat is so loud I can't even hear myself belting out the lyrics but we're all punching the air in unison.

I'm half tranced, high on adrenalin, when a supermodel in a 1920s French flapper costume walks right over to me, parting the other dancers like some Red Sea Moses. I recognize the face but my brain can't place her, so I just grin stupid. Maybe it looks sexy cos she smiles.

'I can't believe it,' she says, hand cupped direct over my ear so I can catch her words. 'What's the deal? Are you gay? I remember Oran said one time you guys fell out about, you know . . . going the whole distance. I never thought . . . Like, holy shit, Tara. You're a lipstick lezzie?'

It clicks. Megan. The one from the kayak. The one from the fire. I shake my head, exaggerated, not quite sure how to react to her words. 'I'm not Tara,' I say. Pivoting Megan around, I point to where Jack and Tara are leaning real close into each other over at the edge of the dance floor. Jack has a pint in one hand, his shoulder up against the brick wall. Tara's holding a bottle of something blue, up on her tiptoes to chat into his ear. So far, I haven't seen them snog, unlike Lena and Joaquim who are lost down each other's throats and intent on causing church scandal with fishnet tights and a dog collar.

'OMG,' says Megan. Her words slur. 'You're the Armagh ones. The Prods.' She's smiling like she's no clue how that just labelled me. Then she glances back at Jack and Tara. His hand is on her waist.

'Isn't Tara just so outrageous?' she says. 'Like she's amazing. Never gives a shit what anyone thinks. And, I mean, I only heard recently myself, but with everything that happened to her nan way back, you'd imagine Tara would never go there with a Protestant but like . . . she's so brave.'

Dee has stopped dancing now too and is by my shoulder. 'There a problem?' she says. I shrug, my brain fogged like it can't process stuff. Megan just turns and waltzes away towards a group made up of a stormtrooper, James Bond and a bad cross between Tarzan and Fred Flintstone. I watch as she points out Jack and Tara. Animated hand gestures. I'm thinking about Jack and the *sshhhh* about him being in a band as we traipsed across Guildhall Square like it was just an *us* joke. Suddenly it doesn't seem so secret or so safe. But Dee and her friends are here with me and, right until Megan smeared it, for the first time it felt like I fitted. The club is warm and Dee's crowd are brilliant. I look at her. She's so out. So confident. So . . . medical-looking. I study her Halloween outfit.

'What actually *is* your costume?' I say.

'Scariest thing I could think of.' She does fake spooky hands and waggles the pocket watch like hypnosis. 'A conversion therapist. One of them religious nut jobs who thinks therapy makes gay people straight.'

'Oh,' I say, thinking about her 'God is Love' outburst. 'Does religion matter to you?'

'Not an ounce. Why?'

'Cos . . .' I'm having to focus hard to string together my thoughts, never mind a sentence. There's an uneasiness in me trying to find words. Stuff about me. Stuff about coming out. Stuff about God. Most of all, it's the stuff Megan said. I'm not even sure whether she meant it bad or how it is between her and Tara since the campfire fight, but the way she called me and Jack 'Prods' and pointed out Jack and Tara to the group of lads, I feel like Jack should know. At least that way, he can make his own call. I study Dee's costume. There's so much I need to learn. So much Dee could teach.

She pulls a funny face. 'What's going on in there?' She taps my head.

I sigh. *I wish I knew.* 'I think I need another drink,' I say. 'And . . . I think Jack and Tara might be better out of here but . . . I'd rather stay.'

Chapter 18

TARA
Derry, 31 October 2019

Jack's still edgy as we queue for the taxi, sliding his hands on his jeans, looking over his shoulder.

'Faith will be grand,' I say, for the billionth time. 'She's with Dee and about five others. You've got to let her make her own choices.'

'But she's sixteen.'

'She's older than me.'

'Yeah.' He smiles. 'But you're streetwise.'

I go hands on hips thinking, *Right. You want streetwise? I'm gonna play you.* 'Wanna go back to the pub?'

He hesitates. Lifts the blue bit in my hair and lets it run through his fingers. 'No.' He grins. Flashes his eyes at me, all rascal.

I'm reckoning it wasn't just me saw the positive in the whole maybe-sectarian thing with Megan. Faith was a bit garbled on the message, but I could see it ticking over two ways in Jack's head. It was an opportunity for me and him to get offside on our own. If Jack felt we should go, but Faith wanted to stay, it would only make sense that I needed to go with him . . . As Jack had toyed with the decision, Dee winked. Nudged me like 'thank me later, you know you wanna'.

It's freezing in William Street. I rub my fingers and blow on them to get the circulation going. Smooth as can be, Jack reaches

161

out and cups my hands in his. Holds them to his mouth and breathes warm air over them. The whole time, he's like turquoise butter-wouldn't-melt eyes staring. Straight. At. Me. I'm trying to act sophisticated and come up with a line, but my brain is stuck in some cheeseball-Hollywood about how I can't even feel the cold any more.

'You're impressively calm today, Miss Connolly,' he says.

'Really?' It's taking every nanodrop of self-discipline not to dissolve in a puddle at his feet. He tilts my black hat at an angle. Lets a hand drop casually onto my shoulder.

'Come to think of it, I haven't even seen you smoke.'

'I quit,' I say. 'No more tasting of ashtrays.'

His eyes go double-intensity-smoulder. Like seriously. Who teaches boys this stuff? He tilts his head, cute-quizzical in the sombrero. 'You got any scientific proof of that?'

'Eh?' Three Rockshore beers and my mental prowess is belly-flopped.

And then. Then. OMG. OMG. This. Is. Actually. Happening. His hand slides from my shoulder down to the small of my back and he pulls me in. Gently. Slowly. Leaning. Leaning. Chest touching chest. Mouth touching mouth. We. Are. SNOGGING. He tastes ELECTRIC. His lips are soft but determined. Our tongues playing. And if I thought I was melting before, now my body is going full-scale thermonuclear and he better keep holding me cos otherwise I'll be peeled off the pavement in the morning all rubbery with the post-Halloween grunge.

In the taxi queue we're like a kiss-fest-tango. Snog. Shuffle up. Snog. When we reach the front of the queue, we almost fall in the taxi on top of each other, then manage a bit of sideways seat shuffling to regain some dignity in front of the driver. Jack's making me giggle, sliding his hand across the seat and tickling his fingers across my thigh. I turn and look at him and bust out laughing. Then he dissolves into giggles too. Our face paint is smeared like Picasso madness. I snog him again and I don't even give a shit about the taxi driver. She must see this glory every night anyway.

On the front doorstep, I pause, wanting to explain about how it's wild important to be quiet. How Nan will probably have the telly blasting *Graham Norton*. But Jack lifts me right off my feet. I squeal with the shock, then wrap my legs tight round his waist. He is so strong. And he is snogging ME. Full on. He slides me down till my feet touch the ground.

'I'm a bit drunk . . .' he says.

'Me too,' I say. 'We gotta be quiet. OK?'

He nods. Mega serious. I turn the key and we tiptoe in. I motion to him to take off his boots. Then I have to bite my finger hard to not blurt a laugh.

What? he mouths.

I'm minding what Megan said. Jack's boots are HUGE. I shake my head like *nothing* and lead him by the hand up to my room, tiptoe-light-treading the staircase and avoiding the squeaky step near the top. When we reach my bedroom, Jack clicks the door shut behind him and for a moment, we just stand there, chests heaving with adrenalin and realization.

We are together.

On our own.

In. My. Bedroom.

Jack puts both hands either side of my face and we kiss. Long. Slow. Forever. When we stop, both of us are, like, lip-biting and then hands over mouths fecking-don't-giggle. The make-up is smeared chronic. Jack does the time-out hand signal. He heads for the bathroom and I go for the make-up remover at my dresser.

When I'm done, he's still not back. In my socks, I sneak across the hall. There's a slit of light where he hasn't quite closed the bathroom door and, if there ever was a God, I'm pure sinner. He's not, like, naked, jeans still on, but his T-shirt is at his feet and he's at the basin, soaping his face clean. I watch the ripple of muscle across his back as he towels dry. He stoops to lift his T-shirt. Then he turns. Sees me gawping. Hesitates. Unsure.

We look at each other through the slightly open door. He holds the T-shirt to his chest, then lowers it. Switches out the bathroom light and walks to me in the hall. Against the banister, we kiss again. I stroke the beard-shadow on his jaw and motion to my room.

'Tara,' he says, as we shut the door for the second time. 'We're a bit drunk.'

'Yeah,' I say. 'We are.'

We stand just inside the door, snogging. He glances at my bed but says nothing. Wraps his arms round my bum and pulls me close, slow dancing even though there's no music. I lift my arms round his neck and lose myself in the turquoise of his eyes, willing his hands to go higher. I can sense he's trying not to. Like I'm the temptress. It's me that pulls him to the bed. For a few minutes we just lie there, on top of the duvet. Clothes still on. Except for his T-shirt.

Instinct takes over. I smooth my hands over his biceps. He's so strong he could do anything he wants right now, but he doesn't. He lets me push him onto his back and I lie on top of him, my elbows propping up my chin on his chest.

'You're so cute,' I say.

'Cute?'

'Like manly cute. I can't believe you actually . . . like me.'

He rubs the back of my thigh. Chews his top lip mad sexy.

164

'You really have no idea,' he says. 'You're stunning. Like original art.'

A wee touch of devilry sneaks into me. 'How come you never fancied Faith?' I say.

'What?' he says. 'I know I'm a Prod but I'm not fecking royalty. No way I fancy my cousin. Besides, you're nothing like her.'

'We look mostly the same.'

'I can tell the difference easy.' He pauses, thinking. 'Maybe it's cos I've known Faith all my life. It's not just the hair or how you talk. She moves different. Everything about her is different. She's like tame and you're . . . wildfire. Fierce. Her eyes are different too.'

'No, they're not,' I say. On this, I know I'm right. I studied them real close again when I did her face paint. Reaching over to the bedside light, I sit up, cross my legs and look at him like, no way you're taking me on over this. 'My eyes and hers are identical.'

He studies me right back and all over again has me pure melted just with looking. He shakes his head. Grins. 'Wrong,' he says. 'You're only after proving my point. Your eyes are completely different. Different in how they look at *me*. Only *your* eyes send me those kinds of messages.'

Heat blushes across my cheeks.

'Do you even realize I feel like the luckiest man on the planet right now?'

Oran never said stuff like that. The thought sneaks in cold. It was always how I could get lucky with him if I played my cards right. Right now I don't want to think about Oran. I tangle my legs with Jack's. Press onto him. He's not lying about feeling lucky. I can feel him on my thigh, even through our jeans. I close my eyes and move. Sliding. Rhythmic. Trying to decide. Trying to think straight. Maybe this is not about thinking. Maybe it's just about being. Even with clothes on I can feel our breathing getting shallower. And OMG. My blood's a riot. Warming. Hotter. Hotter still. There are places I don't know yet. Places we could go. Together. And I've never been anywhere. Anywhere close to this. Except one time. One time. On my sixteenth birthday. In the back seat. Of a car. Oran. Saying we should. Saying why? Why didn't I want to? Saying he'd nothing else to give me. For my birthday. It was a present. His present. To me. Didn't I see that? Didn't I see? Was I scared? It wouldn't hurt. Not too much. Sixteen. It meant we should. Other girls would. I shouldn't think. Just go. With the flow. And let him. But I didn't. I didn't. I didn't.

I stop moving.

Freeze.

The world goes still.

Jack looks at me. Confused. 'Did you . . . you know?'

I'm palms digging into my eyes and shaking my head and OMG. OMG. Apocalyptic mortified. Jack is right here on my bed with me. This is hell-open-up-now-and-swallow-me for I've screwed up everything. Screwed up because Oran's face is blaring loud into my brain. Just like he always does. Wrecking everything. Wrecking. Every. Single. Thing.

I fall off Jack, onto the duvet and bury my face into the pillow. The sobs take over. Horrible, ugly sobs that wrack my whole body. Jack goes quiet. Lies really still. I listen to his breathing. After a while, he turns towards me and rubs my back. Just gentle. I don't know how long we lie there. Saying nothing. He smooths my hair. Not come-on. Just comfort. Then I feel him sit up and put his T-shirt back on and lie back on the pillow.

'Are you OK?' he says after an eternity. His voice wobbles.

I turn and look at him. Expecting anger. Oran was angry. Angry when I said no. It wasn't a no. It was a not yet. A let-me-think-about-it. He'd broke up with me then. For two weeks. Then we'd got back together. Right before it all went crazy. Jack doesn't look angry. He's looking . . . scared. Like he's done something wrong.

'Tara, are you OK?' he says again.

I nod. Then shake my head. 'Are you mad with me?' I say.

He blinks. 'No.' He strokes my hair, looking into my eyes. 'What's wrong?'

And then I spill. Spill everything. The words tumble out and they won't stop flowing and I'm telling him everything. Everything about me and Oran and how he'd wanted to since I was fifteen and I wouldn't and how he kept asking and I just wasn't ready and then he went manic, manic on drugs and crazy on cars and then, then he got shot and had to leave and, and, and how if I'd only slept with him it wouldn't have happened. It wouldn't have happened. If. I'd. Only. Then he wouldn't be dead. He'd still be alive.

Jack's staring at me. His dark hair is gorgeous against the pillow and all I can think is how I've messed this up. So. Bad. He's seventeen. Like every boy I know expects it at seventeen. Instead, I've bent Jack's head with information overload. Never talk to boys about other boys is the rule. It dents their ego. I didn't mean to. I want Jack. Want him like I've never ever felt about anyone. But that's all blown. He's staring like I'm some psychotic eejit that doesn't know which way is up and doesn't appreciate the sheer gorgeousness that is him and it'll serve me right if I'm a virgin for life cos that's what I deserve.

'Tara,' he says, rubbing his thumb across my forehead. 'I know this'll sound crass but . . . you're not to blame. It's not your fault Oran died.'

I sit bolt upright. 'What would you know?' I hiss. 'You weren't there. You don't understand.'

He slides himself up against the headboard. Looks at me right in the eyes. Gulps. Then . . . then he puts his arm over his eyes and his shoulders shift and I know he's crying. Trying not to show it, but he is. I reach out and gently lift his arm down. See the tracks of his tears and his moist eyes – still looking straight into mine. 'Maybe I do understand,' he says. 'Trauma and stuff. Not everything, but at least a bit.'

I don't know how late it is any more. Whether Nan still has the telly on downstairs. Someone suspended time. I'm stroking Jack's arm and he's telling me how he found the noose. Mid-November. Six weeks before his parents split. Right there on the floor of the shed, below a broken rafter. How he knew. Knew from doing pull-ups off those rafters that they didn't break easy. Not unless you weighed more than he did. It could only be his da. But Jack didn't know how to start that conversation with him. His da who blew hot and cold Loyalist for no reason. His da who was proud of Jack Lambeg-drumming in the band but who one day smashed in the skins on his drum only to replace them two weeks later. The da who he'd thought would love the idea of him quitting school after GCSEs and joining the army, but who instead went ballistic. Almost frog-marched him back into his A levels even though he'd never breathed a word about education being important. And then, after Christmas, Jack's mum left. And his sisters. And Jack stayed. Stayed because he'd seen that noose but never told a soul. Stayed because then maybe his da wouldn't try again.

Jack lets a tear fall. Doesn't even try to hide it this time. Then he smooths my hair back with his thumb and kisses me real gentle on my forehead. Leans back against the bedhead and holds both my hands in his, looking at me like heart-on-sleeve, *do you get this, Tara? Oran's suicide is NOT. YOUR. FAULT.*

In the quiet. In the dark. We spoon. Jack's arms around me. Shaped into each other. Clothes on. Just being together. Slowly, everything starts to feel OK. Slowly, I turn to him and smooth his hair. The little spikes of it at the front. I kiss him and taste salt. He kisses me back and it's beautiful.

'Why's your dad like that?' I say.

'Dunno,' he says. 'Something from when he was younger. He used to argue about it with Mum. Always worse this time of year.'

I snuggle my head into his chest and hear his heartbeat.

'Tara,' he says after a while. 'I didn't mean this to be like a one-night thing. Honest to God. I . . . really like you. Can I see you again? We can take it however slow you want. No pressure.'

I suck the blue bit in my hair. Then I just hug him. Real tight. 'Course I wanna see you again,' I say. 'You're epic.'

We're still all hug-snuggling when it happens. Jack hears it first. The key in the front door. I didn't give Faith a key. There's only one person it can be, but how? She's supposed to be working. Jack tenses. Footsteps in the hall. I hold one finger to my lips. Maybe if we stay real quiet . . .

'Whose are the boots?' Mum hollers to Nan.

Shit.

My brain whizzes, excuse-inventing sideways-thinking. Jack grabs my arm, his eyes wide. I'm trying to vibe him like Mam is scary, but just switch on your cool. We didn't actually DO anything. Not really. We're still dressed. But he's up and motioning me to the window. Nosey-neighbouring out the side of the curtains. Because OMG. Ultra OMG WTF. Dee and her friend are on the footpath, steering Faith, a completely plastered Faith, all wiggles and giggles and fallings over, onto our step. The doorbell ding-a-dings like there's no tomorrow.

Holy-Mother-of-God-and-All-the-Saints-in-Heaven. Maybe there will be no tomorrow.

Mam opens the front door.

'Oh. Hi, Miss Connolly,' says Dee. 'Is Tara in?'

Stunned silence downstairs thick as treacle. I'm almost eating my fist. So wired, I desperately need to pee. There's no choice but to face this. Head on. I smooth my clothes and hair. Lifting Jack's hand, I pull him along the hall to the top of the stairs. Breathe. 'Hey,' I say, peering over the banister.

Mam's head turns. Her face drains of blood and her mouth opens like one of those Scream masks the wee kids wear. She takes in me and Jack, then turns back to Faith. Looks at her face. The rainbow T-shirt. Then back to me. Dee senses the get-out-fast vibe and scarpers for the taxi. Mam still looks like she's clocked a ghost. Faith giggles, staggers into the wall. Nan jukes out of the living room – clearly Graham Norton isn't for competing. Then it's a blur. Faith says, 'Oh.' Fires her hand up to her mouth and lurches towards the kitchen.

As we hear her puke, Jack runs, taking the stairs two at a time. 'Sorry, Mrs Connolly. So, so sorry. I'll sort this.'

With heaps of lip-biting, a mega-dose of apology eyes and oh-my-God-please-don't-kill-me grovel, I sidle down the stairs towards Mam and Nan. 'Did Emer say about the girl at the residential, Mam? The one who looked like me?'

Mam nods. Arms hung by her side. 'I never . . . I don't think I took it in, pet. Don't think I wanted to . . .' She holds out her hand like the reconciliation statue at the end of the bridge.

'I'm sorry, Mam. I was going to say. I just hadn't worked out how.' I swallow. Not sure if she'll still be holding out that hand after the next bit. 'That's Faith,' I say. 'She's my half-sister.'

Mam nods some more, like she's still processing this. I reach her hand and she pulls me in tight. Hugs me so much I don't know whether this is for me or her. 'Who's the boy?' she says.

'Jack,' I say, watching him clean vomit off the kitchen lino with a wad of tissues. 'He's kind of Faith's cousin but actually not cos Faith's da isn't actually her da either. We did this DNA thing . . .'

'I think I'll put on the kettle,' says Nan.

Chapter 19

FAITH
Londonderry, 31 October 2019

The table is swimming, or it might be the chair. Maybe the room. They won't even need to preach a sermon on alcohol. I am not drinking ever again, amen. Sat head on my arms at the table in Tara's kitchen, I know I'm a mess. The lights are too bright to look but Tara's nan is clattering mugs and filling a kettle at the tap and Jack has found bleach and is on his knees, wiping where I didn't quite make it to the sink. For some perverted reason, it makes me think of the bible story of Mary pouring perfume on Jesus's feet and wiping it with her hair.

Tonight was the best. So much fun. Me, out in public. Out without disguising who I am. Face paint, yes, but no hiding. No hiding that I'm gay. I hiccup and hold my head. Oh God. I really am lesbian *and* I've celebrated Halloween with every bone in my body. Am I still Christian? All I know is that Tara painted me like Death and I've never felt more alive. It was all great, until it wasn't. I haven't felt so much like, like . . . me. Not since I hit puberty and slowly began to realize. Truth is, the slow bit wasn't the realizing, it was the admitting, the owning of it. To myself.

I raise my head a whisper off the table and rub my eyes, adjusting to the light. Jack's now in the far corner by the pedal bin, hair tousled more than usual and wearing a concerned, sheepish look. Tara's acting the model citizen, helping her nan hoke tea bags out of the mugs and stirring in milk and sugar. Sat right opposite me at the kitchen table is Tara's mam.

'I'm so sorry, Mrs Connolly,' I say.

'*Ms* Connolly,' she says. 'But call me Erin.'

I nod. 'Yes, Ms Connolly.'

There's a wry smile on her face. 'Faith, tell me honestly. Are you just drunk? Did you take anything?'

'Like . . . steal?' I don't understand. The room still spins.

Chairs scrape and mugs clunk the table.

'She means drugs,' says Tara.

'God, no,' I say. My words slur. 'Drugs are illegal.'

Jack slides a mug of tea over and I clasp my hands round it for heat, suddenly aware that I'm shivering. 'Ms Connolly,' he says. 'It probably is just drink. Tonight was her first time drinking alcohol and it was spirits. I should've stopped her . . .'

'No.' Tara's mam glances at Jack. 'Chaperones died in the dark ages. So long as they're her choices, she has every right to make them.' She looks at me. 'And to learn from them if they're wrong.' She sits back on the wooden chair, eyebrows rearranging themselves somewhere between bemused and reflecting.

I try to sip the tea, but my hands are shaky.

Tara's nan disappears, then returns with a blanket to drape over my shoulders. 'Well, I for one saw this lass make a brave choice tonight,' she says. 'Much as I don't know ye, petal, I suspect there's a lot going on inside there.' She smooths my hair. Not for the first time, I'm not following this conversation. How could Tara's nan have seen me before now?

She smiles. 'Ye were on the telly, doll. The late news.' She points to my T-shirt. 'Fair play to ye – giving it lilty with your pals to those religious nuts.'

'Eh?' My brain is still fudge. A chair scrapes. Jack's on his feet. 'TV? We were on TV?'

'Just Faith here, and her friend with the pink hair. Wearing her colours proud.'

'Shit,' says Jack.

Tara's mam gives him a look.

'Excuse my French, Mrs— Ms— Erin . . .' He paces the kitchen.

'OK,' says Tara's mam. 'What am I missing?'

Then my mobile rings. And Jack's mobile. He's quicker on the draw than me. 'Bloody hell.' Then looks at Tara's mam. 'Sorry. Sorry . . . it's my Uncle Philip. Faith's dad.' He lets the phone ring out. Finally, I fish my mobile out of my bag and plop it on the table. Eight messages. Two from my parents.

Missed call. You were called today at 10:37 p.m.

Faith. Where are you? Call us.

Then six from Bethany.

OMG your dad is on the phone.

What do you want me to say?

Missed call. You were called today at 10:43 p.m.

Call me. Quick.

I'm grounded. You were on the news.

Praying for you. Mum says your parents are driving to Londonderry.

I stare at my phone. It's nearly 1 a.m. It rings again. So does Jack's. He sighs, swears under his breath and walks to the hall to answer it. I feel shaky, like I'm not connected to this reality. My phone stops ringing. A tear plops into my tea. Apparently, I'm crying. I put my fingers to my cheek and feel the wet. Half a conversation filters through the kitchen door. *Yes . . . I know . . . I'm sorry . . . You're right . . . Sorry . . . With erm, friends . . . Londonderry . . . Cityside . . . Understood . . . Sorry . . . I'll text you the address . . .*

The hallway goes quiet. It's a full five minutes before Jack opens the door. My heart is racing. He leans on the frame, face pale. 'They're at Bready,' he says. 'They reckon fifteen, twenty minutes tops.' He stuffs his mobile in his pocket and studies the kitchen ceiling. 'They're raging with me. Livid.'

Tara slides back her chair, then goes to Jack and hugs him. 'It's OK,' she says. 'You'll be OK.' She glances at her mum. 'They've stuff upstairs . . .' Her mum nods.

As they leave, the trembling starts. First my hands, then arms, then legs. My mouth is dry. I reach for the tea but instead, I slide off the chair and find myself in a ball on the floor. My chest hurts. I can't breathe. It's like I'm choking. If the room was swimming before, I'm not even sure I'm in it now.

In an instant, Tara's mum is kneeling beside me. Hand on my forehead. 'Breathe,' she says. 'Breathe. In. Slow. Out. Slow.'

Jesus help me. My whole world is shaking. I'm dying. Dying. 'Hold my hand. Squeeze it. Good girl. Breathe. Slow. Breathe.'

I whimper. My whole body is a ball of heat and this must be a stroke or a heart attack. I'm trying to think of the symptoms but all I feel is pain. Fear.

'Breathe. Calm. Squeeze my hand again. Faith? You hear me? Now breathe. Steady. In. Out. In. Out. Slow.'

Racing footsteps down the stairs. Commotion in the kitchen as Tara's nan shooshes back Jack and Tara. 'Don't crowd her.'

For minutes, I'm spiralling, sweating, stomach churning, then it begins to settle. I blink and see Tara's mam smiling down at me, eyes calm. 'Faith,' she says. 'Breathe slowly. Keep breathing. This is a panic attack. You're safe. Just breathe. It'll pass.' She's looking at me deeply now. Studying me. Studying my hair. Worry lines squiggle across her forehead but she keeps smiling.

Slowly the ringing in my ears dulls and the floor feels solid. She helps me sit up with my back against the wall.

'You're going to be fine. But . . . pet, if there's anything worrying you, you should talk to someone. Hear me? Your parents will be here soon. Talk to them.'

I groan. 'That's the whole problem.' Tara's mum sits back on her haunches, and then my tears flood. 'I can't tell them.' I tug at my T-shirt. 'They'll hate me. Everything about me is wrong. I don't make sense any more. Nothing does.'

'Oh,' she says. 'I see. But they already know, honey. They saw you on the news.'

'They can't know. It's not fair. I'm not ready. I don't even know what to say and . . . and . . . I'm drunk. I wanted to do it my way, in my own time . . .'

'They'll still love you. Keep calm now. Don't panic.'

My head twirls and twirls and I'm tugging at the T-shirt, fighting with my own drunk coordination, limbs flailing. 'Get this off. I need this off. I'm not me . . . not yet . . . I can't . . . I want to choose . . .'

'Sexual orientation isn't a choice,' says Tara's mam. 'It's who you are.'

'But I need to choose . . . At least the time . . .'

The doorbell rings. I scream. The sound of it jolts me. My arms flop as my eyes scour the kitchen wildly. I need escape. 'Help me,' I say, but I know nothing can help. I'm a lost cause and this is Judgement Day.

'Jack,' says Tara. 'Close your eyes.'

She strips off her own T-shirt and kneels beside me in her black bra. 'You do have a choice. Maybe your parents didn't see you on the news. It was dark. Maybe they saw me. Get it? Your call.' She holds out the long-sleeved skeleton top. My eyes focus.

I understand. I breathe. Over her shoulder, I see Jack, failing miserably not to peek, particularly at Tara. The doorbell rings again. I nod. As we swap T-shirts, Tara's nan shuffles to the door. Her mum is moving the other way. Backwards. Backwards, until she hits the kitchen wall and looks like she's braced ready to see a ghost. All this time I'd never thought about it. How she might be feeling. She has been like a mother. Or a nurse. When the door opens, I hear Dad. I watch Tara's mum. When she sees him, the colour goes back into her face and she relaxes. Even if we didn't have the DNA result, she's just confirmed, Dad, Philip, is definitely not Tara's father.

My brain goes woozy again with emotion and exhaustion. There are conversations, polite and curt between the adults, abrupt with Jack. My mother's arms hug me, help me to the car. I don't even remember looking back to wave but as we drive in the dark, I glance across the back seat to Jack. He has one knee pulled up to his chin, his head drooped onto it, eyes crinkled tight shut. Nothing is spoken in the car. Everything is unsaid.

Chapter 20

TARA
Derry, 1 November 2019

When I wake, my brain is groggy. Vodka, beer and blue stuff in a bottle. What even was that? Rolling onto my stomach, I bury my face in the pillow. OMG. Bliss. I smile into myself and stretch my toes. Definite. It still smells of Jack. His hair. His aftershave. I hold the fabric tight to my face and imagine kissing him until my stomach goes McFlurry with tingles. Judging by the lack of traffic hum on our street, it's still early. I reach for my phone. 6 a.m. Bedraggled vampires and crumpled zombies across the city will be sneaking home from other-worldliness and misadventures hoping to evade their Derry mammies. At least that's one worry I don't have. My mam already knows it all.

The tone was more resignation than grilling after Faith's parents left. An exhausted shock. I'd watched Mam take two paracetamol and douse her face in cold water at the kitchen sink, the dark rings under her eyes back with a vengeance. Knackered and unsure what bollocking might yet be unleashed, all I could do was gawp. She looked grey.

'Never a dull moment,' said Nan. 'Are you OK, Erin?'

'I had to sign out sick,' said Mam. 'Takes its toll eventually. Too many shifts. Constant understaffing.' She dried off with a tea towel and hung it on the drawer handle. 'Don't know what to make of all this. Not sure I can take much more.'

Nan moved first. Then, when it was apparent I wasn't on a

ticket to a hiding, I followed. We did the Connolly bear hug. Me, Nan and Mam, hugging tight in the kitchen like we always do in tough times when there are no words. Food bank days. Bank letter days. Disability benefits inquisitions. Mam rallied and ruffled my hair. 'Tomorrow,' she said. 'We'll talk about this tomorrow.'

'Are you raging?'

She'd kissed my forehead. 'No,' she said. 'Not with you, anyway. Jaded with minimum wage, good-for-nothing politicians and religious headcases who have girls like Faith so terrified. But I love my girl.'

Then Nan smoothed Mam's hair, one mam to another. 'Go rest,' she said.

Us Connollys aren't a big family but when our world is tight, so are we.

I allow myself one last inhale of everything Jack off the pillow, then swing my legs to the floor, wiping sleep from my eyes. Somewhere in the back of my skull the idea is hatching, forming with a sense of urgency. In the wee hours, before we'd traipsed stupid-tired to bed, Mam had said we would talk today. I want that more than anything now. But not just was-I-or-wasn't-I-with-Jack interrogations and banana revision lessons with my cheeks gone lava. The conversations I want are hardcore. For that, I'm going to need indisputable evidence and, hangover or no hangover, I know exactly where I'm hunting. It's Cluedo time and this game starts in the attic. With the wedding dress.

PJs and slipper socks are not the best combo for the chill under our eaves but I've got to work fast and quiet. My first move is the red suitcase. I twist the copper clasps and lift the lid, shining in the beam from my mobile. The white lace is still beautiful. Running my fingertips over the soft material, I wonder, Mam's or Nan's? I can't tell, but they can. No more secrets. I want the truth – even if it hits hard. As soundlessly as possible, I drag the case over to the hatch to lower down later. Then I turn back to the dusty boxes and piles of junk. This attic has more secrets – I can sense it. The tingling in my blood is entirely different to last night with Jack. Not a lover now. A hunter.

I start in the corner with the papers and boxes of crockery. Same as I did in August, except this time I've switched on my brain. The newspapers wrapping these are old but the contents of the boxes are new. It's not just everyday plates and mugs. Some of it is crystal. Wine glasses and a vase. Why don't we use these? Why eat off bargain-store mismatched plates when we've a secret stash of upper-crust tableware? Then I twig. These are wedding gifts. Unused wedding gifts. Carefully, I unwrap a large bowl. It's nice, but that's not what I'm interested in. The yellowed newspaper tells me more – a sheet from the *Derry Journal*. An article about bombings and the bravery of emergency services. I unwrap a wine glass – images of blast debris outside a Droppin Well nightclub in Ballykelly. Another glass from the same set – dead horses on a road in Hyde Park, London. I keep unwrapping, reading, unwrapping, staring, unwrapping, learning, until I'm sat in the centre of a wide circle of crockery, and everywhere, sheets of uncrumpled newspaper. One year anniversary articles on the Hunger Strikes. Arrests. Protests. Roadblocks. Checkpoints. Blood on pavements. Blankets over bodies amongst rubble. Army. Police. Balaclavas and guns. IRA. UVF. Republicans. Loyalists. Catholics. Protestants. Shootings. Bombings. Disappearances. Funerals. Children walking behind hearses. Men shouldering coffins. Murder. Murder. Murder. How did I not know it was this bad? Why did no one say? It never really sank in before. The Troubles weren't just 'trouble' – where did they even get that name? The lads are always full of *freedom* and *Ireland* swagger. What I'm seeing on these pages is war. War on the streets. Streets I recognize.

I sit with my arms wrapped round my ankles and knees pulled in tight, partly because I'm thinking, partly because if I move, it could trigger a bull-in-a-china-shop-style calamity. After a while, I shift gingerly to my knees and wrap everything up again, plate by plate, glass by glass. The tops of the pages have different dates, but the year in all of them is 1982. As I repack the boxes almost prayerfully, my head does the mental maths. Not far off forty years ago. Mam wasn't yet born but she grew up in this. In 1982, Nan was twenty-three. Mam graced the planet in 1983. There's only one potential owner of the wedding dress and, if I'm guessing right, Nan was already pregnant, but there are riddles I can't solve. What happened to the wedding? More to the point, who was the groom?

I'm still reflective when I turn to the sports bags, jammed with textbooks. Flicking through them, everything is medical. Anatomy and physiology. Nursing. First aid. The ring binders are Mam's – I recognize the handwriting, but this is beyond school. Was Mam a student? If she was at university, why didn't she tell me about it? Why didn't she qualify? Sitting back on my hunkers on the floorboards, I look at my own hands holding the files. No Sherlock Holmes brain blitz needed. The answer's clear. Mam dropped out because she got pregnant. She quit because of me. I set a textbook on 'Nursing Fundamentals' on top of the red suitcase. This stuff's good but it's no holy grail. What I need are photographs, especially photographs of Mam in her late teens. I was born in 2003. Mam was nineteen. Who was she hanging out with? Especially, which boys?

My eyes are drawn to the far corner where I found the black

hat in August. The pile of scrapbooks is calling me, teasing me, like, do-you-really-wanna-know? Manoeuvring round mounds of cardboard and under rafters, I'm thinking about Jack finding that rope. It's not just my family that has secrets. So does his. And Faith's. I start at the top, the dust making me sneeze as I leaf through pages but, although they bring smiles and memories, these scrapbooks are not evidence. They're my primary school projects. Egyptians and pyramids. Ancient Rome. Studies of the Normans in Ireland with motte-and-bailey castles designed in matchsticks glued to the page. Always more attention in my drawings than the writing. How come we did that history and not the *Derry Journal* stuff? Once upon a time, pre-hormones, I used to ace school. Not pure swot but good enough. I sigh and plonk down on my bum.

A glint of light angles up from the hall. The sun is up and soon Nan and Mam will be too. So many boxes. So little time. *Think. You have a brain, Tara. Use it.* I close my eyes. I am a Connolly, just like Mam and Nan. Where would I put something never to be found? Where do Connollys never look? I breathe, in through my nose, out through my mouth, just like Mam told Faith last night, and the way Ingabire says to do when I need calm. It's not a big house. Room by room, I think through each space. Places I used to crawl into playing hide and seek. Places I stashed fake ID or booze. No one ditches all their memories. I blink. There is one place. One thing that has never fitted in our house. It's not even in the attic. I see it every day and I've never opened it or given it a second thought. Hiding in plain sight on a shelf in the living room.

It's impossible to be completely quiet lowering myself, a suitcase and the textbook into the hallway below. Posh houses would have a ladder, we've the wooden-chair-gymnastics approach requiring both nerve and luck. I land with a thud and crouch, waiting to see if anyone stirs. So far so good. Evidence in hand, I head for the living room and stare at the huge leather-bound black book under the fake pot plant on the shelf over the telly. An illustrated family bible. It could be in Latin for all I know. Staring at it, the doubts flood in. Probably, there's nothing in it but God stuff, thees and thous, dos and don'ts. Fifty reasons why I'm eternally hellbound. I think it was given to Mam at my baptism. It takes a stretch on my tiptoes with my fingertips just reaching, to work at inching the book towards the edge of the shelf, bit by bit. My patience goes. I jump and grab, then crash-land on the carpet, ducking as the purple pot plant smashes on the hearth, leaving the plastic cactus looking all forlorn and Poundstretchery. *Shit*.

Upstairs floorboards creak. 'Everything OK?' shouts Mam.

'All good,' I say. Then I look at the bible, open on my lap. Staring out of the book of Leviticus is a holy Trinity – but not in the religious sense. A photo, a news cutting and a detailed pencil sketch. The lines on the drawing are intricate, skilled, the shading subtle, catching the way the light falls on the naked young woman as she lies on a bed with a sheet twisted loosely round her middle to keep her dignity. The artist has caught her smile perfectly. Not just the way her mouth turns up a tad more on the right than left, but also her eyes and the way her left eyebrow raises just a little when she's feeling mischievous. I know that look well, though maybe not so much recently. Mam. My stomach flips a bit *eurrk* cos like, this is my mam, clearly in afterglow, but mainly something in me aches. She looks so beautiful, so in love. This is art. I look to the corners of the sketch and check the reverse of the page. Who drew this? No name.

The photo shows a group outside Barry's Amusements. I

recognize Portrush straight off. When I was wee, once a year, Mam and Nan would take me on the train and we'd skirt the River Foyle and Lough Swilly all the way to the north coast, with me leaving sticky fingerprints on the train windows and footprints on the beach. It's an old polaroid picture. Five teenagers – three girls, two boys, one motorbike. My jaw drops. There's also something else. One black cowboy hat – and it's not on Mam. It's on the boy in the middle, tall, confident. OMG. I remember Mam's face when she first saw me wearing that hat. Was it my dad's? Am I looking at him now? His hair is dark like mine but he's wearing sunglasses, so it's impossible to tell his eye colour.

Upstairs, the loo flushes. Mam's up but I don't care, even if she finds me now, I've enough evidence to face this conversation head on. I turn to the newspaper cut-out. Folded neatly in four, it has the same yellow faded look as the *Derry Journal* pages from the wedding glasses and, on the top, a date: 10 October 1982. The headline in bold black reads: Prison Warden Shot Dead by IRA, but that's not what drops my jaw. Across the entire top of the page is a black-and-white photo. A car, riddled with bullet holes, driver's door flung wide and by the fence a body covered by a blanket, with a dark puddle seeping out underneath. I gawp. This is my street, the body right where the old lady left flowers the other day. My heart pounds as my eyes scan the printed columns, reading, racing, looking for confirmation and there . . . there it is. *Samuel Carmichael . . . leaves behind his mother, father, sister and fiancée Róisín Connolly . . .* My. Nan. But the article doesn't end there and the headline photo is not the only one. My eyes fix on the smaller inset and at first, my brain doesn't even compute, then I make it out. I see it and in the same instant, I know I'll never unsee it. I gasp, hands clasped to my mouth as I leap to my feet. The bible clumps shut, but the page lands right way up on my slipper socks and I sway on the spot, head spinning, staring at the picture. It's a young woman. Her hands and ankles are bound and she's roped round her waist to a lamp-post, her body hanging at an angle with her knees bent and head drooped. She doesn't look at the camera. Her hair is hacked, her clothes torn and her entire body drips black – something too thick to be paint. OMG. I can only think of one thing. Tar. Plastered so thick to her skin she'll have to rub it raw to get it off. WTF? Nan has scars round her neck and hairline. I collapse onto all fours on the carpet. I don't understand. What is this? And why? Why? My head swims because there's no doubt. This is my nan. My wouldn't-hurt-a-fly blue-rinse nan and this picture, this photo? It's torture.

Mam finds me curled in a ball on the sofa. Silent. Too afraid to cry. 'Dear Jesus,' she says, taking in the red suitcase, nursing textbook and the clatter of stuff strewn across the carpet. 'Dear Jesus.'

I'm thinking it's not the bashed plastic cactus has her worried. She sits close and I huddle into her as if I were five, feeling her arms wrap tight around my shoulders. She rocks with me, no idea for how long. Then my tears start. And hers. Warm trickles down our faces that won't stop. Proper box-of-tissues stuff. Still she holds me. 'I've got you, Tara,' she says, over and over. 'I'm here, pet. I'm here.' My PJs are soaked with snot and tears and my mind whirrs, trying to grasp the sense in this butchery. I can't see how any of it gets Britain or Ireland in any way sorted. Something inside me shifts from panic to anger. My nan was tortured. People killed the love of her life. They wrecked our lives. Why? So a bit of ground could be called Irish or British? My stomach turns. The sobs convulse through me. Was it the same people or different sides? Protestants like Faith and Jack? Catholics like most everyone I know? The headline said the IRA shot Sam. My . . . grandad? My head hurts. I moan and Mam squeezes my hand.

There's more traffic now in our street. Out there, everyone thinks this day is just normal and part of me wishes I could start over right back at pillow-sniffing. Another part of me, though, is calming. Somewhere here is truth. Tough but honest. Eventually, my breathing steadies and I lift my head. Mam shifts round and we sit cross-legged opposite each other on the sofa.

'I need to know,' I say.

'Which bits?'

'Everything.'

She nods. 'OK, but you gotta promise me something.'

'Promises suck,' I say. 'No one keeps them.'

She smiles and reaches across to clasp my hands in hers. 'This one's not so hard. Before we start, I'm making us hot chocolate. After we've talked through everything, we'll make pancakes for brunch. Together, we're gonna turn this day sweet again.'

Mam makes cracking hot chocolate. Supermarket own brand but with steaming milk and chocolate digestives for dunking. As I sip, she rearranges the stuff from the floor onto the sofa. 'Rough stuff first?' she says, gesturing to the newspaper article.

I nod. I want this, warts and all. Straight to the point. 'Did Protestants do that to Nan cos she was stealing their man?' I say.

'No.' Mam shakes her head. 'Catholics, Republicans did this to her because she didn't stick to her own. She crossed a line.'

'For love?'

'Yes. Nan fell for the boy next door, or rather three doors up. Sam. His family were Protestant.'

'Protestants lived here? On the Cityside?'

'Thousands. During 1973 most of them left. During the Troubles many Catholics moved house too. Like Bombay Street in Belfast where Loyalists burnt their houses. It wasn't so clear-cut in Derry and people argue about why but, if you ask me, it's pretty simple. Protestants didn't feel safe living here any more. In the Cityside, they'd been murdered at work, in their homes, on church steps. Our side, if there's such a thing, said it was justified – the State was sectarian, prejudiced against Catholics and denying us basic human rights.'

'The voting thing?'

'Sure. *One Man, One Vote* was the slogan. Not too PC these days.' She winks. 'But the peaceful protests were also for Catholics to be treated equally to Protestants in jobs, housing, the right to a fair trial if you got arrested. Stormont didn't even build motorways West of the River Bann or put a university in Derry. Pure inbuilt state discrimination.'

'Didn't government listen?'

'Partially. There was some change but not enough. Protests got banned, the streets erupted and the army were called in. Problem was, state security forces, like the police or army, were overwhelmingly Protestant and they were propping up that biased state. To Republicans, state forces became legitimate targets.'

'And Sam's family? Did they move?'

'Not until the late seventies. By then, Nan and he were in love – difficult, but not impossible. Impossible didn't happen until Sam got a job as a prison officer. 1980. Worst timing ever. Right before the Republican hunger strikes kicked off.'

'The IRA ones? Like Bobby Sands?' I'm remembering Oran going on about the mural in the Bogside and me going foot-in-mouth in Armagh in front of the Gaol.

'Exactly,' says Mam. 'The North exploded and Sam and Nan got caught in the blast. Nan has never talked about it. I don't think she can. Some things hurt so bad you *can't* talk about them.'

'But that's not true.' I straighten up. 'Ingabire says when things hurt bad you *gotta* talk about them. It's the only way change happens.'

Mam rubs her temple. 'Maybe. Regardless, it was your great-grandad, God rest him, took me aside to explain after kids in my school bullied me.'

'About not having a dad?'

'About Nan being a soldier doll.' Mam pauses. 'They'd taunt me in the playground about her screwing a screw . . .'

'A soldier doll?'

'Any Catholic girl who dated a British Army soldier earned the nickname. Often, they earned a punishment attack too. Nan wasn't the only one, there were around a hundred and fifty I think, mainly in the seventies. Tarring and feathering.'

'But they were in love. Nan was in love. Sam wasn't a soldier.'

'Prison offers, screws they were nicknamed, were targets too. Prisoners were fighting for rights. Rights to be treated as political prisoners – they were in jail for fighting state injustice. When Sam and Nan got engaged, Republicans saw her as a traitor and they also knew if they attacked her, sooner rather than later, Sam would come to visit his distraught fiancée. The women attacked Nan and the men laid in wait . . .'

My mug of hot chocolate wobbles in my hand. 'An ambush?' I say. 'Nan was bait?'

Mam nods.

'And it was our side attacked them? Not Brits? Not Protestants?'

'Six days before the wedding.'

I blink, trying to hold back the tears again, but it's useless. Ingabire says tears are important, tears are healing. Poor Nan. No wonder she can't talk about it. It's horrific. Mam's eyes are wet too but she's trying to be brave for me, breathing raggedy, holding my hands. Sam was her da. The da she never met.

'You OK, pet? We can keep the rest for another time.'

I shake my head. 'What about my dad?'

Mam breathes in deep through her nose. Holds the air in her lungs then exhales and lifts the photo. She points to the young man in the cowboy hat.

'This is Ryan,' she says. 'He's your dad.'

My lower lip wobbles. I bite it and look at the teenager in the denims. Then look at Mam. 'Did you . . . love him?'

It's Mam's turn to wobble. She nods, ever so slight at first, then clearer and clearer as her tears stream. 'Yes. I did. Truly, madly, deeply and . . . I was working a summer job in Portrush trying to earn money for starting university when we met and . . . I thought he loved me.'

This time, I squeeze Mam's hands. She smiles through her tears. 'I'm OK, pet. Water under the bridge.'

'What was he like?'

Mam closes her eyes and goes peaceful. Then she wipes her face dry with a tissue. 'Really handsome. Confident. Sporty. Gorgeous eyes – just like yours. He was mad about motorbikes but not just all the macho stuff. He played guitar and sang. Sometimes he sang just to me and . . .' Mam's eyes light up. She lifts the pencil sketch. 'He was a brilliant artist. Just like you.'

For a moment we both study the drawing on the sofa between us. Mam isn't even embarrassed.

'So, what happened? Weren't the Troubles over by then?'

'Yes,' she says. 'It was 2002. The peace deal happened when I

189

was still in school. 1998. That, I know about. What happened with Ryan is a mystery. One thing I'm pretty sure of though – he lied.'

I tip my head back against our chronic wallpaper. 'So, where is he?'

She shrugs. 'No idea,' she says. 'I'm not convinced he even told me his right name.'

'What?' I'm off the sofa, arms locked by my side.

Mam pats the seat but I'm not for sitting down. My face goes screwed-up intense. She sighs. Then step by step she explains every card she holds. Just like Cluedo. Problem is, when she was nineteen there were two players. Sitting in our living room seventeen years on, it's clear, she only knew half the game. Dad said he was called Ryan O'Leary. He said he was from Armagh. He said he was at university in England but was in-between student addresses. He'd write. Send his new phone and address. He'd be in touch. For sure. He loved her. Just one more year and he'd move back. He'd even written a song about her. They could be together . . . Before they parted at the end of August, he'd held Mam tight and seemed honest-to-God emotional to be leaving. That last night, they'd kissed . . . and more. Then, he never wrote. Mam went to university, wondering. Three months later, she finally admitted she was pregnant and took the bus home from Belfast to tell Nan. There was no Ryan O'Leary in Armagh listed in the phone book and in them days, hardly a being had a mobile and no one had yet dreamed up social media. That April, I was born in the USA – Up Stairs in Altnagelvin Hospital and Mam and Nan just got on with it as best they could. The end.

In the room next door there's one hell of a coughing fit. Nan's awake. We hear her drag herself out of bed and across to her Bensons by the clock.

'Tara,' says Mam. 'Don't bring any of this up with Nan. She went through hell. Sometimes silence is best, OK? Let it lie.'

I nod, wondering about the lie bit. Ingabire says stuff is better out than in. Sometimes the lie is the silence.

'Got any more questions?' says Mam.

I do. I'm wondering where Faith's mum fits into the picture. When my da was acting all Romeo with Mam, did he know there was a bun in the oven in Armagh? I glance at Mam but, remembering how drawn she looked last night, I keep the thought to myself. My stomach rumbles. 'Just one question.' I grin, thinking about the promise. 'I hate lemon and sugar. Have we any chocolate spread?'

Chapter 21

FAITH
County Armagh, 1 November 2019

It won't be a good day, more a matter of how horrendous. My duvet is a tangle and my stomach is telling me it's closer to lunch than breakfast, but my brain can't remember half the journey home or how I ended up back in my own bed. What I can remember is chronic – the good bits seem like a different life. A pounding blackness has nested in my skull and my tongue feels like it's coated with sour fudge. I roll over with a groan and fall back into a disturbed sleep.

Waking again, I blink. The autumn sun is drawing angled lines through my bedroom blinds. Outside is bright but the house is quiet. Unusually so. Dragging myself into a slouch against the headboard, I notice fronds of black hair scattered across my pillow like thatch and turn them over in my fingers like a foreign substance before the penny drops. Forget horrendous. Upgrade to catastrophic. With a superhuman effort, I drag myself out of bed and to the mirror, then plonk in a heap on the floor. No hiding now. What were small patches, concealable with clips and hairbands, are now clear spaces of scalp. Pink skin where hair should be. I pick at carpet fluff. The house creaks and I listen. Just the wind. No sound from down the hall.

The diagonal rays of sunshine fade and return, fade and return. I chew my thumbnail. My leg goes numb, then pins and needles, until I finally drag myself to the bathroom. Even with a cold facecloth my brain is fugged. I should shower, but why bother? If I did, would I end up bald? I'm still wearing Tara's skeleton T-shirt. In the mirror over the sink, I face studying my hair again and sense the house breathing in with me. Round the edges of my hairline are smudges of white make-up caked in from last night. I remember the Mexican skull but not washing off the face paint. Was I more dead than alive when I got home? Joggers, a jumper and the now essential beanie hat are all I manage to don before sliding my way along the hall in socks to the kitchen. I pause and listen. No sound of life behind the door. Are my parents out? How much do they know? How much do I want them to know? The silence in the car last night was loaded, thick like you could slice it. I'd slept most of the journey but the feeling of disappointment with an undercurrent of anger clung like November fog in the hollows. Now, the house feels this way. Something is either wrong or brewing.

Nudging the door open, I peer in and sigh. The walls stare back. On the draining board, a single mug, plate and knife. By the breadbin, a granary loaf on a wooden board, breakfast crumbs and butter still sitting. Now, I'm beginning to read this silence. It's the kind that could be scarier than angry parents or lectures. It's the kind that says I'm not the last out of bed this morning. The kind that says my mother is seriously depressed and that Dad has taken to yard work with a vengeance. Definitely November, only made a trillion times worse by my behaviour. The note by the kettle confirms it.

I'm in the sheds. Don't wake your mother. Have some breakfast then we'll head to Gosford for a walk.

When I was little, walks in Gosford Forest Park meant Daddy–Faith time. Duck feeding. Learning to cycle without stabilizers. Time to abandon the shadow haunting my mother in the house and laugh, clambering over the old waterwheel by the car park or playing Poohsticks from the bridge over the river. Dad would smile as I gathered shiny conkers, orange and red leaves. The shadows were always longest in late autumn. Mum's mood changed with the clocks, turning dark like the evenings but then lightening by the time of the Christmas switch-on in town with the costumed Georgian characters revelling in traditional festivities. Recent years seemed easier, although the twentieth anniversary hit home. Bigger numbers brought bigger emotions but still no answers. Every war of words on the television about addressing the past is like a physical kick in the teeth for Mum. I've watched her, pale, glued to the news reports, for as long as I can remember. She wants me to understand. Does anyone?

I fill a glass with orange juice and down it without stopping, then find the paracetamol and swallow two with a glass of water, wondering. I'm not sure what reaction I expected from my parents this morning, probably anger, or at least a serious dressing-down over a stilted family breakfast. I'm blank on my next move. The game plan hadn't factored in TV coverage or an early-morning drunken evacuation in front of Tara and her family. Plan A to Plan Z with no in-between. I make coffee and butter a slice of bread then leave it untouched as I slump at the table, chin resting on my folded arms. Where do I even start with life today? I'm not sure I know how to be me any more.

The coffee is only half-drunk and the bread resembles a nibbled jigsaw piece when Dad arrives in from the yard and kicks off his work boots. I look up, resigned to my fate. He walks over, pauses, leans over the chair, then . . . hugs me. He smells of soil, sweat and chicken sheds. Just like he always does, except for Sundays. Hunkering down, he levels his eyes with mine.

'You had me so worried last night,' he says.

'I'm sorry,' I say. Then my tears come. He's quiet as I wipe them away.

'Come on,' he says. 'You've the hat on already. A walk outside to clear the head and a chat to clear the air. Like the old days. It'll do us both good. Yes?'

The ground at Gosford is springy with slim pine cones and needles. We pull our coats tight and Dad sets a fast pace, past the Girl Guides' hut and towards the millponds. Voices from other families carry through the forest. There are more diverse paths now than when I was little, firmer ground where it used to be boggy. 'We need to talk,' says Dad. He doesn't slow his stride and I keep looking straight ahead as I step in time.

We *do* need to talk, but about what? Mum? My botched lies covering a drunken trip to Londonderry? My parentage? My . . . sexual orientation? I shove my hands deep into my pockets. At the ponds, he stops right by the fence, where we used to throw chunks of stale bread to the ducks.

'Faith.' His face is set somewhere between paramedic and detective. 'I'm hearing two very different stories of last night. Conflicting narratives. What's the truth?' Worry lines wiggle across his forehead. I'm not the only one losing hair, his own is greying at the edges now as his hairline recedes.

I roll a pine cone under my shoe. 'Is Mum really bad with depression?'

In his eyes, he knows I'm stalling but goes with it anyway. 'You know how it is. Maybe too well.' He sighs. 'Sometimes I think we should've protected you more from her trauma. Maybe, with wanting to remember the past, we've forgotten the future.'

'But this year she seems . . . worse.'

'I'll get her to the doctor this week.'

'Does that even help?' I suck my hair. 'He gives her tablets but that's just for symptoms, not the cause. I think she needs . . . answers. She needs some kind of closure.'

Dad runs his fingers through his hair and nods. Then he smiles, kind of sad. 'The whole country does. You know, at our last victims support group they talked about statistics. 3,600 people died in the Troubles. People tend to focus on the dead, not the living. All those bereaved families are still dealing with grief. As well as that, 40,000 people were injured, and the knock-on mental health impact's crazy. They reckon a quarter of our population's still suffering. It's not just our house; walk into any room where people are gathered and guaranteed, someone is struggling.'

Across the pond, quacking from the ducks draws my attention. There aren't ducklings this time of year. In spring they swim in formation behind their mother, learning the bobs and dives. Dad leans on the fence and we watch them together like we always did. 'They look graceful,' he says, 'but underneath, their legs are kicking frantically just to keep moving forward.' He pauses. 'Your mum will pull through, she always does. It doesn't help though, all this politicization of truth recovery. Legislation, compensation, reconciliation . . . it's like they've forgotten the individuals behind the statistics. We're not people any more. We're an issue.'

I think of Mum, lying in her bed with the curtains drawn, laying poppies every year in the graveyard. No answers for who killed her parents. No day in court. People saying we should forget it all and move on. Easy said.

'Even if the politicians could agree, with no government, there's no budget for victim support.' Dad looks up as rain starts to spit. 'Know what else I learned in our group?' He waits until I turn to listen. 'Harm passes through generations. The two sides can fight over definitions, but families know. It's not just those who experience violence or witnessed it first-hand who are victims.' His hand rests gently on my beanie hat. A rain droplet splats on my nose. 'Let's walk,' he says. 'We'll probably never hear the whole truth behind your grandparents' murder, never mind the Troubles, but last night? It was really . . . out of character. What's going on? Who is that . . . other girl?'

We take the winding track that leads to the Arboretum, a huge tree garden. Mud and puddles spark cold onto my ankles as my brain struggles to find words for this conversation. I'm not even sure which conversation this should be. It's a chess match I'm expected to play blindfolded and hungover. How much does Dad know? If he moves first, it would help. I bite my tongue. The air is heavy with pine musk, the chirping of birds high in the trees carrying over the background hum of traffic on the distant road. After a trudge in sustained silence, Dad speaks again. 'OK,' he says. 'I'll start. Of my two sources, one sang truer than she ever did in the choir, the other was tight-lipped as his father and a possible fount of disinformation fit for MI5. I suspect the truth weaves somewhere in-between.'

I dip my head, unable to avoid the grin. Bethany and Jack. Dad's trying to avoid tension, setting it out like he's playing detective but serious at the same time. He tells how he'd been watching the news with Mum when they'd seen me, or a girl they thought was me, in Londonderry. Mum had rewound the footage and paused it. Dad had fetched his glasses, then lifted the phone. First to call me, to see if I was on a sleepover at Bethany's like I'd said, then, when I didn't answer, to call Bethany's mum. After quizzing Bethany, he'd called Uncle Steve. When he confirmed Jack was gone, they'd panicked. Jack didn't answer his phone either. Bethany had blabbed we were in Londonderry with friends from the residential, so they'd jumped in the car.

While we walk and Dad talks, my brain wakes. Maybe it's the coffee finally kicking in or the fresh air chasing away the hangover but what I'm thinking is, Bethany blabbed about the trip. Did she also break her promise and spill about the DNA results? Most importantly, Bethany doesn't know I'm gay. If Jack played his cards close to his chest and Tara's T-shirt switch worked, I might still have a choice about if, or when, I come out. Might I still find my real dad first? As we emerge from the pine forest into the expanse of the Arboretum, I could be out of the woods in more ways than one. But there's still something I need to say. I close my eyes and let the rain fall on my face. These next ten minutes are about to be scary as hell. This could be a conversation *with* Dad, *about* Dad, but does he even know I'm not biologically his? Com-pli-ca-ted.

'What did Jack say?' I ask.

'Very little,' says Dad. 'Though I wouldn't let him leave the car until I'd got something. He said it was his idea, along with his mate Joaquim. You being drunk was peer pressure – his fault.' Dad checks my reaction as we walk. 'Joaquim met a girl in August on the residential but didn't want to travel on his own. Jack dragged you into it because he reckoned you could sort a place to stay with that other girl, your . . . lookalike.'

'Tara . . .'

'Yes.' Dad stops under a tall redwood, painted black with rain and greened with moss. 'Who is she? Bethany said she thinks Jack has a thing for that girl. She also said the trip was your idea. You told her about it at Stormont. You invited Jack.'

I lean against low tree branches: evergreen arms twisted with knots. Bethany has told the truth. Does Dad believe her? I wonder who he thinks Tara is. I say nothing.

'Come on,' says Dad. 'You've got to talk. What's the story with this girl Tara? Is there more behind it? In Jack's version, he's got no real motive for going to all that bother, but neither of them are giving me the whole truth. Bethany's version doesn't stack up. Jack's like his dad – straight cut, red, white and blue. He polishes the buttons on his band uniform every marching season and he's chased girls since he was knee-high to a cricket stump. He wouldn't go for a Catholic who, judging from the TV and the T-shirt, is more than a little . . . confused.'

I blink. 'Confused? Don't you mean gay?'

'Seriously messed up. I'm just being nice about it.'

I stare.

'Look, it's irrelevant anyway.' His voice is rising. 'When I saw her, Tara, in the T-shirt it was a shock, but also a relief.'

I fix my beanie hat and look at my footprints in the mud.

'Bethany also mentioned something else . . .'

When I look up, he's pressing two fingers to his temple, rubbing between his eyes. 'You got results in an email that day at Stormont too. Results of a DNA test.' He pauses. 'Faith, I'm not stupid. It wasn't Jack who walked into our kitchen with swabs three weeks ago . . .' He swallows, closes his eyes, then looks straight at me and speaks with a steady voice. 'This is a conversation we should have had years ago, but your mum couldn't face it. She was so worried what people would think.'

He sits down on a huge trailing branch and runs his palms across the bark. After a second, I sit beside him and hold my breath. He sets his hand over mine.

'You found out, didn't you? I'm not your real dad.'

I can't speak. I nod. My lower lip's gone jelly. Dad's right hand squeezes mine, while with his left hand he pinches the bridge of his nose between finger and thumb, breathing in sharply. When he turns round, his eyes are wet. 'You know I love you? You're my girl. You're always my girl.'

I fling my arms round him and feel the heave and fall of his chest, the damp off his rain-soaked coat. Dogs bark and a family scoot past on mountain bikes. Neither of us say anything for ages. In the end it's me who breaks the silence.

'Sundial?'

He nods. We always go that route. My favourite place in the park. Some of the trees are tall like circus poles, giraffe-necking upwards to the grey clouds. Others have bark-like slabs of once molten rock, aged giants. So many questions are flooding in now. Dad's comments about Tara. *Messed up. Confused. Relieved.* My head throbs. I concentrate on putting one foot in front of the other, avoiding puddles. When I glance at Dad, it looks like he's processing stuff too. Leaving the Arboretum, we turn through black gates onto a gravel path skirting a walled garden. Soon we reach the small courtyard with hexagonal paving. Nothing has changed since we last visited. In the centre, a red brick plinth holds a concrete book, a copper sundial resting on its open pages, embossed with Roman numerals and a starred compass. We stand on opposite sides, the rain coming down heavier now and no shadow falling to tell the time.

'Dad,' I say. 'Who is my biological father?'

Dad claps his hands behind his head. 'I do know,' he says. 'Your mum was totally honest and open with me recovering from the chaos. It was hard, but she loves me and we'd been dating before the bomb and . . . I love her. I always have.' He hesitates. 'I'm going to ask you something hard too. About your real dad – can you wait? Just until I chat to your mum. I think what happened last night, seeing Tara, it's really made her think. She might need to work through some stuff and face up to a slightly bigger picture. Maybe after Remembrance Sunday, when she'll be feeling better? I know it's a big ask but it's her story and . . . it's complicated.'

I run my fingertips over the engraving on the sundial. *L'heure passe, l'amitié reste.* Time passes, friendship remains. I wonder what he means by the 'bigger picture' but it doesn't feel like the time to ask. It's only dawning on me now, how much he must have gone through, how much love and forgiveness he had for my mum, to marry her when she was pregnant by someone else. Slowly, I nod. 'You'll definitely tell me soon?'

'I promise.'

'OK.'

'One thing I need to know from you. The truth . . .'

I feel the blood drain from my face. Is he about to ask? My heart races as the panic starts to hit, the pounding in my skull suddenly back.

'Is Tara related?'

Thank you, Jesus. Of course he would ask that. He's trying to fathom it too. 'Yes,' I say. 'She's my half-sister.'

He nods, and I wonder what hoops his brain is jumping through. By Christmas, I'll know. Before we drive home, he buys me coffee and a muffin from the van in the car park. As we navigate country roads, I try to sort my head. In some ways, things are becoming clearer. In others, I'm more confused than ever. I'd thought Dad would be angrier about Londonderry but I was right about the homophobia. If that was him being 'nice' about it, what does nasty look like? The conversation has been important, but I'm not sure it has helped my stress levels. One thing I do know though – beanie hats definitely aren't part of school uniform. What'll I do on Monday when midterm break ends?

'Am I grounded,' I say as we pull into the yard, 'or can I go visit Jack?'

'Be back for dinner,' he says, 'and no more gallivanting without permission.'

As I approach my uncle's farm, I listen for the chink of tools in the shed but it's silent. The light is already waning, so I make a beeline for the glow of the back door. It's a while since I've been in the kitchen. They could've eaten dinner off the floor when Auntie Bea lived here. I sniff. The sink is full of dishes and something in the bin's a bit rank. TV blares from the living room. When I enter, Jack's sitting on the sofa with his back to me, engrossed in pre-match commentary for the Rugby World Cup.

'Who's playing?' I ask.

He doesn't turn. 'Nine a.m. kick-off tomorrow. England v South Africa.'

'Will England win?'

He shrugs. 'It'll be all about the defence. And the scrum. Their pack weights are colossal. Obviously, I'm rooting for England but it's the first time the Springboks have a black captain in charge. They've serious emotional commitment to the game.'

'Any other emotional commitments from last night I should know about?'

'Yeah, maybe . . .' He stretches his arms over his head and pulls up his hood, but still stays glued to the TV. Boys and sport. I mean, I know rugby is his thing, but after last night, he could at least make me feel welcome.

I plonk myself on the other end of the sofa, grab the remote and press pause. 'Jack, I need your help.'

Jack buries his face in his hands.

And I launch into recounting my head-spin of a day, the he

saids and I saids, and the whole Dad conversation and his relief when he thought Tara was me . . . This stuff is so massive. I need to bounce ideas and think because—

'Are you even listening?' I say. 'I'm falling apart here and you're so into the rugby you won't even look at me.'

He leans forward and reties a shoelace that wasn't even undone. 'OK. You wanna know what I think? You should come out. End of.' He grabs the remote and restarts the rugby commentary.

I go to grab it back and he ups and walks out to the kitchen, leaving me frustrated. I think for a minute and then follow. He's at the sink, head bowed, shoving dishes into suds and then clunking them onto the draining board.

'Jack?'

'What?'

'Is something wrong? Did something happen last night with Tara?'

His hands grip the counter and he kicks his boot off the cupboard base before turning. When I see his face, both my hands hit my mouth. Jack looks really beaten up. A black eye. Swelling round his jawline. A busted lip. 'The bit with Tara was grand.' He attempts a smile. 'The best.' He blushes and a bit of his cheekiness rallies. 'It was the bit with Dad . . . Look, I'm OK. Just maybe next time I won't take it lying down. He caught me off-guard. I thought it was your dad would be most mad . . . clearly, I was wrong. It wasn't even that I'd been drinking or that I'd lied about Londonderry.'

'What then?'

'The DNA test – nothing to do with the biology of it, just like . . . criminal database stuff.'

'I don't get it.'

'Neither do I. He was blind drunk and it'd obviously been playing on his mind since your dad phoned hours earlier. By the time I landed back he was all slurred conspiracy theories, cops hacking DNA databases and rants about Loyalist gangs. When I argued, he lit into me.' Jack shrugs and lifts a tea towel. 'He'll be back soon, but I wouldn't suggest sticking around to ask why.'

As he dries a mug, my phone pings. So does Jack's. We both see Tara's message at the same time.

Meet Dad. The one in the hat. Code name Ryan O'Leary. From Armagh. Current location unknown. Recognize him?

Another ping. Suddenly I'm all eyes on a photo with a teenage boy in jeans, sunglasses and Tara's black cowboy hat. All the faces in the photo apart from Tara's mum are strangers. The noise of the mug smashing at Jack's feet makes me jump a mile. His eyes are wide.

'You recognize him? Any of them?'

Jack shakes his head. 'Not the people,' he says. 'The motorbike. It's Dad's Honda Shadow.'

Chapter 22

TARA
Derry, 5 November 2019

Con-cen-tra-tion. Miss O'Reilly is like proper thigh-slapping, four-syllable lording it over our school running team and I'm minding that last year she said that's what I was lacking. *Men-tal fo-cus.* They've shedloads of it in the posh schools apparently, along with brains, swanky trainers and Garmin watches but I've earphones, my mobile and a wicked playlist with fast beats per minute. All I've got to do is hit play and get with the rhythm, so enough of the pep talk, it's fecking see-your-breath freezing and all I want to do is run. *De-ter-min-a-tion.* One syllable too many but maybe I've picked me up some of that.

Miss O'Reilly has us at the kiddies' playground in the middle of Saint Columb's Park which, like it says on the tin, is crawling with trees, muck paths and hills. Pure perfect for cross-country interval training. Plus, it has a swing so she can sit right here with her stopwatch and coffee flask while we slog five interval circuits.

I'm jogging on the spot and doing the stretches like a notice-me pro because probably my time will be shite. Yang, my classmate, is natural epic-on-legs compared to my five-weeks-off-fags and Lena will ace second slot on our school team because Joaquim's becoming like her Mr Motivator for pure flat belly tone. Once it's six-pack perfection, she's for getting her belly pierced for Christmas, but today is all about thinking beyond December and into the new year. That's when the district cross-country events are held. They're mental craic and, more importantly, mean a whole day out of school with a hint of school celebrity in morning assembly, so long as we're not total shite. Beat the grammar schools and it's playground hero-worship all round. Who am I kidding? My toes feel stuffed in these runners but I daren't tell Mam my feet have gone and grown again, not until the January sales.

The loop is up the hill to the Amelia Earhart cast-iron cut-out, along the Waterside Greenway, through the forest bit where ones go snogging and drinking in the summer, veer left at the Saint Columba statue and then follow the river path back to the playground. Miss O'Reilly sends the juniors packing first, then the intermediates. The rest of us are left like slim pickings, grouped in cliques and scowling, cos, truth is, the running team for our year group has always been a bitch fest. Aged eleven, we were blazing fire-crackers round the courses and lifted the cup but then we got hormones, boy-hype and life crap and it all went wrong.

'Remember, girls,' says Miss O'Reilly 'There's no *I* in *TEAM*. I want fast times and stamina but what I don't want is *at-ti-tude* – not unless it's positive. For the districts I'll be taking the best TEAM.'

I'm like OMG, just let us run. My toes are ice. If we don't run soon, I'll be late to my fourth art therapy session tonight and that is one place I *do* feel the togetherness. No more you-got-this-girl, I'm owning it. I almost bounce out of Emer's car each week.

Looking at the ragamuffin-clatter of year thirteens sprawled round Miss O'Reilly I can see where she's coming from about needing more sense of team. Megan is scowling. I don't even know where we're at right now but I'm not asking. I'm all in for the step count and *men-tal fo-cus*. So help me God or whatever the feck. *Does Jack like belly piercings?*

Miss checks her watch and blows the whistle. It's a few minutes of elbows and under-breath cursing then we spread into some type of line, plodding and head-bobbing our way along the tarmac greenway, then slip-sliding over the carpet of mushed autumn leaves through the trees. Surprising thing is, for the first couple of loops, I'm not half bad, holding my own near enough with Yang and Lena, which is worth the screaming arse muscles simply for seeing the frustration drawn across the faces of Megan and the others who've been track-pounding it the whole term. I wasn't expecting to pull any kind of pace since, far as training's concerned, I've been about as present as school bog roll on Fridays, at least since the whole Oran thing. That my head even recognizes that feels like progress. That I haven't smoked a fag either deserves a whole new category at prize-giving.

Damp is beginning to soak through my runners as my feet pound. None of your fancy Gortex waterproofing for me. I ignore the wet toes and focus on breathing. Cycle of fours, in and out, in time with my steps, keeping my head steady and lengthening my stride. Maybe I have been training more than I've realized. Running up mountains. Running along streets. Running myself ragged.

Up ahead, Yang and Lena are stretching away from the pack. My eyebrows pull into a 'V' as I pick up the pace to get in sync again with my playlist beats. As we stop to catch our breath between intervals, I can tell Miss O'Reilly is plain caught out, surprised by how well I'm doing. She even does that wee recognition nod thing meaning like, 'I see you're back, Tara, now fecking impress me,' except that teachers wouldn't swear, leastways not when they're trying to be all professional. I give her back the nod then look away as-if-I-care in case anyone else is watching.

First three circuits and my times are scandalous good given the shape of me. The fourth one is where the burn really starts to kick into my leg muscles and my breathing goes wonky. I make it back to the playground, still in third place but with Megan and the rest clipping my heels and every part of my body screaming to splay myself on the freezing tarmac in front of Miss O'Reilly and plead for mercy. *Re-sil-i-ence. Stam-in-a.* She's back to the multiple-syllable spouting while the inters and juniors hog the tyre swings and roundabout. The seniors gotta do one last loop. There's a pure knowing in my core that on this one, I've gotta swallow my pride and it ain't gonna be pretty. We're not even up the hill before I feel the bitchiness breathing on my neck and one by one the others overtake and I go redneck from rising shame and anger. The minibus homerun will be pure gloating. I. Am. Toast. My toes are freezing mush jammed into undersize runners and my feet are out of rhythm with each other, never mind the music. Everything in me is screaming *Quit. Double back. Storm off.* I slow to a walk and rip out the earphones. Breathe. Think about Ingabire's mindfulness lark. Count to ten. I am good at running. It's always felt natural. So what if it takes a month to get back to myself? A grey squirrel hops across my path and I listen to leaves fluttering down from the trees. Since Oran, all my running has been running away. Getting back on the team is a goal to run towards. I suck a bellyful of air deep into my lungs and jam in the earphones again, eyes focusing ahead to the mid-distance. Move. Keep padding. Keep pumping.

The climb through the trees is a bastard on banjaxed legs. I crank up the volume. With the twists of the trail, I can't even hear the others, never mind see them. For all I know, Yang and Lena are already finished and I'm just sad dribble. Keep it mechanical. Focus on anything except running to kill the time.

Rebuild that stamina. Mam had some *stam-in-a* to rear me. Nan had some of that *men-tal fo-cus* to not jack it all in after the tarring over Sam. Us Connollys got *de-ter-min-a-tion*, just maybe it shows up different. In my exhaustion, my feet are slipping in muck. Last Tuesday Ingabire said something that's only clicking now. Losing your true north doesn't mean you're lost – it opens your eyes to finding another direction. I'd filed it under 'b' for bollocks but, since Halloween, it's making sense. Oran is still dead. And since, even with a photo, we can't find Da's real name, never mind whereabouts, that feels like a dead end. Nothing has changed except . . . everything. Me. I. Feel. Different. Partly, it's the hot-on-my-thighs memory of Jack and the messages we swap at random times. Partly, it's finding I've a sister. Partly it's understanding more about where I come from. But also, it's something can't-put-your-finger-on-slithery that might be healing. A mending of inside stuff. Jack says life down their direction has gone crazy-eggshells since Halloween. He never spelled out specifics, but neither him nor Faith recognized anyone in the photo, so chances of turning up some old geezer in Armagh who I can blame for all my worldly shite is slimmer than scallions. Maybe, just maybe, that doesn't matter any more. I've an Everest of madness I gotta splurge to Ingabire and Emer tonight – and a favour I want to ask.

My legs are on autopilot, my head chewing over Miss O'Reilly's guru shite when I stumble out the top end of the forest and suddenly clap eyes on Megan. She's sat on the mosaic bench ahead, sporting more hair-flick-lip-pout than a posh ad for perfume. I'm pure sweat-soaked-minging but feck me if I'm not for picking up speed and sprinting past, even if it's murder. I don my best what's-it-to-me bitch face and switch into super-drive, selecting a line close enough for victory eye-balling and wide enough that she can't stick out a leg and have me nose-diving gravel. It's a cracking plan until I catch her eyes and see she's sheet white and shivering. I'm raging. Just when I'm finally full-power-mental-focus something different kicks in and grinds my legs to a halt. I stop a few feet away and turn, feet apart and hands on hips in my best WTF power-stance.

'You're hurt, aren't you?' I say.

She nods, staring at the ground. 'Slipped. Went over on my ankle.'

I saunter over, milking the dominance of the moment and still mad I've even stopped. On Miss O'Reilly's stopwatch my time just went from snail to slug. Then Megan busts out crying, proper mascara-disaster-snot-bubble-sleeve-wiping tears and neither of us have a shred of a tissue. 'It really hurts,' she says. 'I can't even walk.'

'Jesus,' I say. 'Looks swollen.' Next thing, I'm sat on the bench beside her offering sympathies, assurances and OMGs while she winces, trying to rotate it. 'Is it broke? Want me to get Miss O'Reilly?'

Megan shakes her head. 'Think it's just twisted.' She pauses. 'Thanks. The others just ran on.'

I don't know where to look. The bench is all art tiles, turquoise, navy and cream: swirlings of river, oak leaves and wise sayings on peace from the Dalai Lama and Mahatma Gandhi. *You can't shake hands with a clenched fist . . . Peace is a conscious choice . . .* I sit there, not saying anything and wracking my brains to remember what in the name of God ever had me hating Megan Carey in the first place, even before the beach fire or all the Oran stuff. We're not really that different, even our runners are the same 50 per cent off ones from the sports bin bargain-buys. The question spills out of me before I can stop it. 'Did you really go with Oran?'

She gulps. 'He said you'd split.'

'When?'

'Right before Easter.'

I draw circles in the gravel with the heel of my runner. The timing of that's actually true. 'Why do you hate me anyway?'

'Hate you?' says Megan. 'I . . . I don't hate you. It's just that . . . like, you have everything. You ace art, running. You seriously don't give a shit what anyone thinks, you just own it. And boys? They drop at your feet. You always get the best ones. They only want me cos . . .'

When I turn, she's staring dead ahead, studying the Saint Columba statue like she's considering joining a convent. I shouldn't ask, but it's burning my throat. 'Did you and Oran . . . you know?'

She chews at her nail polish, then nods. 'He said you were better at that and all.'

'Bastard.' I jump to my feet.

Megan looks petrified.

I shake my head. 'I don't mean you. I mean him.' My head's fried and I'm gone all hair-sucking and lip-biting but I don't care. My hands are balled into fists and my blood's boiling. Why. Do. Boys. Do. This. Shit? Yes, we'd split. But it had only been days. And he manipulated Megan into bed with lies about me? All this guilt-bender I've put my head through? It wouldn't have mattered buttons if I'd shagged him and, kill me for cursing the dead but he was a pure feck-wit druggie even if he *was* my boyfriend and no, I don't want him six feet under but if he were here I'd kick him in the crown jewels till Saturday fortnight. And some. All sudden, like, something just bypasses my head, fires my fecking-give-a-damn mode and I'm looping my arm under Megan's shoulder and hoisting her carefully to her feet. We're

211

war-wounded-hobbling along the path when Miss O'Reilly appears into view looking concerned.

'Megan,' I say before my brain decides different and the moment goes all teachery. 'Could we . . . just wipe the past? Start over? Like maybe we could even be friends?'

She stops the hop-foot-drag thing and sighs. 'I'd love that.'

Only another three sessions and I'll be an art therapy graduate. I never graduated anything since the wee mortar boards and certificates from nursery school. Already I know I'm gonna fierce miss this. Tonight, I'm quieter. I'm thinking. My skull aches from squishing sixteen years of brain-whirring into this last month but it hasn't all been bad.

Across the table, Dee's like a spring-loaded frog about to boke frogspawn everywhere if she doesn't get Ingabire's attention. Subtlety doesn't suit her. 'Could we get an exhibition?' she blurts.

Ingabire looks up from where she's helping one of the boys with clay work. 'You know art therapy is not about audience. It's about understanding ourselves.'

'But,' says Dee, 'isn't it also about helping us find our voice?'

Around the table there are murmurs of agreement but some people are quiet. Ingabire pulls up a chair. 'Not everyone might want a public voice, Dee. We've never done an exhibition from these classes because they're about healing individuals.'

'But what if our healing could help society?' says Dee. 'Or challenge it?'

Ingabire thinks, then spreads her arms in a wide gesture. 'OK. Let's talk,' she says. 'I'll not rule it in or out but if there *was* an exhibition, it would have to be separate from these classes and no one would be forced to take part or display their work.' She grabs a sheet of wastepaper and scrunches it into a ball. 'Real-life debate. Two ears and one mouth rule – listen twice as much as you speak. You can only speak when you hold the ball. It's a team game – you must pass to another player every minute. What are the views in the room?' She lobs the ball into the air so that anyone can catch it and start.

When it comes to getting people to talk, Ingabire is an A-star wizard. If this was school, I'd be glazed-over-window-staring but round this table, it's different. The stuff we've talked through here is real. Bullying. Bereavement. Fostering. Self-harm. Drugs. Suicide. Parents splitting. Abuse. Mental Health. Listening to the debate, I'm minding what we were like back in week one. Eyes darting, cautious, sceptical, angry, over-loud or freakish silent. This is a miracle. Over the weeks, I've learned that here it's OK to spill my guts onto pages, or into the air. It stays private in the group. There's trust. Respect. Do I want my art on a wall?

The scrunched paper ball is flung my direction and instinctively I catch it. When I hesitate, everyone looks. 'Would it have to be art we've done here, or could we display other work?' I lob the ball and Ingabire catches it.

'That's a good question,' she says. 'What's on your mind?'

She fires the ball back to me across the table and I mess with it in my hands, shredding off bits of the paper as I try and pull together the words. 'I . . . I don't want to focus on my own hurt,' I say. 'Not in public.' Dee is staring at me like 'girl don't diss my dream'. I shake my head like *re-lax*. 'I do have things though that I want to put out there. Things I'm learning. I think they'd be relevant.'

It sparks another flurry of exchanges. After twenty minutes, Ingabire calls the discussion to a halt. Consensus is – hell yes. We're doing an exhibition. Grinning, Ingabire plays her ace. The deal is this. She'll book the exhibition space and set it up for

10 December. World Human Rights Day. She'll sort tea, coffee and biscuits to make it proper posh. But that's it. Every. Single. Other. Thing. Is. Up. To. Us.

Everyone goes quiet.

Us?

Organize it?

Dee and I swap glances. This will take balls. Work. Leadership. I shrug like, 'maybe?'. Dee wrinkles her nose. I smile. We're a team.

'Feck it,' says Dee. 'I'm in.'

'Me too.' I reach across the table and we fist bump.

There's a chorus of support as everyone rallies. We. Are. Gonna. Do. This.

I'm on such a high, I almost forget to loiter at the end. My head's been trying for hours to plan out how to ask Ingabire, but already I know that Emer is up for helping. Conditional like. She doesn't know if my idea is half-wise but, if Ingabire thinks it'd be positive, she's in. Slow packing up my pencils and untangling my jacket, I wait until I'm the only one left, then I unfold the yellowed newspaper that fell out of our family bible and show Ingabire. None of the words go how I've planned. They splodge out triple speed every which way as I explain the last three and a half months all in the wrong order, from pancakes to the Child of Prague, flowers on fences, our attic, Halloween, our youth club trip, the wanting to know, the freaking out and . . . this. This newspaper article from near forty years ago with the photo of my nan. 'She's never talked about it and . . . Do you think it would help? Like I'm sure that woman with the flowers must be a relative of Sam's.'

Ingabire sits down. Her fingers curl round her face as she stares at the picture of Nan clattered in tar and tied to a lamp-post. 'Your poor nan,' she says. 'All that hate. All that silence.'

'Can you help? Emer could find the lady but we'd need you. You'd know how to get them to talk, how to connect.'

Slowly, she nods. 'I'll try. It can't be a surprise though. They'd both have to understand and agree in advance. It'll be highly sensitive. The good things can't be forced – love, hope, reconciliation. Thirty years of war and people think peace can be built overnight? Not everything heals so quickly.'

Chapter 23

FAITH
County Armagh, 6 November 2019

I should be taking the spuds off the hob. I stare at them like they're a major problem without solution. Everything is heavy and my excuses are wearing thin. For three days, I've avoided school because I can't face the fact my hair is falling out. For three months I've avoided the fact my hair is in crisis because I can't face coming out. For over three years, I've struggled with, well, just being me because I can't face my church, my family or even myself. Me being gay doesn't fit. It blows everything apart.

I'm supposed to be sorting dinner for when Mum and Dad get back from the graveyard. They've been gone over an hour so shouldn't be long. Today is the anniversary, so dawn to dusk is a careful choreography of support for Mum and an ocean of tissues. Usually, I'm at school but, having cried off sick, this year I've witnessed everything. Even in the simple act of drinking tea, Mum's head is a hurricane and Dad is treading broken glass to be her calm. This morning, he tied her shoelaces because today, she's not thirty-seven. Today, she's fourteen, violently orphaned and about to be taken into foster care.

I lift the saucepan to the sink and run the cold tap to reduce the steam. The kitchen window drips with condensation. My head aches. It hasn't stopped aching all week and the blackness that I thought was a hangover is proving stubborn. I can't lift my heart. By the kettle is a green-and-white paper bag sealed

216

with the pharmacist's sticker – Mum's prescription meds for the next four weeks. Is this my fate too? Inside I'm so tight strung that something is going to snap, but it's one thing knowing it, totally different knowing what to do. Logic is telling me that Jack's right. There is one solution. Come out. Dobbing school until Amazon deliver a wig isn't exactly an option. It could take a week to get a routine doctor's appointment and I've never booked one without Mum or Dad. It's beginning to dawn on me that even if I do find my real dad, what's to say he'd want to know me anyway? He's shown zero sign up to now that he knows or cares about my existence. Everything's on a knife-edge. Even Jack is refusing to ask Uncle Steve about the Honda Shadow until the situation feels less delicate. Our families are falling apart.

I pull defrosted sausages out of the microwave and fire them under the grill. They should have been cooking at the same time as the potatoes but I can't coordinate my thoughts at the minute, never mind the dinner. I collapse onto a kitchen chair and sigh. Why won't my brain function? *Think.* If I have to face this, is there a right time? Or one that's less wrong? After Remembrance Sunday this weekend, Mum will rally. Once she's stronger, she'll cope better with the shock. If I got help about the hair loss, could I wait until after the church carol service? That way, I could give my parents one last memory of their good Christian daughter, singing 'O Holy Night', before the illusion collapses and I'm banned from darkening church doors.

The sausages spit. I shiver, remembering the pastor speak of hell.

I'm turning the sausages when my phone bleeps. Jack. He'll be on the late bus back from school after rugby practice. Even with the black eye, he won't have missed that.

Check Instagram. Have you seen Bethany's feed? Gone round the whole of Years 13 and 14.

Bethany hasn't been in touch since Halloween and I'm completely out of touch with where she's at. The pang of guilt I feel vanishes the instant I see her photo. It's an edited collage captioned *Spot the Difference*. On the left, an image of Tara from our residential, with red circles like a puzzle-book answer page drawn around her multiple ear piercings and blue hair streak. On the right, a snap of me taken from my profile picture. In the middle, is a freeze-frame from the news coverage at Halloween, zoomed in on me wearing the rainbow T-shirt and leaning drunken against Dee. There's a red circle around my face and a typed label. *No loopy earrings. No blue hair.* Yellow arrows point to my cross necklace in both pictures. *Draw your own conclusions.*

I forget to breathe. The sausages are burning. My teeth clench so tight my jaw hurts. Everyone in school will have seen this and I wasn't even in class. Gossip behind my back, on the bus, in the corridors. I scroll the comments, bracing for the worst. Many of them are *OMG*s, *Goss-ip*, *Scan-dal*. Some have praying hands or shock emojis, but further down a different vibe kicks in, not from my church or Scripture Union friends but from others I don't usually hang with. Their chat isn't about me, they're slating Bethany. Calling her post gay-hate. Sending me positive vibes. *Way to go, Faith!* Rainbow flag emojis. *Wear it with Pride.*

I'm still scrolling when smoke from the grill triggers our alarm and I leap to my feet, grab the pan and wave a tea towel frantically in the air to stop the shrill beeping. Opening the kitchen window, I hear cars arrive into the yard. Three of them. I peer into the darkness. Door slams. Footsteps. Voices. An urgency. First, I make out my parents, then Bethany's dad, followed by the pastor and the other elders from church. For a moment, I assume they're here to pray with Mum and offer pastoral support. Then I hear my name mentioned. Dad glances at Mum, then towards me in the house. 'Perhaps a different day?' he suggests. But the churchmen are already moving to the door.

The panic-attack symptoms bombard me like before. Trembling. Chest pain. Dizziness. I grab the draining board. This time, it's my kitchen. This time, Tara's mum isn't here to help. I'm on my own. *Breathe.* I battle to keep myself calm. Their footsteps reach the back door. *Inhale. Slow. Exhale.* My skin is soaked with sweat. I stagger to the fridge and open the door to feel the cold air. *Breathe.* They're in the kitchen now and everyone is staring, my parents too, staring like I'm an alien species. Oh God. Oh God. I know they know. They know I know. And where is Jack? Or Tara? Or anyone? My lips mumble prayers I can't translate and everything in me wants to crumple invisible onto the cold kitchen tiles. No. Way. Out. *Please, God. Help.*

The pastor coughs. I turn. There are pleasantries. Kind eyes and handshakes. Murmurs of agreement amongst the men. They're here to help. They've seen things. Heard things. It must be a confusing time for me. Stressful. Teenage years can bring worldly temptations and everyone has fallen short, each of us has gone astray. They understand and are sure I do too. Prayer. Prayer would be the order of the day. With a raw scrape, Dad drags a chair into the middle of the room. My mother hugs the corner of the kitchen, sidelined with her grief into the background.

'Sit,' says Dad.

I comply. With my legs gone jelly, it's almost a relief.

Dad's jaw is clenched. I can't meet his eye when he too is urged to lay hands on my shoulders. He is pressing heavily, but his big farming hands tremble. A bible is produced, thick, black, with worn pages. Verses read. *Breathe.* Assumptions flow. The fallen woman who poured perfume on Jesus's feet. I glance at Mum, thinking of the forgiveness and love Dad showed her. The tone from the elders is different. The fallen woman knew her sin but poured out her worship and repentance. *Inhale.* Jesus forgives. He came for us sinners. The dying thief on the cross at the eleventh hour saw the error of his ways. In his penitence the Lord granted paradise. *Exhale.* They feel a deep burden for my soul. I need healing and gladly they will pray for it. Pray for my restoration to my right mind, this is how I want it, yes?

'Of course,' says Dad. No pause for my answer.

Then begin the prayers. It's eyes closed, fervent crescendos and diminuendos interspersed with utterances of 'Yes, Lord' and 'Amen'. My own eyes are dinner plates. Rigid. Unblinking. I am surrounded, caged in, by five middle-aged, married men. They invite the Holy Spirit to minister to me. Mum's face is hidden in her hands. This daughter who has gone astray, chosen an unchristian lifestyle. Banish the spirit of deception. In the name of Jesus, may the devil be rebuked and righteousness restored. Replace the spirit of profanity. Renew in me a spirit of chastity, clean hands and a pure heart. Change me, restore me, renew me in Jesus for His glory. Amen. And, should it be His will, bring unto me a Christian husband and let me bear children, grandchildren for my parents. May they not miss out on this comfort and joy in their old age. Hallelujah. If there is no other way, remove all base desires and strengthen me for celibacy on a highway of holiness washed in the precious blood of the Lord. Bless His holy name. Amen.

My voice is stolen. No words. As they pray, fear ripples in stealth through my arteries. The hairs stand up on the back of my neck and my fingernails dig into the wood of the seat. Everything external is rigid. Everything internal is writhing, freaked out.

Perhaps if I don't see, it will be less real. A dream. I screw my eyes tight shut. *Breathe.* These are Christian men. Leaders I have looked up to. Admired. Their preaching inspires me. Their faith has encouraged me. *Inhale.* What have I done that's so wrong? I still believe. I still love God. Doesn't He love me? Am I forsaken? I didn't choose this. God made me. I think of the Psalms. *He knit me together in my mother's womb.* Jeremiah. *He knows the plans He has for me. Plans for a hope and a future.* Don't these bible verses they preach include me? For years I've wrapped them around my heart and inhaled them into my spirit. God is Love. The prayers of my church leaders snake insidiously inside me, chilling my soul.

Still they pray. Their breath smells of coffee. Heat rises from my neck to my cheeks to my forehead. All of them and only one of me, my heart hammering my ribcage so violently they must feel it through their fingers clamped on my shoulders. Now they sing. Out of tune, old-style mission-hall hymns and choruses 'For Thine Be the Glory' and 'Would You Be Free from the Burden of Sin?' My mother is frozen. My father mumbles lyrics. My brain is slurry. Am I supposed to sing? Sing a new song unto the Lord? This territory is unknown to me. A strange land. Everything in me is burning. Shame. Embarrassment. Humiliation. I do not fit. I am confused. I'm dirt. Sinful. Backslidden. Alone. Very, very, alone. Where are the others like me? Christian lesbians. I've heard of none. Are they all too terrified to come out?

After the songs, the kettle is filled. It's like their good deed is done, victory assured. Burnt sausages and claggy spuds are set aside and the good biscuit tin is hoked out of a cupboard. Though stranded in the centre of the kitchen, I'm invisible, a mere object for the appeasement of their consciences. Bethany's father is advising my parents. I should be encouraged to date. To look feminine. Wear skirts. Braid my hair. Perhaps it would be best if I stayed away from Bethany just so that people are clear there was nothing untoward in our friendship. Perhaps it would be best too if I don't attend church until I've had time to reflect. The choir? Impossible. Clear repentance would be required. Carol singing? Cancelled. As an elder, my father would know this. It's only right. My eyes dart to him. He is nodding, the muscles in his jaw and neck tight, like he's holding back an explosion. He sips tea but when his eyes catch mine, there is anger – or maybe shame.

The elders know of farmers, some with strapping sons. Fine lads. Upright Christians. Some still single in their twenties. Perhaps a little attention would help me come round? Or there is a therapist in Belfast. They're not sure if he does girls. Boys, yes, with some success, dates, marriages, it's a talking therapy, nothing forced, simply a Christian approach to helping those who wish to change. Either way, strict parenting will be required for the foreseeable. The gay lifestyle is sexually promiscuous. Are they aware if I have been . . . compromised?

Ground swallow me now. I am *sixteen*. These men in my kitchen are asking about my sex life.

In unison, their faces turn to me. I feel my whole body shudder. They nod wisely, reading my silence as guilt. Would they put their own daughters through this hell? Their sons? I wrap my arms tightly across my chest and retract into the hard frame of the chair. Dad's hands are fists in his pockets.

'Accountability is a path to healing,' says the pastor. He stares straight at me. 'Would it help if we offered to hear your confessions?'

Jesus, help me. What are they expecting? I have never even kissed a girl.

Their eyes scour me like I'm a leper, a thing unclean. Unworthy. In the intensity of their glare it strikes me, I'm also something else. Christian entertainment. It's sick. Their shoulders are straight. Their legs spread with confidence. My crisis is feeding their sense of purpose. Their self-righteousness. I shake my head. Timid at first, then fiercely, biting my lower lip until I can taste blood. My refusal triggers shockwaves of murmuring. Clunks of mugs on the table. Silently, Mum moves to wipe crumbs and refill the kettle at the sink. Dad clasps his own mug so tight his knuckles turn white.

'Surely, Faith,' says the pastor, each word slowly emphasized, 'you do want to be healed?'

I cannot speak.

'Faith,' says Dad. 'I don't even understand how you can choose this after everything we've taught you growing up.' Mum grasps his hand as his voice raises with frustration. He stares at me. 'You have to repent. This is wrong.'

I stare back. Is he saying this for his sake, or mine? My throat is burning. Tongue stuck to the roof of my mouth. How was he so gracious to Mum despite her choices as a teen, yet here, when I have no choice, he is so harsh?

Outside a cockerel crows. I breathe. In through my mouth, out through my nose. Silently, I pray. Something switches from panic to purpose. This *is* wrong. The kitchen chair screeches as I leap to my feet. I eyeball them. Every. Single. One. Then I am flooded, not with tears but with rage. Rage and peace. A flash of righteous *How dare they*? Tables overturned in a temple. This is about life. My life. My love. I grab the bible from the table. Maybe I'm preaching. Maybe it's a fit of anger. 'Doesn't it say in here that I'm a child of God? Being gay is not a choice. It's not a lifestyle. It's how I was created. Are you saying God makes mistakes? How archaic is your theology? St Paul teaches that slaves should obey their masters. Did we do a U-turn on that one? Do you still support human exploitation? Every human being on this planet is made in the image of God. That includes me. And yes. Here's my confession. I. Am. Gay. Get it? I'm a lesbian and I love God. I'm Christian, and no matter how hard I search, I can't find anywhere in the bible where Jesus tells me I'm a lost cause. There's plenty about grace. Amazing grace. Plenty about loving our enemies. You taught me that, can't you show it? What is it with straight men and their fixation on how people love? Are you scared? Shouldn't you be more worried about how people *hate*? Or how people hurt?'

I look at my mother, ashen and ignored in the corner of our kitchen.

'This is the anniversary of the murder of my mum's parents,' I say. 'Doesn't she matter more than this? Don't you care?'

The pastor pales. Dad groans. I fire the bible across the table and run. Out the back door. Across the yard. Up the lane. Heels kicking, splashing in mud and puddles. My hair flies in the wind as the night air blasts cold onto my cheeks. At first, I just run blind in panic, expecting them to chase or shout, but over my shoulder there is no sound of pursuit, no arms reaching to drag me backwards. Their words worm through my brain, all the more insidious because every elder seemed oblivious to how deep their daggers stabbed. As my feet keep pounding, my heart steadies. I feel the rhythm, the crunch of gravel and find I'm jogging in time to a different voice. On repeat like a meditation in my head – *I will never leave you nor forsake you.* There is a bounce to my stride as I suck November air deep into my lungs and I don't know where the surge of energy has come from. My head clears and I look up. Overhead are a million stars and a bright slice of moon.

I reach the small crossroads past Jack's house and slow to a stop, listening to the familiar sounds of the countryside at night. The rustles in hedges, the low hoot of an owl, a distant bark of a dog. Suddenly, from nowhere, I'm grinning. Ear to ear. Then laughing. I remember my words to the pastor, the elders, my parents and it dawns. I am free. I am out. I fling my arms high to the heavens. There are uncertainties and fears but also a peace, a knowing – no matter how hard this journey, I will never, ever again, deny who I am.

I close my eyes and whisper a prayer of thanks, then shiver. I'm out without a jumper or coat and the breeze has a bite to it. I don't even have my phone. By morning there will be frost. Any sense of panic I felt in the kitchen has evaporated but there is no way I'm going back home, not until I'm sure the church leaders are gone. Even then, I'm not sure. I think of Mum, ignored in the corner on the anniversary. I so want to hug her and see if she's OK. How she reacted to my news is impossible to tell, her emotions probably won't ring true for a couple of weeks. As for Dad, he said all the Amens, laid hands with the rest, but there was a tremble to him. An out-of-character unease. Shock? Exhaustion from the day that's in it? Or anger? Disappointment? Fear that I'd whistle-blow about the pregnancy cover-up at the start of their marriage? My breath ghosts the air. I'll have to face them, but first I need a place to pass a couple of hours and let everything calm. Across the fields, light spills from the windows in Jack's house. After Uncle Steve's rant over the DNA test, I'm not sure how welcome I'll be. At worst though, I can pass a few hours in the shed without turning to ice.

The closer I get to the farm, the more I sense unease. The dogs are barking and the back door is wide open with light flooding the yard. As I reach the gate, I hear raised voices in the shed. Jack and his dad. A full-blown argument. Uncle Steve is yelling and Jack is giving as good as he gets. Slinking back behind the pillar, I crouch, suddenly tired. I'm not sure I can face much more today. Maybe I'll just sneak into the house and borrow a coat or wait in Jack's room. Something brushes my leg and I jump, but it's only the cat. She purrs as I stroke her, then there is a God-Almighty crash from the shed and she bolts. I worry a strand of hair around my finger. The momentary quiet is worse than the yelling. I hold my breath, straining to hear sound. In St John Ambulance training they drill us to know that silence is not always a good sign.

After a minute, there is fresh shouting but this time there is a different sound to it, something sinister, a sneering edge to Uncle Steve's voice, a tinge of fear or concern in Jack's, his voice higher-pitched than usual. I remember the cut on Jack's face at the weekend. His black eye and busted lip. There is a roar, heavy footsteps and a clatter of metal tools on the concrete floor and then a series of grunts, thuds and scuffling. Jack screams. I run and fling wide the rickety wooden door. Inside the shed, Jack and Uncle Steve are in full fight, the power of it terrifying. Rope is strewn across the floor. Clearly drunk, my uncle is flinging arms wildly but when he does land a punch, Jack judders backwards, staggering to keep on his feet, ducking and jabbing. He's moving more defensively, like he's reluctant to put his full weight into an attack and then I see why. The scream curdles from my throat. Clasped in Uncle Steve's hand is a Stanley knife, the razor-sharp triangle blade glinting in the light of the bare bulb hanging from the ceiling. Both men turn. Uncle Steve glares, yells slurred insults then lurches in my direction. I freeze.

In a flash, Jack moves from behind, sliding in his feet to trip his father. They collapse in a tangle on the floor and Jack kicks the knife spinning. 'Run,' he shouts. 'Get help!'

I take a step backwards in horror. There is blood seeping through Jack's T-shirt. As Uncle Steve rallies, he yanks Jack violently upwards by the hair. Jack's neck goes taut as he kicks his heels backwards, struggling to regain his balance. Again, he shouts. 'Phone. Get your dad.'

I blink, then my brain clicks and I race to their kitchen. They still have a landline. In the panic, my fingers slip on the old buttons and I have to redial. The rings are painfully slow.

'Hello?'

'Dad . . .' My sentences all string together and words fail in mind-blank fear because there is more screaming and clanging and heaving and clatter from the shed and 'Dad, please Dad, just come, now. No, forget earlier, this is . . . Uncle Steve and Jack, they're . . . please, quick, they're killing each other. It's punches and a knife – oh my God, Dad, Jack needs you – please, I don't know what to do, they're getting hurt and—'

'On my way. Phone an ambulance.'

He hangs up. I stare at the phone. Another huge crash from the shed jolts me into action and I dial 999. Maybe it's the routine of the four questions that I know from St John Ambulance . . . *Is the patient breathing? What address are you calling from? What number are you calling from? What's the reason for your call?* I answer, clear, precise. My adrenalin pumps and finally I have focus. Possibly a stabbing, they are still fighting. Yes, even over the phone she can hear the backdrop of the violence in the shed and now she is talking, a voice on the other end of the phone advising me to stay safe, keep my distance, but it is her voice becoming more and more distant because I have abandoned the handset on the counter. The shed has gone totally silent and I am walking towards it.

Before nudging the shed door, I hesitate, take a deep breath and steel myself. The door squeaks on its hinges. Slumped by the Honda Shadow, Jack lies crumpled on the concrete, the red stain spread further on the T-shirt across his middle. His shoulder is contorted out of joint. His skin pale. Uncle Steve is kneeling at the far end by the tool bench. He's working at a rope. Tying a slip knot. This time, my slowness is deliberate.

'Uncle Steve? May I help Jack?'

My uncle stares at me, his expression void, then convulsive sobs wrack his body. He folds forward into a ball until his head touches the floor. 'I . . . I think I've killed him. My boy . . . I didn't mean . . .'

'Let me check.' I raise my hands and tread lightly but swiftly over to Jack, keeping my eyes fixed on Uncle Steve as much as possible and trying to remember my first aid. Start with vitals. With one hand I clasp Jack's wrist and check for a pulse. I hold the other in front of his mouth and watch his chest. The pulse is there, but weak. His breath warms my fingers, the rise and fall of his chest laboured, but present. As I lift Jack's T-shirt, I pray. Across his midriff is a gash, long but shallow, seeping blood, but not dangerously. 'Jack?' I whisper. No response. A spanner lays strewn by his forehead. I smooth back his dark hair. There is bruising and swelling by his hairline. I glance at Uncle Steve. 'What happened?'

He staggers to his feet, coiling the rope into his hands. 'Many things happened. Many things that shouldn't have.' He stares at the rafter above him and mumbles something about regrets.

'Did you throw this spanner? Did it hit Jack?'

Uncle Steve nods. He shuffles on his feet as he studies the rope. 'It was an accident. I didn't know. Just a bag, carry a bag. Here to there.'

My eyes scour the shed. There is no bag. Jack is out for the count. How long until Dad gets here? Or the ambulance? Uncle Steve is edgy. I don't trust his movements. 'What's with the rope?' I say.

He smiles, strangely. 'Your mother always wanted justice. What better day?' His words still slur but there is a sadness about him now, something wistful.

My gaze drops from his eyes to the rope and then my own eyes widen. He takes a step backwards and flings the rope high over his head. It loops over the bar, the noose dangling above his head. Now I understand. Jack wasn't attacking. He was trying to prevent a suicide. 'Jack's still alive,' I say. 'You don't want to do this.'

'Don't I? You wouldn't say that if you knew the truth.'

'What truth?'

He hesitates. 'Will Jack be OK?'

'He's concussed. I think his shoulder is dislocated.'

He nods. Tears trickle down his cheeks. 'Tell him I love him.' He moves to tie the free end of the rope to the bench, then changes his mind. As he walks towards me, I step back. Surely Dad can't be far off?

Uncle Steve ties the rope to the Honda Shadow instead. If I can distract him, stall him, even a few minutes . . .

'I saw your bike in a photo,' I say. 'Someone else used to own it.'

Uncle Steve stops. Stares. 'True,' he says. 'He was a brave man. Ryan Craig was a good friend. Didn't get sucked in the way I did. Thought he'd found a better way.' My uncle misjudges a step backwards, crashes against the tool bench and reaches out to steady himself. Behind me, Jack groans.

'Where's Ryan now?'

'Good question. Maybe I'll find out soon enough, but my guess is he's in the other place. No heroes where I'm going.'

Distracted by Jack beginning to stir, I'm not following what my uncle means about Ryan. My head tries to understand, but now my uncle is gazing upwards, zoning out from everything around him. Please, God, please. My dad or the ambulance. Anything. Quick.

'Uncle Steve, what did you mean about carrying a bag? About justice?'

Jack moans. For a split second, I turn. He's groggy, trying to sit, blinking his eyes in the light. Then I hear the scrape of a bucket on concrete and I spin. My uncle's hand is reaching for the rope.

'No,' I scream, running to him. 'Don't. Please don't. Whatever it is, we'll sort it. We'll all help. Jack needs you. We love you.' I reach for his shoulder, but he brushes me away. Stares straight down into my eyes. His are the same beautiful turquoise as Jack's, except already they look dead.

'Here is justice,' he says, swaying on the bucket as he pulls down on the rope. 'Tell your mother I'm sorry. I just carried the bag like they told me. I was fifteen. But I sneaked a peek. A lunch box jammed with wires. A heavy circle fishing magnet taped on top with gaffer.' He reaches out his hand and I take it in mine. 'I knew what it was. I just never knew where it was headed. If I had, I wouldn't have done it. It was never about attacking our own side. Not for me.'

I shake my head. 'I don't understand. What do you mean?'

He leans his head down, right next to mine, clamping his free hand around the back of my skull and drawing me in until our foreheads touch. I shudder. The alcohol on his breath is fierce. There is nowhere I can run from here. He whispers. Each word

230

set out clearly so there is no misunderstanding. 'Once I'd stashed the bag, it was someone else's job to lift it – take it to its final destination and install it. Under a car. A cop's car. It was no IRA bomb that killed your grandparents. It was Loyalists. The UVF. Our Ulster Volunteer Force.' With a swift move, he shoves me in the chest. I reel backwards against the shed wall. He looks over at Jack, then up to the rafter. I pull my arm over my eyes and as the bucket scrapes, I scream. Tyres scrape the gravel in the driveway. Footsteps. Running. Voices. I won't open my eyes. I won't. I won't. No. Please. No. I'm rocking back and forth, back and forth because it was seconds, just seconds. Then I hear hacking, cutting, a blade on rope. Coughing, rasping, tears and paramedics and my dad, my dad's arms wrapping tight, tight, tight around me, lifting me, carrying me out into the yard and holding me against his chest. 'It's OK, Faith. It's OK. I'm here.' Both of us are shaking.

I open my eyes to the blue flashing lights. As well as an ambulance, there's a police car. Jack is being stretchered out of the shed. My uncle is sat on a log by the gate, handcuffed between two policemen, who are talking to him in low voices, reassuring him, keeping him calm, just like I remember Tara's mam talking to me in her kitchen at Halloween.

My legs buckle.

Dad catches me under the arms. 'Let's get you home,' he says.

I look straight into his eyes. 'Do you really want me home? I can't change. It's impossible.'

He looks away, his eyes sweeping across the yard to take in the ambulance, the police and his brother. The hacked rope is lying in the dirt by the shed door. When Dad looks back, his eyes are wet. 'Yes,' he says, hugging me tight. 'Please, come home.'

Chapter 24

TARA
Derry, 8 November 2019

It's like when you got the nit letters home from primary school. Everything itches for no reason except, this time, there is a reason. Anticipation. Any minute they will be here. Emer has brought posh Belgian biscuits, a whole tin, and despite outside being Baltic, Nan has the window wide open on account of having chain-smoked every last Benson on the planet. Even without any grown-up asking, my best behaviour is happening right now, all by itself, because some switch in my core knows this is proper important. The sneaky glow I'm holding in is that, if this works, maybe I'm not such a bad article after all, cos like, it was my idea; but, if it goes tits up, I'm not for taking the rap. The grown-ups all agreed to this too.

Mam, me and Emer are squished into our living room, each of us sitting in weird places on cushions on the floor, Ingabire on the dragged-in kitchen stool, Nan in her armchair, all staring at the two-person gap on the sofa. This kind of waiting would freeze the arse off a bee. There's not enough patience in the world and they're only two minutes late.

'Sure, I'll put on the kettle,' says Nan.

'No,' I say, jumping to my feet, 'I will.'

Her slippers twitch but she stays put. Mam shoots me a smile.

I pace about the kitchen, waiting, and pull out my phone while the kettle grumbles. Two whole days without Faith or Jack messaging. That's normal with Faith and I know she's got shedloads going on with coming out or not coming out or whatever, but like, since Halloween, Jack's been in touch every day, which for a lad is mega. Usually, it's a text straight after school when he's on the bus, or sometimes round eleven at night when I'm kinda hoping he's thinking about me in a whole different way. These last days? Zero. Tumbleweed and radio silence.

I'm rearranging biscuits on the plate for the ten-zillionth time when our doorbell rings.

Mam welcomes them in, all fake-posh and manners, and I gawp up the hall to see the wee Yaris has shimmied itself across the bridge and parked itself right outside our house and the old lady with the pink coat is stood there in our hall with a younger duplicate of herself all scarfed, hatted and Protestant looking. There's handshakes and politeness with triple-dosed awkwardness and then it's a whole teamplay manoeuvre with Emer offering to take coats and Ingabire signposting the ladies into the living room. I've glued myself to the hall wallpaper, come over all toddler-coy. Ingabire gives me a nod and I follow them in, back to my cushion by the telly where I do a whole sit-stand-sit thing cos I never read the rule book on meeting long-lost relatives. I never knew I *had* relatives. It goes communion-quiet, like the ultra-holy moment we got taught about in primary, where you daren't laugh nor pick your nose, and then Nan heaves herself up out of the armchair for a second time with one of them pensioner exhale groans and wheezes her way across the carpet. She does her lip-trembling-eye-rubbing thing, which could be good but may be bad and then – well, then she launches her arms wide, all smiles, and stands there in the world's riskiest don't-leave-me-hanging pose. Risky cos she might actually lose her balance, never mind not be hugged back. Pink coat lady, now pink jumper lady, is helped to her feet by her younger duplicate and suddenly she and Nan, tears tripping them, are hugging like it's already Christmas.

There are a billion nods and some rapid-fire Derry Mammy chat. The pink lady, Cathy, is Sam's sister. Aye, surely, Cathy had married and yes, the other lady is Helen, her daughter. Nan's all, 'This here's my daughter, Erin, and my granddaughter Tara.' Confirmations. Yes, Mam is Sam's daughter. Blushings and hushings. Cathy stands back and studies Mam's face. *Yes.* She nods. *For sure.* She can see Sam in Mam's dark hair and in the way she smiles. Then they're all back to the bawling and wailing: 'How could we not have known? Why ever didn't you say?' The Troubles. The mortification. The stab of sin and shaming from men of religion. The stab of fear in the shadows from men with guns. The distancing of communities. The rawness of trauma. The tension you could slice during the Hunger Strikes. Nan didn't even have a landline in them days either and after the murder, Sam's family had moved house. Out of the city and away from the worst of the violence. Nan and Cathy tut and reminisce, mouth *if only*s.

I'm squatting on the cushion gazing up and at last they're laughing and working out Helen's relation to Mam. They're cousins. Mam smiles like a wee girl just given a teddy and Cathy hugs her in a blur of pink and says, 'Call me Aunt, surely doll, call me Aunt.' Next, more flurries of 'How in ever have we not kept in touch?' 'Wasn't it bad oul' days them Troubles?'

The place is full of lamenting and regret and more hugs and tales told of Sam, with sighs and sad smiles and *God Rest Him*s as grief etches itself across all our faces. Then attention turns to me and eyebrows are raised, like I just magicked myself into the

234

room. I stand up to – OMG – hair ruffling and teddy-tight hugs, cos Cathy is my great aunt and Helen's like a first cousin once removed so her kids are something complicated and cousiny to me and I never even knew that was a thing. My eyes are welling up but, when I look at Emer and Ingabire, they're grinning, so I reckon it must be OK to be feeling gooey and lopsided.

Everyone sits again and, it turns out, Protestants and Catholics are all the same when it's about cups of tea and plates of biscuits. The whole country could've been sorted with better catering. Cathy and Nan both politely refuse the chocolate biscuits on the first tour of the plate, with Mam and Helen both calorie counting and muttering 'doesn't it all just sneak up on you?' as they shake their heads. One whisper from Emer of, 'Sure, it's nearly Christmas . . .', though, and the pattern's almost off the plate with the crumbs. I'm dispatched by Mam for a refill and to stick on the kettle again while I'm at it.

I'm hugging the kitchen radiator trying to understand the glowy feeling inside me when the message lands from Faith.

I've got news. Are you with people?

Chatter and laughter spills from the living room.

Yes. ???

Good. Can I call? It's complicated.

My feet are toeing at the worn lino on our kitchen floor as Faith rabbits on. She's not wrong about it being complicated. My head's fried. Every so often she says, 'Are you still there? Are you following?' I nod, then remember I have to speak, but am not sure if any sound will squeeze out. Jack is in hospital. Recovering. Beat up something horrendous by his own da. Worse, he's terrified to talk to me and swore Faith into keeping her gob shut, but here it is, Jack's da was in the UVF. Ulster Volunteer Force.

235

Proper terrorist style. Like the Prod IRA, only all Brit. Khaki jackets and seventies sunglasses. And if our side was all Free Ireland, the UVF was all For God and Ulster, Brits forever, and somehow it got twisted because Faith says Jack's da was something to do with her grandparents' murder. Not the IRA. Like their own paramilitaries killed their own police. Brits against Brits. It makes no sense.

'Sounds pure messed up,' I say, then glance up the hall thinking a wise move might've been to close the kitchen door.

'I'm not even halfway through it,' she says. 'Sit down.'

I plonk myself onto the kitchen table with my feet on a chair.

'Jack's dad was trying to hang himself.'

'Again?'

Faith goes quiet. Then whispers. 'What do you mean, again?'

'Oh,' I say. And then it's me telling her what Jack had said to me. But not telling the circumstances of it, which still brings a low heat on every time I think on it, which is pretty much all the time.

'Oh,' she says.

Nan's voice carries from the living room and it's all ups and downs, anecdotes and twittering happiness, as though they're weaving a family web of connectedness.

'I didn't know you didn't know,' I say.

Faith sighs. Then she explains how the whole thing went down and the latest is that Jack's da has gone and handed himself in to the cops for questioning and Faith's family is like Armageddon hit early and that's without even the whole handling of her coming out and the religious nuts in her kitchen and I'm all 'OMG, for real?'

'That's not all,' says Faith. 'The motorbike in your photo? It's the one in Jack's shed. When I asked Jack's dad about it, he said it belonged to Ryan Craig. He said he was brave. He called him a hero.'

My heart skips a beat. 'Ryan Craig? Aka Ryan O'Leary? Aka our da?'

'Bingo.'

I pause, not quite sure how to put it. 'He sounds . . . wild Prod.'

'And?' says Faith.

'And . . . nothing. Just, why'd he lie to Mam? Why change his surname?'

'Would she have gone with a Protestant?'

'Maybe,' I say. Then I think on what's happening up the hall. Had Mam mentioned about Nan to Ryan? Had Ryan been hiding something else? If he was friends with Jack's da, was my da also in the UVF? I bite my thumb real hard till it hurts. 'Can we find Ryan . . . Craig? Did your Jack's da say where he is?'

Faith goes quiet again. 'I think my parents know the truth but everything's so mental here I can't ask. Not yet,' she says. 'Thing is, though, we might not need them. Listen carefully. My uncle said Ryan Craig *was* brave. Not *is* brave. It never dawned when he said it, but that night's been on repeat in my brain. I'm sure he used the past tense.'

'Eh?'

'I think . . . we should visit the graveyard.' She breathes deep. 'Tara, I think our dad is dead.'

After feck knows how long, when I don't appear, Emer comes to find me. 'You OK?' she says. 'Bit emotional in there – but in a good way.'

I nod and keep stirring the tea on the stove. It's like tar. Maybe I've been stirring it five minutes. Maybe ten. Teabags going

237

round and round, worn out like my thoughts. Emer lifts the spoon out of my fingers. Sets it on the counter with a clink.

'Tara?'

I sniff. Wipe the back of my hand across my cheeks.

'What's up? You overwhelmed?'

'Not with them ones.' I gesture up the hall. 'Them ones are great.'

Emer does a wide-eyed WTF-then? look with raised eyebrows that won't drop until I spill.

I sigh. 'Faith thinks our da is dead,' I say. 'Why, when life is finally getting sorted, does it have to go arse about face again? How in hell am I gonna tell Mam?'

'Oh,' says Emer.

I'm thinking *oh* is today's stuck record. It's an *oh* inhabited day. Good *oh*s and bad *oh*s and who-bloody-knows *oh*s.

Emer flicks the lid onto the teapot and puts more biscuits on the tray. I watch her like it's rocket science. 'I think,' she says, 'we should go back in and enjoy Nan's moment first. Your new relatives really are lovely. Tara, you've helped such a good thing happen. Can you put on a brave face for another half hour?'

I nod. Pretending comes easy. Honesty is way more difficult. As for truth? It's a total brain-melt. Now that me and Faith are this close to finding it, I'm not sure I want to know. Will Mam?

On our doorstep there are hugs. Hugs with love. Hugs like family. Hugs to heal missed decades. In the hall behind me, Emer is whispering to Ingabire. I want to relax, but my insides are balled tight. With Cathy and Helen safely zooting their way back to the Waterside, I look at Mam. I wanted to find Da to kick out my anger. To have someone to blame. But what if he wasn't just the bastard that left Mam up the duff and never looked back? What if he was worse? Would that hurt? Or the other angle, what if the truth is, he did love her, he just . . . died. Would that hurt more?

As Nan and Mam turn back from the doorstep, I take Mam's hand and squeeze it tight.

Chapter 25

FAITH
County Armagh, 10 November 2019

Remembrance Sunday is supposed to be as choreographed as Christmas. It's not supposed to be Mum and Dad zombified with shock over speculative online local headlines about Uncle Jack and historic UVF bombings. It's not supposed to be messages from my so-called best friend Bethany saying her mum's asked her to sing the Christmas solo because – quote of the century – I missed a week of choir practice. And it's definitely not supposed to be Aunt Bea, Jack's mum, sat at the end of our breakfast table, looking as drawn as her fifth cup of tea. I dip a soldier of toast into my egg.

'Holed up in the house and not speaking to a being,' says Aunt Bea. 'Won't you talk to him, Philip? He is your brother.'

Dad glances at Mum. She shakes her head. Uncle Steve has phoned the house multiple times asking to speak to her, but she won't countenance it. Dad's in an awkward limbo and he's not the only one; Aunt Bea has spent the last half hour speed-talking through how she knew there was something, knew it was bad, but not this. Lord, no. She'd guessed at paramilitary. Sometimes, thick with drink, he'd mumbled in his sleep. Always the bag. The bag with the bomb. Never once had it crossed her mind it was *that* bomb. She'd known it was guilt drove him to drink. If only he'd agreed to counselling, but the stubbornness, that Ulster thranness, was thick on the man and so was the fear.

'But now he's spilled the whiskey down the drain and his guts to the police. And to me. They'd have been better keeping him in but they won't charge him. He phoned me in the middle of last night begging for me to listen. Sober as Good Friday. Begging my forgiveness over everything. Especially over hurting Jack. The man's distraught. This secret's been killing him for years. Nearly did kill him. Twice. We have to help him.' Aunt Bea reaches across the table towards my mother. 'If we don't forgive him, he could try again.'

The silence is so heavy, I can hear washing-up bubbles fizz in the sink.

Finally, my mother speaks. The monotone of her voice is scary. 'His actions killed my parents.'

Aunt Bea pulls back her hand and sits still. 'His actions were to carry a bag. To collect it from a hedge at a bus stop and carry it by night to a back alley. That's all.'

'The back alley near my home. For collection by a bomber who fastened it to my father's car. I was fourteen.'

'He was only fifteen. Younger than Faith here. Younger than Jack.'

'He was part of a murder. Bad enough in its own right but a murder of one of his own community? Unforgiveable.'

'He was a child. Groomed from twelve, sucked in by thirteen. Sworn in over the bible and playing sinister I Spy at fourteen. Carrying sports bags from A to B at fifteen, clueless as to what was really going on.' Aunt Bea leans forward. 'It was the Troubles, for God's sake. He thought he'd be fighting the IRA. Not . . . that. He didn't even know where the bomb was headed. Wasn't even supposed to peek inside to know it *was* a bomb. He saw a lunch box with tape around it and a big bagel-shaped magnet on top. All he was told was to wear gloves and not ask questions.

Philip, he was younger than you. How did your family not notice?'

My dad folds his arms and shifts his weight. 'I don't know,' he says. 'Really, I don't know. I'm only a year older. Guess I was blind busy helping with the farm, putting food on plates. Remember, we'd three younger sisters. Them days were mad. People kept their heads down. By the time I lifted mine, Steve was an unemployed dropout addicted to the demon drink. At least I got him out of that and into the church.'

'Didn't you ever question *why* he drank?'

'Main thing was he stopped – at least until all the media stuff about truth recovery hit recent headlines.'

My aunt shakes her head. 'Main thing was the drink made him useless to the UVF. Gave him an out.'

Dad lifts the kitchen bible. 'Main thing is he found forgiveness in God.'

'And what use is that if he can't find forgiveness from his own family? Isn't there a line in there about forgive us our sins as we forgive others?'

More silence. Mum's hands are clasped tight, fingers knotted. She takes a deep breath in through her nose, holds it in her lungs, then exhales. 'I can't do this,' she says. 'Maybe not ever. Definitely not today.'

Dad drapes his arm over her shoulder, but she brushes it off and stands. 'Some of us have a remembrance service to go to. It's about victims.' She stares straight at Aunt Bea. 'Not perpetrators.' Her chair squeaks as she clanks it against the table and runs from the room.

Glances between Aunt Bea and Dad.

'And what about you, Bea?' says Dad. 'If you think we should forgive him over a murder, are you going to forgive him for how his drinking wrecked your marriage?'

Aunt Bea hesitates. 'I might,' she says. 'If he stays sober and goes to counselling. We're not legally divorced yet. I do love him, you know. It's just . . . he made it impossible to stay.'

Dad tilts his head and folds his arms, surprised. 'Go,' he says. 'She's a lot going on in her head today. Other things we're dealing with. I'll call you.' Then he heads after Mum.

I smush the shell of my egg in on itself, watching how easily the smoothness shatters. Aunt Bea stands, but she doesn't leave. 'Are you OK, Faith?' she says. 'You know you're Jack's hero? And mine.' She pauses to check I'm taking it in. 'Jack'll be discharged soon from hospital. Even your Uncle Steve says you're an angel. If it wasn't for you, I'd have been burying them both.'

I look up. Her eyebrows are furrowed. She holds out her hand like she did for Mum. I clasp it and she pulls me into a hug and ruffles my hair. Then she stops. 'Faith,' she says. 'How long has your hair been like this? Have you seen a doctor?'

I step back and glance towards the corridor. Down the hallway Mam is sobbing and Dad's voice is low, trying to console her. I draw a finger to my lips and shake my head. 'Today's got to be about Mum,' I whisper.

She lifts her coat. 'No,' she says. 'That's where it's all twisted. Our generation was yesterday. Today needs to be about looking after yours.' At the door, she turns one final time. 'By the way,' she says. 'Jack's still struggling with everything that's happened, never mind the injuries. But he did talk a bit yesterday. Filled me in on a few things. Showed me photos. You suited that T-shirt. If you need me, I'm here.'

How my parents section off chunks of their lives into neat boxes, I don't know. I'm chewing over the kitchen conversation as we journey into Armagh but, just like my outburst to the pastor and elders has not been spoken of since Wednesday, my parents make no further mention of Aunt Bea's visit. Now, when I'm ready to talk, it's like they're buffering. Maybe it's timing. Maybe they can't handle it. Or maybe, they can't handle me.

We park opposite the Orange Hall and make our way, slightly late, to the huddle of people at the ceremony. The memorial on the Mall is a grey monolith. The poppies laid reverently at its feet, red, symbolic of blood and peace. This is the choreography I know, and Remembrance Sunday has a solemnity to it that seeps through my coat into my being but, for the first time, I'm questioning it. Our breath whitens the air in witness. We remember the dead with our silence. Is that the right way? The only way? Is it something my family does too well? I used to think my family talked too much about the history but now, I'm realizing, they only talk about certain bits.

As the Old Boys brass band play 'Men of Harlech' and Scouts, Guides, and representatives of various military organizations lay wreaths, I chew over war and forgiveness. Countries make peace with written agreements but how does it work for people? In my heart, already I know I forgive Uncle Steve. I saw the hopelessness in his eyes. But would I forgive him if I were Jack? Or, more to the point, if I were Mum? I glance across to the far corner. Diagonally opposite, other members of our church are gathered. Usually, we'd stand together. Usually, Jack would be here with his dad. Not this year. This year, Bethany is gawping across at me. Do I forgive her? I can feel the bile in my throat even thinking about it. So much for 'O Holy Night'. She's not the only one with razor eyes; I catch the glances from the pastor, the elders and other good-living folk. Apparently, I'm no longer in that category. Dad shuffles uncomfortably. Subtle headshakes, whispers behind hands. I pull my beanie hat down further and stomp my feet to keep the circulation going. At least it's not raining.

Now it's the turn of the police to lay their wreath. My mother links her arm through Dad's elbow. This one has particular poignancy. Two officers walk to the monument, set down the ring of poppies and step backwards in timed respect. A couple of days ago, after Uncle Steve's confession, the police phoned. Mum held the receiver tight to her ear, nodding quietly. Afterwards, I was part of the family hugs, but not the intense living-room conversation with Dad. If they learned the truth, they haven't yet shared it and questions are playing pinball round my head. In the Troubles, police deaths were usually at the hands of the IRA. Why would the UVF target my grandfather? That's the other side. If Uncle Steve confessed to a crime, how come he's sat in his living room? Why hasn't he been charged?

The Royal British Legion are next in line with their poppies. An old man and woman approach the memorial and set down a circle of red. Both wear long black coats. When they turn, I see it's the elderly couple from the graveyard. The British Legion help veterans and their families. Maybe he's a veteran, or perhaps they lost a child. It gets me thinking. Air Force, Navy, Army. What was it Uncle Steve said? *Hero. A better way. A brave man.* Was my dad, my real dad, a soldier? I forget the ceremony and start to puzzle it through. 2001. Only three years after the Troubles ended. It works for Tara's mam's story. He might have trained in England. Openness might have caused him security fears. Might she have mentioned about her own father's murder by the IRA? My dad might have felt the truth was too big a risk to his safety – at least until he knew her better. She was Catholic. From Derry. He wasn't just Protestant, he was army. Or it might have been fear of losing her – honesty from him about being in the British Army could've made her run a mile. Maybe Ryan really wanted to be with her? But what about my mum? Was it just a fling? Crazy days? And, if he *is* dead, how did he die?

I'm engrossed in my train of thought, when, wreaths laid, a hush descends. Then the familiar words of every year.

'They shall grow not old, as we that are left grow old:

Age shall not weary them, nor the years condemn.

At the going down of the sun and in the morning

We will remember them.'

The bugle sounds the Last Post and we stand in silence. For the first time I wonder, as well as my grandparents, am I remembering my father?

After the ceremony, I move to follow the procession to the designated church, but Dad sets a hand lightly on my shoulder. 'Wait,' he says, then heads to our church group. I stand with Mum, wiggling my toes in my boots, the cold rising through the soles from the tarmac. For the first time in days, I sense her studying me, her blue eyes steady, like she's back in the room, released out of a hypnosis. I swallow. With my toe, I scuff a leaf off the side of my boot. At some stage it'll come out, how I've disappointed her. She'll say it more quietly than Dad, I think, with less bible and more heart, but with the same tone of betrayal. If it is harsher, maybe Aunt Bea will help. Her words this morning were unexpected and kind. Across by the railings, Dad is in conversation with Bethany's dad and our pastor. My dad is animated, all hand gestures and head movement. The others are like cut-outs, as responsive as the statue on the memorial.

'Faith.' Mum pulls my attention back. 'What's with the hats? These days you're always in hats, bandanas and Alice bands.'

It's the way she says it. I know she knows. My lip wobbles and I turn away as my eyes well up. She turns me back, pulling me into a hug.

'I'm sorry,' I say. 'I'm so, so, sorry.'

'Ssshh,' she says. 'It's me who's sorry. Sorry I'm struggling to be . . . present. To understand. I'm trying but, this last week or so, I've been wrestling with a lot in my head – facing a few home truths. I promise though, you'll see, I'm getting there.' She glances over at Dad, weaving his way back to us through the stragglers from the ceremony. His hands are buried deep in his coat pockets. 'Later. We can talk later,' she says. 'After the graveyard. When we get home.' That's when I realize, we're going straight to the graveyard. For the first time I can ever remember, we're not going to the church service first.

The black metal bolt. The iron gate. Everything about the graveyard feels familiar but the sensation today is different and I can't put my finger on it. Perhaps it's the light. Perhaps it's that as Dad, Mum and I carry our simple wooden crosses with poppies to my grandparents' grave, my eyes are drawn to the rows beyond. Searching for the possibility of a name. I don't know for sure that he was a local, but, given his friendship with Uncle Steve, there's a good chance he was.

Even the birds are quieter today, like everything gathers in to remember. With a tissue, I wipe the condensation off the gold lettering. It smears a swathe of dry sheen over my grandparents' names. David and Ruth. No one needs to tell us to be silent here. No bugle sounds the Last Post. Looping arms, we pray in silence. I wonder how often over the years my mother prayed for answers, and how much she wished today that the truth could change. The *murdered by terrorists* reads so differently now. Her hand grips mine tighter than usual.

'Have you heard of collusion?' she says, without taking her eyes off the gravestone.

'No,' I say.

She leans her head on Dad's shoulder. 'Philip . . .'

Dad supports her round the waist and strokes her hair. 'Faith,' he says. 'Collusion is when the police shared information with Loyalist terrorists like the UVF. Sometimes in the Troubles, not even the police felt justice could be had within the law.'

'That doesn't make sense,' I say.

'Not everything does.' He stoops over the grave to straighten the cross with the poppy. 'Imagine being in the police back then and seeing other officers, politicians, your friends, gunned down, bombed, maimed. Imagine attending funeral after funeral for years. Witnessing the suffering. Desperate for it to end . . . Now imagine the police knew who the individuals in the IRA were but they couldn't pull their own guns until a crime happened. They couldn't charge terrorists without evidence. Do you follow?'

I shrug, only half following but not sure I should interrupt.

'Imagine you knew other people who owned guns. Other people, on your side, who could unofficially do something to kill off the threat . . . Would you lift the phone? Quietly, albeit illegally, try to arrange the taking of a handful of terrorist lives to save who knows how many innocent ones? Would the ends justify the means?'

I hesitate and think. In my head, I know this is not about a made-up scenario. He's talking about something real, but it sounds more like revenge than justice, at least, not a legal justice. I think about Tara and what she said happened to Oran. How he was shot with no rights. No trial. No chance for his voice to be heard. It's different, but something in it feels the same. 'Shouldn't the police always keep the law? Isn't that their job?'

Mum and Dad stay quiet.

I look at my grandfather's name on the grave and think. 'Are you saying Granda David was a corrupt policeman? That he wanted to break the law and share information to pit terrorists against each other?'

'No.' Mum's voice rings clear as glass. 'The police phoned. They're saying your grandad was a good cop. He was killed by the UVF because he *wouldn't* collude. He was going to whistleblow. Show up his own side and name the corrupt ones so . . . so he was silenced.'

For a second, I can't breathe. My grandfather was murdered because he was too honest? None of us speak. Suddenly there is a new emotion. Not sorrow. A warmth swelling in my chest. Pride.

I hunker down and plant my own wooden cross with the poppy so that our three crosses are in a row. 'I wish I'd known you, Granda,' I say. 'Taking on your own side – you were a brave man.'

Standing, I catch my dad's eye. He pales as if I've uttered something not historic, but prophetic. He nudges my mother and she nods. From her pocket, she pulls another poppy, takes my hand and leads me two rows back to another grave. The headstone is plain cut. Bullet grey.

It's less than ten steps from where I have stood on so many Saturdays. I was so near, yet so oblivious to its significance.

Ryan Craig
Killed in Action in Afghanistan
Aged 20
22 December 1981 – 5 October 2002
Beloved son.

My throat goes dry. I hold my breath and squeeze Mum's hand tight, so tight. 'Is this . . . my dad?' I look at her. She's nodding, unable to speak. Emotion surges, overwhelming, hot tears flowing down my face, flooding my mouth with salt. I fall to my knees and feel the damp cold of the grass through my leggings. After a moment, Mum crouches beside me and rubs my arm. Dad hovers behind. I stare at the headstone inscription over and over.

'He was in the British Army?' I say.

'Yes. Killed on his first tour of duty. Before you were born.'

'It doesn't say father . . .'

'He didn't know. I told no one. Just Philip. Philip had been my first boyfriend. We'd been going out in the months before my parents were killed and then, with the trauma and the shift into social care, I just fell apart. For years, nothing functioned – especially not meaningful relationships. The fling with Ryan, it happened when I was still drinking, still lost. Ryan was drunk too. We weren't even in a relationship. He had a few days home on leave from his army training. He hated the army. Never wanted to join and was determined to leave at the earliest opportunity but, just like Uncle Steve, he'd been getting tangled up with a bad crowd, so his parents made him sign up. Thought it was for the best. He was a free spirit. An artist and musician. He . . . he gave you your voice.'

I lay my poppy at the base of the headstone and lean my head on Mum's shoulder. From high in the trees, birds sing out. 'I need to tell Tara,' I say.

Mum nods and stands.

With my phone, I take a photo of the grave. Later, I'll think of the right words. Later, I'll call Tara and send the image. For now, I stand and bow my head in respect a second longer.

Dad – Philip – coughs. Behind me, there is a nervous shuffling. No doubt, my parents must be finding this hard. I lift my eyes and turn to face them, but neither of them are looking at me. They're looking over their shoulders to where an elderly couple are walking hesitantly towards us. There are nods of welcome as they approach. Mum leans into Dad and he puts his arm around her shoulders to steady her. The elderly couple are holding hands, fingers interlaced so tightly their knuckles are white. The man's eyes are wide. When I'm close enough to see into them, I can see tears welling up. There is a bright sheen over the green irises flecked with brown.

The air feels heavy, a stillness more tangible than when the bugle sounded the Last Post earlier. The men reach out in a handshake. My mother and the lady exchange weak smiles of recognition and then everyone looks at me. As I glance between their faces, trying to read the story, my mum bursts into tears, nods repeatedly, then reaches to pull me in tight before turning me gently to face the elderly couple. We stand together at the graveside and my heart beats so crazily I wonder if it'll bust out of my ribs. Grown-up glances, then, my mother speaks.

'Faith,' her voice trembles. 'I'd like to introduce you to Ryan's parents. Your grandparents. Mr and Mrs Craig, this is my daughter who I mentioned on the phone. Your . . . granddaughter.'

Initial awkwardness. More glances. Then the lady, Mrs Craig, steps forward and clasps my hands in hers. She looks straight into my eyes. 'I knew there was something,' she says. 'From that chance meeting a month ago right here in the rain. You had to be a Craig, your eyes . . .'

'I'm so sorry,' says Mum. 'This shouldn't have been this way and—'

'Ssshh,' says the lady. 'As you know, on the phone it was a

shock but . . .' She looks at me again. 'We are where we are, and this –' she nods '– this is a beautiful place to be. Unexpected, but beautiful.' Her eyes glisten, and then there is light. Light on their faces, in smiles, in hugs and flows of tears, happy tears like sparkles of silver on weathered cheeks. Proper introductions and explanations and all four of them looking at me. Looking at me with love. In between the graves of my real father and my maternal grandparents, we hug. All of us. Something in my mother lifts with the acceptance, the tilt of her shoulders, the way she carries her head is straighter. Every atom in my body is mixed up, buzzing and flipped about, yet somehow it feels like my world isn't upside down any more. It's turning right side up. Remembrance Sunday has shifted from looking backwards to opening our eyes to look forwards. Never before has the graveyard felt so full of life.

Chapter 26

TARA
Derry, 10 December 2019

OMG. Supersized. It's our exhibition day and I'm running around the gallery like a blue-arsed fly meeting myself on the way back. In a few minutes, our exhibition will open. Two weeks until Christmas and I'm already high on Shloer, which really doesn't go with chewing gum, and I'm thinking Ingabire had her head screwed on with the not buying wine for this. And there are people here. For me. People plural, not just one person. Not just Mam. Nan too. And not just cos I hid her lighter until she swore blind she'd come. We're both pulling out all the stops to lift Mam. She's our glue and, since Faith's grave photo last month, it's like Mam's become unstuck. When I showed her Faith's text, Mam didn't speak for hours. She cradled the mug of tea Nan made until it went cold, then she borrowed the cowboy hat and hasn't given it back. Tonight though, she's dug out her lipstick and says she's here with bells on, never better.

Also cheering from the sidelines are Lena and Megan (who is like way more ace and totally sound since I helped her with the balloon ankle thing) and of course, Ingabire and Emer. Shock of the night is that Miss Tierney, my art teacher, has arrived and has glammed herself up so good no one would even reckon on her being a teacher and she's already beady-eyeing my display. The wee Yaris has whizzed my Great Aunt Cathy and something-cousin Helen across the bridge another time cos apparently, they're not for missing anything ever again in our lives. We're even invited for Christmas and I'm betting on it being Crimbo-meets-the-movies with red and green napkins and a stuffed turkey the size of half a cow. I bet their Christmas crackers won't have fortune-telling fish and yellow plastic combs. Mam is happy about that, even though she's still riding the downer about Da. Turns out probable bastard is easier to deal with than white-lie Romeo six-feet-under all these years. I even caught Nan lighting a holy candle, so she must be serious worried.

My nails are bit ragged cos, although Faith says they've near arrived and are just parking the car some place, I won't quite believe it until I see it. It's been six weeks since Halloweengate and her mam and da have driven the whole tour of the north again to get here, except this time, miraculously, they're coming round to the possibility of me being not entirely a pit-of-hell influence on their shiny daughter. Halo-sheen is a long way off yet, but TBH, I still like black. The only gut-wrencher is Jack. Is he my boyfriend? If so, why isn't he coming? Now that my head's totally fifty-billion-per-cent-fine with *moving* on, I'm like WTF is *going on*? Faith better spill cos I don't know if it's *couldn't* or *wouldn't* come to the exhibition, because he's gone so bloody quiet. No wisecracks. No mobile phone pillow-talk at bedtime. No nothing. Even though he's out of hospital, he just never answers. Is my family still cursed with men? I swear, honest to God, I really thought he was into me.

Stood by the lift, Dee is going over her spoken-word piece. It's like a poem, only good. She's gonna be on fire opening the show. Pure obvious. Two of the lads have a song wrote and have got themselves a box-drum-seat thing that sounds class for rhythm. All of us have art on the walls and Ingabire's worked her magic. Everything looks wild professional in frames and with explanation cards beneath them, like we're proper artists. She's got us all rehearsed on how to *e-nun-ci-ate* and told us to imagine the audience in their underwear if we get a run of the nerves, but all it's done is made me wish harder that Jack was here. My nail polish is wrecked and odds is even on the possibility of my fingers being half-ate before we even get to my speech. It'll be right at the end.

At first I was like, sure, bury me if my bit is rubbish, thinking going last is like when everyone's crawling walls in the final lesson at school, but Dee says no. This is different. Performance and art is about a shit sandwich. Start good, bury the crap in the middle and build to brilliance at the end. Dee reckons Ingabire putting me last is a compliment. I wish I had her confidence. What if no one likes my style or they hate what I'm saying? I flick my eyes to the emergency exit but Ingabire catches my glance. She stops chatting to the guitar lads and makes a beeline in my direction. That mind-reading thing must be some female hormone-coding that kicks in to chosen women past puberty. I've not got it, but Emer and Ingabire sure do.

'Nervous?' says Ingabire.

'No,' I say, knowing it's glaringly obvious that I'm shitting myself.

'Art works best when it matters. The more risk, the more reward. You know that, right?' She grins. 'Works for life too.'

I crinkle my nose.

'Tara, your portraits are unique. Powerful. Not just for your age. You're a born artist.' She leans her head in level with mine. 'Own it.'

Suddenly, I'm grinning, total ear-to-ear style, cos, for once, a grown-up didn't just say I got *po-ten-tial* and it wasn't strung in between ifs and try-harders, neither. Ingabire said it *fact*. Inside me, twitchy nervousness transforms into shimmer because art is my bone marrow. This exhibition is my guts on paper. Blood, sweat, shitloads of angst and every bit of *ma-tur-i-ty* and heart-on-sleeve I can dredge up from my big toe. If I can't do us Connollys proud tonight, I never will. Maybe I'm even doing this for Da. Maybe I'm doing it for more than him.

Just before seven thirty, there's a last-minute shuffle at the door and I see Faith cramming in the back with her parents. I wave. Slipping in behind them, quiet and sheet-white, is one last wee Derry woman in a cheap green raincoat. I catch her eye, and she shoots me a nervous half-smile before Ingabire tings a glass and the hum falls to a hush. From now on, it's over to us. Dee walks to the centre of the room, flings her arms wide and turns three-sixty degrees like a born ringmistress.

'Ladies and gentlemen, thanks for joining us. Today is World Human Rights Day. Listen up, because we've got something to say.'

She launches round the room like she owns the place, words and rhythms, reason and rhyme. All of it linked to her huge collage on the end wall. Like me, she's doing a piece about women and generations, but that's where the similarity ends. I won't be performing, just talking. Mainly cos I couldn't perform to save my life but also cos I want my art to do the talking. Dee is on a mission. 'Queer the space . . . clear the space . . .' It's a poetic rant about labels and assumptions, how 'we gotta fight and unite . . . orientation and gender, don't render a nation, blind, unkind . . . it's prej-udice, is blas-phem-ous, not love . . .'

The audience is clapping along, getting into it rightly, but I'm glancing at Faith and her parents, wondering if I should have warned them more clearly in advance. I did mention Dee would be wearing her colours proud. Faith is shy-smiling with admiration or perhaps more than that? Faith's da looks edgy, like he's still working out how queer could be a verb. I'm reckoning, though, that the fact he's still in the room is positive. Initially, Faith's parents were all 'maybe we could give the exhibition a miss?' But when Faith threatened to travel up on her own, they switched into chaperone mode. She says her parents are wild quiet about her coming out and she's not sure they've accepted it yet, but she still has her duvet, a roof over her head and no hint of being chucked out before the Christmas specials hit the telly, so I'm guessing it's going to be OK. Her da has been doing a circuit of different church prayer meetings most evenings and, after hearing what the doctor had to say about Faith's hair loss, her mam has opted to read the bible at the kitchen table rather than attend her usual weekly church women's group.

When the poem's done, everyone cheers and Dee explains about how, before Christmas, the Secretary of State for Northern Ireland is supposed to sign off the paperwork on finally making same-sex marriage legal here. She also talks a bit about her mam's dementia and living in care, and I swallow, then cheer to the rafters when she finishes because, honestly, she's had it so tough it makes my life look like Disneyworld.

There's no doubt Dee is the best, but only in the sense of her confidence and the clear way she gets her message across. Listening one by one to all the others from our gang, every single one of us is saying something powerful. Everyone has their story. For most of us, this is the first time outside of our art therapy group we've ever had the chance, or the nerve, to tell it. It's definitely the first time I've seen people listen like it matters. When the lads sing, they're not half bad. Their lyrics are about peer pressure and online bullying. By the third chorus, everyone's joining in. Not everything is loud though, quiet is also good.

Ingabire holds the mic for wee Jennie, whose hands are shaking. Asks her if she'd rather just let people look at the painting without saying anything, but Jennie shakes her head and after a moment, finds she can talk. Her painting is a beautiful watercolour about learning to hope again after a family tragedy. At the end, her older brother steps forward and bear hugs her.

I don't really take in the story of Kennedy, the boy talking before me. He's sharing stuff about mental health and the real-men-don't-cry lie Ingabire talked over with us in the group. All I can feel though is my jaw tightening and my teeth grinding. I. Am. Next. Holy feck. Heat is rising through me and I'm seriously regretting the gallons of Shloer cos I need to pee. So bad. The green exit sign above the door is pulling my attention and like how is everyone else is soooo good? I'm wishing I'd written down more of what I wanted to say but I hate writing and I thought my head knew it – though now I'm not so sure.

There is a polite round of applause. Then quiet. It's supposed to be me but my feet won't move. I ram hair into my mouth like that'll solve the problem. Everything inside me is spiralling inwards knowing full well that I'm just a bad wee shite from up the Glen that near got kicked out of school and is always arse-of-my-pants flying on the edge of bother. I'm minding the cider-by-night runs with Oran, burning tyre rubber round the back roads. Squeals and laughs in the wee hours. What if that, not this, is the real me? WTF mad-induced moment reckoned I could ever scuff the floor of an art gallery with my clapped-out runners? My throat is burning and I'm thinking back to the bonfire flames licking my arm and how running and kicking were always my best moves cos at least they were moves I knew. No one ever expected me to be any different. But these people? They're here expecting me to do something good. It's scary. My lungs freeze.

Pressure. I look at Ingabire and do a minuscule headshake. No. I won't do this. She better understand. Best I can do is not run. It *is* progress.

The delay is causing mumblings and shufflings in the audience, clinks as people set down empty cups and glasses. Ingabire motions to Dee. Silently holds up five fingers. Dee nods. Steps right up and launches into some other improvised poem. Then Ingabire slides her way over to me and puts both hands on my shoulders.

'Look at me,' she says. Same way she did back in that first workshop. 'Tara, if you can't do this, it's OK. What you witnessed in August was traumatic. You've given one-hundred-and-ten per cent to art therapy and I've never been prouder of seeing how you've started to shine. Just do me one more thing.'

I look into her dark eyes. They're pools of calm, but also understanding. For the first time I wonder what she went through to end up here. She's never told us her story and we've never asked, but somehow, I know she understands horror as well as healing. Probably more than any of us ever imagined. Of all the people in the world, I trust Ingabire.

'OK,' I say.

'Look at the wall,' she says. 'Look at your row of paintings. There's hours, days, of work displayed there. Study those portraits. Hard. The vivid colours, the tangle of lines and shadow. The contrasts. Your work is unique, Tara. Just like you. Look at the eyes in those women you've drawn.'

I lift my chin and take in the seven paintings. Six hang in pairs. Generations. Portraits of Nan and Great Aunt Cathy. Mam and Faith's mam. Faith and me – almost the same except for the debris strewn in the backgrounds behind us. All of it on every painting is symbolic of what we've endured. What we've survived. What we've overcome. The seventh was the hardest. The hardest to draw and the hardest to invite. The lady hiding in the back with her green raincoat still on. Oran's mam.

Dee finishes her performance.

'Tell me now that you've nothing to say,' says Ingabire.

It works. I'm riled yet positive, incensed but clear, just like when I'd put every stroke on the pages. I stride to the centre of the floor and take the mic. Then close my eyes. I am live in front of an audience. *Do not swear. Do not be an arse. For Christ's sake don't screw up.* I feel the calm of the momentary darkness, like a self-induced blindness, and from it, come the words.

'I feel like I've been blind, like I've lived in the dark,' I say. 'I want to call out blindness. Blindness in our communities. Blindness in a system. Blindness in how we've got used to things being the way they are, so we never even ask how things should change.' My voice steadies as I start to speak. 'I don't even know a name for it, but it's broken. Broken for generations. Broken like our government that hasn't met in three years.' There are mumbles of support from the audience. 'It's a system that silences stories that don't fit. It makes people scared to tell the truth and it punishes people who do.' Faith and her parents are nodding. 'A system that puts people in boxes – not just Catholic and Protestant, but women and men, poor and rich. We're easier managed in boxes because in them, we only hear stories of the people in our box. We never get to listen to people who are different, because if we did, we might change the system.' I look at Ingabire. She's nodding. Emer has on her you-got-this-girl smile. Dee is giving me two thumbs up. I'm wondering where the feck I'm getting this from but at the same time I know – it's the real me talking from deep inside. It's there in my art, but now I'm finding words to match. 'Until this year, I didn't even know I was blinded. But then, when things got really dark for me, I found I just had to open my eyes.'

I start to pace the floor, pointing out my row of portraits. 'I could tell you the story of each of these women, but only they have the right to do that. Instead, I've got something of my own to say. Something I've learned. The way the system tells us about *his*tory doesn't properly tell *her*story. The system convinces you that you have to take sides and that power comes from violence or votes, bullets or ballots. The system doesn't understand that courage doesn't hold guns or power. True courage never gets medals or memorials. True courage is getting out of bed in the morning. It's in the keeping going. Turning up to school. The reaching out to understand something. It's the standing in a food-bank queue.'

There's a ripple of applause and my heart is beating mental but still the words come like a busted dam. 'It's Human Rights Day and I want yous all to mind one name. Oran Doherty. Oran was my friend. My boyfriend. At Easter, he got shot in the leg. In August, he killed himself. I never lived in the Troubles, but in art therapy we learned that more people have died of suicide since we got peace than ever died in the Troubles. That's part of a screwed-up system too.' I pause and try to imagine everyone in boxers or high-leg knickers to stop my hands shaking. 'So, here's what I'm saying. Politicians gotta start talking. Get it together or let our generation take over.' More applause. 'This summer I went looking for my da. I'd never met him. I didn't find what I expected and that was tough. What I did find was way more. I found friends. I found family. I found hope.'

Suddenly the emotion of it all floods me. My voice catches and I hesitate. I look at everyone who has come here tonight to support me. Have I made any sense? Mam looks like she could

261

bust out crying any minute and I'm not sure if it's cos I've showed her up or if she's bursting with pride. I clear my throat. 'I guess what I want to say is thank you. Thank you to all the women, but especially to my mam and nan, because every day you show me what matters. The stuff that's worth fighting for doesn't need guns, just guts.'

For a moment, there's silence. Then cheering. Applause. Our art therapy gang runs in for hugs and I feel my feet going as Dee and the crew hike me up high like World Cup glory. Grown-ups are all 'that one's a born politician' and I can hear Emer saying 'naw, she's a community worker,' but all I'm thinking is, maybe I'll be an art therapist.

Afterwards there's mingling and Mam and Nan face-wide grinning. Oran's mam comes over crying her lamps out and flings her arms round me so tight I'm for suffocating. Everyone's looking at my paintings. Best of all, my family and Faith's family are actually chatting. I. Am. Buzzing. Fecking high as a space cadet with not a tab, a smoke or a drink in sight. Faith won't leave my side and neither will Dee and I'm wondering if there's more than celebration in the air between them cos it feels like chemistry and it's class except there's an ache in me. When Dee goes for top-ups of Shloer and shortbread, I finally corner Faith.

'What about Jack? How come he never came?'

Faith dips her head. 'I'm not sure,' she says. 'I think he's struggling.'

'Is he still hurt?'

'Not physically – though he hates that he can't play rugby for a while because of the concussion. He's not himself though. He took a lot of flak in school over his dad.'

'Cos he's going to jail?'

Faith looks at me. 'That's the thing. He's likely not even going to court.'

'Didn't he confess?'

'Yip. Told everything he knew.'

'So?'

Faith tries to explain it simple so I follow. How you can't nail someone on a confession alone. How the cops phoned her mam and said about a *Corpus Delecti* rule which is posh for saying a judge would tell them to piss off unless they can get other evidence. How her mam has a decision to make. Since Jack's da hasn't managed to tell them anything that wasn't already blasted out in public news from the time *and* cos his suicide attempt shows his head had gone la-la *and* cos he was underage when it happened, they don't think there's a case. The cops can't even find the cardboard folder in the archives from the initial investigation and the Public Prosecution Service won't take on the case unless they've at least a 50 per cent chance of winning.

'So, there's no case?' I say.

'Depending on one thing, they've said it should just be dropped.'

'What one thing?'

'My mum.'

'I don't get it.'

'It has to be in the public interest to have a chance of being taken on. Because of the family connection, if the family, meaning Mum, say to drop the case, they will.'

'And?'

'She's still deciding. She has to tell them by the new year.'

'Does Jack know?'

Faith nods. 'He says he's fine . . .' She knots her fingers together. 'He's turned real quiet, not like himself. Doesn't even

263

retaliate to slagging at school. Has he been in touch with you?'

I shake my head and turn to look at all the paintings cos, somehow, it feels like a wee snatch of light is darkening and I'm not quite sure how to say that actually, Jack really matters. My days of hugging Oran's hoodie are ancient history and it's the pillowcase with Jack's aftershave smell that has me aching. I think about everything I've said tonight and everything I've learned in art therapy and how Jack has always just been there – for me, for Faith, for his da. Who has been there for him? It's pure lies that only princesses need rescuing.

On her phone, Faith is taking photos of my art. 'Your paintings are stunning,' she says. 'I'll show these to Jack.'

'Thanks,' I say, still unable to look at her and willing my eyes to not be shiny and give-away wet.

She's quiet. We stand shoulder to shoulder, looking at my portraits. 'Don't give up on Jack yet,' she says. 'I've a mad plan; it'll help you both, and hopefully others. Listen up. I need to know if you're game.'

As I turn to her, she's grinning and I'm thinking *feck me, but is my madness starting to rub off on her?* As Dee weaves her way back, balancing three wine glasses of fizzy grape juice, Faith whispers quick into my ear. Her parents have invited our new-found grandparents to afternoon tea. 22 December. It would've been Ryan, our da's, birthday. Faith is going to ask Jack to come, saying they want to see the Honda Shadow and she'll see if she can convince her mam to let Jack's da, and maybe his mam come along too.

'Christmas is supposed to be about peace on earth,' she says, all Rose of Tralee.

'Aye, right,' I say. 'Our politicians won't even talk to each other.'

'No,' she says. 'But wouldn't it be something if our families did?'

I glance across the room. Great Aunt Cathy, Helen and Ingabire are chatting to Oran's mam. Emer, Mam and Nan are chatting to Faith's parents.

Faith follows my glance. 'I don't just mean our parents,' she says. 'Wider than that. Jack's parents too and . . .' She bites a nail. 'Our new grandparents. I got the impression they'd jump at an invitation to get to know us, more than just us actually.'

'Eh?'

'In the graveyard, when I said your mother's name was Erin, they went really quiet. It's like they already knew her name. I just can't work out how.'

I glance round at Mam and see her chinwagging proud, even though lately at our house, I'm never done lifting her half-drunk mugs of cold tea. It's as if finding the truth about Da, seeing the grave photo, helped me but broke something inside her. Could there be anything left that might help?

Chapter 27

FAITH
County Armagh, 22 December 2019

It's the last Sunday before Christmas and tonight should've been the carol service. We're not going. I'm not singing. It still cuts when I think about it but, this afternoon, I'm choosing to concentrate on the positive. Dee says it helps. So does the bible. *Whatever is true, whatever is noble, whatever is right, think on these things.* Organizing this was my way of putting something different in place, and maybe even starting a new Christmas tradition. Joyous-terrified is how I'm feeling. I brush my hair, again, partly from nerves and partly in wonder and joy from the realization that it's not falling out the way it used to.

It dawns that I can't remember when I last defuzzed the hairbrush. The doctor said that might happen when the stress went; said that baby hair might grow back now that I had come out and could be myself. She'd looked directly at Mum as she'd said that, as if Mum was the one who needed to grasp that and not me, and, now that I think about it, she was right, because I've taken years to get my own head round being lesbian, so if my parents need more time to adjust, or even Bethany for that matter, maybe that's OK, so long as it's not forever. My body's already adjusting. In the mirror, I can see soft downy velvet where the bald patches used to be and, though they're still the same green with brown flecks, my eyes look different too. Brighter.

At any slight sound, I glance out the window to the yard in

expectation, waiting for the cars and sensing the heart-in-mouth wild swinging of emotions racing in my blood. This must work. I'm praying with heart, soul and mind for miracles, just not the type the pastor envisaged. I still don't know what my parents really feel about that – they don't seem to have the vocabulary, but with a little grace and patience both ways, I think we might get there. They haven't objected to me taking Sunday mornings as a quiet time in the house and, judging by the gravel sweep out of the yard, they're still taking the road travelling the other direction, into town and beyond, visiting other churches to sense their fit, or mine. I miss the old hymns but I'm going to learn to sing a new song. It's clear there is no room at the inn for me in our old church. Difference is, for me anyway, I've stopped caring about what they think and started praying for them instead. I've done a lot of thinking about it these last few weeks. If churches can change their thinking on slavery, and on women, what's blocking their perspective on people like me? Fear? Ignorance? The bible didn't change its wording on slavery – what changed was how people chose to interpret it. Back then, church leaders revolutionized their understanding of people and justice. They listened. God didn't stop talking after the final Amen in Revelation.

Our kitchen smells like a bakery. I do a final check on the nibbles warming in the oven and breathe the savoury warmth into my nostrils. Cocktail sausages, chicken bites, mini scotch eggs and quiche. Mum did a dawn raid on the posh delicatessen in Armagh yesterday to avoid the mid-morning Christmas turkey and gammon rush, while I spent the day making mince pies and shortbread. We could feed an army, but will they all come? Dad is meeting Tara, her mum and nan off the bus in Armagh, and Mum is meeting my new-found grandparents in the village so that they don't get lost on the winding country roads out to the farm. It's still icy in the dips from a snowfall yesterday.

My mobile vibrates. Aunt Bea is in the Spar, on her way, searching for non-alcoholic mulled wine and wondering have Jack and Uncle Steve arrived yet? I suck in my cheeks, wondering if mediators in peace processes use white lies too. This could yet be the fatal flaw. Mum and Dad don't know I've invited Uncle Steve. I told Jack and his dad 3 p.m. because everyone else should be here by 2:30, the peace-on-earth gamble being that Mum can't go off on one in front of everyone else and won't want a scene on such a special Christmassy occasion. Going as far as forgiveness won't be necessary, but letting Uncle Steve into the room would be a start. Handing him a get-out-of-jail-free card before New Year would be golden, especially for Jack. But what if my gamble backfires?

I take to mad plumping of cushions, fire stoking and pointless straightening of cookbooks by the breadbin for distraction, then set to whipping cream, the whirr and clatter of hand beaters dulling the doubts, until I hear the cars sweep in convoy into the yard. Outside comes alive with car-door slams and voices as I race to wipe condensation and peer through the window. There's a quiet dignity to my grandmother, how she turns her legs sideways and presses one hand on her stick, the other gripping my grandfather's hand to hoist herself from Mum's car. Mum lifts a bag of presents they've brought and encourages them to the door as Tara spills like a bundle of cooped-up energy from Dad's car. For a moment, they all stop still, looking at each other, sensing history in the making and, as Tara's mam steps out of the front passenger seat, my grandmother's hand touches my grandfather's shoulder.

I abandon the window, running to our front door to fling it wide. With the sound, everyone turns to look at me and, caught in the cold swoosh of air, my split second of confidence evaporates. I look at their faces each in turn and bite my lip. This gathering, it's significant. I look up the empty lane towards Jack's house. Could it be truly magnificent? Is that level of truth and reconciliation even possible in one family? As I wonder, Tara launches herself at me, all hugs and Happy Christmasses. Seeing us together, how alike we look, my grandparents reach for each other in support, mouths wide, then creasing into huge smiles. I think back to summer and the shock of first setting eyes on Tara. Since I met her, Tara's nan has transformed into a bumble of enthusiastic greetings and handshakes despite the wheezing and Mum is in ushering overdrive, steering everyone into the warmth of our living room where the fire blazes orange and deep armchairs beckon and of course there is tea. Gallons of it, because how could you not want tea?

By the time Aunt Bea arrives twenty minutes later, our living room is a buzz of chatter and memories. Mum has out the good china side plates and I'm doing the rounds with a tray piled with savoury stuff. The way my grandmother's nose wrinkles when she laughs, is the same as Tara. And our grandfather rubs his middle finger onto his thumb when he's thinking, same as me. It's strange, the little things, but they feel important, like proof of our connection.

Over finger food, and under the twinkle of Christmas lights, polite twitter gradually changes to banter and anecdotes. Tara's nan is an absolute gem. In between occasional wheezes, she buzzes with life, arms gesticulating like a born storyteller, adopting the role of fussing and mothering everyone from her perch in the corner armchair by the hearth. Tara, sitting on a cushion at her mum's feet, is glowing, eyes wide like they're eating up the atmosphere. She's in dark green skinny jeans, new trainers and a long black roll-neck jumper which hugs her frame and I'm hoping beyond hope that Jack will arrive soon because when he sees her, I know he'll transform. He's been so closed recently, withdrawn and distant. I miss him. Never again will I take him for granted. I check my phone in case he's messaged. There is a message, but it's from Dee, just asking if everyone arrived OK and wondering how it's going. Sweet. There's a flutter in my stomach as I send a quick message back, but for once, no guilt. Maybe there'll be more than one reason to visit Derry in January. It's a new thought and I kind of like it.

After a round of mince pies and cream, it's as if we've all been family forever. With everyone fed and watered, Aunt Bea has settled and even Mum has nestled herself against Dad on the sofa, her shoes off and feet tucked in. It's the most relaxed I've seen her in many a moon. Tara glances at the clock on the mantelpiece and does a concerned eyebrow thing at me. I shrug. Jack and Uncle Steve should've been here by now. She knows it as well as I do. Aunt Bea whispers to me that Uncle Steve is always running behind and not to worry. I chew a nail. I'm beginning to wonder if I should message Jack, when my grandfather coughs and my grandmother tinkles a spoon against a glass.

'We hope you don't mind,' she says, 'but we've brought a few gifts.' The smile lines round her eyes wrinkle beautifully, wisps of her silver-grey hair framing her face, having freed themselves from the loose bun behind her head. 'They're sentimental gifts. Excuse us if we cry a little –' her fingers seek out her husband's hand and entwine a moment – 'but they will be happy tears. Today is the winter solstice – the shortest day of the year. From here on, the dark days lighten and we move towards a new season. It also would have been our Ryan's birthday . . .' She hesitates to draw a breath and blinks rapidly. 'He'd have loved you two girls so much. You're the spit of him. For many years we've cherished his memory alone, so tonight, if you'll allow, we'd like to share some of that with you.' She motions to the bag of gifts at her feet. 'Would that be alright?'

'I know it may take some bravery,' says my grandfather, 'but our Ryan, as well as being a rascal and more of a lad than we realized, was very brave and we are fiercely proud of him.'

Within our living room, there are glances, slight shuffling in chairs and straightening of backs. Tara and I nod enthusiastically. My parents hold hands. Tara's nan grins. Only Tara's mum seems hesitant, her smile flickering like the flames she stares at in the hearth. After a moment, she looks up and nods.

The old man's hands reach into the red Christmas bag and selects two identical books, beautifully printed with blue fabric covers and gold lettering. Photo albums. He hands one to Tara, the other to me. 'Ryan never met you.' His voice trembles. 'But we'd like you to meet him.'

Our parents crowd around, and for the next half hour we are absorbed in anecdotes and images of an impish and creative boy from Orangefield in Armagh. Baby. Toddler. Boy. Teenager. Young man. Always the playful hope twinkling in his eyes – green with brown flecks. His hair is wavy black with a cow's lick over his forehead, his skin fair, his cheekbones and jawline distinct. He cycles with stabilizers, wins egg-and-spoon races and running medals, unwraps Christmas stockings, learns clarinet, stands by a fridge with a display of kiddies' paintings, plays cricket and blows out birthday candles. He is real. At each turn of the page, Mum watches my reaction and squeezes Dad's hand. For Tara's mum, the photos are a revelation – her eyes devour the pages and she worries her knuckles, smiling, but

271

saying little. Sometimes she brushes her finger over an image and closes her eyes, as if connecting. On the final page, Ryan is in his army uniform and beside the photo is a newspaper obituary recounting his death. His eyes, the mirror of mine and Tara's, stare straight at the camera. A quietness settles over the room, the only sound the crackle from the fire.

'It was an IED,' explains my grandfather. 'It overturned their armoured vehicle. He was unhurt at first and carried two others to safety. Going back for a third, he was shot by a sniper. It was instant. They said he didn't suffer.'

The tips of my grandmother's fingers turn white as she presses them into her knees. She nods slightly as my grandfather hugs her tight, eyes closed. Like a keening, they rock together and I lean against my parents and watch how Tara's mum draws her legs to her chest, curled like a teenager. On either side, Tara and her nan reach to hold Erin's hands.

'It's true,' says my grandmother. 'Ryan didn't want to go. We persuaded him, just to get him out of Northern Ireland for a few years, away from bother and bad influences. For ordinary working folk like us, his music or his art, well we couldn't see how it could bring him a proper living. The last time we ever spoke, he was determined that when he came back from Afghanistan, he was quitting the army. He was for coming back home and settling down. He had his reasons, he said. We'd thought the army would put some discipline into him, keep him safe . . .' Her eyes glisten wet as her words fail.

'You weren't to know,' says Mum.

'He painted so beautifully,' says Tara's mum, speaking for the first time in ages. 'And when he sang, everyone listened. It was like a piece of heaven came into the room, like he was holding his heart out for you to touch.'

'Ah, darling . . .' My grandmother curls her fingers against her mouth with a tremble. 'You're right. He had a real talent, and with the benefit of hindsight, so many things might've been different.'

I study the ripple of the blue veins raised on the back of my grandfather's hand as he delves into the bag to produce two more small parcels. One for Tara. One for me. This time they are shaped differently.

'These are symbolic,' says my grandfather. 'Symbolic of other things we've kept of his. When you're ready, you can come visit our house and see if you'd like anything.'

Tara looks at me as she unwraps the purple tissue paper. As it unfolds, she gasps, a set of artist's paintbrushes and an oblong tin of watercolour paints resting in her palm. Her lower lip wobbles as she looks back and forth between her mum, nan and grandparents.

'We have an easel,' says our grandmother. 'And sketchpads and oils. I hear you're an artist.'

Tara nods, holding her gift tight to her heart.

Now it's my turn. The parcel is like a slim but solid chocolate bar, the length of a short ruler, but heavier. As I undo the string, the paper falls away to reveal a B♭ harmonica. The corners of the carboard case are smoothed with use and time, the stainless steel of the instrument polished bright like buttons on a dress uniform.

'We hear you're a musician,' says our grandfather. 'At home, we also have his guitar. The harmonica was special though; it was in his pocket when he died.'

'He carried it everywhere,' says Tara's mum. She closes her eyes as if she can still hear the melodies.

My mother is handed a small, hinged leather box, the size that might hold a watch or necklace. She studies the outside of it before opening it. Her eyes widen, then she crosses the room to

273

hold my grandparents' hands in hers. 'You can't give me this,' she says. 'It's too special. It belongs with you.'

They shake their heads. 'It's his medal for bravery. We want you to have it. You've earned it. All those years keeping going without answers or justice and raising your beautiful daughter.' There are hugs and reassurances and then motions to sit, for there remains one small envelope in the bag.

'Erin,' says my grandmother. 'This is for you. It was in the chest pocket of his uniform when they brought him home. His last letter. We read it many times, searching for clues. Asked his friends but to no avail. Your name was on it, but we never knew who you were or where to find you.' My grandmother's arms shake as she holds out the letter. 'Until now.'

At first, Tara's mum doesn't move, then, trembling, she stretches to take it in her own hands, runs her fingers over the faded handwriting of her own name on the envelope. The paper is yellowed with age, crumpled a little at the corners and stained with marks that might have been sweat. Quietly, she slides the letter out and unfolds it, the single thin page, stiff and crackly. Both sides are jammed with small, neat words in blue ink, and as her eyes skim from left to right, over and over, her tears well, then trickle down her face in lines that catch the light. No one even breathes. Time is suspended. Without looking up, Tara's mum refolds the letter and slips it back into the envelope. She says nothing, but gets to her feet and crosses to give both my grandmother and grandfather a tight bear hug.

'He loved you,' whispers my grandmother. 'He truly loved you, Erin.'

'We're here for you,' says my grandfather. 'It may be sixteen years late, but we've found you. You're part of our family.' He looks over her shoulder and includes us all with a sweep of his eyes round the room. 'You're all part of our family now and if we can help in any way, we will.'

Everyone is crying happy tears, just like my grandparents predicted. Faces crinkled, tissues dabbing, laughs, sighs and hugs. It feels like healing, but in the back of my heart is a dull ache because two people are still missing, one of whom is like a brother to me and I had so willed them to have the courage to be here. Prayed to heal that rift in our family.

As Mum and Aunt Bea busy themselves with further tea-making and food, I gaze out the living-room window across the frosty fields, my heart heavy with if onlys. I excuse myself for a second and Tara follows me into our hall.

'Isn't Jack coming?' She hugs her arms across her ribs and sucks her hair.

I sigh. 'You really like him, don't you?'

She nods.

'I'll try him again,' I say, bringing up his number and hitting green. It rings out and I shake my head. 'Either he's not answering or he's got no signal. He was working on the bike yesterday; I thought he was definitely up for coming.'

There's a clatter at the front door: a simultaneous ringing of the bell and knocking.

'Hello?' The voice is Uncle Steve's, hesitant yet with a desperate ring to it. As Mum and Dad stride into the hall, he stays on the doorstep and holds up both palms. 'Please,' he says. 'Please, no lectures. I need your help. Jack's been gone two hours with the Honda Shadow. He's not answering his phone. Those roads are icy and it's getting dark. He'll be freezing. He didn't take anything else, so I don't think he's done a runner or anything – I'm worried he might have crashed. Help me find him. Please?'

Chapter 28

TARA
County Armagh, 22 December 2019

I've bolted, running, racing with the air numbing my nose and cheekbones, dodging the tree roots cracking under the tarmac of country lanes and trying not to slip on the icy bits at the side that look like spit froze under glass. Nan says I'm always meeting bother halfway. I'm not even full sure what she means but I'm intent on doing it. Somewhere out here is Jack, Jack and a Honda Shadow that used to belong to my da and the others were just taking too long, way too long for my liking, in their adult, organizey don't-panic-it's-sorted-he's-fine mode wondering should they take the van or the trailer in case the bike needs lifting, and all the time Faith's Aunt Bea is going, 'But for gawd's sake, where is he?'

A wee red robin flurries from under my toes at the last minute like I'm an urban inconvenience, as I try to land my feet on the tufts of grass pitching themselves bedraggled out of the ice like a bad haircut. The branches are all frosted white and the skyline across the hills ahead has a belt of vivid orange that fades into turquoise before the black of the near night sky. If I wasn't sprinting, I'd take a photo. It was the way Faith said it, the certainty on her. 'If he's testing the Honda he'll have taken the back roads, the loop by the lake. Always on about how she would corner there.' And how, in the hollow, there's no phone signal unless it's a west wind or some other the feck direction and I'm probably bound for completely the wrong heading but she'd pointed as the crow flies, through the orchard and over by the silhouetted barn and some distant trees, until it was all so country-sounding I half expected the sentence to end 'in yonder manger in Bethlehem'. Any road, I couldn't just be sat waiting by the fire stuffing my gob with shortbread if Jack's out there somewhere doing a Scott of the Antarctic impression or, worse, maybe smashed-up hurt.

As I run, I'm thinking Jack's da looked half decent, like a normal OMG where's-my-wean heart-feared da and certainly not like some insane whiskey-swigging terrorist. Nan's fair come out of her skin since talking about her past so perhaps Jack's da will be all healing crystals and yoga now he's spewed his guts and heart to get rid of the shadows. And my wee mam. Ryan *loved* her. Like proper loved her honest-to-God-and-hope-to-die except that's what did happen and I've never wanted to hug my mam tighter and truer than right there then because, like, that's been her whole life not knowing and now she's ancient, leastways not far off kicking forty, and maybe she'll go mental and have a mid-life crisis, buy a leather jacket and get tattoos done. She looked happy though, underneath all the sad, and I think that's good. Right?

It was the same happy-sad look my new grandparents had on them and the exact same look Nan was sporting on meeting Sam's family after all those years and like, OMG, how many relatives do I have right now? My family tree has turned overnight from beanpole into a proper who-do-ye-think-ye-are documentary. And what's more, they're all nice. But also like, WTF? They're all Prods. I never knew them two things could happen together so consistent and yet here I am running the blazes through a sodden fecking field chasing after another one, except this one I am NOT related to and bloody good job too because I fancy the arse off him. He better not be dead though, or I'll kill him.

I reach the corner of what I'm guessing is an orchard and stop, hands on hips, to catch my breath. Like seriously, I'm definitely high-riding a brain-freeze moment cos I'm fecking clueless about how I'm going to find Jack out here. It's like proper fields and countryside shit and farm animals and OMG my new trainers are clattered. And my jeans. They're the only item in my new the-entire-world-is-not-black wardrobe and now they're more brown than green. I am muck to the eyeballs and if I even did find Jack now I'd be proper mortified. Still, this is not about me. For once, I'm not running *from* something but *towards* something. And that something matters, cos it's Jack. I lift my eyes and study the horizon. The barn buildings Faith had pointed to are on the slope to my left across another infinity of mint frosted grass, and the clump of trees in the distance are where Faith said the winding lake road is.

The air is thick with birds twittering for sunset and if it had wanted to be Christmassy the weather would've fecking known to snow all over the shower but, being Northern Ireland, all it's cut out for is this splatter of frost, slush and muck. I slither to the edge of a gate and climb up to see if it gives me any vantage. Cupping my hands, I shout. 'Jack?' No answer. The cold from the metal bars presses against my thighs. A flash of fear catches in my throat. If Jack is stuck out here hurt, it really is freezing. I jump down with a splat and near lose my footing on the edge of a half-frozen puddle. The straightest way to the woods is across another dose of fields. Thank Christ I'm back at the cross-country training, for this is the real deal. I take to skirting along the hedges at the top end of the slope where the ground seems more solid, and strike a steady pace, counting each field and, thinking back on August, clocking each gate mentally so as not to get lost. The whole stranded in rabbit poo and sheep shite up a mountain lark is not something I'm keen on repeating.

After three fields, I pause and shout again. This time with even more urgency. It's fast turning pitch black apart from a crescent moon glinting a blue-white light off the ground. Still no response. Vaulting another gate, my feet land steady on gravel. The clump of trees are dead ahead and through them, the sheen of water. I'm at a small T-junction with high hedges all about and twigs angled out the tops. Impossible to decide which way might on a lottery whim be the right ticket for a gamble. I ball my fists into my armpits for warmth while I reconsider my own head-the-ball feckin-eejitness. Rather than help, I've probably doubled everyone's trauma. They'll be out head-hunting me now too. I don't even have a coat. 'Jack?' It's more of a theatrical sigh this time rather than hopeful shout.

'Tara?' The voice is tired but clear.

A snap of twigs somewhere up the lane on my right.

'Jack?' This time I give a proper holler and run in the direction of the sound.

'Tara?'

A stronger reply. Definitely Jack's voice. I round a sharp bend and there, splayed out on the lane is a clatter of smashed bike bits. A wing mirror, glass, a bent bit of metal that might be a licence plate. The Honda Shadow is in the ditch, near vertical, back wheel reaching for the night sky. Beside it, Jack is huddled, shivering. When he sees me, he struggles to his feet. I run straight into his arms and hug him super tight, my head pressed sideways against his chest. 'Are you OK?'

'I'd bloody need to be, given how tight you're hugging me.'

I loosen my grip and look up into his eyes. They're the same devilish-cute as ever but he looks drawn. I glance back at the shrapnel and upturned bike. Jack's helmet is in the ditch too. My brain turns over that memory of Oran crashing. The image is still there, but it doesn't stab. Less vivid. More like a blurred sepia photo. I hug Jack again. 'You sure you're OK?'

'I'll survive,' he says. Jack's hands are like ice, even in his biking gloves. I stuff them under the back of my jumper and rub his chest like it'll put some warmth back into him.

He sighs. 'Front wheel hit black ice and the whole bike skidded then flipped from under me when I tried to brake. She's not insured. I shouldn't even have been riding her until I get my full licence. I . . . I'm so sorry. I just wanted to do a final engine check to see she was running perfect for you and your grandparents. She was your dad's bike and all the main parts are still intact, she's fixable, but I didn't know how I'd face you all with this. Not that I can even get her out of the ditch – she's too heavy and I nearly put my shoulder out again trying.'

'I don't care about the bike,' I say.

Jack flinches and turns his head away.

'Well,' I say, 'what I mean is I *do* care about the bike but what I really care about is *you*.'

'Why? I can't do anything right any more. Can't play rugby till my head's sorted. Clearly can't ride a bike. Can't even get a phone signal to call the cavalry. And now the whole world's either slagging, cheering or hating me cos Dad was in the UVF. Get real. I know there's no way in hell you want to be with me now.'

I take a step back and fold my arms. Jack looks beat. His shoulders sag in his leather biking jacket and his head droops so that even the cute bit of spiky dark hair above his forehead hangs down.

'Look at me,' I say, pure doing an Ingabire.

Jack looks up. It's too dark to see his turquoise eyes but I know I've got his attention. 'That's bullshit,' I say. 'You always did right by me. You're one of the good guys, Jack. One of the best.'

He rubs his leg where I'm guessing he must have taken a right jolt off the tarmac. Least he doesn't look like anything's broken.

'Did you hear me?' I say. 'I fancy the arse off you. I properly even *like* you . . . I think, maybe, I think . . . I might even be in love with you, Jack.'

He runs his fingers through his hair and, even though there's a wind kicking up now that would freeze the bollocks off a scarecrow, I'm raging and melted all at the same time because how can he not get that he's a pure hero?

'But my dad . . .' He bites his lip.

'Christ and the crib at Christmas. We weren't even born in the Troubles. Who gives a feck? Anyway, turns out my da was a Brit and my granda was a prison warden so what odds if I've fallen for a Lambeg-drumming Loyalist?'

Jack lifts his chin. 'You really don't mind?'

'Mind? It's a Connolly family tradition,' I say. 'Except, I'd kinda prefer you stick around a bit longer and I don't particularly fancy being up the duff anytime soon either, but I meant it. Now, are we getting this bike out of the ditch or what?'

He looks at me real coy. 'I'd prefer the or what,' he says, and reaching out he puts a hand on my waist and pulls me in close, wrapping his arms around my back. He doesn't kiss me immediately. There's that moment where I know we're gonna, but he's playing me and it's magic. His eyes are smiling directly into mine and I'm pure gone plasticine, moulding in tight, pressed up against the warmth of every bit of him from his thighs

281

to his cheeks. I can feel the heave of his chest. The warmth of his breath. First, he snuggles into my neck, real slow so it tickles, then traces his lips across my forehead, then tilts his head so his nose rubs mine. My blood is fire. Down low, I'm lava. Hot tingles. He teases his lips across mine and I can feel that he's smiling.

'Kiss me already, would ya?' I plead.

He laughs, then locks his mouth full on mine and our tongues are playing and OMG, OMG, I'm up on my tiptoes to get at him better and like I want every bit of him and my insides are speed-flipping somersaults cos he is scrumptious-toffee-caramel delicious. And strong. And like I don't even know how I can feel this much for one person but I do and our fingers wander and it's still fecking freezing and pitch black, and yes we're standing by a ditch with a smashed bike, foundered, but this is like the BEST moment of my ENTIRE LIFE and it has to NEVER STOP. So help me God but I am pure in love. Or lust. Or something. With Jack Duggan. And newsflash – he's totally got the hots for me – absolute cert – and it's fecking brilliant.

Ten minutes later we're still so engrossed in snogging, the headlights of the van sneak up and blind us before we even cop the sound of the engine. Jack's da and Faith's da.

'Oops,' says Jack, the blush of embarrassment spreading beautifully across his cheeks. 'Think we're caught.' He glances at the bike. 'I'm for it now.'

'D'you ever watch old movies?' I say. 'Butch Cassidy?'

Jack grins. 'I love you,' he whispers in my ear.

At the front door there is a whirlwind of hugs, mammy-kisses, oh-thank-Gods and beckonings into the heat. Jack squeezes my hand, but holds back, conscious of his da behind us, unsure on the step. The air stills.

'Mum . . .' Faith sidles up and hugs her mother. 'I'm here for you and . . . it's Christmas.'

Light spills out from the porch onto Jack's da. He steps backwards and shakes his head slightly. 'It's OK, Sarah. I understand. This was only about finding Jack. I've things to be doing on the farm and—'

'Come in,' says Faith's mam, quietly at first, then decisively. 'Come in. You're welcome. You're family. Our family.'

There is a moment's hesitation, then Jack's father steps forward and they both hug, their shoulders shaking in quiet sobs.

'I'm sorry,' says Jack's da, over and over.

'It's history,' says Faith's mam. 'Let's move on.'

We pile back into the living room to give them space. Nan even shoots me a cheeky grin and gives up her armchair by the fire so that Jack and I can huddle in and thaw. Mam smiles at me and raises an eyebrow. I zone out, exhausted and mesmerized by the sparkles on the Christmas tree. It's a real one, I can even smell the pine, and it's decorated perfectly. Silver tinsel. White lights. Red bobbles. I thought Christmas trees like that only existed in the movies. My new grandparents smile with recognition when Jack's da joins us. 'Hardly changed in twenty years . . .' 'One of our Ryan's best mates. . .' Aunt Bea nods subtly and beckons him to sit over by her side. I feel Jack's shoulders lift.

Faith and her mam land in with fresh mugs of tea and, better still, hot chocolate with the works – marshmallows, cream and sprinkles – for me and Jack. He clinks his mug against mine and winks. 'Happy Christmas,' he says.

'That was going to be *my* toast,' says Faith's da, rising to his feet and leaning on the mantelpiece, 'but maybe I'll make a different one.' He holds his mug close to his chest and smiles, taking in everyone in the room in turn. 'A toast to our children. We always say they're the future, but actually, I think they're teaching us a thing or two about the past. And the present.'

He raises his mug of tea and Mam flashes me a wry grin so I know full well she's back to herself and that, though I'm a complete headcase, I'm always her best ticket.

'To our children,' says Faith's da. Everyone echoes it.

'And to family,' I say, lifting my hot chocolate so high the marshmallows nearly wobble off the top.

'To family.' Everyone cheers and the mugs chink.

'And one last thing,' says Faith's da. 'This is important.' He pauses. 'I want everyone to hear my girl sing. She has the voice of an angel.' He looks straight at Faith. 'And I love her. I love everything about her. Exactly the way she is. She's perfect.' He holds out his hand and beckons Faith to stand with him. 'Would you sing us "O Holy Night"?'

Faith nods, joins her da by the hearth and then she begins. The notes ring out clear and true. As she sings, I bite my lip. Something about this night *is* holy. Holier than statues, or first communions or bibles on shelves, and outside, outside the stars must be shining their guts out. Bright. So bright. It's beyond beautiful. And I'm brimming with pride because Faith is my sister. My. Sister. And she's so ace she could be singing in a cathedral or on telly and OMG, life is amazing. Everything is amazing. I close my eyes and snuggle into Jack, so happy I could cry.

The thing about peace on earth is, it's actually easy. Nan had it right all along. All it takes is a few gallons of tea. Then again, in my opinion, the whole place should've converted to hot chocolate years ago.

Author's Note

To every reader of this book – thank you. In a world full of stunning novels, it still feels surreal that people choose to read mine. The stories that we choose to read, write, listen to, or hear around us are significant. In most societies, there are dominant narratives. Those voices say: *This is the way it is, was and always will be.* Often, they fall short of telling 'the truth, the whole truth and nothing but the truth'. If you listen, you will also hear other voices. Diverse voices. They will ask: *Is that true? Is that the only story? Are there other ways of looking at this? Are bits of that story missing? Why?*

The dominant narrative of Northern Ireland in its simplest form is 'Catholics versus Protestants'. For generations it has been a 'them and us' story. It's the story those of us living here are most often told and it's what people elsewhere *expect* to hear from this part of the world. That story is not untrue, but it's also not the whole picture. Dig deeper into any conflict (or peaceful society) and you will find stories that do not fit. Conflict is not always black and white – there are greys. Truth can be messy – and hard to hear.

Truth Be Told is about truth, forgiveness and the stories that do not fit. Up front, it's the story of two sixteen-year-old girls, Tara and Faith – imagine '*Parent Trap* meets *Derry Girls*'. In searching for truths in their own identities, the teenagers uncover more than they bargained for. Sometimes who you *are*, is not what you *expect*. At a deeper level, the novel is the story of women across three generations in Northern Ireland. Stories that are often left untold. *Truth Be Told* is about both 'the Troubles' and the legacy of that conflict today. It's also about social and rights-based issues. Whilst the characters and plot in this novel are fictitious, their context is real.

From January 2017 to January 2020, the regional government in Northern Ireland (Stormont, Belfast) collapsed. Politicians did not meet together there to make practical and policy decisions about everyday things such as health, jobs, justice, environment and education. They also failed to take decisions about more controversial issues, including abortion, same-sex marriage, Irish language rights and legacy issues from 'the Troubles', such as pensions for victims and survivors.

In autumn 2019, the British government (Westminster, London) intervened. It said that if local politicians couldn't form a government to sort things out, it would impose Human Rights legislation to decriminalize abortion and move to legalize same-sex marriage. In October 2019, this happened. In January 2020, Northern Irish politicians eventually reached a 'New Decade, New Approach' deal and got back to work – just before the Covid-19 pandemic hit. In June 2021, a 'Troubles' pension scheme finally opened, 23 years after the end of 'the Troubles'. In July 2021, the British government announced plans to bring forward legislation to ban 'Troubles-related' prosecutions. People who suffered in 'the Troubles' may never get their day in court. Experts appointed by the UN Human Rights Council have been very critical of this. So have victims' groups.

During all of this, people in Northern Ireland just try to get on with everyday life – and much of life here is relatively 'normal' and peaceful. It's a place of stunningly beautiful landscapes, vibrant culture and friendly people. Much of the past hate has been replaced with hope but we are still on a journey. Themes like truth, justice and forgiveness also apply to a much wider context than just within Northern Ireland.

When I wrote the author's note in my first novel, *Guard Your Heart*, I said that I write for empathy – that fiction is a powerful tool for creating empathy and that empathy is a powerful tool for creating peace. I still believe that holds true. Listening to 'other' voices and walking in 'other' shoes broadens our mindsets. It helps us to see our shared humanity and to look at issues from different perspectives. Wherever you live, read diverse stories. Listen to diverse voices. Ask your own questions. Think.

Sue Divin
September 2021

Acknowledgements

Thank you to everyone who has helped me muddle my way through life so far. This book was mainly written and edited during the Covid-19 pandemic and lockdowns of 2020 and 2021. Tough times. *Truth be Told* wouldn't have been written if it hadn't been for that dreaded, yet necessary concept of 'deadline'.

To those who kept me sane by giving of their time for long, socially distanced walks, or coffee and wine in their gardens – thank you. (Maureen 'down the street', you get a special mention here.) To Dawn, for suggesting 'bubbling' yourself and your house with mine to help me swap home-schooling and day job fatigue for occasional writer's retreats 'around the corner' – you're an angel. To Lorraine, who brought soup as I battled Covid, single-parenting and the final chapters of this book in a bleak January – your friendship is a lifeline. More than at any other time in my life, it was the little random acts of kindness that kept me afloat – a card in the post, a phone call, a 'thinking of you' message. There are too many amazing people to thank everyone individually – but a mention to Cathy, Byddi, Emma, Maria, and to everyone who showered me with encouragement when *Guard Your Heart* was published during lockdown. *Buíochas mór.*

Specific to this novel, a huge thank you to the members of 'This Writing Thing . . .' writers' group who assured me in our monthly Zoom encounters that the early chapters were working. Robin, you retain the dubious honour of being my essential 'go-to source' for everything shady, criminal and policing. Bernie, thanks for mentoring me, for freezing with me in socially distanced venues and for writer chats over outdoor coffees. Paul, your dessert-for-breakfast River Mill Writers' Retreats (and lemon tart) proved a catalyst for creativity when the muse vanished. Damian, your book, *As If I Cared*, restored my soul – I'm honoured you gave permission to use an extract from your poem at the start of this novel.

Arts Council of Northern Ireland, thank you for the SIAP funding that paid for the laptop on which I type.

Laura Williams, agent extraordinaire, I remain indebted to your wisdom, professionalism and encouragement (open invite to Derry to hang out where all my mad characters roam). And to my editor, Venetia Gosling, and the team at Macmillan, a hundred thousand thank-yous for taking me on and for putting this book onto shelves and into readers' hands – you truly make the magic happen.

A tribute to all those who work for truth, justice and reconciliation. During the entire Covid-19 pandemic, peace work continued in Northern Ireland. Communities continued to connect with those in need. I remain inspired by those who, on a daily basis, turn up to make a difference. Keep the faith. Your commitment has helped focus my understanding of many of the issues in this novel and I hope, in its own way, that this book can help build peace.

Finally, to Mum, Dad, Anita and Ethan – thanks for being there over the years with love, hugs, and those vital cups of tea.

About the Author

Sue Divin is a Derry based writer and peace worker, originally from Armagh in Northern Ireland. With a Masters in Peace and Conflict Studies and a career in Community Relations, her writing often touches on diversity and reconciliation, borders and the legacy of the Troubles today. Her début novel, *Guard Your Heart*  (Macmillan 2021) was joint winner of the Irish Writers Centre's Novel Fair in 2019. Her short stories, flash fiction and poetry have been published in literary journals and anthologies including *Her Other Language*, *The Caterpillar*, *The Cormorant*, *The Honest Ulsterman*, *The Bangor Literary Journal*, *Splonk*, *North West Words* and *The Bramley*. *Truth Be Told* is her second novel.

© Ethan Divin